THE JOURNEY TO
NEW CANAAN

GLENDA ALLEN REID AND
LUANN ALLEN PAYNE

CROSSBOOKS
PUBLISHING

CrossBooks™
A Division of LifeWay
1663 Liberty Drive
Bloomington, IN 47403
www.crossbooks.com
Phone: 1-866-879-0502

Scripture taken from the King James Version of the Bible.

Scripture taken from the Holy Bible, New International Version®. Copyright © 1973, 1978, 1984 Biblica. Used by permission of Zondervan. All rights reserved.

First published by CrossBooks 09/14/2011

ISBN: 978-1-4627-0652-5 (sc)
ISBN: 978-1-4627-0653-2 (hc)

Printed in the United States of America

This book is printed on acid-free paper.

To the Holy Spirit who led us to write this book.

PROLOGUE

"1860 WAS HIS YEAR," HE thought to himself. In three short months he, Gabriel Lyon, would be graduating from Amherst College, with many more wonderful events to follow. All his plans were finally coming together.

What a difference April was in Amherst Maine compared to his native Baton Rouge, Louisiana. Here it was cold, the type of cold that hurt your bones. Baton Rouge was warm and sunny, he closed his eyes and he could almost feel the sun on his face.

The thoughts filling his head raced with speed. He remembered the kind brown lined face of Liza, his only memory of what mother meant. She had always been there to pick him up if he fell, brush tears away if he cried, sat by his bed, and nursed him back to health when he was sick. Liza whispered stories to him at night of his beautiful mother, and of her love for the Lord. She told him of his mother's kindness to others and of her outward beauty that was second only to her inward beauty; she was the mother he never got to meet, because she had died in childbirth…. his birth.

Gabe remembered at the age of five he'd learned of the horrible meaning of slavery at his father's knee. He had begged his father to allow him to spend the night with Liza and her family, only to have his heart broken when his father explained why he could not. What would his dear friend Charles think? Charles could very well have been one of his father's slaves had he been born in Louisiana. What would "She" think if she knew about New Canaan? He offered up a prayer, and quickly finished dressing. He slipped the small box off his dresser into his pocket. He had an important appointment to keep.

CHAPTER 1

"THIS IS THE DAY THE Lord has made," Gabe thought as he pulled his coat tight around himself and stepped outside into the cold wind of Amherst.

Walking quickly down Main Street, his mind was full of images of his past. He thought of how God had always had his hand on his life for as long as he could remember. It seemed he couldn't think when he hadn't felt as though God had guided his every footstep. Even when his father really hadn't wanted him to go to Amherst College and especially when he found out his son planned to be a pastor. Yet God made a way where none seemed possible. Then to top it all off, God had sent Josie Hall into his life.

Josephine, as her family called her, was Professor Hall's daughter. Professor Hall was a kind man, a great teacher and most of all he loved the Lord with all his heart. He was in his fifties, tall and silver-haired. His smile made you think he had always been your friend, and his hand-shake was firm. Josie was definitely his daughter. How she loved the Lord! She was kind, compassionate and always quick with a word of encouragement. She was petite with eyes as blue as the sky and hair the color of wheat.

"Lord," Gabe said out loud, "I know she's the one you have chosen to be my wife. Please be with me and give me the right words to say when I ask her father for permission to marry her. Thank you, in Jesus' name."

As Gabe hurried down the street, he neither heard the city sounds nor the horses and buggies on the busy street. He didn't notice the people around him hurrying to their destinations, for his thoughts were elsewhere. Suddenly, he became aware of someone urgently calling his name several times. He stopped mid-step and turned.

"Gabe! Gabriel Lyon!" Out of breath, Charles Wood, his good friend and study partner, ran up to him.

"Charles what's the hurry? Is something wrong?"

"Gabe, you've received a letter of great importance and it was delivered by hand. I thought I should find you and bring it to you quickly." Breathlessly he handed the letter to Gabe.

Gabe glanced at the handwriting on the letter and his heart pounded. There, in his father's shaky handwriting, was his name, Gabriel Lyon. Gabe quickly thanked Charles and tucked the letter into his pocket.

"Shouldn't you read it now?"

"I don't think I will. I'm on my way to see Professor Hall and Josie." Gabe waved good bye to Charles and hurried on his way.

"I can do all things through Christ who strengthens me," Gabe said over and over to himself. He approached the pretty white house and quickly went up the steps and knocked on the door. It seemed like forever had passed before the door opened, and there stood the love of his life, Josie.

"Come in quickly, you must be so cold!" She led him to the fireplace in the small but homey sitting room. "Father is in his study, he's been waiting for you. Please take time to warm yourself first. I'm so nervous for you. I'm sure father will say yes!"

Gabe took her hand. "I'm nervous too. I've prayed he'll say yes, but that's not all I'm nervous about." Josie looked at Gabe questionably with her big blue eyes. "I'll tell you after I speak with your father. First things first," Gabe said, smiling down at his lovely blond angel. The smile on her face took away all his anxiety about talking with her father. Squaring his shoulders, he walked toward the doors of Professor Hall's study.

Gabe knocked on the study door with what he thought was confidence, but he really wasn't sure. It didn't matter; he knew what he wanted to do.

"Come in!" Professor Hall answered quickly.

Gabe entered the study which reflected the professor's personality. It was both warm and comfortable. Book shelves lined the walls on all sides of the room. In the middle was a large mahogany desk with many papers scattered on top. Not messy, but organized in the professor's way.

"Gabriel Lyon! How are you?" The professor stood and shook hands with Gabe.

"I'm doing well, sir. How are you?"

"Doing well, doing well indeed! Have a seat, young man, and let's talk. What's brought you out on such a cold day as this?" Professor Hall asked with a twinkle in his eye.

"Well, sir, I've come to speak with you, or rather ask you…sir, I've come to talk with you about Josephine."

"Yes?"

"Sir, you've known me a long time, and as you know, in June I'll be graduating. I've also been offered a pastoral position with a small church, Christian Fellowship. There is small pay… but it has a parsonage, and sir… I love your daughter, and I wish to ask for her hand in marriage," Gabe finally blurted out. Nervously, he searched the professor's face for his answer.

The professor was thoughtful for a moment, and then stood with a smile on his face. "Now that wasn't so hard was it? You are a fine young man and you'll make a good pastor. I know you have a heart for the Lord. I think I'd like it very much to have you as my son-in-law! Yes, you may marry my Josephine." Then he added laughing, "She has said yes to you, hasn't she?"

"Yes sir she has, but only with your blessing," Gabe replied quickly.

Gabe didn't know what to do next. He just stood smiling like an idiot. Then he held out his hand to Professor Hall. The professor walked around his desk and took Gabe's hand saying, "I've been wondering how long it would take you to ask. I've seen the way you two are with each other. I've always wanted her to find the love of her life as I found with her mother. A love like that is hard to find. It only comes from a higher power. Remember to always put God first in your marriage, and your blessings will be overflowing."

All Gabe could do was say, "Yes sir. Thank you, sir. Thank you."

"Don't you think we should call Josephine in here and let her know?" asked Professor Hall with amusement.

Josie paced up and down the sitting room wondering what was taking so long. "How much longer will I have to wait? It shouldn't be taking this long!" she said to herself. Josie thought of her mother, who had gone to be with the Lord two years earlier. "Mother would have surely enjoyed seeing me like this. I wish she were here! Mother always knew what father was thinking even before he did." During this dialog with herself she heard the study doors open. Quickly sat upon the nearest chair and tried to act as if she was merely waiting for their return, but in fact, her heart was racing. Yes, her Mother would have really enjoyed seeing her this way.

"Josephine, my dear, I believe you and this young man have a wedding to plan!" Her father exclaimed. Gabe stood beside her father, smiling.

Josie ran to her father, and hugged him and kissed him on his cheek. "Oh, thank you Father," she joyfully whispered in his ear. Gabe held out his hand to her, and she took it. Looking up into his eyes, she could see the love he had for her. She would always remember this moment.

After a small celebration of tea and cake, Gabe reached into his pocket and removed the small box. Feeling all eyes upon him, he opened the box and took out his mother's small, white and yellow gold rose ring. Looking at Josie, he asked, "May I have your hand?" Slowly, Josie held out her hand. Gabe slipped the ring on her finger. "I love you Josephine Hall, with all my heart."

Josie, with tears of joy in her eyes, looked up at Gabe and said, "I love you too Gabriel Lyon." She felt a blush rise to her face as she remembered her father was in the room. She quickly looked down at her ring. It was so dainty. It was a perfect rose made of yellow gold with small leaves of white gold. Never had she seen anything so lovely in her life. Surely this must be a most cherished family heirloom.

Clearing his throat, the professor said, "What's this you've dropped on the floor, Gabe?" The professor leaned forward and picked up the letter Gabe had forgotten was in his pocket. Handing the letter to Gabe, Professor Hall asked, "News from home?"

"It's a letter from my father. I haven't read it yet, but I think I will now. Whatever it says involves the three of us. We're family."

"Is this what you were talking about earlier?" Josie asked.

He nodded. "Yes, it is." Gabe opened the letter that simply stated, "You are needed at home. Return at once." No signature, but then, none was needed.

Gabe read the letter out loud to the professor and Josie. The professor sat with a thoughtful look upon his face. Then after a few moments asked, "Do you know what this means, Gabe?"

Gabe looked up from the letter and then back down. He thought if he kept his eyes upon the words he would see what wasn't written there. "No, Professor, I have no idea. I do know for Father to call me home at this time, his reason must be important." Then he turned to Josie, "This means I'll have to go home soon, before we're married. It will give you time to plan our wedding for when I return."

"Gabe, your graduation! What does this mean? You've only a few short months left. Even if you left now, by the time you returned, it will have passed!" Josie's soft voice rang with concern.

Sighing, he looked into Josie's blue eyes, wishing he could take her in his arms. "I have to do this. I have to see what my father needs. When I received this letter on the way here, I knew it might be something urgent. My father is a good man but a man of few words. In all the time I've been here, he's only written me three times, so I know this is important. Now, about my graduation, I'll just have to pray and leave it to God. Professor, what do you advise?"

The professor was silent for a few moments. "My boy, you have to return home as you've said. I'll see what I can do regarding your graduation. I need not to remind you, your position with Christian Fellowship depends upon you graduating from this college in June. You will need to notify them as soon as possible, so they can find a suitable replacement. Remember, you'll need to make your travel arrangements home soon, if you're to leave within the week."

"You're right, there is much to do, Sir," Gabe said agreeing with him.

"Josie, with your father's permission, I'd like to come for you tomorrow for a buggy ride. It's Saturday, and I have no classes, weather permitting of course. Is this acceptable to you?"

"Indeed it is," she said with excitement. "Father, may I?"

"Of course, my dear, be sure to dress warmly."

"Then I'll call for you at eleven o clock," Gabe rose slowly to his feet with Josie standing with him.

"I'll walk him to the door, Father."

Professor Hall merely nodded his head.

Standing at the door, Gabe took Josie's hand in his. "I have much to discuss with you, my love, on our ride tomorrow. There's a lot about my family I need to tell you, now that you're to be my wife." Taking her hand to his lips, he kissed her hand and said good night.

Josie stood at the door watching Gabe walk out into the cold night and down the path. She wondered what tomorrow would bring, after such a wonderful day as this. Slowly, she closed the door, and offered a prayer of thanksgiving for this wonderful man.

Gabe hardly noticed the cold as he walked toward the college. He had a lot on his mind. He had to tell Josie about his family, about his father, but most of all, about New Canaan. What would she think? Would she still marry him with her abolitionists' background? Would her father allow her to marry after finding out? What about graduation? What about his position which depended upon him graduating?" These were the questions that played over and over in his mind.

When Gabe entered his small dorm room that he shared with Charles, he was cold and tired. All he could think of was going to bed, getting under the cover, and getting warm. Glancing toward the other bed, he saw Charles was deep in study. Not wishing to disturb him, Gabe quietly went about getting ready for bed.

Charles didn't glance up from his Bible. "If you think you're going to go to sleep before you tell me what was in that letter, you're wrong. I saw the look on your face! Is it bad news?"

With a look of pure misery, Gabe let out a long sigh, and sat down on the end of his bed. "It's a letter from my father. He's requesting I come home as soon as possible."

"You're to go home before graduation?" Charles asked loudly. "You can't Gabe! You'll miss the final examinations! You won't be able to graduate! You won't be able to take the position at Christian Fellowship, and you won't be able to marry Josie!" In one breath Charles had voiced all of Gabe's fears.

"I know, I know, Charles. What am I going to do? I asked Professor Hall for permission to marry Josie tonight, and he gave it. I even gave Josie the ring. That was before we read the letter."

"So, does Professor Hall and Josie know?"

"Yes, they do. Whatever am I going to do? What am I going to do?" Gabe repeated with doubt clinging to each word.

Charles couldn't believe what he was seeing nor hearing. The one man he thought who truly knew how to obtain answers, who had more faith than anyone he knew, was now sitting here, in this room, asking him what he should do? Well, there's only one thing to do, Charles thought!

Closing his Bible, Charles sat up on his bed quickly. "I'll tell you what you're going to do, you're going to pray, and that's what you're going to do! You need advice from someone who knows what tomorrow will bring. The One who has his hand on your life!"

"That's not all; I have to tell Josie about my family. Things that may make her change her mind about marrying me. Things, I haven't even told you." Gabe's voice held deep concern.

As he spoke, he felt as if a dam had broken loose. Gabe began to tell Charles about his father, his mother, his life in New Canaan and the calling God had placed on his life. He told Charles how he had always wanted to preach Gods word. Then he told him of his hatred for slavery and the guilt he carried because of it.

Charles sat silently until Gabe finished. He was trying to understand all Gabe had said. Trying not to judge, trying to remember this was his friend, and his brother in Christ. Slowly standing, Charles walked over to Gabe and said, "You're my best friend. More a brother than a friend; nothing will ever change that! You can't do anything about the past, yours or your fathers. What you have to do is change the things you can. To be honest with you, I don't know if we could have been friends if I had known this before. It doesn't matter! The fact is, we are best friends, the type of friends God places together. Where Josie is concerned, I can't speak for her. I believe now is the time to pray Gabe."

Charles knelt to his knees. Gabe followed kneeling, closing his eyes and bowing his head, as he joined Charles to pray.

"Heavenly Father," Charles began out loud. "Your word says you have not given us the spirit of fear, but of power, love and a sound mind. I ask you to remove fear from Gabe, and give him peace in its place. Give him a sound mind, so he may know your will in the task that has been set before him. Psalms thirty two says that you, Lord, will instruct us, and teach us in the way we should go. You will counsel us and watch over us. So, we ask you to give Gabe this wisdom. Teach him and counsel him. We ask you to send your Angels to protect and keep him safe on this journey. Thank you, Father, in the name of Jesus, Amen."

The two men remained on their knees, praying silently. For this little room had become a holy place. They knew the presence of the Lord was with them, and both men felt it as surely as if they had stepped out into heaven itself. Neither wished to disturb it, as they were flooded with peace and love which only the Heavenly Father could give.

After what seemed like hours, but was only minutes, both men stood to their feet. Silently they finished readying for bed. No words were exchanged, for what could one say? No words could describe the encounter they just had with their Heavenly Father.

The next morning, Gabe woke up early feeling refreshed and free from worry. His God had let him know what to do. Not in a vision, or in a loud voice, but in the quite still way God talks with his children. Looking across the room, Gabe noticed that Charles must have gotten up with the sun, for he was by himself.

Taking his time dressing, Gabe planned his day. He knew tomorrow morning he would be leaving for home. He had to buy his train ticket, rent a horse and buggy, talk with the elders of Christian Fellowship and go to Josie's. Taking the money box out of his dresser, he removed the money his father had sent him, on the few occasions his father had written to him. It was more than enough to pay for everything planned for today, and pay for his trip home. Grabbing his coat off the chair, he was out the door and down the street, a man on a mission.

Several hours later, Gabe drove the rented buggy toward Josie's house. He was thinking about all he had accomplished. He had bought his ticket, this was the easiest task. He had talked with the elders of Christian Fellowship, not so easy, but it was done. The elders appreciated being informed early, so now they had time to find a suitable replacement. They were understanding, but clearly didn't like the position they found themselves in, though they did wish Gabe well. All Gabe had to do now was talk to Josie, and leave his letter of withdrawal from Amherst with Professor Hall. He had accomplished his tasks and felt encouraged.

Pulling up to Josie's house, Gabe tied the horse and buggy to the hitching-post. Walking to the front door, he took a deep breath and knocked. Almost immediately Professor Hall answered the door, allowing Gabe entry.

"Hello Gabriel." Professor Hall took Gabe's offered hand in a firm hand- shake.

"Good morning, sir."

"Did you sleep well? I know you had a lot on your mind when you left here last evening." The professor asked, leading Gabe into the sitting room.

"Yes, sir, I did. I have a lot to tell you when Josie joins us. What I have to say, I'd like to say to both of you."

"Are you sure you want me here when you talk to her?"

"I'm sure," Gabe replied.

Josie could hear the men talking from her room, but couldn't quite make out what they were saying. Looking into the mirror, she tried to smooth the few wisps of hair that had found their way out of her swept up bun. Grabbing her bonnet, she went to join her father and Gabe.

"Josie, how lovely you are!" Gabe said walking toward her as she entered the room. Her beauty and grace always amazed him.

"She's as lovely as her mother," her father said.

Blushing with embarrassment, but smiling with joy, she politely thanked them. Taking her hand, Gabe guided her to the couch, and sat beside her.

The professor remained standing at the fireplace. Gabe looked into Josie's loving eyes. "I've a lot to say and there's no easy way to tell you."

Josie nodded for him to continue.

"First I'll tell you my plans; I have decided I will be going home tomorrow. I've already bought my train ticket, and talked with the elders of Christian Fellowship, and they're going to find someone to replace me. I have a letter for the Headmaster of Amherst, which I will give to your father. Sir, is this agreeable with you?" Taking the letter from his pocket, Gabe stood and handed it to Professor Hall, who nodded. Sitting back down he continued, "I know all of this is sudden to you, please have faith that I have to leave, and what I am doing is right."

The emotions Josie felt rushed one after the other. She knew they played across her face, but she didn't know what to say. She certainly didn't know how she felt. Josie stood suddenly, and turned her back to him. Gabe rose quickly and stood behind her.

"Gabe, I don't understand. I don't know what to say. Tomorrow is only a few hours away. It doesn't leave us much time together before you have to go," she said with emotion ringing in her voice.

He gently turned her toward him saying, "Josie, you know I didn't make this decision by myself. I've prayed about this, and God gave me His answer as surely as I stand before you. Please trust me. I don't know where this will take me, but I do know God's hand is on me, and He is control. Do you understand? Do you trust me? Do you trust God?" He could see the tears in her eyes, and he could understand her disappointment, but this was something he knew he had to do.

"I do trust God and I do trust you!" she said softly but firmly.

Gabe took her by the hand. "Let's go for our ride and talk." Looking up, Gabe's eyes went to where the professor had been standing. Sometime during their conversation, the professor had quietly slipped from the room.

Gabe pulled her into his arms and whispered, "I love you, Josie!"

Laying her head on his chest, she whispered back, "I love you too!"

Standing there in each others arms, Josie knew she would treasure this moment. She knew he had to go.

When they found her father, and said good bye, they were off in the buggy. Dressed in their winter coats and with their lap blanket tucked around them, they began their drive. Neither one noticed the cold. They barely recognized their friends who waved to them as they passed. They had eyes only for each other.

"I don't know how to begin, and I know you have questions for me," Gabe said as he maneuvered the horses down the street.

"I have many, but first I'd like to ask you what you want to tell me about your father?"

Gabe quickly looked at her. Josie could tell she had surprised him with her direct question. She smiled as he regained his composure.

"As you know my father lives in Louisiana. What I haven't told you is… he's a plantation owner in Baton Rouge." He waited for her response.

"Does this mean?" Her question trailed off to silence. Josie knew he would know what she meant.

"Yes, my father owns slaves." Gabe took his eyes off the road long enough to look at her. He wanted to see what her eyes were saying. Then making a quick decision he said, "Josie, this buggy ride isn't working out for us to talk. Let's take the horse and buggy back to the stable, and from there we can walk over to the church where we'll be warm, and be able to talk without distraction.

"I think that would be best. This way we won't be in a hurry or so cold we forget what we need to say."

Gabe quickly turned the horses around and headed toward the stables. When they arrived, he helped Josie down, as the stable owner approached.

"Is it too cold for a ride today?" The stable owner asked.

"Something like that," Gabe replied handing him the reins.

Offering Josie his arm, the couple walked the short distance across the street to the church. How Josie loved this church! It had been a haven to her on many occasions. It was always opened for anyone who wanted to come pray. She had come here when her mother had taken sick, and again when she died. She often came here when she needed to pray, and last night she had slipped away after Gabe left, and her father retired to his study. She had come to pray for guidance, wisdom and understanding. God always met her here, ready to talk, comfort her, and answer questions. It was the perfect place to be, Josie thought.

Opening the door, the couple stepped into the sanctuary of the church. The pastor, standing at the front, turned toward them smiling his greetings.

Both smiled back in return. The pastor made himself busy at the pulpit, knowing if they needed him, they would call but propriety demanded he not leave them alone.

Sitting down in a back pew, Gabe continued his conversation in a low voice.

"I want you to know my father is a good man, Josie. The plantation has been handed down to my father from his father. He's been good to his slaves as long as I can remember. He's better than most of the plantation owners there."

Josie gave him a look of pity. "To own another human being Gabe, is not being better than others. It's still a sin," she said, placing her hand on his arm to soften what she said.

"I have more to tell you before you judge," his eyes pleaded with her.

Removing her hand, Josie nodded, "I'm sorry, please continue."

"As I was saying, father has been good to his slaves. There are about thirty families in all. They're given food, and clothing, but I think better could be done by them. The estate is about 700 acres. Some two hundred acres are farmed during the seasons. The plantation grows corn, cotton, rice and some sugar cane. There's a large orchard on the back acres, and lots of animals too. There are the usual horses, cows, sheep and a few pigs. Most of the land is used for grazing, timber, and such. It's a beautiful place Josie, you should see it. There are great oak trees with Spanish moss hanging from their branches, the Magnolia trees with their large white flowers, the flowers of amaryllis, Iris and roses bushes. The air at times is filled with their fragrances so heavy, that if you closed your eyes, it seems you could pick the flowers from the very air you breathe."

As he spoke, Josie watched Gabe closely; she could tell he loved his home.

"My mother died in childbirth having me. I only know her by the stories Liza has told me as child." Gabe looked away as he stepped into the past.

"Who's Liza?" Josie asked.

"She's a slave. The housekeeper, but to me, she is the only mother I've ever known. I've always knew Liza loved me. It didn't matter my father owned her, that wasn't her choice. She knew it wasn't my choice not to have a mother. She didn't love me because of it; she loved me in spite of it." He told her softly. "Now, none of this is to excuse my father. I knew at a young age I didn't want this to be my life. I've a calling on my life that cannot, no, will not be ignored Josie. God has something planned for me in his work, and not of a plantation owner. I've hated slavery since my understanding of it, and I will not be part of it!"

"Be careful, Gabe, about what you say you will not be part of," Josie said softly. "You know not what God may ask of you. I know you hate slavery, and I know you've been ashamed of your family's involvement in it, but you don't know what God has planned for you!"

"I know he wants me to preach, I know that! I don't believe he would have me come all this way to prepare for the ministry, and not use me. I know he wants us to marry, and to begin a life together; to begin a work together that will glorify Him!"

"I know it too!" Then she added, "Things don't always go according to our plans; it's always according to God's plan. His ways are not our ways."

"I will be back." Gabe searched Josie's face looking for a sign of doubt. "You do know that, don't you?"

"Yes, I do, I have no doubts," she replied laughingly.

"Then in spite of this, my family's legacy, and what I have told you, and your abolitionists' ideas, you still intend to marry me?"

"Of course I do!" She was shocked by the very idea he'd thought otherwise.

"What about Professor Hall?"

"You leave Father to me! With your permission, I will tell him everything you've told me, and when you return, sir, our wedding will be planned and ready to take place!"

Relived, Gabe took her hand and holding it tightly, he looked into her eyes thinking how God had blessed him with this woman.

The pastor approached the couple saying, "Is there anything I can do for you?" Both Gabe and Josie looked up. They'd forgotten about the pastor and being in the church.

"Yes, sir," Gabe said. "When I return will you marry us?"

"Why yes, I will. Return? Are you leaving us?" The pastor asked slightly confused.

"For a while, I have to return home." Gabe was feeling confident now.

"Then, we'll pray together for your safe journey, and your safe return."

So the small group bowed their heads as the pastor prayed. Thanking the pastor, Gabe and Josie left the church. They walked in a comfortable silence toward Josie's house.

"What's its name?" Josie asked breaking the silence.

Gabe looked down at her, not understanding.

"Every plantation has a name. What's the name of your father's plantation?" she explained.

"It's New Canaan, my love," he said to her tenderly.

Oh, my! The New Promise Land," she translated in a whisper to herself.

This very well may have God's hand in it, more than she or Gabe realized. Smiling to herself, she kept those thoughts within her.

Once they arrived at Josie's house, she turned to Gabe. "Will you stay and have supper with us?"

"Yes, I will." He wasn't ready to leave her just yet.

Entering the house, the couple was greeted by Professor Hall. Josie informed her father that Gabe would be staying for supper. This delighted the professor immensely. He enjoyed Gabe's company because the conversations were always challenging, and they both enjoyed a good debate.

The conversation at supper was light, and filled with laughter, as the three ate the meal Josie herself had prepared. Josie wouldn't have it any other way. She wanted her last few hours with Gabe to be laughter, not tears. She watched and listened, as her father and Gabe debated over the Democrat's position on the newly formed Republican Party, and if they would lead the United States to Civil war should they win the upcoming election. They laughed over the Know – Nothings, the new third party that had been formed which ignored all issues of importance. She voiced her concerns when she could, which wasn't often. When these two men of her life got together talking politics, they would become so intense in their debate, she could barely get a word in.

When the conversation began to dwindle, Professor Hall rose from the table along with Gabe and Josie. Together, they went into the sitting room. They had enjoying each others company so much; they'd remained at the dining table a long time. Noticing the time on the grandfather clock in the corner of the sitting room, Gabe knew he'd have to leave soon. They all knew, especially Josie. She'd noticed the glances at the clock from Gabe and her father, and she dreaded the time he would leave her.

"Thank you for the delicious supper," Gabe said to her. "You are a wonderful cook."

"A great asset in a wife," Professor Hall said with pride.

Laughing, Josie said, "Men! You just fed them, give them a good debate and they're happy." Both men laughed.

"I know you'll be leaving soon Gabe," said the professor. "I have something for you to take on the journey. I have to get it from my study."

The professor left the room, giving the couple a few minuets of privacy.

"I'm going to miss you." Gabe walked over to stand by where Josie sat.

"I'll miss you too." Her gaze studied him closely.

"Have I got something on my jacket?" he asked laughing.

"No. I'm just making a memory. I want to remember everything about you to keep with me while you're gone," she said still holding her gaze upon him. She knew she was being forward, but she didn't care. She wanted to remember his handsome face, his dark hair, his green eyes and the way his smile lit up his whole face.

He laughed and held out his hand to her. She took it and stood. He took her in a tender embrace, telling her of his love. When they heard the study doors open, the two parted, but not before he had given her a tender kiss.

Professor Hall entered the room with his gift for Gabe. Walking over to where Gabe stood, he handed it to him. Taking the gift, Gabe was glad to see it was a book.

"Professor, this is one of Hans Christian Anderson's latest books, On Judgment Day. I've wanted to read it for some time now. Thank you, sir!"

"You're welcome my boy! Now, you'll have something to read on your trip. I know you'll be taking your Bible with you, but this is just something different," he replied.

"I have something for you too!" said Josie. "It's a little more personal."

She walked over to the side table and removed a package from its drawer. Handing it to him she laughingly added, "I got this gift before I understood how warm it may be in Louisiana."

Gabe opened the gift, taking time to put the ribbon from it into his pocket. Inside the box was a pair of black leather riding gloves. "I'll wear them and think of you," he said softly.

She smiled. He couldn't think of how she'd been able to get him such a gift when there had been little time to do it, and to cook the meal too. One thing was for sure, she could do anything that she sat her mind to. He would have to remember that fact.

"I suppose it is time to leave," Gabe said looking from Josie to the professor.

The professor stepped forward placing his hand on Gabe's shoulder, saying "You be careful on your journey, and God speed. Return as soon as you can."

"I will, sir," he said. He was thankful for this man's friendship.

"I'll walk him to the door Father," Josie said coming to stand next to Gabe.

Shaking the professor's hand one last time, Gabe took Josie's hand, and walked to the door slowly.

"I'd like to see you off at the train station," she told him as he put on his coat.

"It'll be too early for you," he said gently. "It would be better to say good bye here. It'll be a lot warmer for sure!" he added jokingly trying to ease the tension of the moment.

"Oh, Gabe!" she cried softly. "I'll miss you so! Please be careful. I'll be praying for you every minute that you are gone!"

Putting his arms around her, he pulled Josie close to him. "I'll miss you my love, so very much! Thank you for your prayers, and know I'll be praying for you. I love you."

"I love you," she answered holding her tears back.

He kissed her gently. Then releasing her, he opened the door and disappeared into the shadows of the night. Josie stood watching until she could no longer see him. Closing the door, she felt the held back tears fall on her cheeks. She felt her father, more than seeing him, behind her. He put his arms around her, comforting her in the way only a father could. She cried on his shoulder until she couldn't cry anymore.

The hardest thing he ever had to do, in a long time, was to leave Josie. He knew he had to leave, and the sooner he returned home, the sooner he could come back and marry her. Gabe pulled the collar of his coat up higher as the cold wind blew around him, while he walked toward the dorm. He still had to pack for his trip. "It's a good thing," he thought, "I don't have much." College life isn't one where you could have a lot of things. Then again, college life meant you couldn't afford a lot of things. His father may have paid for his education, but for the other necessities he needed, he had gotten himself by doing odd jobs.

He entered his room glad of its warmth, and took off his coat. Laying his coat on the chair, he pulled out his case, and laid it on top of his bed. He remembered the last time he packed, how he'd been full of excitement. Now, he was full of curiosity as to why his father needed him home. "I'll find out soon enough," he thought, and started packing. When he finished and closed the case, Charles came in.

"You've finished packing?" he asked.

"Yes, just now," Gabe replied, taking the case and sitting it on the floor.

"Can I do anything for you?"

"Could you keep some of my books for me? I'm not sure if I'll be back in time to remove them."

"Sure, the books and anything else you need to leave behind. It's not like you're not coming back. You don't need to take all your things," he told him.

"Thanks, Charles. I just don't know how long this will take with Father."

"Did you say good bye to Josie?"

"Yes I did. She handled it well. We spent the day together talking. She even cooked me supper," he added laughingly.

"Lucky you! I had to eat here, and you know what that means! I had to eat a supper cooked by the freshman students! Charles made a face then ask, "Will you need help taking your things to the station tomorrow?"

"No, but thanks anyway. I'll be fine," Gabe assured him.

"Are Josie and Professor Hall seeing you off in the morning?"

"No. I thought it would be better if they didn't. It's something I need to do by myself, and anyway, it will be too early and too cold," Gabe said as he got ready for bed.

Charles was already in bed but still continued to talk to him. "I understand. If you want company to the station, I'd be glad to go with you."

Getting into bed, and pulling the warm quilt to his chin, Gabe said, "No, its okay. I'll say goodbye to you in the morning. Go to sleep! You may not need it, but I sure do!" Both men laughed and within a few minuets were fast asleep.

The light was bright and shone all around. He closed his eyes and took a deep breath. The air was so sweet, mixed with the perfume fragrance of flowers he couldn't quite name. He opened his eyes to find himself standing on the lawn of New Canaan amidst giant oak trees laden with Spanish moss. The grass was soft beneath his bare feet. Looking down he realized he was barefooted and in his night clothes. "What is this?" he thought looking up. The landscape colors which surrounded him were more felt than seen. The colors brilliant and pure, along with the fragrances of the air, assaulted his senses with wondrous delight. He knew this was New Canaan but yet it was wonderfully different. Standing a few feet from him was a man he hadn't noticed until now. The man was familiar to him, but he didn't know why. He was tall, with a face that was neither young nor old. Gabe couldn't tell what type of clothing he wore because of the brilliant light shinning around him. The man approached Gabe saying, "Come and follow me." Then he turned and walked away slowly, and motioned for Gabe to follow. Gabe did as he was asked, and tried to catch up with the stranger who was always ahead of him. It didn't matter if Gabe walked or ran, he couldn't catch up with him. The stranger kept getting further and further away. Finally, the stranger stopped and turned toward him smiling. Then, he waved as if to say goodbye and disappeared leaving Gabe standing alone.

"Gabe, wake up. It's time to get up!" Charles said as he shook Gabe's shoulder.

As he opened his eyes, Gabe felt confused. "A dream," he thought. "It was just a dream!" It had felt so real. Gabe knew he would never forget it.

Gabe prayed as he dressed for his trip. He needed God by his side.

"Thank you, Father, for your word that says you will never leave us nor forsake us," he said out loud.

"Amen" said Charles as he handed Gabe his coat.

Picking up his case, taking his coat and assuring Charles he would write as soon as he could, Gabe said goodbye to his friend. Then out the door he went, heading to the train station as the sun began to rise above him.

CHAPTER 2

GABE STEPPED OFF THE TRAIN tired after his long journey to Baton Rouge. He was hot; after all, he had dressed for the cold when he left Amherst. Here, it was warm, and not a cloud in the sky. There wasn't even a cool breeze, and a coat was definitely not needed. It was hot on his arm as he carried it with him to retrieve his case. Making his way down the train station ramp, Gabe looked around him, and all he could see was injustice. Slavery was everywhere he looked in some sort of fashion. He saw black men carrying the white man loads, and black women caring for the white woman's children, as well as black children doing a man's work. "Oh, what will happen when sleeping justice awakens?" he thought as he picked up his case.

Gabe made his way through the busy town toward the livery stable. He noticed how much things had changed since he'd been gone. New shops stood everywhere. He recognized few people. The old familiar landmarks seemed different standing next to new buildings. The town had grown. "If these are the changes here, what can I expect when I get home?" he thought as he crossed the busy street.

The smells that hit him as he entered the livery were leather, and those usual smells that come with animals being kept in a stable. He saw a young boy of color cleaning out a stall. This child could have been no more than ten years old. His shirt was so worn and tattered that Gabe could see his ribs. The child had no shoes on his feet, and they were dirty. The boy looked up and stopped what he was doing. He waited for Gabe to say something.

"Hello there," Gabe said smiling at the young boy.

"Mornin," the young boy answered shyly.

"Is Mr. Allen around?"

"Yez sah, I go an fetch him fo ya," the boy said, dropping his shovel as he ran to do his errand. In just a few minutes he returned with Mr. Allen.

"Gabriel Lyon, is that you?" exclaimed Mr. Allen holding out his hand.

"Yes sir, it's me," he said shaking Mr. Allen's hand.

"Long time no see! I understand you've been to school up north to be a preacher."

"Yes sir, I have, but I'm home now, as you can see. I've just arrived by train. I need to get a horse and buggy to drive out to my father's house. Is that possible?"

"It sure is! Little John here can ride along with you and bring back the buggy so you won't have to make an extra trip," Mr. Allen said motioning at the young boy standing beside him.

"Thank you, sir. I think Little John will be doing me a great service by coming with me." Gabe noticed the young boy stood up straighter at this unexpected praise.

Gabe waited a short time for Little John to hitch the horse and buggy, and then he said his goodbyes to Mr. Allen.

As Gabe maneuvered the horses through the busy town traffic, Little John remained quiet beside him. Gabe suddenly had an idea, so he pulled the horses to a stop in front of Hebert's General Store. "I'll be right back," he said to Little John, and jumped down. Little John merely nodded as Gabe went into the store and came out quickly. When he was seated back in the buggy, the two continued their trip to New Canaan. Gabe took in the scenery as they drove the seven miles. How green everything looked. Flowers were blooming everywhere. It was good to be back but just for a visit he reminded himself. His thoughts went directly to Josie. How he missed her! Most of all he missed the way she laughed. He was glad he had asked her to marry him before he left.

"Ya be's a preacher?" Little John asked breaking Gabe away from his thoughts.

"I will be soon," he answered looking down at Little John.

"You's shur be lucky!"

"Why's that little John?"

"Cause ya can read Jesus' words and my maw says dat dem words holdt a treasure. Shur wisht I cud read dem words."

"Maybe someday you will!"

Little John didn't answer. Reading and writing was too much for him to hope for. Gabe felt a deep compassion for this child of God that had the desire to read the words of Jesus. Neither one spoke for the rest of the drive, each lost in their own thoughts.

Turning off the road to the long drive that led to his father's house, Gabe stopped the buggy. The beauty of New Canaan never ceased to amaze him.

The two story white house, with the columns along the front, looked the same. All he could think of was all those rooms for one lonely man.

The rocking chairs he spent so much time in listening to the stories Liza told him, still remained lined up across the front poach. The flower boxes remained laden with flowers. The tall Oak trees still lined the drive to the house, and shaded the green manicured lawn that was spotted only with the colorful flowers that grew wild. It was still picture perfect. Urging the horses forward, he knew in his heart that nothing much had changed here in all the time he had been away.

Reaching the end of the drive, he pulled the horses to a stop. He thought it odd no one heard him arrive. Getting down and taking his case out of the carriage, Gabe looked up at Little John, who now was holding the reins.

"Little John, I thank you for coming with me today. You have been perfect company," Gabe said. Reaching into his pocket, he pulled out a small brown bag and handed it to Little John.

"That's for you, look inside."

"Fo me sah?"

"Yes, for you. Don't you want to look inside?"

Opening the bag, Little John looked inside. "Candy fo me?" Wonder filled the little boy's eyes.

"Jus fo me?" he asked again to make sure it was his.

"Just for you! You've done me a favor by coming with me, and taking the buggy back. I want to thank you for what you've done."

"Thank me? Why, thank ya sah, thank ya!" The delight that shone in Little John's eyes was all the thanks Gabe needed.

"You be off now, and be careful."

"I's will sah, I's will," he promised, holding tight to his reward.

Little John headed the horses up the drive as Gabe stood watching until he disappeared from sight. Picking up his case, Gabe said a prayer for the boy's safe return, and then headed up the steps.

Opening the massive oak door, Gabe stepped inside. "Hello!" he said loudly so that he could be heard through the big house. No answer greeted him.

"Where is everyone?" he thought. Was there no one to greet his arrival, and no one to answer his hello? Something was wrong. He could feel it! Setting his case down in the foyer, Gabe repeated his greeting. "Hello! Is anyone home? Father? Liza? Hello?" he almost shouted.

Hearing foot steps, Gabe continued on into the large sitting room, looking about him to see if anyone was there. Suddenly, he was surrounded by a whirlwind. Liza came running toward him, holding out her arms. It had been a long time since she had seen her boy.

"Massa Gabe, Massa Gabe! My eyes can't b'lieve dey beholden ya!"

Throwing her arms around him in a big welcoming hug, she told him how much she had missed him, and how glad she was he had come back. Gabe hugged her back with the same affection.

Liza sent a young slave woman upstairs with orders to get Gabe's room ready for him. Turning to him, she anxiously placed her hand on his arm.

"I's be glad ya here! De Massa be sick, chil. I's knowd dat he done writ to ya. Ya gona stay fer a spell?" she looked at him hopefully.

"Yes Liza, I'll be here for a while. Where is everyone? Where's my father? Just how sick is he?"

"He be upstairs in da bed. Been dat way fo sum time now. Doc says nofin dat he can do." Her eyes glistened with tears. "De uders be a workin in da fields. My Ben's be scared Massa would up an die afore ya could git here. But here ya is! Praise da Lord! Ya goes on up dar and see'd him. It be powerful good fer him."

"I'll go, but first I need to get my case, bathe and change clothes."

"No Massa Gabriel, my Jonah fetch ya case fer ya, and draw ya bath. Ya member my boy, Jonah? She didn't wait for him to answer. She just went on, "Ya be needin ta see'd de Massa first!"

"You're still as bossy as ever," he told her laughingly, then bent and kissed her brown cheek. He knew she loved it when he teased her.

Going up the spiral staircase, Gabe stopped at his old room. He washed quickly at the basin, and changed into clean clothes he had left when he'd gone to school. Once he changed, he knelt and prayed. He asked God for His guidance and for words of comfort for his father.

Gabe entered his father's darkened sick room. His father looked so small in the large four posted bed. As he got closer, he noticed how much his father had aged. His hair had turned white and his sleeping eyes were sunken. He was not the same vibrant man of fifty eight he had left. His breathing was so shallow, Gabe had to watch carefully to see the rise and fall of his chest.

Here, in this room, was change and Gabe didn't like it. Quietly he went around to the side of the bed.

"Father," Gabe said touching his thin pale hand. Ezra Lyon opened his eyes slowly and looked up.

"Son, you're here," he said so softly that Gabe had to strain to hear him.

"Yes, I'm here."

"I've so much to tell you." The man struggled weakly to sit up, but couldn't.

"I'm going to be here for a while Father. You don't need to tire yourself."

"Not much time left for me."

"Don't say that! You just need to rest."

"Rest… there will be plenty of time for rest when I die," his father said coughing.

"Father…." Gabe said softly, "don't talk that way."

"How was your trip? How's your life in Maine?"

"It's well. I've asked Josephine Hall to marry me."

"What did she say?" His father asked with a faint smile.

"She said yes."

"When do you plan to marry?"

"As soon as I return to Maine… after you're well," Gabe said smiling.

Ezra Lyon was quiet and thoughtful for a moment. Looking up at Gabe, he motioned for him to sit before he continued. "I need for you to make me a promise."

"What is it?"

"I need you to promise you will take over New Canaan when I die."

"Oh, Father…" Gabe didn't know what else to say.

"You have to promise me son. I want to die knowing you will do this for me."

Oh dear Lord, Gabe prayed silently, what am I to do? Then almost immediately he shocked himself. He couldn't believe his own ears as he said, "I promise Father."

"Good! I know you'll keep your promise. I think I need to rest now. We will talk more later," he said smiling. Then his father closed his eyes and was asleep.

Gabe sat at his father's bedside still in shock. It had been as if he opened his mouth and someone else spoke. He had no intention of promising his father he would take over New Canaan. Quietly Gabe left his fathers room. He had to find Liza. He needed to talk.

Making his way through the big house, he found his way to the kitchen. He stood watching Liza going about her chores like he had in years past. She had not heard him because she was busy preparing supper and humming a tune that he remembered was her favorite. Liza was a small thin woman with chocolate brown skin. Her face showed signs of hard work and age. Her brown eyes flashed with wisdom one has when you reach a certain age and what life's experiences can give you. Not that she really knew how old she was, because she didn't. No one had taken the time to record her birth at the plantation where she was born.

"Liza," Gabe said softly so he wouldn't startle her.

She turned at the sound of her name with a questioning look on her face.

"I think someone needs to stay with Father at all times. Do you know anyone who might be able to do this?"

"My girl Hannah, she be trainin ta be a healer fer a time now," Liza replied.

"Where is she now?"

"She be in de field, takin de men folk a bite."

"When she gets back, would you ask her to come see me? Oh, she may need someone to help her too."

"Yez sah, I's will."

"Liza?"

"Yez sah?" she asked raising her left eye brow.

"I don't think Father has much time left."

"No sah, he don't."

"I'll be in the study if you need me." He turned and left the kitchen.

In his fathers study, Gabe sat in the big leather chair by the fireplace. He desperately needed someone to talk to. If only Professor Hall were here, he thought.

"I'm here," came a whisper of a voice.

Startled, Gabe sat forward in the chair looking around the room to see who had spoken. He was the only person in the room.

"I'm here with you," came the voice again. Gabe was worried now. Either he was really tired, or he was losing his mind! Standing to his feet he asked,

"Who is there? Show yourself."

"Did I not promise you that I would not leave you, nor forsake you?" came the voice again.

"Heavenly Father!" Gabe exclaimed, falling to his knees as he could no longer stand on his own. "I am so sorry" …was all Gabe could get out for his voice had failed him.

"I will instruct you and teach you in the way you should go; I will counsel you and watch over you. Fear not!"

"Thank you, Heavenly Father," Gabe whispered.

Then he began to pray, repenting for not coming to the Lord first with what was on his heart. He made God a promise it would never happen again. Gabe remained on his knees, worshiping and praising the Lord of his life. Finally, after feeling Gods release, he sat back in the chair. In all his life he never thought he would have been blessed to hear God's voice as clearly as he did today. Soon he would tell Josie how his God had visited him and spoken to him.

Josie was about her evening chores when suddenly she felt a strong urge to pray for Gabe. She stopped what she was doing and bowed her head as she lifted a prayer up to God for him.

A soft knock sounded on the study door. "Come in," Gabe said.

A young Negro girl of about twenty entered the room. Her clothes were worn but clean. Her head bowed, she said, "Ma says ya be needin me sah."

"You must be Hannah, Liza's daughter. I remember when you were just a little girl. Your mother tells me you're studying to be a healer."

"Yez sah, dat be me."

"I wanted to ask you if you would tend to my father. You may need help after awhile, so I think it would be wise if you chose someone that could relieve you. It's hard work, and you'll need rest. Doing this will be your only job," Gabe told her.

"Yez sah, I's take good care of da Massa," she said softly.

"Thank you Hannah, I know you will."

"Massa, ma wanta know'd ifen ya be hongrey? Supper be awaiting on ya."

"Tell her I will be right there."

"Yez sah," Hannah replied, backing out of the door.

Sighing, Gabe went to the dinning room to eat. How lovely this room was yet lonely with only him at the table. After he said grace, he tried to eat supper. He wasn't hungry because he had a lot on his mind. He knew in order to face tomorrow he needed to rest. As he thought about what tomorrow would bring, Liza entered the room like a mother hen caring for her chicks.

"Gabe Lyon, yo best be eatin! Ya gona nee'd all de strength da good Lord be agivin ya," she fussed at him.

"I'm tired Liza," he told her with a small laugh.

"Makes no never mind ya best get ta it!"

"Would you sit and talk with me awhile?" he asked.

"Aint rite, ya knowd dat!" she said with surprise.

"Who's going to tell? I won't if you don't," he said laughing at her.

"De others ifn dey see'd us, why dey be thinking I's be uppity and such."

"Then let's go into your kitchen where it won't matter at all."

He stood and led the way to Liza's domain. Settling into chairs at the stove, Gabe started talking. He told Liza of Josie and their plans to be married as soon as he returned to Maine. He told her of the plans he had for his life, of the promise he made to his father, and how the promises changed things now. Liza sat listening quietly, taking in his every word.

"Now that I've filled you in on what's happening, I'd like to know what you think."

"Right now I's knowd ya be tired. A askin dis ole woman what I's be thinking," pausing she became more serious. "Afor I's give ya da answer, I's be de mind of prayin first. Does ya understand?"

"Yes I do, I learned that lesson today!" Changing the subject, Gabe asked,

"Would you see Hannah is comfortable in Father's room? She may need a bed in there. I've been thinking, we could put it in father's dressing room so she can be near by."

"I's be seein to it!"

Gabe got to his feet slowly. He was tired. Leaving Liza to her task, Gabe returned to his room. His bath water was cold but he didn't care. He bathed, dressed for bed, and said his prayers. He was asleep before his head had laid on the pillow.

Gabe rose early the next morning rested, and after dressing, he walked the short distance to his father's room. He found Hannah sitting in a chair, at his bedside. Walking quietly over to her, Gabe whispered to her that she should go and rest. He would take the watch for her. Smiling her thanks, Hannah left, leaving Gabe alone with his father. Ezra Lyon looked up at his son and smiled a weak smile.

"How are you feeling today, Father?" Gabe asked gently.

"I'm tired son, but better now that you're here," he answered weakly.

"Do you feel like eating something?"

"No, Hannah's already seen to that."

"Do you feel like talking?" Gabe asked.

"Yes, for awhile. Why?"

"I have to talk to you about taking over New Canaan. I need to know a few things about the plantation. You know, the business end of it."

Ezra began to tell his son where he could find all the important papers. He told him of the finances, who he could trust in business dealings, and who he couldn't. Gabe took it all in as fast as he could. After a question and answer session, Gabe cleared his throat. Looking at his father, he asked him,

"Father, what's your relationship with the Lord Jesus Christ?"

"I've been wondering when you were going to ask me," his father said.

"Well… what's your answer?"

"When your mother was alive, I thought I knew. Then, she died and I lost faith," he said sadly turning away from Gabe.

"Do you want to see her again?"

"What do you mean?"

"Mother was a Christian. She's gone to Heaven, and in order for you to go to Heaven to be with her, you have to ask Jesus into your heart. He has to be your Lord and Savior. Have you done that?" Gabe asked gently.

"Always thought I had time."

"Father, if you've asked me to take over New Canaan, then you already know you don't have the luxury of time. Let me tell you about my Jesus and what he has done for you and me." Gabe began to tell his father of Jesus' love, and how God so loved the world that he gave his only begotten son. Whosoever believes in him would not perish, but have ever lasting life. He told him how Jesus had died on the cross for their sins. Then he told him how to ask Jesus into his heart. When he had finished, with tears in his eyes, he looked at his father and asked, "So, are you ready to ask Jesus into your heart?"

"Yes I am. Will you help me?" his father looked at him hopefully.

Leading his father in prayer to ask Jesus to come into his heart was the happiest moment this father and son had ever shared.

They spent the rest of the morning talking of things they'd never spoken of before. They talked of his mother, and how proud she would have been of Gabe for his love of God. Gabe told his father all about Josie and the calling upon both of their lives. They spoke of old memories and shared new ones, until Gabe could see his father was tired.

"You rest now; I'll be here if you need anything," he told him.

His father closed his eyes and rested comfortably for the first time since Gabe had arrived at home.

The next few days Gabe spent mostly in his father's room talking or watching him sleep. Gabe honestly thought he might get better, but that wasn't to be.

Gabe was awakened by a soft knocking on his door. Grabbing his robe, he answered, "Yes?"

"Come quickly sah. Ya father be askin fo ya," Hannah told him when he opened the door.

Running to his father's room, with Hannah at his heels, Gabe went to his father's side. Ezra Lyon's breathing was shallow and raspy. He knew he was dying. Holding out his hand to his son, he told him for the first time in many years he loved him. He thanked his son for coming to him and telling him about Gods love. Then he closed his eyes and was on his way to Heaven.

The whole household was in mourning. The grandfather clock in the main sitting room stood silent. Its pendulum stopped as tradition, at the time of the master's death. Gabe took Hannah aside and thanked her for the tender care she had given to his father. With tears in her eyes, she could only nod. Then, going to Liza, he asked her to gather all the slaves to the back yard.

Gabe stood on the back porch, waiting for the slave to come. He needed to talk to them. He needed to calm their fears as he knew they were already aware of his father's death. As he stood looking over the slave quarters, his heart dropped. "How could things have gotten in such disrepair? Another thing he needed to add to his list," he thought. He'd started the "list" since his encounter with God in his father's study. It was questions he needed answers to, and answers to questions that he hadn't asked yet. God was with him. His heart hurt because he wouldn't be able to see his father on this earth again, but joyful that he would in Heaven. Gabe thanked the Lord for giving him such precious time with his father.

The slaves were slowly making their way to the main house. Gabe could see them coming from where he stood. Liza and her husband, Old Ben, had been such a help. Old Ben had gathered the men while Liza gathered the women and children. He could see the men taking their hats off before they reached the porch. "There's so many!" he thought, at least thirty families, as far as he could tell.

When the slaves had gathered quietly at the steps, Gabe spoke. "I'm sure by now you all know of my father's death. I wanted to let you know I'll be taking over New Canaan in his place. I don't know much about the workings of the plantation, so I'll be depending on all of you for help. Starting now and for the next three days, only the jobs that are of necessity will be done. Then after that, we'll go back to working as usual. I'll be coming to see each of you soon to talk. I want you to know there will be no selling of anyone so please do not be afraid. I want to thank you for your loyalty and your services to my father. I hope I can earn the same respect. Once again I thank you."

Gabe could tell the slaves didn't know what to think. He saw their surprised expression while he spoke. He saw their relief at knowing they wouldn't be sold. He saw them whispering to each other as they left and returned to their quarters. Little did they know change was coming.

The next three days were a whirlwind of activity. Gabe had been so busy making all the arrangements he barely had time to sleep. The one thing he had made sure of was his time alone with the Lord. He would never again let God be second no matter what was happening. Without God he was nothing.

The funeral for Ezra Lyon was held on the second day. Many people from the surrounding parishes came to pay their respects. Gabe met the owners of the neighboring plantations and their families. He had so many names floating around in his head he was sure he wouldn't be able to remember them all. Everyone asked him the same questions. They wanted to know if he was staying, was he going to sell his slaves, and most of all did he want to sell New Canaan? They were quick to mention, after all, he was just a preacher and not a plantation owner. Gabe answered all their questions and noticed the other plantation owners didn't think he could do it. He didn't care because he had other plans. He'd even sent Josie a letter telling her of his father's death, and he would be taking over New Canaan. He also told her when to expect him to return so they could be married. They would be returning to Baton Rouge afterwards. Gabe told her of his love, how he needed her, and asked for her understanding.

For the next few weeks Gabe continued making the plans he felt God had led him to make. He even talked audibly to him as if he were standing in the room with him. It never occurred to Gabe the household slaves could hear him through the closed door. They thought he was talking with his father who had just passed away not to his Heavenly Father. It didn't really matter; he would've done it anyway.

Josie, with letter in hand, walked home as fast as she could. Gabe was coming home! "Father, Father!" she called excitedly almost running through the house to her father's study.

"What is it child? What's wrong?" Professor Hall asked with concern.

"It's a letter from Gabe! He's coming home soon. We'll be married in June as soon as he arrives! Isn't it wonderful?"

"Is that all he had to say?" asked her father laughingly.

"No, he told me his father has died. Here, let me read the letter to you."

Josie read the letter to her father, leaving out only the things young ones in love say to each other.

"Liza," Gabe said as he entered the kitchen. "I need to speak with Ben. Could you send someone to get him for me? Oh, I will need you to come with him. We have some plans to make together."

"Yez sah," she said not questioning him as to why she needed to be with them. She'd seen the changes in him the last few weeks which let her know he had a reason, whatever it was, for this request. Liza left immediately to go to the fields to get Ben.

Old Ben and the other slaves were working hard. It was hot for the end of May. Standing to wipe the sweat out of his eyes, Old Ben saw Liza scurrying across the fields toward him. "Now, dat be a sight!" he thought watching her make her way to him. "Dares be somin wrong!"

Liza came up to him, motioning for him to come away from the rest of the slaves. Whispering in his ear she told him, "Young Massa be needin ya ta cum now!" Dropping his hoe, he followed her out of the field. The others looked up, watching them leave, then continued their work. The ground had to be ready for planting.

Gabe took Liza and old Ben into the study. They both refused to sit down. Looking at Liza, then at old Ben, he said, "There are things I need to talk to you about, so please sit down as this may take a while." Then Gabe sat down and slowly Liza and Old Ben sat down on the sofa, but only on the very edge. He realized this was something they weren't used to, but things would be changing, not only for them, but for all of New Canaan. "I'm going to be leaving at the end of the week," Gabe began. "I'm going back to Maine where I'll be marrying Josephine Hall and we'll be coming back here to live."

Liza and Old Ben looked quickly at each other with Liza smiling from ear to ear. Seeing their approval, Gabe continued. "Ben, while I am gone you'll be in charge and when I return you'll be my overseer. You've been here the longest and know this plantation like no other. You know all that has to be done in order to get the crops planted and harvested. You also know how to care for the animals. I know, just as my father knew, you are the most trustworthy of all."

Gabe noticed Old Ben sat up straighter with pride, knowing the Master of the house depended upon him.

"Liza, you're to be in charge of the house, as if you weren't already," Gabe added smiling. "I'm depending on you both to take notice of what needs to be repaired. If we can fix it, we will. If it needs to be replaced, then we'll buy it. See where we need help and who we can entrust with responsibility. I want to know any ideas that'll improve New Canaan. When I return, I want to meet all the families. I need to get to know them, and they need to know me. Are there any questions?" he finally asked.

"Yez sah, bout how long ya be gone?" Ben asked.

"Two weeks. Five days there, get married and five days back," Gabe answered.

"De house be aready fo ya, jus' hurry on back," Liza exclaimed happily.

"I'm not gone yet!" Gabe teased her.

The trio stood to their feet. Gabe held out his hand toward Old Ben. Old Ben wiped his hand on his pants and then took Gabe's hand in a firm hand-shake. Liza stood by looking proudly at her two men, knowing they would become good friends.

CHAPTER 3

THE FAMILIAR SCENERY OF AMHERST came into view as the train slowed to a stop. "Thank you, Lord!" Gabe said as he stood to gather his things. It had been a long trip. Finally, he would see his Josie. It had been two and a half months since he had last seen her. That was two and a half months too long he decided. Stepping off the train, he saw her waiting for him, as beautiful as ever. He could tell she had seen him too. She was smiling, waving and calling his name. It was all he could do not to run to her. She must have been thinking the same thing, for at that moment, she took off running toward him. He ran to her, picked her up and twirled her around in the air. Never had he been so happy to see her. He didn't care who knew it! Passer-byer's looked at them in shock at their public display of affection. He just had this big silly grin on his face; but Josie blushed from the top of her head to the soles of her feet. He put her down to ease her discomfort while laughing at her. Other than her blush, she didn't seem to mind what he'd done.

"You're beautiful!" Gabe whispered as he held her.

"I've missed you! She whispered back smiling.

Professor Hall and Charles came up to the happy couple. Greetings, handshakes and laughter were exchanged. Everyone was excited Gabe had returned. Quickly making arrangements to have his luggage delivered to the hotel, the four friends walked the short distance to Professor Hall's home. Josie at Gabe's side, held tightly to his arm.

"Home at last!" Professor Hall exclaimed as he ushered the group inside.

"Everyone sit, Gabe, you must be tired after your journey. Would you care for something to drink?"

"Yes, I'd love some tea."

"I think tea would be good for all of us," Josie said as she went to get the refreshment.

"Tell us all the news Gabe," Charles requested.

"I will, as soon as Josie comes back. I don't want to leave her out. It shouldn't take her long."

So the men reminisced of times they had shared together, that of the teacher and the students. Their laughter drifted into the kitchen where Josie hurried about her task. She didn't want to miss anything they were sharing. She didn't want to have Gabe out of her sight.

Josie entered the room with the refreshments; the men stood waiting for her to be seated. When she had seated herself on the sofa next to Gabe, and served the tea, the conversation continued with Gabe saying, "I've so much to tell you, I don't really know where to begin!"

"How about at the beginning," Charles volunteered.

"That's a good place to start!" Gabe laughed.

"When I arrived at New Canaan, I discovered my father was gravely ill. The last few days with him were wonderful. He received Jesus Christ as his Lord and Savior. We talked about memories, about God and you Josie," he said turning to look into her beautiful blue eyes.

"How wonderful God gave you those last moments with him," Josie said softly.

"The most wonderful part is yet to come! I was in my father's study wishing I could talk with you Professor Hall. When, just as you hear me now, I heard the voice of the Lord! Now don't think me daft, it happened! The Lord reminded me he would not leave me, He would be my counsel, and He would lead and protect me! I can't explain in adequate words what this has done to me. I fell to my knees, I couldn't stand, and I couldn't talk. I just started worshiping the Lord. Then this peace came upon me, like the Bible says, *Peace that surpasses all understanding.* I truly know what it means now. Then, as the days passed, I began making "The List." This list I'll share with you later. Now, I want you to know everyday I talk with the Lord, not in a prayer but something like a prayer. I talk to him out loud and He answers me! Not in a voice like he did to get my attention, but he floods my mind with solutions and answers. Why, I even have answers that have no questions! That's how the list came about. I wrote everything down. This experience has changed my life so much! I can't begin to tell you the difference in me now. I know what I have to do. I have no fear, and no doubts! I may be taking over New Canaan, but I'll definitely be doing God's work. So will you Josie, we'll be partners in this adventure with God!"

"What I wouldn't give to have such an experience!" Charles exclaimed in awe.

"Truly something to be treasured," Josie said softly.

"I've wanted to experience that my whole life! To hear the Lord's voice audibly, Gabe, you've surely been blessed," Professor Hall said with passion.

"Now, when I read the Bible, I know he's talking to me!" Gabe stated emphatically.

Everyone nodded in agreement, no one said a word, and each was lost in their own thoughts about what Gabe had just revealed.

Gradually they began to make small talk. Gabe, looking into Josie's eyes, asked with a mischievous smile, "Now, tell me, when will I be married?" Everyone started laughing at his question.

"You sir, will be getting married day after tomorrow on Sunday. So you have a lot to do between now and then," she told him smiling.

"What's there for me to do? All I need to do is show up and here I am!"

"Well, if that's all you have to do may I ask if you've gotten the rings? Just who do you want to invite? You've only one day to personally invite who you wish. I've sent invitations out to a few friends. I want this to be a small wedding. The only ones I care about being there are Charles, Father, my friend Mary, and of course you and me."

"I stand corrected, I do have a few things to do! I hope you aren't disappointed we won't be taking a honeymoon. We have to get back to New Canaan as soon as possible."

"That'll be enough of a honeymoon trip for me," Josie told him assuredly.

"Well Charles, are you going to be my best man? Gabe asked.

"It will be my pleasure," Charles said standing and bowing.

"See? I've already accomplished two things for the wedding! I have my best man, and my invited guest. I'm almost through with my part," he told them laughing with a wave of his hand.

They talked for awhile about the wedding with Josie telling them of the plans she had made. All were in agreement the wedding was to be small.

"Tell me Charles, how was your graduation?" Gabe inquired.

"It was a day of celebration!" Charles exclaimed, barely keeping his excitement down. "Josie and the professor came. My parents, like you, couldn't make it. They did send me their congratulations in a letter. We all went to a reception afterward, which was the social event of the year. But that's not all! You, my friend, owe me congratulations! You're now looking at the new principal of Silver Springs Academy for young men ages six to fourteen."

"Praise the Lord! Congratulations!" Gabe said standing to shake Charles' hand. "You're following the same path as our own Edward Jones. Charles, do you know what this means? It means you have access to books. I wonder, could you help me get the McGuffey Readers?"

"I can get the publishers address and the books. Is that what you need?"

"Yes! Thank you!"

"Just what do you need with these readers Gabe?" he asked.

"It's all part of the list, my friend!"

Josie, who had been listening carefully, placed her hand on her heart. She suddenly realized what he was going to do! She quickly thanked the Lord for revealing this to her.

"I can't wait to see this list of yours," the professor told Gabe. "I must admit, it has captured my curiosity."

The afternoon passed quickly as the group talked of many things, and enjoyed each others company. Gabe was amazed, it was as if he never left, but that's how it was with family. Looking at the grandfather clock, he was shocked at the time. "I'm going to have to leave soon. I have to go to the hotel, but I'd like to invite all of you to join me for dinner as my guest."

"We'd love to join you," Josie said quickly while the others agreed.

"So, we should meet within the hour?" Gabe asked.

"Yes," They all agreed at once.

"Charles, I have some lesson plans you might want. Come to the study with me and see if you can use them," the professor told him. Both men rose leaving the room, finally Gabe and Josie were alone.

"I've missed you so much!" Gabe said standing taking Josie in his arms.

"I've missed you too, I can't begin to tell you how hard it's been for me."

He could see the misty trace of tears in her eyes, how his heart hurt for her.

"It was hard for me as well, I have so much I want to share with you," he told her lovingly.

Pulling away from him so she could look at him, Josie laughed and said,

"We'll have five days of travel to share with each other!"

"I love you Josie, thank you for being so understanding, I'm moving you away from everything you know. I noticed your father didn't bring it up, as a matter of fact, everyone seemed to avoid the topic all together," Gabe said.

"Father and I have discussed it many times. He was the first to bring it up, just after you left."

"He did?"

"Yes, but that can wait! I just want to look at you!" she said.

Taking her by the hand the two stood whispering words of their love. After a kiss that told her he missed her, the two walked to the door.

"Tell your father and Charles my goodbyes," he said putting his hand on the door.

"I will," she replied, hating to see him go, even for just a little while.

"I'll see you very soon," both said in unison. Then he kissed her quickly and left.

Smiling, Josie went to her father's study, and found her father and Charles in deep conversation. "Men," she thought, then said, "excuse me gentlemen, Gabe has left. He's asked I tell you goodbye. We're to meet him within the hour for supper, so I will be in my room getting ready. Please, let's not be late," she said looking directly at her father. She knew when these two got together time slipped away from them.

"I promise we'll be ready to leave when you are," replied her father.

"I promise too!" added Charles.

Smiling at both of them, Josie went to her room to get ready. There she took out her favorite blue dress. She was glad she had not packed the dress with the others in the trunk for her trip to New Canaan. Standing and looking around her, she noticed she didn't have the same feeling for her room as she had in the past. It was as if this was no longer her room. It could have been a stranger's room, or a hotel room. It didn't hold the same security as it once held. In truth, she told herself, it wasn't her room. In New Canaan was her room, the one she'd be sharing with Gabe as his wife.

She dressed as quickly as a woman could dress, and fixed her hair. She wondered what the fashion would be in Baton Rouge. She wondered, "how does one dress as a plantation owner's wife? Did she have to change the way she dressed? Probably for the heat," she thought. "How was she to handle or behave with servants? All she knew was she'd treat them as her equal. What would they think of her? What would Gabe's friends think of her?" Her mother had raised her in the proper manners and graces so she knew that wasn't a problem. What she did have a problem with was she'd be a wife of a slave owner. She prayed for God to give her guidance and understanding. She was depending on God to do just as he had promised in James1:5 *If any of you lacks wisdom, he should ask God, who gives generously to all.* She believed this with all her heart. Putting on her bonnet, she went to see if her father and Charles were ready to leave.

Gabe saw them enter the hotel lobby where he waited. There she was, as beautiful as ever, on her fathers arm. His heart always raced when he saw Josie; soon she would be his wife. He had no doubts about their life together. Tonight he had to share her, tomorrow he had to do his errands without her, but Sunday he would marry her. Then they would be off on the adventure God had planned for them.

Walking over to the small group, Gabe offered Josie his arm, and escorted them to the dining room. As they were about to be seated, the professor stood back and put his hand on Charles' shoulder. Smiling, Professor Hall looked at Gabe and Josie and said, "I think Charles and I will eat over there. We have a lot to talk about and I know you and Josie do. Remember Gabe, we're still your guest!"

"Are you sure you won't sit with us?" Gabe asked, pleased the professor had thought of them.

"We're sure," Charles assured him.

The two men walked away to their table leaving Josie and Gabe by themselves..

"Father is trying to give us time to be alone," Josie whispered.

"I've noticed!" Gabe said laughing. Their conversation remained light until after they ordered their food.

"I know moving to New Canaan is difficult for you," Gabe began, "The heat of your first summer there will be trying."

"Should I buy cloth and bring it with me for lighter clothes?"

"I have an idea, why don't you wait until we're there, and then you can buy as much cloth as you need."

"You don't want to have to carry anything extra with us. After all, with my things, there will only be two more trunks."

"Just two?" he inquired jokingly.

"I could arrange for more."

"No, it's quite all right, but please bring everything you want to bring. I don't know when we'll be coming back,"

"Then I'll bring one more trunk, I want to bring some things that were my mothers."

"By all means do," he told her sincerely.

After their food arrived and they said the blessing, Gabe began to tell her about all the things he wanted to change about New Canaan. She listened carefully with wide eyes. He could tell she was impressed with his ideas. He told her of "the list" and its importance to him. He pointed out to her the things she would be in charge of if she agreed. When he finished, he asked her, "So, what do you think?"

"I think it's from God!" She exclaimed, "Do you understand the responsibility of this? Do you not realize in the south the majority of "the list" is against the law?"

"Yes. my love, I do! We're going to have to pray our way through this whole project. I know we can do this together."

"I know we can too! I know God will be by our side the whole time. I have some ideas I'd like to share with you. You're not the only one God has been talking to."

Josie began to tell him of her ideas. He couldn't believe what he was hearing. These were the same things God revealed to him. He didn't want to spring too much on her at one time, so he hadn't told her everything. Now, there wasn't a single doubt in his mind. He knew these things would be accomplished, and here was his confirmation. The couple finished their supper with the promise to continue this conversation when they reached New Canaan, in the privacy of their own home.

Long after their meal, Josie and Gabe strolled arm in arm. The professor and Charles walked a short distance behind them; the two men were deep in conversation as they made their way back to Josie's house.

"I've a few errands to run tomorrow morning, but I'd love to come and see you in the afternoon. I don't want to spend any more time away from you than I have to," Gabe told her.

"You can come anytime after you have finished. You know that! Will you stay for dinner?" she asked

"Yes, of course," Gabe said looking into her eyes.

"Good!" Returning his gaze, she continued, "Do you think Liza would teach me to cook all your favorite dishes?"

"She would love to teach you. The only thing you have to worry about is her letting you cook once you've learned. You have to understand the kitchen is Liza's private domain!"

"I don't want to step on any toes Gabe, all I want to do is learn. The main problem for me is having servants and slaves. I'm really nervous about it. You know me, I do everything for myself. I hope I don't offend anyone, most of all Liza," Josie confided in him.

"Just be yourself and she'll love you," Gabe assured her.

"That's all I can be!" she warned him.

They added Charles and the professor to their conversation as they neared the house. Josie invited Charles to dinner on Saturday which he accepted. They laughed at Charles bemoaning his plight of being the single man out come Sunday. Everyone agree they would pray for him a mate, which he told them was acceptable, and asked they do it soon. When the group had reached the steps of the house, Gabe gave a quick kiss to Josie on the cheek, telling her he'd see her tomorrow, and shook hands with the professor. Saying good night, Charles and Gabe left them standing on the front porch waving good bye. The two friends, walking back to town, enjoyed each others company, laughing and talking about the days to come and the days past.

Waking early on Saturday morning, Gabe was ready to face the day. His only project was to get the wedding rings. Bounding down the hotel stairs, Gabe didn't stop for breakfast. Out the door he went in search for the perfect wedding rings. The only place he knew to go was the small jewelry store down the street which is where he headed. Walking into the jewelry shop, Gabe was greeted with a nod from the man behind the counter. Gabe asked the man to show him the wedding rings he had available.

"How much do you want to spend?" the man asked with indifference.

"Cost is no problem," Gabe informed him.

The jeweler lit up at hearing cost was no problem. It was all Gabe could do not to laugh in his face. How sad to think this man would treat someone with money any different than anyone else.

The jeweler began to show Gabe the most expensive rings in the store. All were beautiful but he had to pick out a Josie ring, one that looked like her. He looked at all of the rings, commenting on their beauty. None met his mental picture of the ring he wanted. He told the man he wanted something different, something special for his wife to be.

Grinning, the jeweler pulled out a little black case. Opening the case slowly, he showed Gabe a ring. It was definitely Josie! It was a plain yellow gold ring with a small engraved cross in the middle. This was it! This was the ring he wanted. He then picked out a plain yellow gold wedding band for himself, paid the jeweler and left. Gabe made his way to the nearest bookstore, here he purchased the wedding present he'd be giving Josie. It was a white family Bible with gold trimming on the cover and pages. This would be the Bible to record the births of their children.

Gabe hurried to the house to join Charles, Professor Hall, and Josie for the rest of the day. Josie and Gabe were full of excitement as they laughed and talked about the wedding to take place the next day. They enjoyed the dinner Josie prepared for them but they teased her how she'd soon become lazy having someone else to do the cooking for her. She laughed along with them good naturedly, and assured them the one person they needed to worry about was her father. He would after all, be eating his own cooking. Professor Hall informed them he was going to hire a housekeeper. No one should suffer by eating what he cooked, especially him! When the sun started to set the group stood on the porch.

"You know Gabe," Charles said teasingly, "you won't be able to see Josie until the wedding. You'd better kiss her quick, because this will be your last time kissing her as a single woman."

Josie blushed at Charles' words. Taking her hand, Gabe raised it to his lips and kissed it saying, "Until tomorrow," then he said, "Goodnight." He left a blushing Josie at her father's side.

Sunday morning found Josie both nervous and excited about her wedding. Her father was as nervous as she. She wondered if Gabe felt the same way. Mary Mangum, her best friend and maid of honor, had shown up early to help her dress. Josie's white satin wedding gown was beautiful. The high collar was trimmed in the smallest lace which accented her slender neck. The sleeves were long and came to a point on her gloved hands. The tight fitting bodice showed off her tiny waist and the skirt was full, trimmed with lace that touched the floor. It was the most beautiful dress either girl had seen. Mary's dress was made similar to Josie's. It was light pink and trimmed with small dainty roses along the bottom of the skirt.

"You remind me of your mother," Professor Hall said in a husky voice from the doorway of Josie's room.

"I wish she were here," she said softly to her father.

"We both do," her father assured her.

"I think its time for us to leave. How you got the pastor to do the wedding before Sunday services is a miracle!" Mary said, as she gathered their bonnets.

Josie took her white satin bonnet from Mary and placed it over the many curls framing her face. "There," she said, "I'm ready now."

Taking her fathers arm, Josie and Mary made their way to the waiting carriage.

Charles watched Gabe pace back and forth in front of Amherst Church of God. Laughing at him only caused him to walk faster, not going anywhere, but in circles. "You must calm down Gabe! You're going to wear a hole in your boots!"

"Laugh if you will my friend. When it's your turn, I'll be sure to remind you of this very moment!"

The carriage came within sight of the church, and Josie could see Gabe standing there handsome as ever. She couldn't remember Gabe looking as stunning as he did this day. His tall stature was accented by the black jacket he wore, the tails of his jacket moved as he paced in front of the church. Josie had to laugh. He was as nervous as she!

When the carriage pulled up to the front of the church, Josie descended gracefully and carefully placed her hand in Gabe's. Her beauty took his breath away sending his heart racing as never before. Charles helped Mary from the carriage and Professor Hall followed. The wedding party stood holding hands as they said a prayer for the happy couple before entering the church.

The ceremony was beautiful as they stood before the Lord. The words exchanged were a promise, not only to each other, but to God with family and friends as witnesses. The rings exchanged represented God's unending love as well as their own. The promises they vowed were sealed with a kiss. They were now husband and wife.

"Congratulations! May I present to you, Mr. and Mrs. Gabriel Lyon!" the pastor almost shouted.

Hand-shakes and tears were shared by the friends and family as they congratulated the happy couple. Excited and holding tight to each others hand, the newlywed's left the church. Gabe helped Josie into the carriage that was to take them to Professor Hall's home and said, "Are you ready?"

"I will be as soon as I change from this dress!" She assured him.

"No regrets?"

"What about? Leaving, no, leaving father…I feel a little guilty, but as he has said many times, he knew this day would come."

"Ah, so that's what you meant by the two of you discussing your leaving."

"Yes, it is. Just goes to show you how God prepares one for the future," she assured him happily.

Gabe and Josie stood at the train station saying good bye to their friends and family. Professor Hall had a brave smile on his face, because the last thing he wanted was for Josie to feel bad about leaving. After giving her father a kiss on the cheek and promises to write, she and Gabe boarded the train. Destination, New Canaan!

CHAPTER 4

GABE LOVED WATCHING JOSIE'S EXPRESSIONS as they passed through the different states to Baton Rouge; she loved looking at the new scenery. She had even ventured out with him onto the landing outside the compartment door, wanting to get a closer view as the train passed through the towns and countryside. The sleeper car was not comfortable to him and it held no privacy, it didn't seem to bother Josie who slept well enough. She was a bundle of excitement as she waited to see what was around the next bend. Their long journey hadn't seemed to tire her as she asked many questions about New Canaan and its people. It seemed she had committed everything he said to memory. She never ceased to amaze him! In the evenings they spent time reading, praying, and talking about the changes coming to New Canaan. He couldn't wait to get home.

"Josie, time to wake up," he said to her gently, for she had fallen asleep on his shoulder. "We're here."

"Oh my, Gabe we're here already?" she asked with a sleepy voice.

"Yes, my love, we're almost home."

When the train came to a stop, they gathered their things and disembarked.

"I'm having trouble keeping my balance after being on that train for so long," Josie told him laughing.

"You'll get use to it quickly."

"My word, Gabe! Between the heat and humidity here, I'll be drenched before we reach New Canaan!"

"It takes some time to get use to the heat, but I promise you will. We need to go to the livery stable and get a carriage to take us the rest of the way. It's just across the street."

They left their luggage at the train station. Then Gabe, with Josie on his arm, crossed the street. When they'd entered the stable, Gabe spied Little John hard at work.

"Hello Little John," Gabe was glad to see the boy looking well.

"Sah," Little John answered excitedly, happy at seeing the man.

"Is Mr. Allen here?"

"Yez sah, I's be a getin him fer ya!"

"Oh Gabe, I've never seen anything so sad! How can you stand this slavery?" Josie whispered, not wishing for anyone to over hear her.

"It's the way of the South for now my love," he whispered back.

"Gabriel Lyon! Who's that with you?" Mr. Allen asked returning with Little John.

"Mr. Allen, Little John, I'd like for you to meet my wife, Josie," Gabe said making the introductions.

"It's nice to meet you Mrs. Lyon," Mr. Allen bowed slightly.

"How do you do," Josie gave a polite nod. Then turning to Little John she smiled. Little John in turn smiled back shyly, happy to be acknowledged by the pretty lady.

"I'm here to get a carriage again. I'll need Little John to go with us, if it's acceptable."

"That'll be fine, just fine. My family and I were sorry to hear of your fathers passing. He was a fine man and I know he'll be missed."

"Yes, he will, but thank you for saying so."

"I just found out yesterday you'd gone back up North. Who did you leave in your absence to oversee the plantation? Word has it you are going to be taking over yourself. Is it true?"

Knowing Mr. Allen had alternative motives for his inquiries, Gabe answered him clearly so there wouldn't be any doubts of his intentions. "Why wouldn't I take over the plantation? After all, it was my fathers and I am his only heir and son. So, yes, to answer your question, I'll be running the plantation and just so you know, I won't be selling the land nor anything or anyone either. Now, as to who's been taking care of the plantation in my absence, let me assure you, Mr. Allen, I left it in capable hands!"

All the while Little John had been hitching the horses to the carriage.

He was so happy to be going with the good preacher and his pretty wife.

When he was with the preacher he felt good about himself. He didn't know why, he just did.

Mr. Allen's face turned bright red as Gabe finished his speech. He was well aware Gabe had made a distinctive effort to inform him about his intentions. He felt like a fool! He wouldn't be listening to his wife anymore! Deciding to make up for his foolish questions, Mr. Allen looked sheepishly at Gabe and said, "If you need Little John, you may borrow him for a few days to help your wife get settled in."

"Thank you, I'll send him back to you day after tomorrow," Gab agreed.

Little John was careful to hide his excitement but his heart filled with joy.

"Will you inform Little John's family where he'll be and when he'll return?"

"Little John's family doesn't live here. I bought him from your father two years ago," Mr. Allen explained.

"Very well then, thank you for your generosity," Gabe said as the two men shook hands.

Gabe, Josie and Little John went to the train station, and after retrieving their luggage, they continued to New Canaan. They rode talking and laughing at Josie's awe of the new countryside. Little John didn't say much, but an occasional giggle could be heard from him. Josie really liked this little boy. She was already trying to figure out how to keep him with his family at New Canaan.

Gabe stopped the carriage at the drive of New Canaan. Josie let out a small gasp before saying, "It's beautiful! I don't believe I've ever seen anything like it!"

Laughing, Gabe said, "Welcome home Josie!"

They continued down the drive with Josie entranced with the beauty she saw. He was pleased she admired it. He felt the same way each time he saw it. It was always as if it were the first time. As the house came into view, Gabe was surprised to see every slave on the plantation standing in front and along the drive. He couldn't believe his eyes. Everyone had come out to welcome them home.

"Gabe, what is this?" Josie whispered in his ear.

"We shall soon see!" He whispered back.

Little John was scanning each face they passed, looking for his mother and father. Stepping down from the carriage, Gabe held his hand out to Josie. Gracefully she descended. With Josie at his side, he turned toward the assembled group and before he could say a word, a shout of "welcum home" came from them. Liza rushed forward with Ben behind her holding his hat in his hand, waiting for introductions. Gabe realized how little he knew of these people. He would make certain he would know everyone by their name. Smiling at the group before him, he began the introductions.

"Thank you for this warm welcoming. I'd like to introduce you to my wife, Josie."

As if on cue, Josie did her first duty as mistress of the plantation.

"I'd like to thank you for making me feel welcome by coming out to greet me and my husband. I hope to get to know each and every one of you soon. I'm sure I'll need your help in learning to do many things here. So, I thank you in advance."

When she had finished, Gabe turned to Little John. "Little John, do you see your Mother and Father?"

"Yez sah, I's does!" he said so softly.

"Where are they?"

"Over dar, sah," Little John pointed toward the large group.

Turning to face the slaves, Gabe asked, "Will Little John's mother and father please step forward?"

A couple from the back of the group made their way to the front. The woman, in her late twenties, was holding the end of her apron, twisting it nervously with her eyes cast down. She was followed by a tall, proud muscular man, about the same age. Smiling at the couple, Gabe said, "Little John has come for a visit! I'd like to come to your home soon and talk with you both, but for now, Little John, go with your family."

Little John jumped from the carriage and ran to his mother, throwing his arms around her waist. She wrapped her arms around him, crying, telling him how glad she was to see him. His father put his arms around them both then, looking up at Gabe, he said, "Thank ya, sah. Ya be givin us a blessin."

It was all Josie could do to keep from crying. Her composure was on shaky ground. All the slaves gathered around Little John and his parents. They knew what a rare occasion this was; to be reunited with a love one that had been sold. Such things never happened. Not even for a visit.

Old Ben stood tall and dismissed everyone. Taking the horses by the rein, he led them off toward the stable. Liza, acting like the mother hen, shooed Josie and Gabe toward the house. Stopping at the door way, Gabe reached down and picked Josie up in his arms and carried her across the threshold. Josie blushed, but Liza laughed at them. Sitting Josie on her feet once again, Gabe made the introductions.

"Josie, this is Liza. Liza, this is my wife Josie."

"It's such a pleasure to meet you Liza; I've heard such good things about you!" Josie shocked Liza with her warm embrace.

"I's hear'd good thangs bout you!" Liza smiled, happy her boy had cared enough to talked about her.

"Later you must tell me all about Gabe when he was a little boy," Josie told her in a loud whisper making sure Gabe heard. Gabe only laughed.

"I's be morin happy ta do jus't dat! Ya'll be tired. I's done fix't da Massa room fer ya. Ya'll rest and I's call ya in a while when da dinner is ready. Follows me, I's showd ya'll ta ya room."

"Lead the way!" Gabe told her, just happy to be home.

Josie had always heard of big beautiful homes like these. She had even been in a few in Maine, but nothing had prepared her for the beauty of this house. Holding tightly to Gabe's hand, they followed Liza up the spiral staircase. Instead of turning right at the top of the stairs, Liza turned left taking them toward the west wing of the house. Gabe had no idea where Liza was going! Slowing down at the big oak double doors, Liza turned to Gabe and said,

"Massa, I be a hopin ya don't mind, but des here be ya mama's favit room. Me an my Ben fixit fer ya an da missus." Liza opened the doors. Josie couldn't believe her eyes. It was the most beautiful room she had ever seen!

There was a mahogany four poster bed sitting caddie corner in the room with the rest of the other furniture made of the same wood. On each side of the bed were night stands with glass lamps. On one wall was a dressing table with a chest of drawers beside it. At the end of the room was a fireplace with two large leather chairs sitting on a beautiful cream colored Asian rug.

The most beautiful of all was what appeared to be a large window with long cream colored curtains with red roses that matched the coverlet of the bed. Nothing prepared Josie for the moment Liza parted the curtains. French doors were revealed which lead out to a balcony over looking the most beautiful flower gardens below.

"Oh Liza, it's beautiful! Thank you so much!" Josie said with misty eyes.

"I'll thank Ben in person, but thank you for doing this for us," Gabe told her.

"Twas notin, Massa Gabe. I's be glad ya'll be home at last." Turning, she left the room, closing the doors behind her.

"Do you realize this is the first time we've been alone since we've been married?" Gabe asked Josie.

"Yes I do," she told him shyly, as he took her in his arms and kissed her.

As Liza worked in her kitchen preparing dinner, she wondered how that little snip of a girl survived the long trip from her home to here. She was so tiny and dainty. Liza noticed Josie hadn't complained about one thing since she had arrived, not like the other women she'd met from the other plantations. Why, even standing out in the heat earlier, she hadn't even swooned. Yes, she definitely was the proper mate for Gabe!

Little John sat in the comfort of his mother's arms, telling her how much he'd missed her. He told her about his life with Mr. Allen, and the work he did. His father looked on with pride, realizing his son was strong despite being so young. His father wondered what the master wanted to talk to him about. All the slaves were talking of the young master and his pretty wife. Big John and his wife had been bought by the old master just after the new master went away to school. The old master had been good to him, but he'd never done what the young master had done. He didn't know of any master who had done anything this kind before. Maybe old Ben was right. Maybe changes would be coming.

After they had bathed, rested and changed into lighter clothing, Josie and Gabe came down to have dinner. After all, it would have insulted Liza if they were late.

"I've got to see the rest of this house!" Josie told Gabe with delight.

"It's yours to do with as you please," he said, leading her to the dining room.

"Do you think you could make me a map so I won't get lost?"

"I could, but I don't remember much about the west wing. My old room was on the east side and so was father's. I can make you a map from our room to the kitchen. How about that?" he asked laughing.

"Why sir, that would be mighty fine of you," she said trying her best to mimic a southern draw. This sent them both into a fit of laughter.

"Now dat be music to my ears! Dis ole house aint heard laughin in a while," Liza said entering the room with a platter.

Gabe noticed Liza had set the table with the finest china and linens.

"I was just telling Gabe I'll need a map to find my way around this house." "No need fer dat. I's learn ya."

"Thank you, Liza! I'd appreciate it very much."

After saying the blessing, Josie was greeted with the different foods that are traditional in Louisiana. She tried cornbread for the first time and loved it.

The fried okra and green beans were wonderful. Not that she hadn't had green beans before, but not seasoned this way. She tried sweet potatoes with brown sugar and turkey that had seasoning she couldn't name. It was a taste adventure. Gabe noticed she tasted everything. He was thankful Liza had taken in account Josie hadn't had Louisiana food before and made a meal easy for her to eat.

After dinner, Gabe left Josie in the capable hands of Liza. He wanted to find Ben because they had a lot to talk about. He soon found him in the stables.

"I thought I'd find you here!" Gabe said as he walked toward him.

"I's sur glad ya be back Massa! Them nosy Broussard's been here askin bout whar ya be. I's tol em ya be out. Dey came by yestada askin all kinda questions. I's didn't tell'em nothin."

"I'm glad I came back when I did too. I spoke with Mr. Allen at the livery stable. He said he'd just found out I'd been away yesterday. News travels fast enough around here. I thank the good Lord they only came once."

"Shur enough!"

"What I would like to do Ben is start meeting with the families. I'd like to start tonight with Little John's family. Could you take me there and introduce me?"

"Shur sah, it be this way."

As Gabe and Ben walked toward the slave quarters, they could hear singing coming from that direction. They walked passed the row of small cabins. They all looked as if they needed repair. He couldn't believe how his father had let them live this way. Ben broke Gabe's thoughts as he stepped in front of one of the smaller cabins.

"This here be little Johns pa's place."

Gabe didn't know quite what to do. The door wasn't much, but still he knocked.

Little John opened the door with his father standing behind him. Both were surprised to see Gabe. "Massa, cum on in," Little John's father's voice was husky from being so nervous.

Entering the small two room cabin, Gabe was appalled at what he saw. A fireplace that was too small, a rickety old table, two straight back chairs and a small pallet on the floor he knew was for Little John.

"I've come to introduce myself. I'm Gabriel Lyon. My friends call me Gabe. I hope we'll become friends. What are your names?"

"I's be big John an this here be my Delia," putting his arm around his wife, he pulled her close to him.

"I want you both to know how sorry I am my father sold Little John to Mr. Allen. I'm going to do my best to get him back. He shouldn't be without his family." Delia started to cry and the big black man had tears in his eyes. Little John's face showed hope for the first time since Gabe had known him.

"Thank ya, Massa, Thank ya! Big John said and then they shook hands.

Gabe didn't miss the big man's grip. One thing about it, Gabe needed to build up his strength. Leaving the cabin with Ben, they made their way to the next cabin. There Ben introduced him to another couple who had five children. Then they moved on to the next. They continued in this fashion until Gabe had met everyone. Their names swirled in his head. He'd have to rely on Ben to help him with names. Gabe stayed out longer than he'd intended and it was late. He hurried back to the house after thanking Ben for his help and making arrangements to meet with him the next morning.

He came through the back following the laughter. He found Liza and Josie in the kitchen sharing Gabe stories. Knowing his wife was tired after a very long day, he stole her away from Liza, taking her upstairs with him for much needed rest.

It was Tuesday morning. Little John had to return with the carriage to Mr. Allen's. After a tearful good bye with his mother, little John got into the carriage. Walking over to him, Gabe reached into his pocket and brought out a nickel. Giving it little John, Gabe told him this was his payment for his services for taking the carriage back to Mr. Allen. Also for the hard work he'd done along side his father while he was there. Little John was speechless. Gabe would have given him more, but he didn't want the little boy to get in trouble. Waving goodbye, Little John set off for town.

The next few weeks were spent with Ben showing Gabe around the Plantation. As they walked through the fields, Gabe made sure he spoke to each and every person he saw, calling them by name with Ben's help. If it was only a hello, he made sure he did it. While Gabe was on his tour of the land, Josie and Liza were busy too. Liza introduced Josie to all the women and children, and was quick to point out each woman's talent. She told Josie what the smaller children did, and the age they went to work either in the orchards, the fields or in the barns.

Josie made her list and Gabe made his. At the end of each day they would meet in the study to compare notes. They would kneel and pray, asking the Lord for his guidance in how to proceed next. When it was time to go to bed they were tired, but excited. They would lie in bed whispering to each other about what they would be doing soon.

One morning Josie woke up before Gabe. It was still dark outside as she stood on the balcony in her night gown, thanking God for all his many blessings. She worshipped the Lord in this quiet time. Suddenly, a bright light emerged from the darkness. It started out as a small light, but then it grew bigger and brighter. There, standing in front of her, was what Josie could only call an angel. He was dressed in brilliant white with his wings spread wide from his shoulders. He smiled at her and said, "Its time to begin!" then he was gone. Josie just stood there a few minutes in awe, then her adrenalin kicked in. Rushing over to where Gabe was asleep, she jumped on the bed, calling to him urgently.

"Gabe, wake up! I have to talk to you, Wake up!"

Sitting up with a start and sleepy eyed, Gabe woke up. "What's wrong? Are you okay?"

"I'm fine! You're not going to believe what I saw! I saw an Angel, an Angel from God!"

"Are you sure? Tell me what happened," he thought he must be dreaming.

"I was standing on the balcony praying, when all of a sudden, a bright light broke through the darkness and this Angel was standing in the garden smiling at me! He told me it is time to begin!" she said excitedly.

Gabe was wide awake now. He knew she'd seen an angel from God. It had to be! Because he'd felt the Lord leading him in this same direction.

"Then we had better put our list into action," he told her, taking her hand, they thanked God for their message. After a quick kiss and hug they got out of bed and dressed quickly. Running to the study, they got out the list. First thing on the list was going to be done immediately. Gabe rushed to find Ben and Josie went to find Liza. Ben was given the request to have all the slaves assemble at the back porch after breakfast as soon as possible. Josie was excited as they waited for them to arrive.

"Here they come!" She told Gabe softly as he reached down taking her hand.

When everyone had gathered, Gabe began, "I have three announcements for you today. Starting tomorrow, which is Sunday, there'll be no working. We are to remember God made the Sabbath to rest. The only things to be done are feeding the animals. We have to take care of the animals because the Lord gave us responsibility for them. The second thing is, we're going to have church services. We'll meet here tomorrow about ten in the morning. It's time we started doing things God's way. The third thing is, I want all the couples who have jumped the broom to step forward." The couples began moving toward the front. Once they were there Josie counted them and Gabe continued. After Church tomorrow, I'll be marrying you to your partner. Everyone should be married in the sight of God according to his word. From now on there will be no more jumping the broom. I'll marry anyone who wants to get married. Tomorrow after the weddings, we'll be holding a big celebration in honor of all the newly wedded couples. Everyone is invited to attend! Bring your children, family and friends. I want everyone to come!

The women began to giggle and the men looked at Gabe as if he had lost his mind, but they couldn't help smiling. Then they cheered loudly and everyone began talking at the same time. They had every Sunday off from now on and they were getting married.

Josie knew she had her work cut out for her. She wanted every woman getting married to have a bridal bouquet and a flower wreath for her hair. After all, she had a flower garden at her disposal, and every woman needed to feel special on her wedding day. Liza jumped into action too. She had lots of cooking to do and food to bring up from the storehouse. She commandeered the younger children and had them running errands from the storehouse to her kitchen. Josie got the smaller children to help her cut flowers. They laughed and talked with the Missus, not really understanding what the excitement was about, just happy to be part of it.

Josie, Liza and her daughter Hannah worked late into the night. Liza made the largest pot of red beans she ever made, and the women all helped by baking bread. Liza had given them all the ingredients they required, and handed out any pans that could possibly be used to bake bread.

Liza was beside herself, she was getting married! Just like the good Lord intended. Gabe, Ben, Big John, and Ben's sons Jonah and Caleb, worked along side each other making and setting up tables for the big celebration. The men talked as they worked, sharing stories, hopes and dreams. Ben was proud of his new master who wanted to do things God's way. Ben knew a little about God's ways, and if this was what his master was doing, he wanted to be part of it.

Sunday morning arrived with excitement. The sun seemed to know it was an important day. It was a beautiful day, warm but not too hot. There was a slight breeze blowing, filling the July air with the fragrance of flowers, it was perfect. Even though they had gone to bed very late, Josie, Gabe, Ben and Liza were up and about with the sun putting the final touches to the first Sunday of worships and weddings. Liza was wearing her good dress. In reality it was her only other dress. It was dark blue with a crisp white apron. Her every day dress was black with a white checked apron. Ben was dressed in his best, his only other white muslin shirt and work pants.

Liza and Ben talked and laughed while working side by side. "Today we's be wedded proper like," Liza told Ben with excitement.

"Maybe so, but I's always member jumpin de broom wid ya. Dat be my fondest membrance of all," Ben said softly. Delight shown, in Liza's face, to think he held the day as a fond memory.

Gabe and Josie were having their own conversation of memories. He helped Josie gather the flower bouquets and hair wreaths for the weddings and placed them gently into a basket.

"I think it's wonderful you've thought of the women. Now they'll have their special day. All the flowers are simply beautiful," Gabe told her kissing her on the cheek.

Giggling Josie kissed him back. "All little girls dream of having flowers at their wedding. I don't think it would be any different if you've jumped the broom or not. A wedding means flowers!" changing the subject she asked him, "Have you got your sermon ready?"

"I do!" Realizing what he'd said caused both of them to laugh at the irony of the situation. "Now let's go find Ben and Liza!" Taking Josie by the hand, Gabe led the way. Turning briefly, he picked up the flower baskets as they went.

"Everything is ready," Gabe thought as he stood on the back porch. Today the back porch would serve as a pulpit. Soon he'd see about building a church. He watched the people coming from the slave quarters. Everyone looked spick and span in the best clothes they had. He was going to do something about clothing for these people. They deserved better. As the slaves got closer, Gabe noticed some were carrying chairs from their homes. The little children were skipping, holding flowers in their little hands. Everyone appeared happier than when Gabe and Josie first arrived.

After everyone had settled into their places for the service, the adults in chairs and the children on the ground, Gabe began speaking to them.

"Today we make the first changes to New Canaan. Soon there will be many more, according to the way God will lead us. Thank you all for coming, let us pray. All bowed their heads. "Father, today we ask your blessing upon this service. May it glorify You in every way. We ask for your blessings upon the union of all the couples who will marry today. Lead us and guide us as we all travel upon this journey you have placed before us. Bless everyone with peace, happiness and health, in Jesus name, amen." After lifting their heads, everyone looked at Gabe expectantly.

"Today I'm going to talk about Gods creation. It comes from the first book of the Bible called Genesis." Gabe read to them the creation story. He explained to them God saw Adam was alone. So, He made him a helpmate, Eve, and God saw it was good. He explained to them the importance of marriage and how to keep it holy. He told them God had rested on the seventh day, and from this day forth, they would be doing the same in observing God's day. He didn't talk long, because he knew to teach them about God's love and ways, he'd have to take it slowly. As if on cue, Hannah stood and sang the sweetest song Gabe had ever heard. It came from the Bible. He recognized it from the book of Psalms. "It may not be so hard after all," Gabe thought to himself. It seemed these people already knew more about God than he thought. Oh, what a foolish man he was, thinking they didn't know God. Gabe asked God to forgive him. After Hannah finished her song, the group before him stood and gave a loud shout. Gabe would later learn this was called a ring shout, shouted by Negros after a worship service. He was the one who had a lot to learn!

When the service ended, Josie went about gathering the women who were to be married to the right side of the yard. With help from the younger girls, Josie placed flower wreathes in the bride's hair, and gave them each a bridal bouquet of beautiful flowers. The women were giddy; each complemented the other on how pretty they looked. Women are women, no matter what their lot in life may be, and they loved pretty things. While Josie was with the women, Gabe gathered the men and had them stand on the other side of the yard. He told them when their partner stepped out they should go to them, walk to the steps, and stand holding their hand. After making sure they understood what to do, Gabe made his way back to the porch. He turned toward the group, and then nodded at Josie who sent the first woman out. It was Delia, looking pretty as ever. Big John met her as Gabe had instructed. Then together they walked toward Gabe holding hands. Ben stood on the right side of Gabe and Liza on his left. They were to serve as the witnesses to the marriages. One by one, Gabe married the couples in turn. He had decided he would marry each couple separately to make it special to them. The ceremony was brief, but would be memorable to each bride and groom.

Finally, the last couple to be married was Ben and Liza. Old Ben held tightly to Liza's hand and looked at her with love that would last a life time. It blessed Gabe, as well as Ben and Liza, for him to marry them. In the last hour and a half Gabe had married thirty couples. Some who had jumped the broom and a few who were marrying for the first time.

Gabe couldn't believe the size of the group. There must be at least one hundred and forty slaves and what appeared to be more on the way. Soon he'd have a meeting with all the men of the families and speak to them about what they'd be doing next. But for right now, it was time to celebrate, and celebrate they did!

Food came out of the kitchen so fast it almost made Gabe dizzy. The meal was simple with red beans and rice, bread and butter, cake for desert and lemonade to drink. Everyone was laughing, talking and having a wonderful time. Gabe scanned the crowd looking for his Josie. He spotted her helping serve the children. He watched as she helped a small boy with his cake. She looked as if she were having the time of her life. It did not go unnoticed by those there, this woman was not afraid to serve. The day ended with a beautiful sunset as everyone made their way home. Gabe stood with his arm around Josie as they waved good bye. The last to leave was Ben and Liza.

The older couple came to say good night when Gabe said to them, "Ben, Liza, I was wondering if you would mind moving into the house with us?

There's plenty of room. Just think about it for tonight and when we meet tomorrow morning, you can give me your decision." The couple agreed, then walked slowly to their cabin holding hands.

When everyone had left, Gabe and Josie walked tiredly toward their room.

"May I buy some cloth the next time we are in town? Josie asked Gabe as they made their way up the stairs.

"Sure, I don't see why not."

"May I buy a lot of cloth?" She inquired sheepishly.

Yes Josie. What are you up to?"

"I want to make new clothes for the little ones."

"The big ones need them too. How about you buy cloth for each family? The women of each house can make clothes for the adults and then help with making clothes for the children. How would that be?"

"That will be fine with me. Thank you for allowing me to do this," she told him as they entered their room.

"Any time," he told her yawning, and then added, "It's been a long day."

"It's been a long two days for me," she answered him almost asleep.

Josie couldn't believe she had slept so late. "Gabe's probably been up for hours," she thought to herself as she got out of bed. Liza will think I've become lazy. There, waiting for her, was a bath. She couldn't resist. If one is late, one is late. No matter how fast you get there, late is late!" she told herself as she got into the tub. She would enjoy this for now.

A while later, feeling rested and refreshed, she went in search of Gabe. Passing the study doors, she heard voices. Then she remembered the morning meeting with Ben and the men. Slipping past the doors quietly, she went to find breakfast.

Most of the men had never been in the "big" house as they called it. Here they were, in the study, feeling out of place. The master needed to talk to them in private and if he needed them they would be there. They listened carefully while Gabe told them about his plans. He told them he wanted to rebuild or repair their houses and he asked their advice on how much lumber they needed. The men made Ben their spokesperson so they told him, in hushed voices, what they needed for each family. Ben relayed to Gabe this information and he wrote it down. Next they turned to the subject of the barns, store houses, the animals, and then to the crops in the fields.

When they'd finished their meeting, the men left and returned to their work except for Ben, whom Gabe asked to remain behind. With everyone gone, Ben and Gabe discussed the repairs that needed to be done. Gabe thought the housing should come first and Ben was thinking of the barns. In the end both agreed work on the cabins was to be first. Everyone needed a safe place to live with a good roof over their heads. Alone at last, Gabe bowed his head and asked the Lord who he should put in charge of the project to rebuild cabins. He asked the Lord for a definite sign and thanked him for his direction. As he sat meditating on God's words, he was filled with a peace that let him know his prayer had been heard. Getting up from his desk, he left his study.

Walking thoughtfully through the house, he passed Josie in the kitchen with Liza. He stopped, not saying a word, took Josie in his arms and kissed her on top of her head. Letting her go, he went to Liza and placed a kiss on her cheek and then continued on his way out the door. Liza and Josie turned and looked at each other baffled as they watched him leave.

Gabe continued on his way. He had no idea where he was going. He was just walking. He found himself walking toward the stables. For no reason he turned and went inside. There Gabe found Caleb working with the horses, talking to them in a soothing voice as if the horses knew what he was saying. Gabe watched for a while before making himself known.

"Hello there, Caleb."

"Massa Lyon," Caleb answered with a nod of his head as he continued with his task.

"Any problems here I need to know about?"

"No sah, none come ta mind." Then almost as if it were an afterthought he added, "Massa Lyon, I's be a wonderin ifn ya been ta de ole cabin in da wood since ya been home?"

"No I haven't. I'd forgotten about it to tell you the truth."

"Would ya be of da mind ta go dar wid me?"

"Sure, why?"

"I's somethin ta shows ya Massa."

"It's Gabe."

"Sah?"

"My name is Gabe, Caleb." He hated being called master.

"Yez sah, Massa Gabe," Caleb was confused as they walked out of the stable toward the woods where the old cabin stood. He didn't understand just what to call the young master.

Gabe couldn't imagine what Caleb wanted to show him. As they started down the path leading into the woods; Gabe told Caleb about stories of being a young boy, playing there and his adventures. Into the woods about fifty yards, stood the old cabin surrounded by a well kept lawn, scattered with wild flowers. The old cabin looked in better shape than Gabe had remembered. He was surprised. Opening the door, they went in and walked around. It smelt of old wood and leaves. It had four medium sized rooms with small windows that allowed sunlight in.

"Why did you want me to see this?" Gabe asked not understanding.

"I's be a ponderin on it. Dis here would make a rite nice church." Caleb told him.

Gabe immediately got excited and said, "of course it would! We could knock out a few walls to open it up. Put a new roof on it, put some benches in here, and it will do just fine. You know what else? It'll make a good place for a school too! Gabe was so excited he gave Caleb a friendly slap on his back and laughed in spite himself. "Good thinking Caleb, good thinking! Thank you, God, for this unexpected gift!" he shouted.

All Caleb heard the master say was, this would make a good school. Surely he had heard him right! Caleb had always wanted to learn to read.

"Not a word to anyone Caleb. I need to talk to Josie. Then, I will start working on the roof and benches. You're a good man Caleb!" With that, they left the cabin. Gabe wondered what Josie would think when she saw it, and Caleb dreamed of going to school. After letting Caleb get back to his work in the stables, Gabe made his way to the house to talk to Josie.

CHAPTER 5

JONAH WATCHED FROM HIS HIDING place as his younger brother walked with the master. He didn't like it at all. This young Master had changed everything. He had his mother, father, and now his younger brother eating out of his hands. He'd even seen his sister, Hannah, warming up to him too. Didn't they know slavery was still slavery, even if the master was good to them? The master had easily won over his family, but it wouldn't be so easy to get him! All he had to do was wait, and then he'd make his move. Watching, as the master made his way toward the house, and Caleb returning to the stable; Jonah slipped away unnoticed. At least he thought he had.

Gabe entered the house as he always did through the kitchen. He was greeted by the busy activity two women make when they are on a mission. He couldn't believe his eyes! His dainty wife was dressed as a cleaning woman! She was bare footed and her long hair was in a single braid hanging down her back. She also had smudges of soot streaking her face. Gabe couldn't help it; the sight of her sent him into a fit of laughter.

"Just what is so funny Gabriel Lyon?" Josie asked, glaring at him.

"I just don't believe I've ever seen you this way!" he told her trying to control his laughter.

"Liza and I are cleaning the rooms off the kitchen. You can't possibly know what a mess it's been! How could you expect Liza and Ben to move into something that dirty? Gabe, stop laughing!" Josie stomped her bare foot.

"Gabriel Lyon! Ya be alevin dat yongin alone rite now!" Liza fussed at him as she came to see what was keeping Josie. "We's got work ta do!"

Gabe just stood in awe as he watched Liza give orders to the men she'd commandeered to move furniture to the attic. Then she turned on him.

"Ya be a helpin ifn ya get ta workin with us. Da Missus be a wantin de rug frum da sun room!" Liza stood with her hand on her hip looking expectantly at him.

Chuckling, Gabe went to retrieve the rug as requested. He was shocked when he brought it to its appointed place. What he'd thought all these years were storerooms off the kitchen, were in fact living quarters for the household staff. The apartment had three rooms connected to the main room where he stood. Josie and Liza had transformed the main room into a sitting area; this was where the rug was needed. To the right of it was a small room, which was made into a bedroom for Hannah. After all, Josie told him, she was too young to be living alone with her brothers in the cabin. To the left was a room big enough for a sewing room. Then straight back from the main sitting room was a bedroom, which was to be for Ben and Liza.

The walls, the floors, and the fireplace had all been scrubbed clean. The furniture filling the rooms Gabe recognized from his adventures in the attic as a young boy. Now, he knew why his wife looked the way she did. She must have cleaned the fireplace! With this realization, laughter hit him again, but so did a broom! He just wasn't sure who did it because both women stood glaring at him when he turned.

"If you want something to eat Gabe, there's biscuits and ham on the kitchen table," Josie said to him sweetly.

Not wishing to push his luck, Gabe went in search of the food before he enticed the wrath of both women at the same time.

Food in hand, Gabe returned to the sanctuary of his study. Pulling out the financial books of the plantation, he began to study them. If he handled the expenses with good sense, he'd be able to do what was needed to making the changes God had laid upon his heart. After all, his father left him with more than enough money. With that assurance, he began to make a list of needed materials for repairs to the cabin in the woods and the new slave quarters.

After checking his list a second time, Gabe wrote a letter to Charles asking for his help in getting church and school supplies. He explained to Charles, in his letter, it was necessary for these things to come from his school. Finishing, Gabe sat back in his chair. He needed to show Josie the cabin in the woods. He needed to go to town and get building materials; also he needed to find someone other than himself to be responsible for overseeing cabin repairs. He'd already asked the Lord for this person, so, he'd wait until he came! "Thank you, Lord, for your answer!" Gabe spoke out loud looking upward.

Getting up from his desk, Gabe went in search of Josie. Surely he'd stayed out of her way long enough, it had been hours! He found her in their room reading. He went to her and placed a kiss on her cheek," now, you look like my wife!"

Smiling, she closed her book and looked at him with love in her eyes.

"When we found those rooms I just had to help Gabe. I know it isn't proper in the south, I just hope I haven't done anything wrong."

"Don't change one thing about yourself, Josie! You're a servant of God, just as I am. In everything you do you must hold fast to this truth. You owe no one an apology, nor do you need to ask for forgiveness when you do something you know God has laid on your heart! Now, I will tell you, wife, you may have to watch yourself when we have company. That doesn't mean you have to change your sweet, loving and caring nature. It means you, my love, will have to watch your temper."

"Watch my temper? What do you mean?" She asked him surprised.

"It means, here in our world, it's very different than what you'll see in town or on other plantations. Soon we'll be going to town, and we'll be invited to parties. You're going to see you've been isolated from the real truth of slavery. In other words, the slavery you've seen here is nothing compared to what's really out there. I already know it's going to make you angry."

"I understand what you're saying Gabe, but isn't there anyone in this parish that believes the way we do?" he noticed the concern in her voice.

"At this point, I don't really know. I'll have to feel the others out and see, but only when the time is right. I'll know the right time when God tells me. So, for right now, we have to be careful. Anyway, what I wanted was to show you something. Since its late now, it'll have to wait until tomorrow. By the way, I need you to get a list of supplies you and Liza need for the household. I'm going into town on Saturday and place an order for building materials. Then, on Monday, I'll be taking Ben and a few other men to pick them up. As a matter of fact, if you want, you can go with us."

"I'll think about it. So what is it you want to show me tomorrow?"

"It's a surprise! You'll just have to wait!" He told her grinning.

Knowing she wouldn't be able to get anymore out of him, she didn't try. She knew she'd be seeing whatever it was in the morning.

The next morning Josie and Gabe set out walking. They went past the barns, the stables, crossed the meadow, and then headed toward the woods. Unable to suppress her curiosity Josie asked, "Is my surprise in the woods?"

"Yes, it is, just enjoy your walk. You'll know it when you see it," he smiled and took her hand.

When they started down the path into the woods, Gabe watched Josie closely to see what her reaction would be. When they approached the cabin, he saw it in her eyes.

Quickly she turned to him and exclaimed, "Gabe, this will make a great church!"

"Wait until you see inside!" He opened the door and swept her in.

She couldn't believe her eyes. It was exactly what they needed!

After a closer inspection of the interior, Josie's excitement bubbled forth.

"This is big enough for a school and a church!"

"That's exactly what I thought! I just need to take out some walls and give it a new roof. I can do the repairs myself. I wouldn't have to take anyone from their work. It's back here protected from nosy neighbors who might drop by unexpectedly. As far as the school goes, you could do the teaching, right?" Josie's nod told him she was excited. "I've already written to Charles asking for help with the church and school supplies. I'm sure he'll commandeer your father into helping as well."

"We're going to school everyone, aren't we?" she looked at him expectantly.

"Yes we are my love, I just haven't figured it out yet, but the teaching is up to you."

"Wonderful! I can't wait to get started!"

As they left the woods hand in hand, they talked about their plans for the church and school. Gabe told her how Caleb brought him here with the idea of it being a church.

"God is working here!" Gabe exclaimed.

When they started to pass the stables, Gabe stopped. "Have you seen the horses?"

"No, I've been waiting for you to show me. I'd love to learn to ride."

"I need to tell Caleb I'll be needing a horse for tomorrow's trip into town. My father was known for his love of horses. He was the envy of the whole parish for the Arabians he owned. Father had them brought over from Europe."

"Caleb? Are you here? Gabe called.

"Yez sah, I's in da tack room," he answered coming out to meet them. "Is dar sumptin ya be a needin?"

"In the morning I'll be going to town. Would you have a horse ready for me about seven o'clock?"

"Yez, sah, Massa Gabe, ya be a needin me ta go's wid ya?

"Yes, thanks Caleb, I'd enjoy the company. Just be sure to saddle a horse for yourself, because we won't be taking the wagon on this trip."

"Yez, sah, I be ready!"

"I'd like you to show Josie the horses," Gabe requested.

This simple request brought a light to Caleb's face. He loved showing off his animals.

Josie watched the young slender man of eighteen who was definitely Liza's son. The delight he took in showing her the "finest" horses in the land was also present in the way he cared for the animals. Caleb took them to a stall that held the loveliest chestnut mare.

"This one be gentle enuf fo ya ta ride, Missus," he told her shyly.

"I don't know how to ride," Josie confessed.

Caleb looked surprised; quickly he turned and looked at Gabe questionably.

"I'll teach her soon!" Gabe said, bringing smiles to both Josie and Caleb. "We'll be off now, thank you for taking the time to show Josie around."

Saturday morning found Gabe and Caleb on their way to town. Gabe was riding a favorite horse of his, Judah, a black Arabian stallion that stood sixteen hands high. Judah was high spirited, but Gabe handled him easily. He often thought it was because he treated the horse with respect. Even animals needed to be treated kindly. He pitied the man who would treat this horse differently. Gabe had seen the results of it once before, and he had no desire to see it again. He remembered the day his father's friend tried to ride Judah. Gabe had tried to warn the friend of Judah's temperament, but the man didn't listened. In trying to show the horse who was master by using a riding crop harshly, the horse threw the man on the ground and tried to stomp him. If Gabe hadn't been there it would've ended gravely. Thankfully, Gabe had interceded and both man and horse lived to tell about it. Gabe noticed Caleb was riding the mare he'd shown Josie. He knew Caleb was getting the horse used to having someone on its back. No telling how long it had been since anyone had ridden her. It was a thoughtful gesture, which Gabe appreciated.

"We need to go by Reid's saw mill and place an order, then to Hebert's General Store, afterwards; I would like to go to the livery stable to see Mr. Allen. I'd like to see if he has a saddle for Josie," he explained to Caleb as they approached town.

Making their way to the saw mill, Gabe noticed people on the busy street stopping and staring. It was always this way when he rode Judah. The horse was magnificent.

Reaching the mill, Gabe dismounted the horse and handed the rein to Caleb. "Would you mind watching the horses? I won't be gone long."

"Yez sah, massa." Caleb like the fact his master always asked him, never told him, and then thank him for what he'd done.

Gabe was quick about placing his order, telling Mr. Reid he would be picking up the order on Monday. Mr. Reid was surprised at how much lumber he wanted, but assured Gabe it would be ready on Monday afternoon at the latest.

Gabe and Caleb made their way to Hebert's General Store and placed Josie's order. Mr. Hebert was in awe of the size of Gabe's order. He too assured Gabe the supplies would be ready as requested on Monday.

The final stop before home was the livery stable to see Mr. Allen. When they arrived, they found he was already waiting for them in front of the livery, which meant Mr. Allen knew he was coming. Imagine that! The news of Gabe being in town had traveled quickly.

"Good Morning, Gabe!" Allen said smiling.

"Mr. Allen, how are you?" Dismounting Judah, Gabe handed the reins to Caleb.

"Doing just fine, that's one beautiful horse you have! Your father had the finest horses in the Parish! He never would sell any of them. He just kept them to himself. Yes sir, that's certainly a fine horse," Mr. Allen repeated as he circled the horse inspecting it closely.

Gabe saw Little John standing in the entrance of the stable, so Gabe smiled and waved. Little John smiled, waved back, and then stepped back inside.

"What brings you here?" Mr. Allen asked still eyeing the horse.

"I need a saddle for my wife and if my memory serves me right, you make the best."

"I do indeed. I'm known for the quality of my work."

"How about you showing me what you have in stock."

The two went inside where Mr. Allen bragged at length on himself, and the high quality of his saddles. Gabe tried to listen, but soon tired of Allen's endless ramblings. Pointing to a black saddle he asked, "How much is that one?"

Mr. Allen quoted him a price and Gabe agreed. When he paid and walked outside, Mr. Allen asked, "How much would you be willing to take for this horse?"

"How much you willing to give?" Gabe asked just for the fun of it.

"Well, I'm not a man of means like you. What would you take for the animal for an old friend of your fathers?"

Gabe could see Little John standing in the doorway watching again. He knew what he had to do. Gabe put his hand on Mr. Allen's shoulder and pulled him aside. "How about you and I step over here and talk some horse trading?"

Mr. Allen broke out in a big grin as they walked away. Caleb was shocked. How could his master ever consider trading or selling this magnificent horse?

After a long while, Gabe and Mr. Allen shook hands. A deal had been struck. Leaving Gabe, Mr. Allen went into the stable and came out with Little John. Caleb couldn't believe what he was seeing! The young master had traded his favorite horse for a negro boy! He surely didn't understand!

Caleb took the saddle off Judah and led the horse into the stable at Gabe's request.

Little John stood silently looking confused. Gabe asked Allen if he'd keep the saddles for him until Monday when he would return. Mr. Allen was quick to agree. Gabe walked over to Little John and looked down at him. "You're going home with me." Turning, Gabe mounted the mare Caleb had been riding. Caleb and a confused Little John followed close behind on foot as they set out for New Canaan. Not one word was spoken until they were well out of town. Bringing his horse to a halt, Gabe got down. "Little John, you ride for a while. I need to talk to Caleb." Little John did as he was told hesitantly. He would have done almost anything at that moment. He wanted to ask if he was truly going home. The only reason he didn't was he feared this was just a dream and he would wake up.

"Caleb, you have to understand," Gabe began as they walked side by side. "I had to do something to get Little John back with his family. I know Judah is a good horse, but he isn't worth more than the little boy. That boy needs his family and they need him. Judah will take care of himself. If Mr. Allen doesn't do right by him, the horse will definitely let him know. I warned him. So he knows. Do you understand?"

"Yez sah, I's see'd," Caleb told him, having a newfound respect for Gabe.

This was how they traveled home, Gabe and Caleb walking, and little John riding the master's horse. Little John still couldn't help but wonder if this was true and not a dream. Caleb was in awe of this man who thought one little Negro boys life was worth more than a very expensive horse. Then there was Gabe, praying that no one saw him walking while his slave rode. Not that he really cared, but he just didn't want anything to mess up his plans. They arrived at New Canaan a few hours later. Before going to the house, Gabe took Little John to his mother and father, telling them Little John would be staying for good. Leaving them to their reunion, he started toward the house.

The news of Little John's return swept through the slave quarters like wild fire. Big John and the other men all gathered around Caleb as he recounted the story of the best trade ever.

When he got home, Gabe told Josie the whole story of little Johns return while he ate a cold supper. She cried tears of happiness that ran down her cheeks. Hearing them in the dining room, Ben and Liza came in and listened. Neither could believe what they were hearing. It was truly a miracle from God.

Sunday service was on the Parable of the Lost Sheep. Gabe read the story to them from Luke 15:4-7. *"What man among you, if he has a hundred sheep and has lost one of them, does not leave the ninety nine in the open pasture and go after the one which is lost until he finds it?"* *"When he has found it, he lays it on his shoulders, rejoicing. And when he comes home, he calls together his friends and his neighbors, saying to them, Rejoice with me, for I have found my sheep which was lost!"* *"I tell you that in the same way, there will be more joy in heaven over one sinner who repents than over ninety nine righteous persons who need no repentance."*

He explained to them saying, "Every person is important to God. God wants them no matter what they've done in the past. By accepting Jesus as their Lord and Savior, they can return to God." He then went on to say how happy he was to tell everyone Little John had returned home. The service ended with a prayer followed by a song from Hannah.

Later that day, Gabe asked Ben to get as many men that be could spared, to make the trip into town to bring back supplies on Monday. He explained they'd need at least four wagons because the order included lumber. Ben had no trouble getting volunteers, because the slaves would do almost anything for their new master. Then Ben gave the remaining men their instructions and asked Big John to stay to make sure things ran smoothly while they were gone. He also asked big John to keep an eye on his boy Jonah. He told Big John he was afraid Jonah was up to something. He'd caught the boy trying to sneak off a couple of times, leaving his work to be done by others. Big John agreed and reassured the old man he would do his best.

The next morning it took three wagons to bring all the supplies back. Gabe was grateful he'd brought the fourth one. It was used to bring back a few extra things and the men. He was ready to get started on making living conditions better. He'd stopped by to see if Mr. Allen and Judah were getting along, and to retrieve his saddles. Mr. Allen said they were doing just fine together, but Gabe couldn't help noticing a bruise on the side of Allen's cheek. It was all he could do to keep from laughing. Maybe Mr. Allen had learned his lesson with Judah. If not, then Gabe would offer to buy him back, but in no way was Mr. Allen getting anything more than money from him!

Josie decided not to go with Gabe to town. It was too hot. July brought the heat with an intensity she could hardly handle. She even opted not to wear more than one petty coat under her dress. "There had to be a way to dress for this heat! She for one would find it!" These were her thoughts as she went through the house looking for Liza. They needed to make plans for sewing clothes for the children. Josie felt overwhelmed. Lifting a prayer up to the Lord for guidance, she went to the kitchen. Not seeing Liza anywhere, she called out, "Liza! Where are you?"

Receiving no answer, she went outside to see if anyone was about. To her horror she saw Liza running behind Big John, who was carrying a little girl about five years old. In her breathlessness, Liza explained the little girl, Sara, had been overcome by the heat while hoeing in the cotton fields.

Josie was scared. Little Sara's eyes were closed, her lips were pale but she could see the rise and fall of her chest.

Quickly making their way into Liza's sitting room, Big John laid the girl on the sofa. Liza sprang into action by taking herbs from a well laden chest, and began mixing them together. Taking little Sara's head in her hand gently; she put the mixture to the child's lips. After taking a few sips, little Sara started moaning. Quickly Liza started placing wet cloths on the child's head and body. Josie jumped in alongside her and copied everything Liza did. Finally, after an hour of applying and reapplying wet cloths, while giving sips of the mixture, little Sara set up. At this time, Liza started giving her water to drink and before long little Sara was asking for her mother.

Pulling Big John aside, Josie asked him to go and get the little girl's mother.

Big John went without a word. While cradling the little girl in her arms, Liza began to talk with Sara in a soothing reassuring tone. While waiting for her mother to come, Josie began to ask questions.

"Do all the little children work in the fields in this heat?"

"Yez um," Liza said looking up at her.

"Can the work be done without the children?"

"My Ben shud knowd," came Liza's reply as she continued to rock Sara.

"It's too much for them! I didn't even think! Josie said, and started to cry.

That's how Big John found them when he returned with Sara's mother.

Liza was rocking back and forth with Sara in her arms, and Josie was on her knees beside them crying.

"I's brung da chil's mama, Missus."

Josie quickly wiped her tears and moved so the little girl could see her mother. After a few minutes of consoling her child, the mother thanked Liza for her help. Josie looked up at the same time the woman turned around. Josie froze. The poor woman was with child! Clearly she had been working in the fields too! From the looks of things the baby was due any day now.

Clearing her throat, she asked "What's your name?"

"I's Molly, Missus, de wife of Henry," she proudly stated.

"I'm so sorry about this, Molly! Please take Sara home and stay with her."

Molly looked distressed at what she said and quickly Josie assured her, "It'll be alright, I'll take care of everything. If you need anything let us know. Now, go and rest."

"Thank ya Missus," she said shyly.

Big John reached down and picked the little girl up and carried her out with her mother not far behind.

"Liza, I am going to talk to Gabe as soon as he comes home about this.

Those children have no more business working in the hot sun than I do!

We can't let this continue! The worse thing of all is, I didn't think of it! I'm sure Gabe hasn't, or he would have done something. I am just so sorry!"

"Now, now Missus, it be da life," Liza told her softly.

"But it shouldn't be the life, Liza! It's wrong! I can't stand the thought of it! What would have happened if you hadn't been here? I wouldn't have known what to do! I'm grateful for what you do. You must teach me, along with Hannah, so I will know."

Agreeing to do that for Josie, Liza stood and said, "Be mighty careful missus of whatcha be sayin. Ya not frum de south, thangs be diffrant."

"I know Liza, Gabe told me the same thing. It's just hard." Standing to her feet, Josie kissed Liza's cheek and then went to her room. She needed to lie down and have a good cry.

That's how Gabe found her when he returned from town. Liza met him at the door and filled him in on the details of the day. His poor Josie, he was going to have to do something about the children soon. He knew Josie felt overwhelmed, but then, so did he.

Entering their room, Gabe could hear Josie's sobs; he had never seen her cry like this.

"Josie?" he said softly touching her shoulder.

"Oh, Gabe!" she cried throwing herself into his arms. Then she told him about her day. She told him how she had asked God to forgive her for not thinking of the children.

After listening, he looked at her and said, "What we'll do is pray. I'll be honest with you, I don't know the answer. I just know we have to protect these children. Will you pray with me?"

Together they kneeled and asked God for answers. For only God knew what they should do.

They went to bed early that night, both exhausted, not only from the heat but from the dilemma of the day. Resting well for Gabe was out of the question. He awoke to the chimes of the grandfather clock striking three o'clock in the morning. He didn't understand why he was so tired, and yet so wide awake. Getting out of bed quietly, so he wouldn't wake Josie, he lit a candle and went to his study. If he couldn't sleep he might as well get some study time in.

He entered the room and walked to his desk to retrieve his Bible. To his surprise he did not find his Bible, but an old ledger he had never seen before. Picking it up, and wiping the dust off, he noticed it was one of his father's older ones. Sitting in his chair, he opened the book and started to read. Gabe was amazed. This was the ledger his father kept on the buying and selling of slaves. Documented on each page were the name and the cost of every slave that was on the plantation! Who could have possibly put this on his desk? If he didn't know of its existence, then no one else did. One thing was for certain, he knew it wasn't a human being. As he turned the pages reading the names' and the cost of each person, it broke his heart. "How can you put a monetary price on a human life?" he asked himself. The Lord Jesus Christ, the son of God, was the only person to pay a price for a human. It was with His blood that purchased each and every person's salvation, if only they would accept Him as their Lord and Savoir. Jesus

Christ's blood paid for man's redemption. How could anyone, even his own earthly father, sink so low to put a dollar value on these people who were Gods' children? Gabe put his head in his hands and started praying. He asked God to forgive his father for the sin of slavery and he asked God to forgive him, for he was no better.

Gabe asked God to show him what to do. He continued in prayer until the early morning sun shone thru the windows of his study. He had a burden that was almost too much to bear. Feeling confident God would guide him, he returned to his room and got ready for the day.

Gabe met with Old Ben that morning like he did every morning, but he could tell something was different. He could see it in his master's eyes because he looked so sad. After asking Ben to sit down, Gabe took a deep breath. "Ben, how long have you been here?"

"Well sah, ya granpa boughtin me when I's a youngin. I's member when yor pa waz born. Why sah, I's heped build des house! Can't recollect de years, dun been too many."

"Do you remember your mother and father?"

"Sah, I's shur do. My mama and papa wuz da best workers in Missisippe. My ma wuz rite prudy. Sung lika song bird, she did. My papa wuz strongest, in da county, like I's told ya. Dey knowd de Lord too, sah, jus like yo! Whys, I's b'lieve, papa be a rite fine preacher ifin hed been allowd."

"So you're from Mississippi, moved down here when you were just a boy."

"Yez, sah."

"What about Liza?"

"Well, sah, she be a comin frum Loozeanna. Best day ever fo me wen da Massa brung her here. I's a young buck den. She be da prudiest thang I's ever see'd. She be feisty little thang too! Missed her ma and papa fer a long time. Nobody saw her cry tho, she made shur ob dat. I's catch'd her cryin one nite hind de barn. When she'd looked at me wid sorrow in dem eyes, it wuz all I's could do ta keep frum cryin wid her. I's jus puts my arms round her and let her cry. Whys, I's fell in love wid her rite den and dars. She swore me ta secret to. Said ifn I's said a word to anyone bout de cryin shed make my life hard! She'd dun it to!" Ben laughed then continued. "We's jus stayed together after dat. I's love her an she love me. We's jump da broom sometime after dat. Ya knowd da rest."

"Did you ever hear from your mother or father after that?"

"Naw sah, aint like white folks. Ya'll rite and such, slaves don't rite or read, lost track of dem sometime ago."

"Well Ben, that's all about to change. We will have a school. Everyone will have the opportunity to learn. That's one of the many things I want to talk to you about this morning. Let's begin with the rebuilding of the cabins. Who do you think would be good to put over this project?"

"Sah, yo knowd Big John, he be a carpenter slave afore he kum here. He be doin a good job fo ya."

"Then we'll talk with Big John later, I trust your judgment. Now I want to tell you about the cabin in the woods that Caleb showed me. I'd like to turn it into a church and school. It was Caleb's idea to use it for a church, and I'm so thankful he thought of it. These are the kind of ideas I want to hear from everyone, anything to improve our lives' here, yours and mine. I'll do the repair to the cabin in the woods myself. I don't expect this to be added to someone else's work with the corps still in the fields. I just want you to know that's where I'll be tomorrow if you need me for anything. The next thing is the children. The heat's too much for those children or anyone else to be working in. So, what do you think about breaking up the day and having the work done during the coolest parts of the day?"

"I's don't knowd Massa; it'll be hard ta do. De crops needin harvesten startin in September wid de rice. Den, Oktoba be a bringin de corn and hay. Den, Novemba brang de cotton harvest. De heat a bein worse in August and Septemba, tho it can be longer. I's ponder on it," Ben said with a thoughtful frown.

While the two men continued their meeting, Josie and Liza were having their own. Having decided the children needed at least two sets of clothes each, they made their plans. Pulling out the cloth Gabe picked up for them, they started laying it out to cut. They began with the smallest children first. That meant the babies that were coming got priority. Then those children from newborns to five would be next. Then they'd move on up till they got to the adults. Seeing they needed more help, Liza went to the slave quarters to see if Molly would be willing to help. Not only was she willing, she was excited they had asked her. Liza assured her it would be just fine to bring little Sara with her. The three women then set up their sewing in the sunroom, since the only thing left in the room was a large table big enough to hold the cloth for cutting. It was perfect for them!

They began their task with an energy none knew they possessed. Molly was in awe of the fine cloth and Josie in awe of both Liza and Molly's skills. Josie and Liza laughed and talked as they worked in that comfortable way they had with each other. Molly, shy at first, joined in soon. They talked about raising children, husbands and those things women talk about when they get together. Laughter rang out as they made patterns and worked. For once Josie felt like she was doing something that would help make things right. Noticing little Sara watching, Josie ran to her room and retrieved a large picture book on birds for the little girl to look at. When she handed the book to her, Josie opened it to show her the pictures. The little girl didn't know quite what to do. Slowly she began to explore the book. The women then went back to their sewing.

Gabe and Ben went to talk to Big John. As they crossed the fields of corn looking for him, Gabe took in how many children were in the fields and their ages. Seeing Gabe motion to him, Big John came out of the field with hoe in hand. After speaking to him, Big John was delighted he'd be overseeing repairs to the cabins. Gabe told him he could pick three men to help him. Depending on the progress of the work, it would change if he needed more help, all he had to do was let Ben know. Gabe also told Big John he wanted to make the cabins bigger, either by adding on to the existing structures, or building new ones altogether. The homes needed to big enough for individual families, and all were to have wooden floors. All decision would be left up to Big John, and construction would begin the next day. Gabe could tell he'd pleased the man by the excitement showing on Big Johns face. After many "thank ya sah," Gabe and Ben made their way to the next project.

Gabe could see two riders coming in the distance, "now what?" Gabe thought, "This is all I need now, company." Gabe and Ben hurried to greet the two men on horse back. It was Mr. Broussard and Mr. Allen and they seemed in a hurry.

"Mr. Broussard, Mr. Allen, hello!" Gabe greeted them as they brought their horses to a halt. Gabe noticed that Mr. Allen wasn't on Judah. "What brings you all the way out here?"

"We came to ask you to attend an emergency meeting of the plantation owners," Mr. Broussard said still sitting upon his horse.

"Emergency meeting? Why? What's wrong?" Gabe was curious now.

"It's better left to discuss in private and not in front of slaves," Mr. Allen said eyeing Old Ben standing behind Gabe.

"Oh, you mean Ben here? Why he's here to tend to your horses if you should wish to dismount." Both men dismounted and handed their reins to Ben.

"Ben, would you water Mr. Allen's and Mr. Broussard's horses for them?"

"Yez sah Massa," Ben replied leading the horses away.

When Mr. Broussard thought Old Ben was out of hearing range, he began. "The meeting is tonight at seven o'clock at the bank. There's a uproar due to the rumors of a civil war, if Lincoln wins the next presidential election. You know he wants to do away with slavery! We won't stand for it!"

"Mr. Broussard," Gabe began, "The election is too far off for anyone to be worrying about who will or will not win, much less if there'll be a civil war. I call that buying trouble. As the Bible says, worrying won't change anything. God's in control. All we can do is pray for the right man. If that's all this meeting is about, then I won't be coming. I, for one, put my trust in God. Sitting around and talking about what if's isn't going to accomplish anything. It's just wasting time and energy, both of which, I don't have to waste on something that's only a rumor. As you know, since my father's sickness and death, I have many things to tend to here, which I can control.

Sorry gentlemen. Count me out. If something more than rumors comes up, then I will attend. I see no need of it now."

"Is that your final answer?" Mr. Allen asked.

"It is." Gabe didn't know how to make it any clearer and these men were testing the limits of his patience.

"Then we'll be off. We have many stops to make before we return home. If you should change your mind, the invitation still stands." Mr. Broussard said.

"Ben, would you bring Mr. Allen and Mr. Broussard's horses? These gentlemen need to leave."

Ben brought the horses over and the two men mounted and left. When they were out of range, Gabe shook his head. "What foolish men! Do they have so much free time on their hands, that all they could do is make trouble? He and Ben then went into the house to Gabe's study.

When Gabe was finally alone, he thought over his conversation with Broussard and Allen. He didn't know what it was about those two men that put him on edge. It seemed to take a lot out of him just to deal with them. It left him feeling tired. But then he had been up since three o'clock in the morning. Deciding to take a nap, he laid on the sofa, and almost immediately he fell asleep.

It was at this time God answer Gabe's prayers. In a dream he filled Gabe's mind with plans for the plantation. He saw the children and others walking in the dawn of the morning to the fields, then he saw them returning to the cabin in the woods when the sun was high in the sky and the heat was most intense. Josie stood in front of them teaching the A B C's. Then he saw the slaves return to the fields with a cooler evening breeze blowing on them. Next he saw the ledger of slave names. God's finger pointed to the column of the price of each slave. Then he heard a voice say *"He has fulfilled his purchase!"* Even in his sleep, Gabe knew this was God. At that point of realization, Gabe went into a deep restful sleep.

It didn't last very long for he felt an urgency to complete the assignment God had given him.

Gabe rose from the sofa and went directly to his desk and pulled out paper and pen. This is what he wrote:

> I, Gabriel M. Lyon, do hereby grant freedom to the slave known as Ben of New Canaan Plantation. He is from this day forward, granted all rights and privileges recognized to absolute freedom. No earthly Master owns this man. This declaration of freedom is to be instituted on this day, July 15th 1860. Signed by, Gabriel M. Lyon - New Canaan Plantation of East Baton Rouge Parish. Then Gabe applied his seal and taking another sheet of paper he then wrote one for Liza.

Gathering his ledgers and the letters of freedom, he went to find Josie. Gabe found her in the sun room sewing by herself. He walked over to her and asked her to come with him. Together they went to the kitchen where they found Ben and Liza with their children, talking at the table. All looked up at Gabe and Josie in Surprise. Ben and his boys started to rise, but Gabe motioned for them to keep their seats.

"Ben, Liza, you've served my grandfather, my father and me with not only your hard labor, but also your loyalty. Your labor has well exceeded the price paid for your slavery. As of this day, I am granting you your freedom. You may go, or stay with us. The decision is yours. If you choose to stay, you'll receive a wage for your work here. You may continue to live here in the house with us. Whatever decision you make, I want you to know how much your friendship has meant to me. No one will ever be able to replace you in my heart and memories. I thank you for all you've done in raising me, teaching me and helping me through all these years."

He handed the letters of freedom to Ben and Liza. The room was so quiet you could hear a pin drop. Josie found herself in tears again. The surprise in Ben's eyes changed from unbelief to thankfulness. Liza was the first to find her voice. She jumped up and ran toward Gabe, throwing her arms around him crying softly, repeating her thanks many times. Ben stood up tall, grinning from ear to ear and extending his hand to Gabe, he repeated his thanks while Gabe still held Liza in his arms.

"You know this means you no longer call me master. My family calls me Gabe, understand? Since your children were born here and not bought by my father, they're free too. Your papers will be ready for you in the morning. The same arrangements will apply to you, and if you choose to stay, you'll be paid a wage for your work just like your parents." Jonah, Caleb and Hannah just stood there, unable to move. Their parents went to them enfolding them in their arms. Each child thanked Gabe for their freedom.

Ben, Liza, Hannah, and Caleb all asked to stay on the plantation. Jonah told Gabe he'd let him know what he was going to do, but he had to think about it. Gabe then told Ben that all the slaves would be given the same opportunity to work and purchase their freedom, but the ones that had been there the longest would be given their freedom now. Then, on Sunday, he'd tell the rest of the slaves about his plan. Gabe asked them not to say anything until then, and everyone agreed.

Then Ben looked at Gabe and said, "Sah, I's thank ya fo my families freedom, but I's cant be a callin ya by ya given name. Just aint in me, I's been a slave too long. I's mean no disrespect, so I's be a callin ya Mr. Gabe. I's a freed man now, an I's choose ta be a callin ya dat. Dat be okay wid ya?"

"I understand Ben and it is okay with me." And it truly was; it was the one thing Gabe couldn't change over night. Slavery left its mark on everyone, one way or the other.

CHAPTER 6

GABE WORKED HARD TO FINISH the repairs to the roof on the cabin in the woods. He was grateful for the shade provided by the trees, which allowed him to work during the hottest part of the day. He felt the need to get it done before Sunday. It wasn't that God told him to have it finished by then, it was just an urgency he felt deep down in his soul. He'd learned early in his Christian life to obey those feelings and nothing was going to stop him. After hours of working, he paused to stretch his back. Gabe looked around at all God put him in charge of, and gave thanks to Him for giving his family this little church. Family, the word made him smile. He considered every person here his family, and it was growing quickly. He felt responsible for them like a father does to his children. He wanted them to learn the ways of God, and the skills they needed to survive on their own if they chose to leave.

Deciding he was thirsty, he climbed down the ladder in search of the water bucket, and when he'd found it, he also found Caleb waiting for him.

"Morning, Caleb!"

"Mornin, my chores be dun, an I's time on my hands, so I's cum here ta see'd ifin ya be needin help."

"Why, bless you! I can use your help no matter how long you can stay!"

"Where ya be wantin me?"

"How about working inside? If you could start taking down the walls, we could have this done in no time."

"My ma says I's be good at tearing thangs down. I's git right to it!" Caleb said laughing. Picking up the hammer and crow bar, Caleb went inside.

Josie and her staff had just increased by one; Hannah had offered to help them sew! If only they had a sewing machine! Why with that thing, they could do the work in half the time. As quickly as the thought passed through her mind, she reminded herself they'd just have to make do, and be grateful for what they had. The women attacked their sewing with a vengeance leaving no doubt it would be done soon.

Big John worked just as hard as anyone else. Already he and his men had completed repairs to the first cabin. A new door, which had been white washed by Little John, hung in its place, the new roof had made the cabin watertight. Window panes with glass replaced shutters, and a new wooden floor replaced the dirt one. Big John felt a sense of pride in the work Henry, Little John, and he had done. He knew the master would be very pleased too.

Sunday arrived with the mid morning heat bearing down on New Canaan. Gabe was grateful they'd be having services in the Church instead of on the grounds. The shade from the trees would provide a cooler church, and hopefully God would bless the day with a breeze. This was the prayer Gabe prayed while dressing.

Everyone knew the church was finished and they would be meeting there. Knowing the benches hadn't been made, the slaves brought something to sit on. Chairs and blankets filled the church. Laughter and the hum of fellowship could be heard coming from the church as Gabe and Josie approached.

"Yes, Lord, this is how your house should be! Full of laughter and love from the family of Christ," Gabe softly said to the Lord. When he had entered and walked to the front of the room, he looked into the smiling faces that looked back at him expectantly. "Today will be a different type of service. This is a day of celebration! For what you may ask? Well, I'll tell you soon. Will the following people come forward as I call your name?" A small low murmur came from the slaves as Gabe called the names: "James and Amie, Dan and Suzie, Joseph and Josephine, Jerome and Nolee, Philip and Laney, Dave and Tamis and last but not least Ben and Liza."

Gabe waited until they stood before him before continuing, "You have been here at New Canaan the longest and most of all you've served my grandfather, my father and me unconditionally. So today, I tell you, you are now free men and women! Since your children were not bought by my family, they too, are freed. You may stay or leave, the choice is yours. Should you choose to stay, you'll be paid wages for your work. You can live here, and you'll have the benefits of going to school, a share in the profits from the sale of crops, and five acres of land to farm for your own personal use." While he spoke, Josie handed the letters of freedom to each man, woman and child. They held their letters as if they were gold. Josie knew each person wanted to read the words on the pages giving them their freedom. Praying they would stay, she returned to Gabe's side.

"Every slave here has the same opportunity to earn their freedom. You automatically have the same benefit as the others. At anytime you may use your part of the profits to buy your freedom. Then you have the same choice to make, to stay here or go, it'll be up to you.

Hallelujahs went up all over the room. "Shouts of amen and thank ya Massa rang out. Gabe and Josie stood holding hands while watching their congregation rejoice at their new found opportunities. When things had settled some, Gabe got their attention by saying, "With these new opportunities comes only one request. I ask that you tell no one about what we're doing here. If anyone outside of New Canaan finds out, there will be consequences. Josie and I would be arrested for breaking the law for teaching you to read and write. Then, the plantation would be confiscated and sold. God only knows what would happen to the rest of you. Your very lives depend on this being kept a secret."

Big John stood and then motioned for the rest to stand. When all stood, Big John said, "Massa, we's be a talkin amongst us. We's knows ya be a man of honor. Whatcha's says ya do, ya duz. Whatcha be givin us, words can't tell! We's be kepin de secret, sah. Any man dat don't, has ta answer ta me! We's thank ya." The congregation agreed in unison.

"Josie and I thank each and every one of you and we trust you'll keep your promise. So I guess the services are over!"

Gabe expected everyone to leave and was surprised when not one person made a move. Instead, they all kneeled and started thanking God for their new freedoms and opportunities. Gabe even heard them thanking God for him and Josie. This blessed his heart so. Not because they thanked God for him, but they'd thanked God first for their blessings. Church didn't let out for quite a while after that. It was decided by the congregation praise and thanksgiving should be given before anyone left. Singing rang out from the rafters. Gabe's family was growing up.

The next day Gabe could see a change in everybody's outlook. Smiles could be seen from everyone he met as he made his way to the church. Men found their way to the cabin to help in their spare time by building benches and tables for the church and school. Some came by with their thanks, and others to tell Gabe they wanted to stay. By the end of the day all those with freedom papers had decided to stay. He sent them to Josie to have her write their names in a new ledger called payroll.

The night brought relief from the heat, and a covering of protection, as one by one the men of the slave quarters slipped into the woods. Old Ben had called for a meeting at the church. All the men needed to talk without the hindrance of women and children, and the church was the perfect place. Ben knew Gabe wouldn't mind. He even thought Gabe would understand why he'd chosen not to tell him about this meeting.

"We's got thangs ta discuss men," Ben said after they'd all gathered in.

"I's be a needin ta knowd ifn ya'll gona keep da Massa secret? Member, ya'll be'd in da house of da Lord. Only truth be spoke here!"

Ben addressed each man by name; all forty of them and each man gave his promise.

Big John stood up and said, "I's sez we's take a mark. De mark be de sign of de promise. "De women and chilen should do de same, dat way de Lord and Gabe be knowin we's be a kepin our wurd."

"What be de mark we's be a takin?" Old Ben asked.

"How's bout de mark of de cross?"

"De mark of de cross be serious, Big John. Is ya a b'liever in da Lord Jesus Christ?" Old Ben asked him seriously.

"I's b'lieve in him! Saved my soul by die'n on de cross, and he be de son of God," Big John assured him.

"Hows bout de rest of ya? How ya'll be a standin wid de Lord?" Ben asked looking closely at the group.

Then just as he had done before, he called each mans name, asking the same question. When Ben got to the men who hadn't accepted Jesus Christ as their Savior, he and Big John led them through the scriptures of salvation they knew by heart. Then, Ben led them in the sinner's prayer, so they could ask forgiveness of their past sins, and ask Jesus into their hearts.

It was quite a night. If only they could've seen the sight surrounding the little church. Angels standing side by side protecting the church until the Lords business was done. The men left the church changed. Assured in their salvation, they slipped out quietly into the darkness with the promise to return in two days to begin their marking.

The activities began to increase on New Canaan plantation. Everyone was busy. During the day, they worked the fields and their assigned areas. At night, they would slip into the woods to receive their mark. Using ink borrowed from Gabe's study, and a sharpened quill, a small cross was etched into the skin at the base of the palm of their right hand. Nearly everyone received the mark. The only one that hadn't was Jonah. Ben would take care of that! If Jonah was going be staying at New Canaan while trying to make up his mind about what he was going to do, then he was definitely going to take the mark and keep the promise.

Ben searched the grounds for Jonah. He even went to all of Jonahs favorite hiding places. Ben was determined to talk to him and wouldn't quit until he found him. After searching for several hours, Ben found Jonah standing idly against a tree. Anger shot through Ben, how dare the boy eat and not work! "Jonah!" Ben shouted.

Jonah turned in surprise. He'd been caught! He could tell his pa was angry by the sound of his voice. Just how much didn't sink in until he saw his face. "I's not afeard of him. I's ain't no boy!" He thought to himself.

"Yez pa?"

"Boy, we's a gona talk!" Ben took his son by the collar and led him into the woods.

With August fast approaching, Ben and the workers wanted to get as much done as they could before the real heat set in. They worked as long as they possibly could, having the younger children only to bring water and food to the fields. Josie and Gabe noticed this change. Gabe figured Ben had something to do with moving them out of the heat and was glad. Older children were assigned to areas such as the barns and the orchards. The pregnant women were now helping with the sewing, safely out of the intense heat of the sun.

Gabe felt good about the way things were coming along. He had only one concern, and that was Jonah. He had not told Gabe whether he would be staying or not. Gabe decided not to push the issue, but he didn't want Jonah, who was known for causing trouble, to let their secret out.

Jonah was angry at his father. He'd made him take the mark! He'd have to make up his mind soon. Right now he didn't want to stay, but then he didn't want to go either. Soon he'd leave. He just had to choose the right time.

Little John, who had been working with his father, saw the rider fast approaching the house. Quickly he pointed this out to Big John who told him to run and tell the master. Running to the woods he called out "Massa, Massa!"

"What is it Little John?" Gabe said setting down his hammer.

"Dar be a rider cumin to de house!"

"Its okay, Little John, lets go see what he wants."

"We's ain't in trouble is we?"

"No, I don't think so. We'll just go see what they want." Gabe had the same thought to cross his mind. They'd reached the front of the house as the rider made his way up the front steps.

"Hello there!" Gabe didn't recognize the stranger.

"Hello, are you Gabriel Lyon? The rider inquired.

"I am," he replied.

"I'm Miles, Mr. Fontenot from the train station sent me, and you have several crates from Maine waiting on you. If you want, I can bring them out tomorrow, or you can come and get them today. It's up to you."

"We'll come and get them today, but thank you for your offer." Turning to Little John, he said, "Go ask Caleb to hitch the wagon for us and bring it around."

"Yez sah," Little John said heading toward the barn.

"I'll go on ahead and tell Mr. Fontenot you're coming."

"That's fine. Please tell Mr. Fontenot I appreciate him sending you out."

Miles tipped his hat as he rode off toward town.

Hurrying inside, Gabe called out to Josie as he went up the stairs to change. Following his voice, she went to him. "What's going on Gabe?"

"I'm going into town with Caleb. The books have arrived from Charles!"

"Praise the Lord!" Josie shouted.

"Better get your teaching shoes on!" He said as he grabbed her and twirled her around. After changing clothes, and giving Josie a quick kiss, he was down the stairs and out the door.

Josie was so excited! Running down the stairs, she went to tell her news to the ladies in the sewing room.

"Liza! Guess what!?"

"Whatcha cited bout?"

"The books are here! Charles sent the books! Gabe's gone to town to pick them up! Isn't it wonderful?"

"Fo shoor! Dat be a meanin we's can git startin wid da readin an writin!"

"It sure does!" Josie said laughing. The women returned to their sewing excited and to wait for Gabe's return.

Gabe hurried to get back home. How he wanted to look in those crates. His heart raced when he read the labels on the wooden boxes. One was from Charles, the other from Professor Hall. How clever of those two men! No one would be able to guess what was in either. Josie was really going to get the surprise of her life, he thought, as they pulled up to the house. Apparently Josie was waiting for them. She shot out of the house like a bullet, and behind her came Liza just as excited. Neither one could wait to see the treasures the men brought home.

Gabe and Caleb brought the crates into the study. Taking a crow bar, Gabe opened the first crate from Charles. It was filled with books for basic reading, writing and math. It contained lots of slate tablets, paper, quills, chalk, pens and ink. Charles had thought of everything. At the bottom of the box was a letter from Charles. Gabe opened it and read it out loud.

> Dear Gabe, Josie, and Friends,
>
> I hope this letter finds you all well. I've sent you supplies I thought were important for your adventure. Please tell your students to study well, and learn as quickly as they can. In this day and time it is critical for them. If you need any further assistance, please do not hesitate to ask. Who knows Gabe; you may very well have a future senator, lawyer or doctor in your midst!
>
> Your friend always,
>
> Charles

"Sah, he don't knowd who ya'll be a teachin. Goin on wid us be'in doctors and such." Caleb couldn't believe what he just heard.

"Caleb, Charles and I are best friends. We went to college together in Maine. He graduated and I didn't. Now, he's a head master of a school. The thing you should know about Charles is, he's a negro just like you. He is very proud you're going to be learning to read and write. He knows what a difference it'll make in your life."

"Fo shoor?" Caleb asked in disbelief.

"Yes, for sure, you see, only you can put limits on yourself. If you want something bad enough, all you have to do is go after it, with study and prayer. You do your part and God will do his. Understand?"

"Yez sah, and he be yor best friend?"

"Yes, he's my best friend!" Gabe assured him.

Walking over to the next crate, Caleb took the crow bar and opened it.

"Don't knowd whut dis be," he said as he removed the straw.

Josie sure did! With a shriek of delight, she started jumping up and down.

"Oh Liza, Gabe, do you know what this is? It's a sewing machine! I can't believe it. Father sent a sewing machine. Seeing an envelope attached to the inside of the box she took it and read it immediately.

Dear Josie,

I wish I could be there to see the surprise on your face when you see this machine. I hope you enjoy it as much as your husband enjoyed arranging this gift for you. I think it's a wonderful thing you and Gabe are doing in New Canaan. The news here is civil war is on the horizon. You and Gabe need to keep up with the news and the political changes occurring around you. I'll keep you in my prayers. May God's protection and blessings be with you in all that you do, I love you. Write soon with updates.

Your Loving Father

"Oh Gabe! This is wonderful. Thank you so much! What made you think of a sewing machine?"

"I saw the need my love, that's all," he said as he leaned over and kissed her.

"Liza, we're going to be able to make clothes twice as fast, as soon as we learn how to use this thing," Josie said giggling.

"I's be de one a wantin to knowd! Ya'll be a takin dat thang in da sun room. Me en Josie be a wantin ta see'd des here better," Liza said looking at the two men, "Git ta movin it!"

Laughing and obeying, Gabe and Caleb got busy. When Liza had that determined look in her eye, you had best do what she said. Both had learned that early in life over her knee!

That evening Gabe wandered through the house looking for Josie. He had searched everywhere he knew to look. Standing at the bottom of the stairs he called out, "Josie, where are you?"

"I'm in your study!" Came her reply.

"I wondered where you'd gotten to."

She sat on the floor with all the books and school materials around her. Looking up she smiled. "Isn't it wonderful? Soon school will start. Oh, when can we begin?"

He helped her to her feet. "Think you can have a lesson plan by Monday?"

"Yes, I can!"

"Well then, on Sunday I'll make the announcement school will begin on Monday. We'll just have to take it one day at a time after that. Okay?"

"Agreed!" Josie knew Gabe was excited, but not as much as she was.

By Sunday, Josie had her first lesson plan made, and Liza had the new sewing machine conquered. Come Monday morning, they'd be doing a new job, both were excited about the changes. It was all Josie talked about as she and Gabe walked to church.

Standing in front of his congregation, Gabe was amazed at all the smiling clean faces and new clothes. How different everyone looked. They'd certainly changed before his eyes. Before he could speak, there was a wave of hands from everyone in front of him. Confused, he just waved back. This brought the whole room into a fit of laughter.

Standing up from his chair, Old Ben quieted everyone down. "Mr. Gabe sah, afor ya begins, we's gots sumptin ta says ta ya."

"Go ahead, Ben." Gabe smiled for Ben hadn't called him master.

"Well sah, we's wantin ya ta knowd dat we's be a kepin ourn promise. We's be a wantin God ta knowd too. So, we's took da mark, so ya knowd fo shoor, and we's took it afor God!"

"What do you mean Ben?" Gabe wasn't sure he understood.

"Ya see'd everybodies rit hand?" Gabe looked closely at the raised hands. But he still couldn't see what Ben was talking about.

"Yes?"

"Dat be da mark. Cum on down here and see'd, sah."

Stepping down from the little rise serving as a platform, Gabe walked to the person nearest him. Taking their right hand, he saw a tiny cross tattooed at the base of the palm. He then went to the next person, and then the next. Doing this until he reached Ben. He looked at Ben's tattoo, and then raised his eyes to meet Bens.

"We's all dun it, Mr. Gabe, tis our promise ta God and ta you." Ben looked into Gabe's eyes to see if he understood.

Gabe was speechless. He thought for sure he was going to cry. He didn't know what to say. This show of loyalty hadn't been expected.

"I's a sin ta confess, I's taked da ink frum your study," Ben admitted.

Gabe started laughing, at first it was a small laugh, but then it became loud and uncontrollable, as if it came from the depths of his soul. Then Ben started laughing and soon laughter erupted from the whole congregation. Gabe reached forward and took a surprised Ben into a hug. Letting Ben go, he turned and motioned for Josie to join him. Still laughing, he showed her the tattoos on every man, woman and child. It took him a while, but he finally regained his composure. This service was certainly going to be different from what he planned.

"What we have here, my friends, is what the Bible calls a Covenant. He went on to explain how God had a blood convent with his children, through the blood of Jesus, which was shed on the cross. To make it binding, Gabe said, Josie and I will take the mark too. Ben, will you do the honors?"

"Yez sah, I's proud ta duz it fo ya." Taking the ink and sharpened quill from his pocket, Ben tattooed both Gabe and Josie in front of everyone.

"Before we leave today, Gabe said, I want to thank each and every one of you for your loyalty. You don't know what this day means to me! Thank you from the bottom of my heart. Before I forget, I've some good news for you, tomorrow school starts! The children will begin at nine o'clock, then break for dinner at noon. Then the adults will join them after dinner till four. After that, you'll return to your work to finish what you can by supper. We'll try it this way for a few days to see how it works. I know the harvest begins soon, so if we need to change it, we can. Now let us pray. "Lord, I thank you for my family. Please watch over us and keep us safe. We ask your blessing on all we put our hand to, in the name of Jesus, Amen."

The next morning found Josie deep in thought, as she walked to the school.

She had one full month before the harvest began to teach as much as she possibly could, because everyone would be needed in the fields for the harvest. The children, she knew, would be easier to teach than the adults. But this didn't bother her, God was in control. She entered the school in high spirits. She noticed Caleb had set out books, and slate tablets along the benches, one for each child. Josie figured she'd have around thirty children this morning, ranging in the ages from six to twelve. The children above those ages were considered adults by their own standards, and would be working until noon. She honestly didn't believe she'd be able to get everyone in the room and teach them like she wanted, but she knew God would direct her. While she sat there thinking on these things, the door opened and a young black girl of sixteen walked in.

"Good morning," Josie said smiling.

"Morin Missus. I's be Emlee. Miz Liza say I's should be a lettin ya knowd dat I's can read and rite sum." The young girl was shy and soft spoken.

"You've been taught to read and write? How? I don't understand." Josie was confused at what the child said.

"Well Missus, I's frum Virginee afor da Massa buyed me. Ain't agin da law ta read and rite dar. My ma learned me, anyways, Miz Liza be of da mind I's mit be a help ta ya."

"How old were you when you came here?" Josie asked in shock.

"I's be about ten missus, but I's can count ta a hunder, I's knowd da ABC's, and I's can add and subtracts sums. Not da big'ins, jus enuf ta take care of moneys. I wuz de market girl."

"How about you reading to me some from this book," Josie asked, as she handed her the primer reader.

Emlee read the first page like an old pro. She then said the ABC's and wrote them out for Josie. Then she showed Josie her skills in adding and subtracting with Josie giving her basic math problems. Josie was amazed. This young lady would be able to help her! God had answered her prayers quickly, but that was just like God. When he wanted something done, he made sure it happened!

When all the children had arrived, and taken their seats, Josie began their day. First with the alphabet and the standard A is for apple and so on. Then she taught them their first lesson in writing. As the noon hour approached, Josie stopped and read them a chapter from The Wind and The Willow. The children were captivated by the story. When she'd finished the first chapter, the children didn't want to leave. She had to promise them she would read to them again, and she shooed them out the door to have lunch.

Not all the adults, slaved or freed, wanted to go to school. Josie noticed at least one person from each family had shown for classes, that would do for now. Josie asked Emlee to take the younger children outside to play under the shade of the trees, so she could focus her attention on the adults. Hearing a burst of laughter from outside, she walked to the window to see what the children were doing, as she went thru the ABC's for the second time that day. Josie was happy to see Emlee sitting with the children around her, teaching them to count. She showed them the number on her hands and then wrote the number on a slate tablet for them to see. She said the number, and the children repeated it. Josie smiled at what she saw. She knew beyond any shadow of doubt, Emlee was a blessing.

The days started flying by for everyone concerned; everyone was busy learning, and working. By the end of the month they knew their ABC's, could count to fifty, and write their names. Josie felt very blessed.

September brought the rice harvest, but attendance wasn't affected. It seemed they only tried harder. Josie still kept the children separated from the adults in the afternoons, with Emlee's help. It proved to be very effective.

October was the driest month for New Canaan. The corn and hay were harvested within two weeks. A very quick harvest time, but Gabe couldn't have been happier. The crops had surely been blessed. It was the best harvest, so far, in New Canaan's history according to Ben. The cotton wouldn't be harvested until November. We're going to make it! Gabe thought as he entered the house going to his study.

Gabe found Liza waiting for him. He could tell by the look on her face something was up. She approached him quickly.

"Ya gots a visitor sah," her tone warned him it was someone being nosey.

"Thank you Liza, that will be all," he said loudly, then in a whisper, "Go get Josie."

"Yez sah," she said obediently. So much so, she made Gabe smile in spite of himself. Walking into the setting room, there sat Mr. Broussard.

"Mr. Broussard, how are you?" Gabe asked politely.

"Gabe, my friend, I'm doing well! Where's that lovely wife of yours?"

"She's out on the grounds. You know how women love their flowers." Gabe didn't want to lie, but it wasn't any of this man's business where his wife was!

"In this heat? Why, my wife wouldn't take a step out of her room, much less be outside!" Mr. Broussard laughed at the thought.

"Well sir, I know you didn't come all the way out here to talk about our wives and the heat. So, what brings you here?" Gabe hated being so direct but he didn't want any more questions about Josie.

"Right you are. I've come to invite you and your wife to the Annual Harvest Ball. It's my turn as host, so it'll be at my house on October twentieth. My wife and I hope you'll come."

Josie chose this time to enter the room carrying a basket of flowers on her arm to Gabe's relief. Mr. Broussard stood to his feet as she entered.

"Mrs. Lyon, how are you?"

"Mr. Broussard! Fine, thank you, how's your wife?" Josie asked politely.

"She just fine, thanks for asking. I was just telling your husband here about the harvest ball. We're hoping you'll be attending."

"I'm sure we will be Mr. Broussard, thank you for inviting us. This is such an honor." Josie was not only polite but sweet to the man.

"Well good! We'll be seeing you both soon. I should be leaving now; my wife is expecting me home for supper. Goodbye and stay out of this heat!"

The last remark was directed at Josie.

Walking Mr. Broussard to the door, Josie and Gabe thanked him again for coming and for the invitation.

When the door closed, Josie and Gabe broke out in laughter. "I can't believe you walked in with that basket of flowers on your arm. I didn't know what to tell him and that just came out."

"Lucky you! I heard what you said from the dinning room. So I grabbed this basket from the kitchen, and the flowers from the vase on the table, and just made my entrance! Besides, you weren't lying, I was on the grounds and I do love my flowers!" she told him laughing.

"Thank you for being such a smart wife!" Gabe said taking her in his arms and kissing her.

The next two weeks pass quickly for Josie. She and Gabe worked from sun up to sun down. Often Liza would have to remind them they hadn't eaten, fussing as she placed food in front of them. Both were tired, but they were happy with their busy life. Never had Josie experienced anything like this before, it was a feeling of fulfillment. Doing Gods work gave an inner peace, strength, and joy beyond expectation. How she loved it!

Josie couldn't believe she was getting ready for her first ball. She felt both excited and nervous. Nervous, only because she didn't want her abolitionist ideas to slip out at any time and endanger what she and Gabe were doing. She prayed, "Lord, please put a guard over my tongue have me say what only you would want. Thank you, in Jesus name, amen." Feeling better, she ran down the stairs to the kitchen for Liza.

"I know you're busy Liza, but could you help me get dressed? I don't know how to put this thing on without your help! Josie held up the corset for Liza to see.

"Yez, my girl, I's help ya. Come along now, afor the men folk come and see." Laughing they went upstairs to Josie's room.

"Are you sure I have to wear this? I can't breathe, Liza!"

"It be made ta make ya prudy, not comfortable!"

"I'm sure glad I don't have to wear this thing everyday. I just wouldn't do it!" Josie declared. Laughing at her, Liza picked up the hoop and had her step into it.

"Am I going to wear petticoats with this too? Josie knew the answer, but asked anyway.

"Now Missus Josie, don'tcha be a complainin! Des here need dem petticoats ta make ya skirt stand out. Ya best be practicing sittin whilst I's getcha petticoats and dress. Go ahead on, sit!" Liza commanded.

While Liza went for the dress, and the rest of the petticoats, Josie practiced. Her first try at sitting wasn't very lady like, as the front of the hoop flipped up nearly covering her head. Josie couldn't help laughing. The second try was worse; the hoop almost flipped her backwards. Determined to get it right, she kept practicing. Soon Josie found if she sat on the edge of the chair, she was in control of the hoop. It would at least remain down.

After practicing several more times, she was confident she wouldn't be embarrassing Gabe, or herself. Liza had returned during Josie's second attempt at sitting, but couldn't bring herself to say anything. She just stood at the door, laughing, until Josie noticed her there.

"Liza, one day you'll have to wear one of these things, and I'll get to laugh at you!" Josie teased as she sat again without incident.

"No thank ya! I's be like a duck out of water in sumethang like that. No ma'am, not me!"

After helping Josie into her petticoats, Liza brought out the new ball gown.

It was beautiful. It was the lightest pink, and seemed to shine when the light hit it just right. It was off the shoulders just enough to be fashionable, but not indecent, with short puffy sleeves, and bows on each shoulder. The bodice was made of satin with tiny pink pearls scattered across it. It fit her like a glove, showing off her tiny waist. The satin skirt was full, with double rolls of lace along the hem touching the floor. She wore pink satin slippers with the same tiny pearls at the toes. Looking into the mirror, Josie couldn't believe it was her. Picking up her white gloves; she turned and headed down the stairs.

Gabe saw her coming down the stairs gracefully. He felt as if the very breath had been knocked out of him. She was beautiful! Coming to stand in front of him, Josie whipped out a fan, holding it to her face, she batted her eye lashes and said, "I am ready sir," in her best southern drawl. Gabe and Liza laughed at her.

"Ya's be prudy as a picture!" Liza told her beaming.

"I second that!" Gabe said taking her by the hand, "you'll be the prettiest one there; all the men will be envious of me!"

"Thank you both, you're looking handsome yourself my husband," Josie said, while making a small curtsey.

"I think it's time to go. We don't want to be late, but we don't want to be the first one's to arrive either." Gabe guided her to the door.

"Ifn ya mama could be a seein ya now, shed be rite proud!" Liza said then added in a whisper, "member ya hoop an yor sittin Missus!" This caused both women to break out in laughter. Then Gabe and Josie dropped a kiss on Liza's cheek and told her good bye, laughing as they went out into the night.

Liza turned to go back to the kitchen when she saw Ben and Caleb standing in the doorway. Both had grave looks on their faces. Her heart fell.

"What be de matter?" She demanded. "Ya'll best be a tellin me now!"

"Jus cum ta da kitchen, we's be a needin ta tell ya sumethang," Ben told her softly as he lead her there.

Sitting in her chair, she asked again "Whatcha needin ta tell me?"

Ben took his wife's hand and said, "Jonah up and left. Jus told Caleb he be a leavin."

"Did he be sayin where he be goin?" she asked Caleb.

"No mama, he jus sayd he wuz is all."

"Be he gone now?" It was all Liza could do to hold back her tears.

"Yez Liza, he be gone." Ben put his arms around his wife as her tears began to flow.

Josie felt like a princess as she danced with Gabe in the ball room. The room was exquisite. Never had she seen such excess, but it was beautiful. "Do we have a ball room?" She couldn't remember seeing one.

"Josie, are you telling me you haven't explored our house yet?" Gabe couldn't believe she didn't know.

"Gabriel Lyon! You of all people know how busy I've been. No, to answer your question, I have not. But I can assure you I will as soon as I can!" She whispered to him as he twirled her around the dance floor.

When the dance came to an end Gabe could tell Josie was tired.

"Would you like to sit for a while?"

"Yes I would and something to drink please."

"It appears we're about to have company!" Gabe whispered as he escorted Josie to the setting area. He'd noticed the couple approaching them.

"Gabriel! Good to see you. You haven't met my wife have you?" Mr. Broussard asked as he ushered his wife between the two.

"No sir, I don't recall meeting her."

"No? Well allow me the honor. Inez, this is Gabriel Lyon and his wife Josephine."

"Pleased to meet you," Gabe and Josie said.

"Mr. and Mrs. Lyon," Inez Broussard said with a nod as she took her seat.

"Gabriel, we plantation owners are having a little impromptu meeting in my study now. Would you care to join us? Our wives can get acquainted while we're gone." Mr. Broussard said with a satisfied smile.

"Trapped!" Gabe thought to himself as he turned to Josie and said, "Do you mind dear?"

"Trapped!" Josie thought as she replied, "Not all," with a forced smile.

When the two men departed with a promise to return soon, Josie turned to Mrs. Broussard. "This is a lovely party. Do you have it every year?"

"No. This was just our year. Each year it's held at a different home. Next year will be your turn. Actually, this was your year, but seeing that your father-in law just passed away and the two of you being newly married, my husband decided we should have it."

"How thoughtful of you, Mrs. Broussard," Josie told her.

"Oh well, think nothing of it," she assured Josie. "But you must call me Inez."

"Inez, thank you, you must call me Josie."

"How quaint, a little nickname for Josephine I take it?"

"Yes, it is. My father called me Josie from the day I was born and it's just stayed with me." Josie informed her with a tight smile. This woman was rude!

"My husband tells me you're from the north...Maine isn't it?"

"Yes, your husband is correct." Josie felt heat rising to her face.

"Tell me, just what does your father do?" Inez quizzed her.

"My father is a professor at Amherst College."

"Oh... A professor, how nice for you," Mrs. Broussard said slowly through her fake smile. "Oh anyway, we must bear what we must bear. Tell me Josephine, you don't mind me calling you Josephine do you?" Not waiting for an answer, Inez continued. "My husband tells me Mr. Lyon and you will be staying to run New Canaan."

"Yes, we are," Josie smiled as her anger rose.

"I just don't understand it! I mean, after all, your husband is just a preacher! He knows nothing of being a plantation owner and growing crops. Does he really think he can do it?" Inez asked with her fake smile.

"Mrs. Broussard, by what you are saying, you must believe because my husband is a man of God, he can't run a plantation?"

"Well, yes, that's exactly what I'm saying! I don't think he can, not like my husband!" the hateful woman hissed.

"Let me ask you this, Mrs. Broussard," Josie stood. "Is your husband going to hell? I mean, after all, he is not a man of God, like my husband! He's just a plantation owner!" With that said, Josie left a shocked, open mouthed Inez Broussard sitting by herself.

Gabe was holding his own in this impromptu meeting of The Plantation Owners Association. As soon as he could get out of there, he was getting Josie and going home! Mr. Broussard had his nerve, Gabe thought as he looked around the room. These so called Christian men needed to know their God! As soon as this thought went through his head, the man sitting across from him smiled, almost as if he could read Gabe's mind.

Before Gabe could think anything, much less say something, the man across the room rose and walked over to him. The man interrupted Mr. Broussard's long winded speech on the importance of slavery, by saying, "Gabriel, my name is Michael Guerrier. I noticed your cotton crop in the field on my way here earlier today. May I come by and visit you at your home tomorrow? I've some business to discuss with you."

"Yes sir, you may. Would you like to meet my wife?"

"Yes, I'd love to!" The two men turned and left the room, leaving the rest in a stunned silence.

Finding Josie getting some much needed fresh air, Gabe took her by the hand and led her toward Mr. Guerrier.

"I have someone for you to met Josie. This is Mr. Michael Guerrier. Mr. Guerrier, my wife Josie Lyon."

"How do you do?" Mr. Guerrier asked politely.

"I'm better now, thank you." Josie replied unthinking. Mr. Guerrier threw his head back laughing while Gabe just looked at her in shock.

Clearing his throat, Gabe continued, "Mr. Guerrier will be coming to our plantation tomorrow Josie. He wants to see our cotton crop. Possibly even buy it. You see, he is a buyer for a company in France."

"Well then, we should leave now Gabe, so we'll be well rested to give Mr. Guerrier a tour of New Canaan. Mr. Guerrier, it has been such a pleasure to met you tonight. I look forward to seeing you tomorrow."

"Indeed, it has been a pleasure, Mrs. Lyon. Until tomorrow," Mr. Guerrier smiled and gave a slight bow.

Josie then took her confused husband by the hand and led him to get their things. She wanted to go home now! As they went out the door, she spied Mr. Guerrier watching them. He had the biggest smile on his face, as if he was enjoying a private joke.

Chapter 7

Josie couldn't wait to tell Gabe what happened while he was in his meeting with The Plantation Owners Association. As soon as they were on their way home she began, "Gabe, that woman is absolutely dreadful! I don't think I've met anyone with such rudeness and hatefulness! Do you know she had the nerve to tell me since you're a man of God you wouldn't know how to run a plantation?"

"It doesn't matter what she thinks Josie, we aren't running the plantation like the others. We're running the plantation according to Gods word. You should've heard Mr. Broussard, going on and on about slavery being a good thing. Then in the next breath he's talking about cutting food rations to his slaves to make more of a profit! Why, if Mr. Guerrier hadn't interrupted him, I would've walked out, I've never heard such nonsense!"

"Have you ever meet Mr. Guerrier before tonight?" Josie asked.

"Now that you mentioned it, I haven't. Though, he does seem familiar to me. Anyway, I was thankful to get out of there!"

"I know Mr. and Mrs. Broussard claim to be Christians, but I don't think they know our God! I can't believe I allowed that woman to get to me!"

"What do you mean?"

"I lost my temper Gabe. I'm feeling bad about it now, but it sure felt good then!"

"That's the way it usually is Josie, what did you say?"

Taking a deep breath, she confessed her sin, "When she told me she didn't think you could run the plantation because you're just a preacher, I asked her if her husband was going to hell, because he was just a plantation owner!"

"You didn't!"

"Yes I did!" Josie couldn't believe she'd said it either.

It was all Gabe could do not to laugh. Leave it to Josie to get straight to the point in as few words as possible. Her temper rose with the slightest injustices. After a few minutes of quiet, which actually was him regaining composure, he patted her hand. "Well Josie, if you feel bad about it, ask God to forgive you, and the next time you see Mrs. Broussard apologize."

"An apology isn't necessary, I feel like I just pointed out something to Mrs. Broussard she didn't see! I feel bad about how I allowed her to make me angry. I'll pray about it and what God tells me to do, I'll do."

Gabe was grateful Josie couldn't see him in the darkness, if she could see his face, she might think he wasn't taking her seriously. It was hard not to laugh! He knew something like this might happen, he just didn't think it would be this soon.

When Gabe and Josie entered the house, Ben, Caleb and Liza were waiting for them. All three had worried looks on their faces, and Liza appeared to have been crying. Ben stepped forward, "Mr. Gabe, I's be needin to talk wid ya."

"Of course Ben, is something wrong?"

"Yez sah, our Jonah done up and left wid out saying nothin to his mama or me, jus told Caleb here, he was a leavin."

Gabe was silent as Josie rushed to Liza. "I'm so sorry!" she said. This caused new tears to flow. Putting her arm around Liza, Josie led her to the kitchen. There they could talk, and the men would be alone to discuss what needed to be done.

"Mr. Gabe, I's don't knowd ifn I's should goes after him, or just let him be." Ben stood shaking his head, not knowing what to do.

"He's a free man now." Gabe felt the same dilemma.

"I's knowd dat, he'd jus don't knowd how ta be freed! He can't read or rite, but he can work ifn he puts his mind ta it. I's jus gots me a bad feelin, dats all, jus got my soul a churnin bout him."

"Well, we can't do anything about it tonight. We need to pray for some guidance Ben. Then we'll do what the Lord lays on our hearts, so let's do it right now." The three men bowed their heads. "Father, we come to you now asking for your guidance on what we should do about our Jonah. We want to do what's right for him. If we should go looking for him we will, if you want us to let him go on his own, we will do that too, we just ask you lead us. We pray your protection over Jonah right now, lead and guide him wherever he is, in Jesus name, amen."

"Thank ya Mr. Gabe, I's knowd ya would help, and I's knowd you'd pray. I's be waitin on de Lord afore we does anything. I's be goin an get Liza now, de missus probably got her calm down some. Caleb, you goes back ta de cabin case he come back."

"Yez sah, pa." Caleb left with a heavy heart. The cabin was going to be lonely tonight.

Gabe and Ben found Josie with Liza at the kitchen table deep in prayer. The men stood quietly, waiting for them to finish. When they were done, Ben went to his wife and led her to their rooms, Liza cried softly as they walked away.

"It's been a long night Josie. I think we should go to bed now, I have a feeling it's going to be a long day tomorrow." Gabe took Josie by the hand and led the way upstairs.

Jonah had been walking for hours and was tired; he needed to find a place to sleep for the night. He stopped and searched the land before him, and spied an old barn up ahead in the bright moonlight. No one seemed to be around, so he quietly made his way there. Deciding the hay loft would be the better place to sleep and stay hidden should anyone come in, he climbed up to the loft, made his bed, and lay down. In the darkness he started thinking, "dey's sure ta be missin me now! I ain't ever goin back. I's don't need dem and deys sure ta be sorry I's gone." Feeling satisfied with himself, he closed his eyes and went to sleep.

The morning brought the bright hot sun with no breeze to be felt, as everyone readied for Mr. Guerrier's visit. Gabe continued in prayer for Jonah as he went about his morning activities. There wouldn't be school today because they had a visitor coming. Josie had instructed Emlee to take all the smaller children to the woods to play, and to use the school for whatever she wanted. They just needed to stay out of sight and out of the hot sun until their visitor had left. Ben and Liza were unusually quite this morning, but who could blame them? They were both earnestly in prayer for their missing son.

Gabe headed for his study, when there came a knock at the door just as he passed the foyer. When he opened it, there stood Mr. Guerrier.

"Good morning, Mr. Guerrier, I'm so glad you've come. Welcome!"

"Good morning to you! Isn't this a glorious day the Lord has made?" Mr. Guerrier asked, shaking Gabe's hand.

"Yes sir, it is! Mr. Guerrier, I didn't know you were a Christian!"

"Please, call me Michael," Mr. Guerrier insisted.

"Then you must call me Gabe, how long have you been a Christian?

"I've been confessing Jesus is Lord and the son of God since the very beginning!"

"How wonderful, it blesses me so to find someone with the same heart for the Lord as me!"

"It blesses the Lord more than you can imagine for someone to seek him out and put their faith, and trust in him." As Michael spoke, it was as if fire flashed from his eyes. Gabe knew this was no ordinary man.

Jonah was awaken with a hard blow to his back. Jumping up in fear and pain, he didn't understand what was happening. It didn't take him long to realize he was in big trouble! Five big rough looking white men surrounded him and he had no way to escape.

"Looks like we found us a runaway slave, boys, I betcha he'd be a good worker by the way he jumped up so fast." A bald heavy- set man laughed as he walked toward Jonah.

"I's be freed!" Jonah shouted at the man once he regained his breath.

"Freed? No one around here is freeing any slaves. If they were, we'd heard about it. Where you from?" The bald man stood inches from Jonah's face.

"I's gots my papers sah, jus let me shows dem to ya," Jonah begged.

"Go ahead and get'em. You best not try to run either, cause we can catch you and when we do you'll be sorry! Understand?"

"Yes sah, I's understands." Jonah reached for his bag, taking out the papers, he handed them over to the bald man.

"Well, well, looks like that preacher Lyon gave this boy his freedom. I think Mr. Broussard might be interested in this information. Why, we might even get us some money! Come on boys, tie him up and take him to the shack!"

"Sah, my papers, I's be a needin dem!" Jonah was desperate to get them back.

Laughing, the bald man walked over to where the four other men held Jonah, and punched him in the stomach. Jonah lost all ability to breath, and as he was gasping for air, the men tied him with a rope. His arms were tied behind him, and then the rope was looped around his neck. It was the last thing he remembered before he passed out.

Gabe presented Michael to Josie. She'd never met anyone with such a commanding appearance in her life. He was about thirty, with a muscular build. Michael was well over six feet tall, with long bond hair, and steel blue eyes that seemed to spit fire when he talked about the Lord. His stance was of someone in authority and not to be argued with, but his smile was both warm and comforting, and she automatically liked him.

"Gabe, we must see to Michael's horse, it's been standing out in the hot sun for a while now," Josie reminded her husband.

"No need to worry Mrs. Lyon, I've been dropped off at your doorstep," Michael assured her.

"Will they be back to pick you up later?" She asked.

"Not to worry, I have a way back. Now let's see this cotton of yours!"

Not wasting any words or time, Gabe took Michael on a tour of the grounds as they made their way to the cotton fields. Gabe was thankful for the breeze blowing to cool them as they walked. Michael asked questions as they strolled, and Gabe answered them in return. Gabe really enjoyed being in the presence of this man. They talked about the crops, but mostly they talked of God. Gabe was so impressed with Michael's knowledge; he just had to ask him about his education. "Where did you go to school? I have to know! I don't believe I've ever talked with anyone so knowledgeable about the Bible."

"I know of these things from my father," Michael answered him quietly. As I said before, I've known these things from the beginning. It's just the way my family is."

"I think it's wonderful! Its how I want to raise my children," Gabe told him.

"Your sons will be powerful men of God, Gabe. Just continue in the direction God is leading you, and you will not fail."

Emlee chose this exact moment to come out of the woods, the children following close behind her in single file. They were singing their ABC's at the top of their voices. Gabe didn't know what to do. Seeing the two men, Emlee froze. She stopped right where she was, causing all the children to run into each other, fall to the ground laughing. Then thinking quickly, Emlee turned, and started walking back toward the woods. The children all jumped up, still laughing, and fell in behind her. Then to Gabe's surprise, they all began to wave as they disappeared into the woods.

"Are those your children?" Michael asked, laughing at the sight.

"Yes, they all belong to me," Gabe smiled as the last little dark head disappeared into the woods.

Beau Broussard was livid! He talked out loud to himself as he paced back and forth in his office. "How dare that young know nothing, Gabriel Lyon, invite Mr. Guerrier to New Canaan to see his cotton in front of the whole Association! Of all the nerve! He, Beau Broussard, had the finest cotton in the state of Louisiana. Everyone knew it!" A knock on his office door stopped Broussard from his ranting and raving.

"What do you want?" He yelled without opening the door.

"Mr. Hanisee here to see ya, sah," came the reply of the house keeper.

"Now, what did that old coot want to see him about? How many times did he tell him not to come to his house in person? He was supposed to send a message, and then they would meet somewhere. I'll remind him just this once, but he better not show up here again!" Mr. Broussard thought as he yelled "Show him in! What are you waiting for?"

"Hello there, Beau!" Mr. Hanisee held out his hand as he entered the study.

"What do you want?" Mr. Broussard ignored the man's outstretched hand.

"Why, I've come to give you some important information. I figure you'll find this tidbit worth some money." Mr. Hanisee sat down without being asked.

"What could you possibly tell me that I don't already know?"

"Seems I've found a slave hiding in one of your barns this morning."

"A runaway?" Mr. Broussard asked.

"Nope, now, this is where it gets real interesting. Seems this slave was given his freedom. I've got the papers right here in my pocket," Mr. Hanisee said as he patted his shirt. "That's where they'll stay too, unless you want to pay to see them. It'd be in your best interest to see them, if you know what's good for you."

"How dare you come in here and ask for money, you no good thief, get out of my house!" Mr. Broussard's aggravation raged in his voice.

"Well now, I can sure do that, but you need to see these papers. If word gets out to the slaves about someone near here giving out freedom, you just might loose a lot of your own slaves!" Mr. Hanisee stood to his feet.

"Are you telling me, a plantation owner in this parish, is giving out freedom papers to slaves?" Mr. Broussard's disbelief was evident.

"That's exactly what I'm telling you. Now, if you wish to see these papers, I believe twenty dollars should cover it, but if you want the slave, and I know you will, it'll cost you fifty," Mr. Hanisee assured him defiantly.

After a moment's hesitation, Mr. Broussard took out his wallet and handed twenty dollars to Mr. Hanisee. "If it isn't worth the twenty dollars, I'll take it out of your hide!" Handing the papers to him, and taking his twenty dollars, Mr. Hanisee sat back down and watched Mr. Broussard as he read.

"Why, that no good preacher! I knew something was wrong with him when I couldn't get him to commit to joining the association. So this is what he's been up to. Say, you have his slave?"

"I sure do, got him out at your old fishing shack, back in the bayou."

"I think I'll just go and have a little talk with this slave!" Mr. Broussard in his anger tore Jonah's freedom papers into tiny bits.

Gabe didn't know how he was going to explain to Michael about the children. Lifting a prayer up to the Lord for the right words, he turned toward Michael. "Come with me, I'll show you the cotton later. First, I'm going to show you something here."

Leading Michael into the woods, Gabe stopped a few feet in front of the cabin. To the left of the cabin, sitting under the shade trees, was Emlee, reading to the children seated around her. She lifted her head, and seeing Gabe, she jumped up and ran to him.

"Massa, I's so sorry! I's don't knowd why we's came out. I's jus didn't think."

"Not to worry Emlee. I'm so proud of you for the way you have taken such good care of the children. It's okay. I promise."

"We's not in trouble?" Emlee's eyes were bright from her unshed tears.

"No, we aren't," Gabe assured her.

A small movement caught Gabe's eye. There, standing in front of Michael was a little boy of about three. He was smiling and holding his hands out for Michael to pick him up. Bending down and gently lifting the little boy in his arms, Michael smiled at him saying, "Hello Isaac."

Isaac leaned forward and whispered into Michael's ear. Pulling back, Michael smiled and nodded his head yes. Then he leaned forward and whispered into Isaac ear. The child smiled as if they shared a great secret. Michael hugged him, and then sat him back on the ground. Isaac ran giggling to join the others.

Gabe was confused! How did Michael know the child's name? Emlee must have said it! That had to be it! His reasoning made him dismiss the worry. Feeling he could trust Michael, Gabe took a deep breath. "This is our church, and it doubles as a school. What Josie and I are doing here is what we feel God is leading us to do. First we teach the word of God, and then Josie teaches reading, writing and math. It's our ministry. I know it's against the law to teach slaves to read and write, but that's mans law, not Gods. Josie and I feel slavery is wrong and will soon be abolished. We feel the responsibility to teach them to survive on their own."

"This is what God wants you to do Gabe, there's no misunderstanding. This is truly your ministry. You were born for such a time as this!"

Michael's words washed over Gabe, giving assurance he was on the right path. "Not all the people you see here are slaves, Michael, many are free. They've chosen to stay with us, and have sworn to keep what we do here a secret. Those that aren't freed are earning their freedom."

"All the freed ones chose to stay?" Michael's asked.

"All but one, Jonah, who left yesterday, and he's unprepared for the life he'll encounter out in the real world."

"I see," Michael said quietly.

"We're praying for him, and asking God to show us what to do. I don't know if we should go after him or not, after all, he is a free man now."

"Yes, wait upon the Lord. I too, will ask Him for guidance in this, in the mean time, you should be praying for the protection of your whole family," Michael waved his hand toward the children.

Finally, they started toward the cotton fields, and as they did, the sky darkened suddenly. The threat of rain was evident. Almost immediately the wind started blowing hard, chasing everyone from the fields. Gabe and Michael ran back to the school, gathering the children together, and seeing them back home. By the time they'd finished, the rain started coming down hard. Lighting shattered the sky, followed by loud rolls of thunder. Praying as he ran, Gabe asked God to protect the people of New Canaan, the crops and his family. He and Michael were soaked by the time they reached the safety of the house. "Didn't that feel wonderful!?" Michael's eyes and voice rang with excitement.

Mr. Broussard didn't notice the sudden change in the weather. He was too busy with the business before him. "So, tell me, why did you leave New Canaan?"

"I's a freed man! Massa Lyon gave it ta me! Jonah told him.

Nodding his head at one of the men, Mr. Broussard smiled an evil smile. "You should be careful how you talk to me, boy!" With another nod, the man took out a whip and hit Jonah several times. Holding up his hand for the man to stop, Mr. Broussard continued his interrogation. "You're going to tell me everything I want to know or else! Do you understand? I want to know everything about Lyon's cotton! I hear it's a fine crop. Is that right?"

"Yez sah, de cottons be big as a growd mans fist, and be white as can be. Massa Lyons harvest be twiced frum last years, ifn not more." Jonah clenched his teeth in pain.

"What's he doing different?" Broussard's anger seemed to grow with each answer.

"Nothin, I's knowd of!" Jonah had to concentrate to talk now. The pain was getting worse.

"Nothing? Well, I'll give you time to think on it before I ask you again. When I do, you better answer me or else! How come he gave you your freedom?"

"I's don't knowd sah, Massa jus did, dat be all. I's be surprised at it." Jonah would keep his promise if it killed him and it looked like it would.

"I don't believe it; I don't believe it for one minute! If you won't tell me what I want to know, then my friends here will beat it out of you! With a nod from Mr. Broussard, the four men converged on Jonah with whips and fist, while he and Mr. Hanisee watched.

"Wonderful? Michael, have you lost your mind?" Gabe laughed.

Michael smiled, "I like nothing more than a good run, or feeling the wind flow around me. Why, the rain to me was just a bonus! I love the way it feels on my face. I assure you Gabriel; I have not lost my mind!

Josie and Liza hurried toward the drenched men with towels, laughing at the sight of them. Josie then turned toward Michael, "You must stay for dinner and the night. The weather is just dreadful and you won't be able to travel in this!"

"Thank you for the invitation. I will stay for dinner, but let's see how things progress before I accept your invitation to stay the night."

The men retired to the Gabe's study, while Liza and Josie started preparing their meal. In no time the women made a supper that was delightful.

Gabe and Josie convinced Liza, Ben, Caleb and Hannah to join them. Their conversation consisted of Michael telling stories of Angelic battles of the Bible. They laughed at Liza's stories of her own battles with raising Gabe and her sons. It was truly an evening of warm comfortable companionship as the storm raged outside.

Jonah didn't think he could endure much more of the cruel beatings. He felt his very life being beaten out of him. Closing his eyes he took a deep breath and cried out "Lord help me! I need you now!"

Mr. Hanisee's men stopped only long enough to make fun of him for crying out to the Lord. "You'll need more than the Lord by the time we finish with you!" one of the men jeered. Jonah tried to see his assailant, but his eyes were so swollen all he could look through were tiny slits. Jonah kept crying out to the Lord, praying God would hear him and end his pain.

Josie, Gabe and Michael retired to the study. Darkness fell as the storm continued outside. The noise from it didn't bother anyone. A sense of peace filled the room. During a lapse between thunder rolls, Josie heard pounding at the door. Excusing herself, she went to investigate. Opening the door, she found an elegant looking man who resembled Michael, standing in the rain. Bowing slightly, he politely said, "Michael Guerrier, please."

"Do come in! Follow me; he's in the study with my husband." Closing the door she led the way.

"Michael, you have a visitor." Josie stepped aside to allow the man to enter the study.

"Thomas!" Michael said as the man came toward him.

Stopping in front of Michael, Thomas placed his fisted hand to his chest and bowed. "Sir, I have an urgent message for you."

Michael stepped forward as Thomas leaned close and spoke softly. Michael straightened and nodded. "You know what to do."

Thomas stepped back. Then placed his fisted hand on his chest and bowed again. "Yes sir!" Turning on his heels, he left the room. Josie walked quickly behind to escort him to the door. He once again smiled and without a word went out into the stormy darkness.

Josie closed the door behind him. Suddenly there was a crack of lighting so bright that it lit the room, followed by a hard roll of thunder that shook the very door she held her hand on. Quickly she opened the door to call Thomas back in. Finding no one there, she stepped out onto the porch. All she could see was the darkness of the night and rain.

When Josie returned to the study, she looked at Michael who was standing at the window. "I believe your friend, Thomas, is the fastest person I know!"

"Why's that?" Gabe asked her.

"Well, one minute he was going out the door, the next he was gone!"

"It is raining. I believe I'd hurry on my way too!" Gabe assured her.

Turning from the window, Michael quickly walked toward Gabe. "We're going to need two horses."

"Two horses? Why?" Gabe jumped to his feet.

"We have to go find Jonah!" Michael's eyes flashed with intensity.

"In this rain?" Gabe asked in disbelief.

"Yes, in this rain! Do you not feel it? You and I both asked God to tell us what we should do about finding him. I believe He wants us to go looking for him now!

"Yes, yes I do!" Gabe could feel the urgency within him.

"I do too," whispered Josie.

"Then we must be off!" Michael rushed from the room with Gabe behind him.

"He's no good to us now Beau, I believe he's passed out," Mr. Hanisee said laughing and pointing toward Jonah.

"Well I can't very well leave in this rain, pour some water on him, and wake him up!" Broussard commanded.

"If we beat him anymore we'll kill him!"

"So? Who's going to know? He's just a slave! Mr. Broussard's nonchalance towards murder was frightening.

"I ain't killing anyone!" the man holding the whip exclaimed.

"You'll do as I say or else!" Mr. Hanisee sneered.

"Men, men, just calm down! We'll give him some time and see what happens. We have all night you know," Broussard assured them.

Gabe and Michael flew on their horses for miles in spite of the rain, and darkness. Gabe had no idea where they were going. He was following Michael's lead. It seemed Michael knew exactly where they were headed, and that was alright with him. Gabe had been praying for direction and God seemed to be giving it to Michael.

They made their way down a winding path through a heavily wooded area being careful of the fallen trees. Gabe immediately realized where he was. This had been his favorite fishing place as a boy. Then, he realized it was Mr. Broussard's property. They slowed their horses as they neared the old dilapidated fishing shack. Dismounting quietly, they tied the horses to an old tree. Quickly Michael and Gabe made their way around to the window of the shack hidden by bushes. Angry gruff voices could be heard coming from inside. Michael motioned for Gabe to look through the window.

Taking his position, Gabe slowly stood to peer inside, being careful not to be noticed. What he saw was not only shocking, but sent hot anger through him as if someone had shot an arrow into his soul. Not caring if he could be heard or not, Gabe quickly ran around the shack and kicked open the door.

"What do you think you're doing here!?" Gabe shouted as he entered.

Mr. Hanisee and his men jumped in surprise, and then threateningly started toward Gabe.

Mr. Broussard held his hand up, stopping the men from advancing on Gabe.

"This is none of your business Lyon! Leave now or I won't be responsible for what happens to you!"

"None of my business? That's my man you have there! Let me have him!"

Gabe's anger made him unafraid of the man's threats.

"Your man? Ha, you can no more prove he's your man, than he can prove he's free! Mr. Broussard's laugh was cold and hard.

"Yes I can!" Gabe said slowly to make sure Mr. Broussard understood.

"Yeah? Just how? There's not a mark on him proving he's yours!

"I'll show you!" Gabe walked slowly toward Jonah, keeping his eyes on Hanisee and his men, lifting Jonah's right hand, he turned Jonah's palm upward. Gabe said, "See this mark of the cross? That's the mark of New Canaan!" Then pulling up his sleeve, he showed Mr. Broussard the same mark on his wrist. "You've nearly killed him! How could you do this? You're supposed to be a Christian!"

Mr. Broussard threw his head back with an evil laugh. "You're nothing but a naive preacher!

"That would be incorrect Mr. Broussard; he is a Man of God!" Michael proclaimed as he walked up behind Gabe. Michael took Gabe by the arm and pulled him away from Jonah. Slowly he and Gabe backed up until the door stood behind them. Broussard, Hanisee and his men stood in front of them with their weapons ready to charge.

"You have to answer for what you've done here!" Gabe shouted staring unyielding at Mr. Broussard.

"There isn't a court in Louisiana that'll touch me! I have too much money and know too many people, besides, it isn't against the law! Mr. Broussard sneered. "Men, I think we ought to teach this meddling preacher and his loud mouth friend here a lesson."

With a signal from Mr. Broussard, Hanisee and his men started toward Michael and Gabe. When they came within a foot of Gabe, the group of men froze in their steps. Their faces changed from surprise to total fear in just a matter of seconds. Gabe slowly turned and looked behind him to see what caused them such fright. Gabe was stunned at what he was seeing! There standing behind him were seven large angelic beings. Their wings were spread out wide. The angels were dressed in battle gear of bright gold breast plates with swords drawn, standing in a ready stance.

In awe, Gabe turned toward Michael. In a blink of an eye, Michael transformed into a brilliant white angel, dressed in the same battle gear with his sword drawn and its end pointed at Mr. Hanisee. Gabe was unable to speak. Hanisee and his men paled in fear, dropping their weapons and ran screaming from the cabin, leaving Mr. Broussard alone. It appeared Mr. Broussard hadn't seen, or couldn't see what the others did. He still stood looking arrogant and angrier now because his men had ran.

"It would appear, Mr. Broussard, you are alone," Michael informed him.

"Yes, well, you can have your beaten slave!" Mr. Broussard said as he made his way to the door slowly. "I have no need of him!" Then he ran out the door and into the night.

"Michael? Are you really an angel?" Gabe asked still in shock.

"Yes, I am Michael, the Arch Angel of God's Heavenly warriors! I will answer what questions I can for you later. We have to get Jonah help now or he will surely die!"

Turning to see the angelic warriors one more time, Gabe saw Thomas. With a smile and slight bow the angelic warriors disappeared in a flash of bright light. Gabe turned back to see Michael leaning over Jonah, but this Michael was a human, not the Angelic being that had been standing at his side. Together they carefully picked up Jonah.

The rain had stopped as Michael and Gabe, with Jonah, made their way home. Reaching the house, Gabe wasn't surprised at seeing Ben and Caleb running toward them to help. "Ben, we're taking Jonah to my old room, get Liza and Hannah. Caleb, go to town and bring back the doctor," Gabe shouted as he dismounted his horse. Running to Michael's horse, Gabe carefully eased Jonah down. When Michael had dismounted, the two men carefully took him in and up the stairs. Josie met them in the hall. Hurrying, she opened the door to Gabe's old room. The two men carefully placed Jonah on the bed.

Liza hurried in carrying her herbs and cloths. Tears poured from her eyes at the sight of her badly beaten son. She went to work quickly. "Why's ya go an leave us boy? Does ya see'd what de world done ta ya? Here ya be loved. Here ya be sumbodies. Here ya be protected and ya be blessed. Mr. Gabe done risk he's very life ta git ya back. Out there ya be nothin but a slave. A nobody. Here ya be free! It be evil an nothin fo ya out there!"

"I's sorry ma. I's not knowd till now." Jonah couldn't speak anymore. The pain was more than he could bear.

Michael and Gabe left the room. Neither one said a word as they made their way down the stairs and out into the night. When they'd reached the grove of trees on the front lawn, Michael stopped and turned toward Gabe. "There are many things I can not tell you, but I can tell you this. Thomas was assigned to Jonah, but he couldn't do anything until Jonah asked. When Jonah cried out to the Lord, that's when Thomas came to me. I have been assigned to you. This will not be our last meeting. The Father is pleased with you Gabriel! It has been both an honor and privilege to serve you! You must not tell anyone of my identity! Oh, by the way, Gabriele, the Lord wishes I remind you of shoes."

"Shoes?" Gabe was really confused now.

"Yes, shoes! It will be getting colder, and all need shoes." Laughing, Michael placed his hand on Gabe's shoulder. "Your people have been praying for them! It is time for me to leave, but I shall see you soon!

Michael started glowing brightly, then transformed into the Arch Angel once again. Spreading his wings wide as he started to lift upward, he said, *The Lord will keep you from all harm. He will watch over your life .The Lord will watch over your coming and going both now and forevermore.* As he cleared the top of the trees, he was met in the air by his angelic warriors. Then, in a flash of bright streaking light, they were gone. Gabe fell to his knees and began to praise and thank the Lord for what He had done. As he neared the end of his prayers, he assured God he would get the shoes.

The next morning Dr. Gaharan arrived, and carefully examined Jonah. He told Gabe and Ben, Jonah would live, but it would be a long recovery. As Gabe showed the good Doctor out, Dr. Gaharan became chatty. "Some weather we had last night, wasn't it? I heard several twisters touched down. Did you know Beau Broussard's place got hit? I understand it was nearly destroyed."

"Really?" Gabe didn't care if he ever saw Broussard again.

"Yes, lots of fallen trees, and damages to his crops. His cotton didn't make, it from what I hear."

"I'm sorry to hear that."

"Oh well, just take good care of that young man. If you need me for anything, you know where I am!" Dr. Gaharan mounted his horse. "I doubt if you'll need me though. His mother knows just what to do." With a wave of his hand, he rode off.

"Lord, what would you have me do?" Gabe knew God was dealing with him about Mr. Broussard. "He has to be the meanest man alive, but I know he's a neighbor in need." Gabe prayed as he went to join Ben.

Gabe wondered if the crops survived the night. He saw Ben coming from the fields, he should have known it'd be the first thing Ben would check on. "It all be good, Mr. Gabe! De crops be jus fine and my boy be too!"

"The Lord really was with us last night on both accounts. Not everybody did as well as we did last night." Gabe was testing the waters with Ben.

"Whatcha mean? Did de twister harm sumbodies?"

"Yes it did. This may be hard for you to hear, but just hear me out. Broussard's place took a hit from the twister last night. Seems he has a lot of fallen trees, and he lost his entire cotton crop. I've just been praying about it. I feel in spite of everything that has happened, maybe we should take some men and ride out there and see if we can help."

"Ya be a feelin da Lord wants ya ta do this?"

"I do, but I want to know how you feel," Gabe assured him.

After a minute, Ben looked at Gabe. "Den we's best be getting ta it! I's be a goin with ya."

"Alright, let's get Big John and some of the others. We'll load a wagon with tools and go out there in the morning. You know Ben; the Lord will bless you for this work."

"Like da good book says bout da enemy, do good to him and tis like heapin burning coals on his head, and de Lord will reward ya."

Laughing Gabe said, "Very good! You've been reading!"

The next morning, Gabe went to check on Jonah. The swelling was still evident, more so now than before.

"How's he feeling today?" Gabe asked Liza.

"He be a doin sum better. He be takin sips of water an broth."

"Is he asleep?"

"Jus now, sah. My Ben says ya'll be goin ta Broussard's place."

"Yes, we'll go this morning. Is it alright with you?"

"Tis fine by me. Even wid whut he done!"

"Thank you Liza," Gabe said.

"De Lord says we be doin this, rite?"

"Right!"

Gabe found Ben and the men waiting for him in the wagon. It was a prayerful ride to Mr. Broussard's plantation. Gabe didn't know what would happen or if their help would be accepted. As they pulled into Broussard's drive, Gabe was amazed at the damage he saw. Shutters had been blown off the house, trees down on the lawn, and not one barn stood intact. "Well, at least the house is standing," Gabe thought. Pulling up to the back of the house, Gabe went to the door. Knocking, he waited for someone to come. He waited so long he thought for sure no one was inside. As he started to leave, Mr. Broussard opened the door and stepped out. He was clearly a broken man.

"What do you want?" He grumbled at Gabe.

"I heard you got hit by the twister. I brought some men with me to help clear some of the damage, if it's alright with you."

"Yeah, it's okay with me, but why are you doing this?"

"The Lord sent me. You're a neighbor in need." Gabe stepped off the porch ready to work.

Gabe and his crew got to work quickly. Broussard's slaves had been hard at it for hours and looked tired. A little boy of about five years old came up to Gabe. He was the skinniest child he'd ever seen. His ribs showed through the dirty, tattered and torn shirt he wore.

"I's hep ya Massa. My name be Eli. Jus tells me whatcha be awantin me ta do."

"I'll tell ya what Eli, how about you working with Big John here. He's a good man but sometimes he needs help."

"I's be morin happy ta have ya workin wid me! Cume on." Big John took the little boy by the hand and headed for a fallen tree.

The men worked hard in the hot sun. The humidity was high and threatened another storm. At noon they stopped to eat the lunch Liza packed for them. Gabe noticed Eli had left their group. What a talker the child was! Scanning his surroundings looking for Eli, Gabe saw him sitting by himself under a tree. He wasn't eating or drinking anything. Gabe walked over to him. "Eli, have you eaten?"

"No sah, I's be waitin ta see ifin there be any leftover."

"What do you mean?" Gabe was hoping he misunderstood.

"Well sah, de Massa says I aint worth fedin cause I's be small. Aint got no ma or pa. So's I jus waitin ta see'd if anybodies gots leftovers I's can have."

Gabe's was sick at his stomach and his heart hurt. What kind of man was Broussard that he could starve a child?

"Where do you sleep Eli?"

"I's sleep in da barn sah, least wise I's use ta. It be better than dem cabins over dere, but now de barns be gone." It was as if Eli realized for the first time he had no place to lay his head.

"Come with me Eli, you'll be eating with us. We have more than plenty to share with you, you won't be eating leftovers today!" Taking the child by the hand, Gabe led him over to where his crew was eating. Everyone shared their food, and the child ate like he was starved. Big John and the others made sure Eli had plenty to eat now and for later. Gabe couldn't eat; all he could do was pray for this child of God's which knew hunger at such a young age.

After lunch Gabe and his men finished all they'd set out to do. The shutters were back on the house. The front lawn and drive were clear of all debris. It had been a productive day. Walking back to the house, Gabe once again knocked on Mr. Broussard's door. Gabe didn't have to wait long for an answer this time.

"What?" Mr. Broussard demanded.

"Just letting you know we're finished here. It shouldn't take much longer for your slaves to clean up the rest. They've done a fine job already."

"What do I owe you?" Broussard demanded angrily.

"You don't owe me anything. Like I said, you're a neighbor in need. We just wanted to help. That's all."

"I don't take charity! What do I owe you?" Gabe could see Broussard's temper flaring.

"I tell you what. How about you give me little Eli over there and we will call it even."

"You can have him! He can't work much and he isn't worth feeding. I got stuck with him. Just take him and go. Don't come back!" Mr. Broussard slammed the door closed.

"I will be more than happy to do just that!" Gabe said to the closed door.

Gabe signaled for Ben and the others to load the wagon. Just as he came around, Eli came running to him. Throwing himself at Gabe's feet, the little boy wrapped his arms around Gabe's legs.

"Please sah, don't be aleavin me here! Takes me wid ya. Nobody knowd I be gone! Nobody knowd I's here. I's work hard for ya!" The little boy begged.

"Eli, it's going to be just fine. I'm not going to leave you behind! You're going with me and live at New Canaan. I promise, you'll like it there. So come on, get into the wagon with us."

"We's can't be stealin da boy Massa!" Big John whispered to Gabe anxiously.

"I'll explain on the way home. Let's just get out of here. We aren't stealing him!" Gabe could just see it. Preacher wanted for stealing starved child. It could have made him laugh if it hadn't been so sad.

Gabe explained to Big John about his conversation with Mr. Broussard.

Big John shook his head sadly. "He be livin wid me and Delia ifin ya don't mind sah. Little John be needin a brother anyway. My Delia be proud ta take him in."

"If you need more room at your place, I'll help you build on. Thank you Big John, from me and Eli."

The ride home was not a quiet one. Eli was so excited when Big John told him he'd be living with him. That child had more questions than one could imagine much less answer. He made everyone laugh in spite of themselves.

When Gabe returned home, he went to see Jonah again. He found him sitting up in bed and in a talkative mood. His face was still swollen but he seemed in better spirits.

"How are you feeling today, Jonah?"

"I's feelin better than yesterday," Jonah answered, trying to smile.

"Is there anything I can get for you?"

"Naw sah. I's wantin ta thank ya fo cumin fer me."

"It was God who led me to you Jonah. You know that don't you?

"Yez sah, I's knowd dat. Massa Gabe? Does ya believe in Angels?"

"I sure do. Why?"

"Cause, I's believe I's see'd one! I's member I's couldn't take de pain anymore. I's prayed Massa Gabe, and asked de Lord to help me, then dis big angel came to me and carried me to dis real prudy place. He put me under dis big tree and gave me sum sweet fruit ta eat. It made me feel better. I's jus sat under dat tree wid the breeze blowing a restin. Then I's woke up here. Dat be all I's member. I's sorry fer all I's done, does ya forgive me?"

"Of course I do. But you need to ask your mother and father for forgiveness. You know that, don't you?

"Yez sah. I's gotta ask the Lord to forgive me too.

"Have you accepted the Lord Jesus as your savoir Jonah?" Gabe asked him.

"No sah, but dats what I be wantin to do. Wouldcha help me?"

"Yes I will! It would be my pleasure."

Gabe read the salvation scriptures from the Bible to Jonah, and led him in the sinner's prayer. Jonah was very tried, but extremely thankful for being home, and his new place in the Kingdom of God. It would be a while, but Jonah would soon heal and find his path with the Lord.

Christmas was less than a month away. Josie had so much on her mind. What should she get for Gabe? What should she get for their extended family here on New Canaan? She was on her way to find Big John, with all the crops in now, she knew she had a chance to find him at home. As she walked down the path to the hired hands quarters, what she preferred to call it, she admired Big Johns craftsmanship. He had transformed all the cabins into pretty homes that showed each person's own taste. Some had flower gardens, some had vegetable gardens, and some had both. It was wonderful to walk this way now. The children all waved as they played outside as she passed by. Coming to Big John's house, she slowed down to watch Little John play with Eli. She was so glad Gabe had brought Eli home. The two little boys ran to meet her.

"Hello there! Are you two having fun?" Josie asked.

"We's shur is!" Eli answered for them.

"I've come to see your father. Is he home?"

"I's get him fer ya, Missus!" Little John ran to get his father.

"Missus, come on in," Delia said from the door. "We's be havin readin time."

"I was wondering if I could speak with you and Big John without the children," Josie whispered to Delia.

"Little John, Eli, ya'll goes to da garden an bring back a mess of greens fo me, please." Quickly the boys left to do as they were asked.

"I wanted to talk to you about Christmas!"

"Christmas? Why Missus, we aint never had Christmas afore. We's has it in our hearts, but not wid presents and such," Big John said with surprise.

"I'm sorry it was like that before, but it's not going to be that way now! I was hoping you would help me, if you didn't mind and have the time.'

"Whatcha be needin me to do? Big John asked.

"I was thinking with your craftsmanship with wood, you could make some wooden toys for the boys, and blocks for the littlest ones. Delia, I was hoping you could help me make some dolls for the little girls. As for the bigger ones, I was thinking bonnets for the girls, and shirts for the boys. If you have any idea's, I'd appreciate hearing them."

"I's can do that!" Big John said catching the excitement.

"I's help too Missus. Why my ma taught me how to make ragged dolls with button eyes when I was a youngin. We's can do this! Delia exclaimed.

"Good! Shall we start soon? We don't have long till Christmas. I better get my list ready for our town trip. Will you go with me Delia?'

"Yez Missus, I's go wid ya." Delia was delighted at being asked. "I's walk with ya to the house and we's can make plans."

The two women walked while they made Christmas plans. Delia noticed dark circles under Josie's eyes. "Missus? Ya be mighty pale. Be ya feelin poorly?"

"Oh no Delia, I'm fine. I just ate too much today."

"We's can't be havin ya sickly Missus, we's be needin ya."

"I'm fine. I promise!" Josie wasn't concerned about what Delia had said. She'd always been pale; after all she did come from Maine.

Josie knew Gabe was in his study. Things had slowed down a lot since the harvest. "I thought I'd find you here. What are you doing?"

"I've been going over the books and ordering shoes," Gabe said nonchalantly as he turned the pages of a catalog.

"Ordering shoes? Whatever for?" Josie asked surprised.

"New Canaan is in need of shoes. Everyone is barefooted Josie. It's already getting cooler and come January it'll be cold. The few that do have shoes, well, they're worn out or they're too big or too small. Everyone needs new shoe."

"You're right, I didn't think about it. How are we going to get their sizes? Gabe, there are over a hundred and forty people!"

"I know, so I just prayed about it. I've ordered ten of every size. Boots for the men and boys, ladies shoes for the women and girls. Not those fancy ones with the funny heels, but those flat ones. See?" Gabe showed Josie the picture in the catalog.

"Not bad for a man. I'm surprised you were aware of it." She handed the catalog back to him. "We have tiny feet to cover too. I think I'll ask Hannah if she would make some booties."

"That's a good idea. Make a list and we can go into town to get what we need," he said.

"Okay, I'd like to go and Delia said she'd go with me," she replied.

"So, now we've got that settled, what are we going to do about Christmas?"

Josie told him about her plans. Gabe was glad she had been thinking ahead of him. In turn, he told Josie about the profits they would be sharing from the sale of the crops. They talked long into the evening about the list, the plans and the things they'd accomplished so far. Soon it was time for bed.

It was Christmas Eve. Josie was trying her best not to feel bad. The house was decorated from inside and out. The rest of the families homes were decked out too. Everyone was excited about tonight's Christmas feast. She just had to get over feeling so bad! She couldn't understand what was wrong with her! Deciding she needed to talk to Liza, who had an herb for anything that could possibly ail a person, she went to the kitchen. Josie found her alone. "Liza do you have anything for an upset stomach?"

"Who be needin it? Liza was surprised at her request. She didn't know of anyone being sick.

"I do. I don't know what's wrong with me! I'm fine one minute, then the next I'm sick to my stomach."

"You sit rite down there. We's be needin to talk women talk!" Liza pulled out her chair and sat her down. So Josie and Liza began their talk. Liza asked all the questions first and then Josie asked some. After an hour or so Liza stood and wrapped her arms around Josie. "Tis nothing ta be afeared of, I's be here ifin ya needs me."

All Josie could do was nod. "Is there anything you can give me for my stomach?"

"I's be rit back wid ya something!" Liza went to her herb chest with a knowing smile.

The roasted turkey could be smelled throughout the house. A giant Christmas tree stood in the ball room, decorated from top to bottom.

It had to be the most beautiful tree Caleb had ever seen. Never in all his life had he celebrated Christmas. He'd seen it from far away, the way slaves do while the master had his party. Now here he was, ready for his first Christmas. God's son needed a birthday party, and he was helping give it! All the tables were laden with food and drink. Nothing had been left out.

All he had to do was wait for everyone to come, and they would be here in just a few short minutes. Caleb was dressed in his finest. He'd saved his newest shirt and pants for a special occasion, and this was just the night. The night Jesus was born! Now he had to help Jonah come down for the party. Jonah was steadily getting better with the help of prayers and his mother's tender care. Jonah would tell you it was his best present ever.

Gabe couldn't wait to share the news. He was excited about Christmas as much today, as he was as a boy. He had surprises for everyone. Taking as many presents as he could carry, he headed for the Christmas tree. Liza and Ben had presents to go under the tree too. This was definitely a Christmas to be remembered.

The family of New Canaan had Christmas cheer. The children were in awe of the big Christmas tree in the corner. Men, women and children were all dressed in their best. As Gabe and Josie entered the room everyone broke out in a cheer. Gabe smiled as he and Josie took their place at the table. "Lets all hold hands as we say the blessing. Father we thank you for this day, the day of our Lord Jesus' birth. We thank you for the many blessings you have bestowed upon us. We thank you for our family. We thank you for this feast, and ask your blessing to be upon it. We also ask your blessing upon New Canaan, and all those living here in the coming New Year. In Jesus Name, Amen."

The feast was wonderful, but the fellowship was better. Gabe couldn't remember enjoying Christmas this much. It blessed him to see the happiness that filled the room. He prayed all their Christmases would be as good as this one. When they'd finished their meal, Emlee read the Christmas story from the Bible. Then Hannah led them in singing Christmas Carols. Some songs Gabe and Josie knew. Those they didn't were slave songs. All were beautiful and gave praise to the Lord.

When the last song had been sung, Gabe stood. "I want to thank each and everyone here for all your hard work. I can't begin to tell you what it means to Josie and me. You've stayed by our side through lots of changes and never complained. You've taught us so much and I don't know how I'll ever repay you. I do have a surprise for you! Good job everyone, may God bless us next year as much as he did this year."

Big John stood. "Thank ya Mr.Gabe. I's ta speak fer everybodies here.

We's wantcha ta knowd we's proud ta be here. Ain't nobody like ya and the Missus. Ya'll been good ta us an we's thankful dat God see'd fit to give ya to us. May de good Lord bless ya sah!"

"The Lord blessed us with you, but you're welcome!" Gabe exclaimed.

"I think it's time to open the present!" Josie announced with excitement.

The family was stunned at this announcement, all except Eli. "We's get presents? I aint never had no present afore!" He caused the room to break out in laughter. The truth was, Eli just said out loud what everyone in the room was thinking.

"Well Eli, if you and Little John come on over here, you two can help me give the gifts out! Running as fast as they could, Eli and Little John joined Gabe at the Christmas tree. Reading the names off each package, Gabe prayed they hadn't left anyone out.

It was almost as if the group didn't know what to do with their presents. Finally, Josie told the children to go ahead and open their gifts. They didn't need any further prodding. They opened them as fast as they could. The little girls received dolls, bonnets and new shoes. The older girls received a Bible, bonnets and new shoes. The little boys received wooden wagons with their names on them, wooden farm animals and new shoes. The older boys were given a Bible, straw hats and shoes too. Baby booties, blankets and blocks were given to the new babies that had arrived and those that were on the way. Both the men and women received Bibles, blankets and shoes with an added surprise of bonnets for the women and hats for the men. Eli said it best when he shouted "Merry Christmas" causing everyone to laugh.

"I have a special Christmas present to give," Josie said after everyone had quieted down.

"What would that be my love?" Gabe asked.

"It's mostly for you Gabe, but I want everyone to share it with you."

"Yes?"

"Well, Gabe, we're going to have a baby!"

"What? I mean…we are? You're sure? He stood to his feet and took her in his arms forgetting the crowd watching them.

"I'm very sure!"

Gabe swept her off her feet and kissed her in front of everyone.

"I's knowd it! I's told John it be so!" Delia shouted. "We's got a present fo ya too Missus. John brings it here!"Coming from the back of the room, Big John brought their present. It was covered and tied.

"Go ahead on, Missus. Open it!" Big John urged Josie.

Opening it with shaky hands, she removed the rope and covering. It was the most beautiful hand carved baby cradle Josie had ever seen."It's beautiful John. Oh Delia, this is wonderful! Thank you so much!" Josie stepped forward and surprised both Big John and Delia with a hug and kiss upon the cheek.

"We's all got sumthing fer ya!" Liza said laughing.

Josie and Gabe received baby gifts made with love from each person: Baby booties, blankets, gowns and a beautiful rocking chair. What a blessing they received from the youngest to the oldest.

Gabe walked to the tree when things had settled down. "Would the head of each family please come and stand by the Christmas tree?"

The men looked at each other questionably as they made their way to Gabe. When they stood there, Gabe continued. "You've worked hard this year and God has blessed us abundantly. I've something to give you." Taking a pouch from behind the tree, Gabe stood before them. Beginning with old Ben, Gabe placed five ten dollar gold piece in each of their hands. Making his way down the line, he thanked each man personally for their work and dedication. "This is your part from the sale of our crops," He told them when he had finished.

The men didn't know what to say or do. They looked down at the money in their hands then back at Gabe in wonderment. Never before had they held so much money. Most never had any money of their own. With trembling hands, they held it gently, then turning it slowly as if to memorize what it looked like and what it felt like. It seemed they stood a little taller when finally realizing they were able to support their family.

One by one the men went to Gabe and thanked him. "Don't thank me, you deserve this! All I did was provide the ground. It's your hard work and knowledge that made this money.

Families gathered around their husbands, fathers and sweethearts to see what they held in their hands. No one would be the same. It was a good day to begin anew. Christmas truly held the hope of everyone's tomorrow.

CHAPTER 8

IT SEEMED AS IF IT happened over night. Lincoln had been elected president, and Louisiana had seceded from the United states. Now it was part of the Confederate States of America. What had this world come to? Rumors of war were in full swing. The Plantation Owners Association called an emergency meeting and Gabe had to be there. "No way out this time," he thought, as he went upstairs to see how Josie was doing. Since her announcement of the baby, Liza made sure Josie had plenty of rest. "Thank you Lord for Liza," Gabe prayed as he went to their bedroom.

"How are you feeling, Josie?" Gabe saw she was awake.

"I'm fine, I'm getting lazy. Liza won't let me outside unless I have a nap!"

"You're not lazy, Liza loves you. She just wants you to take care of yourself, that's all," Gabe assured her.

"I know, it's just hard, I'll take my naps like a good girl, and let Emlee teach in the afternoons, and she's been teaching the older ones too. That child is such a blessing, you know Gabe, I think Emlee and Caleb are sweet on each other."

"It doesn't surprise me! I've seen those two paired up at church, and then afterwards at Sunday dinner. Caleb's even asked me if he could buy five acres near the school!"

"I see it happening, I just hope they wait a little longer, they're both so young."

"I don't know, we'll just wait and see. I think its funny how they look at each other." Then he changed the subject, "Do you have mail needing to go to the post office?"

"No, I've already written to father, Jonah took it with him yesterday when he went to town."

"Jonah's come a long way, hasn't he?"

"He sure has, his mother and father are so glad he's saved."

"We need to baptize him soon. I'm thinking next Sunday will be Baptismal Day. What do you think?"

"I think it's a great idea! Maybe you should have services in the afternoon when it's warmer."

"Good idea! I'll pass the word on to Liza. She'll get the word out." Gabe knew Liza would get the job done.

"I saw you got a letter from Charles. What did he have to say?" Josie asked.

"He's concerned about an impeding war. He and your father believe you should go back to Maine until you have the baby."

"Oh no, I wont go! My place is here with you. I'll protect the baby, you'll protect us, and God will protect you! We're all under the protection of God Gabe, and I will not be away from you while I'm having this baby."

"Now don't get upset. I have no intentions of sending you anywhere right now."

"Not now, or ever! Just get that thought out of your head!" She told him with her temper flaring. "Promise me you won't send me away!"

"I promise! Though I do have that option should war break out," he told her seriously.

"Either we trust God or we don't. I for one do! What about you, man of God?"

Shocked she would even think such a thing, he was quick to answer.

"Of course I trust God! How could you say that? Look at all we've been through and what God has done for us."

"Then you'll have to trust him with our lives. War or no war, there will be no more talk of sending me away! Do you agree?" She asked him softly.

"Okay. You'll stay no matter what."

"Good, now I believe I'll take that nap." She turned on her side and closed her eyes.

"Before I leave, I want to remind you, I have to attend a meeting tonight with the Plantation Association in town. But most of all I want you to know I love you."

"I love you too, Gabe. You have fun at your meeting with the boys tonight," she added with a giggle. Laughing, he left the room.

Gabe worked hard to control his horse, Cana, as he rode toward town. It seemed the horse could sense something Gabe couldn't see. This was the only part of the road the trees covered thickly like a canopy and could hold real danger. Gabe could feel the hair on the back of his neck rising as he became aware of his surroundings. As he started around the bend, Cana reared and snorted in fear. As he wrestled for control again, Gabe looked up ahead of him. There standing in the middle of the road was a rider on a magnificent white horse, and the rider was some one he knew.

"Michael! You're scaring my horse!" Gabe exclaimed with excitement at seeing him.

"Sorry about that! It's just my over whelming presence," Michael said laughing. "I did travel with you a while so your horse could get used to me, but it doesn't look like it worked."

"I bet you got a good laugh at me!" Gabe was embarrassed that Michael had seen him struggle with the animal.

"Actually I did! You handled your horse very well. Why did you name him Cana?"

"I didn't, Caleb did. He loves the story where Jesus turned the water into wine. Cana was the name of the village where it happened, but you already knew that didn't you?

"Yes, I just wanted to see if you did. By the way, Cana means reed. I just thought you would like to know," Michael said laughing.

"I have a feeling you're here for something more than inquiring about my horse's name. Am I right?"

"Yes, you are. As you can see, I'm here as Michael Guerrier. I'm going to the meeting with you."

"Are we going to fight our way in or out?" Gabe couldn't help but grin at the memory of the last time they went somewhere together.

"Neither, God sent me to assist you in a matter that will be coming your way shortly. We'll discuss it after the meeting."

"How are we going to explain you being here?" Gabe's voice showed concern.

"It's simple really. The others think I am a cotton dealer from France. I'll just be checking on my interest. That's all."

Michael and Gabe turned their horses toward town. Cana still wasn't happy about their company, and required much of Gabe's attention.

The meeting went just as Gabe thought it would. It was apparent the Association was ready to go to war to save their livelihoods. Gabe searched the room to see if Mr. Broussard was present, but couldn't find him. Leaning to the person next to him he asked. "Mr. Broussard isn't here is he?"

"No! Haven't you heard? He's left town. Sold all his slaves, closed down his house and moved to Texas! Seems he lost everything in that twister last November. Apparently he has some family in Texas willing to take him in."

"Has he sold his plantation?" Gabe asked with interest.

"No, seems no one wants it." The man informed him as he turned his attention back to the speaker. Well ..well, Gabe thought as he settled back in his seat.

"Hold on to that thought!" Michael whispered grinning.

Gabe had a lot of questions, and Michael seemed to know it judging by his smile and quick looks he gave Gabe as they rode toward New Canaan.

"Well, are you going to let me in on what's going on, or do I have to guess?" Gabe asked him.

"No, you don't have to guess, I'm waiting until you clear all the junk from your mind. It's important you have an open mind about what I am going to tell you. So, as soon as you clear out all those questions, the sooner I can tell you why I've been sent to you."

Gabe relaxed and cleared his mind the best way he knew how, by praying for God to help him. They were nearly home when Michael started talking.

"Soon you will have an important event to attend. You'll be receiving an invitation to the inauguration of President Lincoln. There, you with me by your side, will meet with the President. Josie won't be going with you." Gabe quickly looked at Michael with concern on his face. "Not to worry, the baby is fine and so is she. She won't want to go because she wants to take care of herself and the baby."

"Why are we meeting with President Lincoln? He doesn't know me. I don't even know anyone who knows him."

"Yes you do! The Lord knows both of you. Fear not Gabriel! The Lord watches over your coming and goings! By the way, would you like to know what it is?"

"What do you mean, what it is?" Gabe hated being confused.

"The baby! Do you want to know if it's a boy or girl?" Michael asked grinning again.

"You can do that? I mean… you can tell me what my child is?"

"Yes, the Lord said I could if you wanted to know."

Taking a few minutes to think about it, Gabe smiled. "I believe I'll wait with Josie to find out."

"What makes you think Josie doesn't already know?"

Before Gabe could say a word, Michael added, "Until we meet again!" Then with a blink of a eye, both horse and Angel were gone.

Gabe just sat there in stunned silence thinking, does every Christian have these experiences? Or is it just me?" Out loud he said, "Lord you must have a sense of humor to have Michael as your Arch Angel!"

Gabe could have sworn he heard laughter in the distance, but then again it could have been the wind.

Sunday was a perfect day to have a Baptism. It was as if the Lord himself was there with them as they stood on the bank of the pond. Today, they'd be Baptizing Jonah and anyone else that had received Jesus as their Lord and Savior. As far as Gabe knew, it would only be Jonah.

After a Sunday service of explaining how Baptism represented the death, burial and resurrection of Jesus, all who had accepted him as their Lord and Savior are to be baptized, they went to the pond. Jonah took his place at Gabe's side in the water. A happy Ben and Liza watched with tears in their eyes as their oldest son went into and came out of the water. Then to Gabe's surprise, Big John and his family, including Eli, asked to be baptized. What began to be just one, ended with nearly everyone present being baptized. Making sure each was saved, Gabe asked the question if they had accepted Jesus as their savior, and prayed the sinner's prayer for forgiveness. Each said they had, and even told who had led them to their salvation. Gabe was amazed at God's goodness. Each time it seemed God out did Himself. New Canaan was now full of Christian men, women and children that were not only free in Gods sight, but mans too. There was not one slave among them.

Gabe was getting worried. The inauguration of President Lincoln would be in one week. He still didn't have his invitation. The only thing Gabe knew was he had to go Washington. He knew he could get there, but he didn't know how he was going to get into the ingurgitation without an invitation. Deciding to step out in faith, Gabe mounted his horse and headed for town to buy his ticket. Praying as he went, he asked God for guidance and direction. By the time he arrived at the train station, it had begun to rain. Not a hard rain but a gentle one. It made Gabe remember the night he and Michael brought Jonah home, except this time there hadn't been a storm to precede it.

Dismounting and going inside the station, Gabe greeted Mr. Fontenot. "Hello there, Mr. Fontenot!"

"Hello Gabe, good to see you as always. What brings you in town today? Planning a trip?"

"Yes sir, I am. I need to buy a ticket."

"I'm glad you came out today, you've saved me a trip. I have a letter for you." Mr. Fontenot handed Gabe his letter. Opening it Gabe almost shouted

"Hallelujah," for this was the invitation he needed! A sense of relief flowed over him.

"Now, where did you need that ticket to?" Mr. Fontenot asked him.

"I need it for Washington D.C., please."

"Washington D.C.? Why would you be going to Washington?"

"I've some business there this coming week. I shouldn't be gone long. I've got rice to get planted," Gabe rambled trying to throw Mr. Fontenot off track.

"Going to make a big rice deal are you? You know since we seceded from the United States, I'd make them Yankees pay a high price for that rice!"

"We'll sir; you can never tell what'll happen!" Gabe paid for his ticket and left in a hurry to avoid any further questions from Mr. Fontenot.

Once Gabe arrived home, he hurried to see Josie. Finding her in his study he closed the doors and went to sit down beside her. "Did you have a nice trip to town?" she asked as he kissed her cheek.

"Yes, I did. Josie, you aren't going to believe this, but I got some mail today. Look at what I have."

Taking the envelope from his pocket he handed it to her. Josie opened it and was speechless. "Gabe, this is an invitation to the President's inauguration! How did you get this? Are you going? Who knows about this?"

"Yes, I'm going, and only you and I know about the invitation. As for who sent it, only God knows."

"Do you want me to go with you?"

"No, I don't think now's a good time for you to travel. Mr. Fontenot knows I'll be going to Washington, but not why. But anyway, I need you here to keep nosey people away."

"I'll miss you, but I'm glad I won't be going. This child of yours likes his naps and comfort!" She said laughing. "When will you be leaving?"

"In three days, that should get me there one day ahead of the inauguration. I don't want anyone to know about this. You should tell anyone who asks I've gone to Washington on business, but I'll be back in time to plant the rice. Mr. Fontenot thinks I'm going to make a rice deal. He'll have that rumor spread before I leave."

"Okay, I can do that. I just don't want to lie to anyone, Gabe."

"You won't be, its true Josie, I will be going on business. It's the Lord's business, after all, only God could have sent this!

"I wonder why?" She asked.

"Who knows? We'll just have to wait and see."

Gabe watched the scenery pass by as he looked out the window of the train. "Where was Michael?" he thought, as he turned away. It's not like Michael had given him much information. He'd just told him he was to meet the President, and then he was gone. But Michael had said he'd be there. Since this was a mission from the Lord, he wouldn't worry, after all, God was in control. Closing his eyes he went to sleep.

Some time later, Gabe was awakened by the train slowing. Opening his eyes and looking around, he noticed people getting their things as they were getting off. Sitting up in his seat, he looked out his window to read the name of the train station where they were stopping. He couldn't believe it! He was already in Washington. Gabe stopped an elderly gentleman in the aisle. "Excuse me sir, what day is this?"

"It's March third of course!" He gave Gabe a look clearly indicating he thought Gabe had lost his mind.

"Thank you." Gabe was confused. How could he have slept for two days straight! He hated being confused, but since taking over New Canaan it seemed to be part of his everyday life.

He went to retrieve his baggage and looked around to see if Michael had come to meet him. Not seeing him, Gabe made his way to the hotel. Because of the inauguration, every hotel he'd been to was full. Gabe was starting to worry. Making his way to a hotel recommended by the last hotel manager, Gabe began to pray for a room. He prayed until he stepped up to the counter. "Do you have a room available?"

"Yes we do, it's the last one. You sure are lucky!" The clerk behind the counter said as he handed Gabe the key. "Please sign in."

Offering a prayer of thanks to the Lord, Gabe signed in and then went to his room. Walking over to the window and looking out at the busy street beneath him, he began to pray. "Lord, I'm here. I thank you for the room. You've done some wonders in my life! I've seen Angels, the salvation of all the people of New Canaan, and I've slept for two whole days without waking up. What are you going to do with me next?"

Gabe couldn't believe he'd slept through the night, but he had. He also couldn't believe he was getting ready for President Lincoln's inauguration, but he was. Taking his time, he began making a plan. He would hire a coach, and then go to the Capitol and see what would happen next. Not much of a plan, but it was a start. He picked up his coat and went out.

Gabe was overwhelmed with excitement as he stood at the Capitol's East Portico listening to the President address the Union. This man was something else! He believed in getting the United States back on track. Gabe would love to talk politics with him, but he knew it was impossible.

When it was over, Gabe started to leave the Portico when a solider came up and stopped him, saying, "Mr. Gabriel Lyon?"

"Yes?"

"Please come with me," The solider asked, then turned to leave.

Gabe followed him. The Solider led him to a door off the East Portico where the President had given his speech. Entering the room, the Solider announced "Mr. Gabriel Lyon!" then stepped aside.

Gabe stood there, gripping his hat in his hand. Nervously he looked around. There, standing beside President Lincoln was Michael, looking as if he belonged and had been there many times before.

"Mr. Lyon, please come in," President Lincoln said.

"Mr. President, it's a pleasure to meet you," Gabe extended his hand.

"The pleasure is all mine, I assure you," President Lincoln said as he shook Gabe's hand. "You know my friend, Mr. Guerrier? He tells me you're good friends."

"Yes sir, we are." Gabe's nervousness showed.

"Please, everyone have a seat. I need to sit myself. My speech today was longer than I intended, may I call you Gabe?" The President asked.

"Please do sir, it would be an honor."

"I'm sure you're wondering why you're here. I know you'd rather be at home as Michael tells me your first child is on the way."

"Yes sir, I am curious as to why I'm here."

"Michael's told me about all the things you've done with your plantation in Louisiana. I must tell you I'm impressed! He also told me you're a man of God and you're honest and can be trusted. You only want what's best for all your people, that brings me to why you are here. I need your help. I'm wondering if you would allow your home to be used, on occasion, to have meetings with my men who are under cover in the seven states that have seceded. I also will be asking you to send any information you find out, directly to me. Its apparent war is about to begin. Would you help me with this Gabe?"

"I'd be proud to help you sir. We can provide you with all you've asked. I just have one question."

"What's that?"

"When will this war begin?"

"Within the next thirty days." The President said sadly. "I wish it could be different."

"There's no other way?" Gabe asked.

"No. My hand's been forced. Maybe with your help and God's, it won't last long." The President stood to his feet.

Taking his cue the meeting was over, Gabe stood to his feet. "It's been a pleasure and an honor to meet you sir. My family and I will be praying for you. May God bless you and keep you," said Gabe.

"I too have to be going," said Michael. "Congratulations on the day and I hope to see you soon." The two men shook hands with the president before leaving together. They walked to the street and called a coach.

Michael followed Gabe up to his room. Once inside, Michael began to speak. "You have done well Gabriel. What you've done here tonight will save hundreds of lives."

"Did you hear what he said? War will begin in thirty days!"

"Yes and with that knowledge you know what to do. You have time! Do not waste it!"

"No, I won't waste a minute of it! I have a child on the way Michael, is he to be born in the middle of a war?

"Yes, Gabriel, he'll be born in the middle of a war. But he'll also be born into a loving family that will raise him to be a mighty man of God. He will not be harmed by the war that rages on the outside, because the love that God and you have for him protects him. Do you understand?" Michael asked him.

"Yes…I do."

"Then, until we met again, *The Lord is your light and salvation, whom shall you fear?*" Michael proclaimed and then was gone.

Gabe was glad to be home, and thankful that Caleb had brought Cana to the livery stable for him. Now he rode as fast as the night would allow him toward New Canaan. He had a lot to do. He wouldn't tell Josie everything, but they would make ready for the coming war. His mind raced with thoughts of what needed to be stored and what needed to be planted. There would be less cotton this year. Food crops were going to be needed in mass quantities. No telling how long this war would last. He had a lot of people he was responsible for, and he had to see them through this.

He wouldn't show fear when he told them; they needed to be prepared for what was coming. Gabe prayed, asking God's protection over his family, extended family, and over his land, and animals. As he reached the house, he rode Cana to the barn, waking a startled Caleb from his sleep.

"Why are you sleeping in here?" Gabe asked him.

"I's jus had me a feelin ya'd be home ta nite, Mr. Gabe."

"Your feeling was right Caleb, I would call that the Holy Spirit talking to you."

"It was mighty strong! I's be in my bed and jus kept getting up, I's jus had de feelin ta come here. I's able ta sleep then. All go well wid ya trip?"

"Yes it did, but I'll tell you Caleb, I've got a lot on my mind."

"Be there anythin I's can help ya wid?"

"Not right now, but tomorrow, would you get the men to the church about ten o'clock? We need to have a meeting."

"Yez sah, theys be there," Caleb promised then added, "I's take care of ya horse, you go see'd yor Missus."

"Thank you Caleb, good night."

"Good nite Mr. Gabe, I's pray bout yor burden."

"Thank you, I need it more than you know, Caleb."

Gabe found Josie dressed in her night gown reading her Bible in the study.

"You're home!" She exclaimed jumping to her feet.

Taking her into his arms he kissed her soundly, "Yes, I am."

"Tell me all about your trip!"

"First, tell me why you're still up? Shouldn't you be in bed?"

"I couldn't sleep. I had you on my mind, so I've been praying and reading." She held up her Bible to show him.

"This candle light will ruin your eyes, use the lamps next time, it gives more light."

"Gabe you're stalling for time. I know you better than you know yourself. What happened?" She asked.

"I met with President Lincoln."

"You what…I mean how? Why?"

"I met him after the inauguration, Michael Guerrier arranged it all."

"You're serious?"

"Yes, I am. It seems President Lincoln and Michael are very good friends. Apparently he's told the President about what we're doing here at New Canaan and the President even said he was impressed with us."

"He did?" Josie hung onto his every word.

"Yes he did. Now, here comes the part about why he wanted to talk with me. It seems he needs our help."

"Our help? Why?" Josie asked curiously.

"Well, Josie, within the next thirty days or so, our country will be going to war. He wants us to help him by obtaining information, and using our home for meetings with men who are working undercover in the states which have seceded."

"What did you tell him?" She asked.

"I told him we would. Would do you think?"

After a moment she answered, "I trust you. If you feel we need to do this, then we will."

"We'll have to tell the others dear. We're going to need all the prayers we can get to get through this. No telling how long this war is going to last. We've only got thirty good days left to prepare."

"We need to make a plan and get organized," she said.

"That's what I've been thinking too. I don't think we'll plant much cotton this year. If we can keep the sugar cane from ruin during all this, by November's harvest it should bring a good price. We need as many vegetables as we can raise, and store as much meat as possible. We need to fill the smokehouses, and the storehouse. I don't know what else to do. Have I left anything out?"

"We'll need lots of cloth and household staples. Liza and Hannah need to gather herbs. Are our wells okay?" She asked.

"Yes, they're fine, but that's good you thought of them. I need to talk with Ben, but it's late, tomorrow will come soon enough. I found Caleb asleep in the barn. He said he had a feeling about me coming home tonight, and was waiting on me. So, I know God is with us," he sighed heavily.

"Yes he is!" Josie stood and took her husband by the hand. "Now it's time for sleep. You won't be any good to anyone if you're tired or sick. Let's go to bed, and we'll talk again in the morning."

The next day Gabe found the men waiting for him at the church. Greeting them, he took a seat next to Ben. Ben already knew what was going on because Gabe had informed him during their usual morning meeting. Gabe knew he could count on him for support.

"I wanted to meet with you today to tell you what I learned on my trip to Washington. I've chosen to speak with just the men so we wouldn't worry the women and children. After our meeting, you may tell your wives and older children what we've talked about. What I'm about to tell you needs to remain here. No one outside of New Canaan is to know. Do you agree?"

"Yez sah, we agree's," Big John said, while the others nodded.

"Okay then. While I was in Washington I met with President Lincoln. He told me many things, but the most important is a war between the states will begin within a month's time." Gabe paused to let this sink in as the men began to talk among themselves. He could tell they were surprised.

"What's dat be meanin Mr. Gabe?" Henry asked.

"It means we need to be prepared. We're going to plan this whole thing out from supplies to crops. I, at first thought, we shouldn't be raising cotton this year, but after talking with Ben, I've decided we should go ahead and plant half of what we planted last year. We're going to increase our gardens. Ben said the sugar cane would be ready by November to harvest. I believe it'll be our money maker. For right now we need to fill the smoke houses, and the store houses with as much as we can. The orchards in the back need to be pruned. We're lucky we've been told ahead of time. There are lots of people going to be caught unaware. So, I suggest we do as much fishing and hunting in our spare time to add to our store houses and smoke houses. It couldn't hurt." That's about it, anyone have any questions?"

"Does ya think we's shud be tellin the women folk? Jarome asked.

"Yes sir, I do. I've already told my wife and I want you to tell yours. We need their thoughts and help if we are going to take care of our families during this war.

"We's be wid ya, Mr. Gabe," they all said.

"Good, we need to pray everyday for God's guidance and protection. That's really important. This way we stay ahead of trouble."

"Yes sah, we's knowd that fo shur. We's prayed for shoes and we's got em." Dan said, causing everyone to laugh.

"Just as you had faith for the shoes, have faith we'll all get through this without having to go hungry or losing anyone."

"We's best be gettin ta work den. Dey's be a lot ta do." Ben said as he stood. He looked over to Gabe. "I's be havin a meetin wid everybody tonite ifin it be alright wid ya, ta answer the questions dat be comin after they's be thinkin on it awhile."

"That'll be good Ben, thank you. Are you going to make sure they tell their wives?"

"Yez sah, I's be doin jus that." Ben smiled his reassuring smile.

Everyone had gotten to the meeting early that night. Emlee and Caleb had the children outside playing, while the grown-ups met with Ben.

Jonah stood proudly at his father's side as the meeting began. "Anybodies here gots questions bout what be a comin?"

"We's be wantin ta knowd ifin this war be takin away ours freedom?" Henry asked.

"Aint nobodies freedom goin be takin! We's got de Lord and Mr. Gabe a fightin fo us. Sides, des war be bout freedom fo everybodies," Ben assured him.

"Cant never tell! Mr. Gabe, he jus might wanta take it back!" shouted someone from the back.

Ben looked to see who'd said it before he answered. "Anybodies dat knowd Mr. Gabe knows dat hed be wantin ta preach Gods word mor'in bein a plantation owner! He be a man of God first, we's jus mighty bless God see'd fit ta give him ta us. He done gone through lots ta set us free. Jus ya be membin dat James!"

"Whats we be needin ta do? Big John asked.

"We's be needin ta fish and hunt," Jonah said as he stepped forward. " We's need ta be fillin de smoke houses full. I's got me a plan. We's can have us a huntin group, and we's can have us a fishin group. De women be cleanin what we's get, and my pa be smokin it. Dat ways we's all be puttin food in store houses so's Mr. Gabe don't do it all. We's be doin dat even durin da war. Nothin can stop what de good Lord be givin us frum da land."

A murmur of agreement went through the room. Big John stood to his feet.

"Now dat be done, we's need ta be discussin sumptin else. Mr. Gabe done lots fer us. Now we's gona take cared of him an de Missus. When dis thang breaks out we's gona kept us eyes on em makin sured deys be safe.

Nobodies cares bout slaves. Mr. Gabe and the Missus might be in harms way. Everybodies okay wid dat?"

Everyone shouted amen, including James. Ben was glad to see it, but he was going to keep his eye on James for awhile anyway. "Can't be tellin what a bodie be doin under pressure," he thought. Happy with the way things had gone, Ben turned the group over to Jonah so he could assign men to fishing and hunting, then the meeting was over. The only ones that remained behind were Old Ben, Big John, Caleb and Jonah. They had plans to make on protecting Gabe and Josie.

For the next two weeks everyone worked hard at planting, hunting, and fishing. It seemed as though no one slept. You could hear some kind of activity all night long. Something was being built or something being stored.

Gabe spent most of his time in prayer; he found he worked harder while he prayed. Josie and Liza made several trips to town to stock up on salt, flour and other staples they might not be able to get during war time. Each time they went, they came back with stories of soldiers trying to recruit young men for the Confederate Army. It was happening faster than Gabe thought it would. Here, at New Canaan, the children still played and went to school in the mornings. The grown- ups had stopped all together because of the work needing to be done. Church services still continued without one person being absent. Gabe was glad to see everyone was putting their faith in God.

On April 12, 1861 Civil War began, not in Louisiana, but in South Carolina. Many lives were lost. Having done all they could in such a short time, Gabe felt they were prepared for whatever might happen next.

Late one night, shortly after the war had begun, Gabe was awaken from his sleep to the sound of men shouting from outside his bedroom window. Quickly he ran to the window and peered out into the night. He could only see silhouettes struggling in the flower garden. Quietly he made his way downstairs in the darkness to his study to retrieve his gun. Then he made his way out the door to the side of the house. The moon's light was all he had to go by and it wasn't very bright which was to his advantage. Slowly, he rounded to the back of the house to the garden. Standing up straight he called out, "Who's there? I have a gun and I'll use it! Tell me who you are now!"

The struggling silhouettes stopped and separated. There stood two men, but Gabe couldn't tell who they were. Finally, one of the men answered.

"It be me Mr. Gabe. Jonah! I's catch'd dis man sneaking round de house!"

"Good job Jonah! Mister, step over here and let me see who you are! Jonah, you stay behind him!"

"Yez sah! Jonah shouted back.

The two men walked toward Gabe who by now had stepped out into the moon light. Gabe didn't recognize the man standing in front of him.

He was tall and dressed in dark worn clothing that looked to big for him.

His face certainly didn't match his clothes. It was too clean and he was shaven.

"What are you doing here?" Gabe asked.

"I've been sent here sir," he replied.

"Are you telling me someone sent you here to sneak around my house?"

"No sir, I'm telling you I've been sent here to speak with Mr. Gabriel Lyon on behalf of a mutual friend from Washington."

"If that's true, why are you here at this time of night in the back of the house? Gabe didn't lower his gun.

"Are you Gabriel Lyon?" The man asked.

"I am."

"Well sir, I got here earlier than I thought I would. So, I thought I'd sleep in the garden until early morning, before I woke the house. But your man here caught me by surprise, and before I could say anything knocked me to the ground. You know the rest."

"I's don't trust him, Mr. Gabe!" Jonah told him.

"Come with me to the house and remember I have a gun," Gabe commanded. Then looking at Jonah, he motioned for him to follow. Gabe took the stranger quickly to his study, keeping the gun on him all the time.

Gabe shut the study doors quietly. "Jonah, I'm trusting what you hear tonight will go no further than this room. Okay?"

"Yez sah, I aint leavin ya alone wid him fo shoor!"

"I'm Lieutenant Jacob Sanders with the Union Army, the solider informed Gabe. " I've been sent to show you this." He removed a folded paper from his pocket. Gabe stepped closer to the Lieutenant. "If you'd kindly lower that gun sir, it would make this a lot easier." Gabe lowered the gun while he watched the Lieutenant unfold the piece of paper and place it on the desk. Jonah stepped forward with the lamp.

"It's a map!" Gabe exclaimed.

"Yes sir, it's a map of the exact location of our Union infiltrated areas between Mississippi and Texas. As you can see, it also shows the exact location of our men here in Louisiana. What I've been asked to do, is set a meeting up here at your place for these men stationed in this area, and Mississippi. What I'm hoping for is the men in Texas will be able to come if given enough notice. Your place is here." The Lieutenant pointed it out on the map. "It seems it's a good place for our meeting, since it provides safety and cover. It also cuts the travel time down for most of our men."

"When would you like to set up the meeting?" Gabe returned his gun to its place.

"In three weeks time. That should give everyone time to get here, and for me to look your land over for security. Though I've been told we can depend on you, I'd like to have an escape route should one be needed. You can't be too safe in a time of war."

"Understandably so, how many men will be coming?"

"Around ten sir, that's what I've been told, but that can change without anyone telling me. Can you trust everyone here?" The Lieutenant asked.

"Yes you can, as you know, it seems we have our own security here." Gabe motioned to Jonah.

"Can you trust all your slaves?" The Lieutenant kept his eye on Jonah.

"There isn't one slave on this plantation, Lieutenant; you can trust everyone here with your life, as I do."

"Very well then, I'm just not sure everyone should know what's going on here, just in case it should leak out."

"You'll just have to trust me on this. Even the smallest one here will protect you with their life. Everyone working here will be told of your presence, and that we'll be expecting more company soon. You'll never know whose help you may need now or in the future."

"Yes sir, but…" The Lieutenant began, but was interrupted by Gabe.

"Jonah, as soon as morning comes, have everyone meet at the church. Men, women, and the older children. I need to go wake Ben and let him know what's going on now."

"He be a knowin, Mr. Gabe." Jonah whistled a high pitch whistle.

Out from the shadows of the room stepped Ben holding the biggest stick Gabe had ever seen. They could see Caleb and Big John standing outside on either side of the opened window now. Laughing, Gabe turned toward the Lieutenant. "No secrets here, everyone will be told. It's more for your protection than anyone else's, Lieutenant. That's the way it's going to be!" The only thing the Lieutenant could do was nod his head in shock and disbelief.

The meeting to inform everyone of their upcoming company went well. The men were excited about being able to help. Keeping Lieutenant Sanders out of sight had been a worry for Gabe. It shouldn't have, for Lieutenant Sanders and Jonah had become fast friends. Jonah dressed Lieutenant Sanders in his old clothes and darkened his skin with a walnut stain mixed with lard. Liza promised it wouldn't come off easily. The Lieutenant blended in as Jonah showed him around the fields and wooded areas. Even Gabe had to take a second close look. The whole incident had the entire plantation laughing, especially now that the Lieutenant was staying in Jonah's cabin. Gabe could only imagine what Lieutenant Sanders' commander would have to say.

Josie was nervous about all the cloak and dagger. She prayed almost all the time she was awake and late into the night. She just felt that prayer in advance was needed to protect everyone involved. She'd even gotten to where she sang Psalms ninety one as she went about seeing to lesson plans for the children, and her sewing. Now that she definitely showed she was with child, it was harder for her to walk long distances without getting short of breath. Soon she would give the children a break from school, but that just presented another problem, what to do with the children during this break. Oh well, she thought as she walked to the little school, that too will work itself out.

Josie stood at the back of the class room listening to the children read out loud to Emlee. How careful the dear girl was making sure no one was left out. Some read faster than others, but Emlee made sure to praise everyone the same.

When Emlee noticed Josie, she smiled. "Missus Josie be here ta listen ta ya read." All eyes turn toward Josie. Smiling, she walked to the front of the class saying hello to every child as she passed. When she had taken a seat at the small table in front, Emlee said, "Missus Josie, we've been a hopin ya be coming ta see's us. We's gotcha a surprise!" One by one, the children showd Josie what they excelled in, some read out loud, some did math and the smaller children sang their ABC's and counted. So much had been accomplished by Emlee!

"I'm so proud of each of you!" Josie told them smiling. "You've learned so fast! Emlee, you've done a wonderful job."

Emlee was proud the Missus could see how hard she'd worked with the students. Maybe sometime soon she could talk to the Missus about her and Caleb. For right now, she would just wait.

It was a cloudy dark night that threatened rain, as shadows slipped out of the woods, and crossed the fields toward the house unseen. In reality the night had many eyes watching each movement. Already Jonah and Lieutenant Sanders had counted fifteen people.

"That's more than I was told would come," Lieutenant Sanders whispered to Jonah. "Something must be up!" Quietly, Lieutenant Sanders and Jonah followed the shadows from a distance, making sure each one was suppose to be there. Judging from their uniforms, they were all union.

"Why dey be wearin uniforms? Dey gets caught fo shoor come daylight!"

Jonah whispered to the Lieutenant.

"Let's pray they all get here before sun up. We need to let Mr. Lyon know they're here."

"He knowd, my pa and Caleb done told em. Ifin we's can see'd em, then fo shoor dey can."

The Lieutenant had to grin. Jonah was right. This was just how he wanted it. He could see them, but they couldn't see him. Trouble could be averted should the Confederates happen by, which was not likely.

"I guess its time for me to go in," The Lieutenant said more to himself than Jonah.

"Ifin ya be needin me, jus whistle. We's be watchin till ya say not to."

The Lieutenant left his hiding place and moved toward the house. Ben had already been to the house to let Gabe know the soldiers were on the property. Ben even laughed saying they were trying to be quiet and not seen, but he and the others could not only see them, but hear them as well. Gabe had everything ready. Josie and Liza had food and coffee for the men knowing they would be hungry. A knock at the back door took Gabe from his thoughts. Opening it, in stepped a Union solider asking, "Gabriel Lyon?"

"Yes, come in quickly." With a motion of his hand the soldier signaled the others to follow him.

Gabe led them up the back stairs to the west wing of the house to the old library which stood empty. It was large enough for them to hold their meeting. A big table with chairs and several lit lamps were all that occupied the room. Gabe stood at the door as the men filed in, lighting their way. The last to enter was a General from the appearance of his uniform, and the respect he was shown by the other men.

"Mr. Lyon, I'm General Ulysses Grant," he said, as he shook Gabe's hand.

"It's an honor to meet you General Grant. Welcome to my home. Will this be all the men coming tonight?"

"Yes. It seems I'm missing one Lieutenant Sanders. He would be here, wouldn't he?"

"Yes sir he is, he's changed a little since you've last seen him though. I thought I should warn you in advance. In order to have him here without being noticed we had to change a few things about him."

"What do you mean?" The general asked.

"You'll see, here he comes now." Gabe smiled as Sanders entered the room dressed in his uniform with his dark skin. Sanders saluted the General.

"General Grant! What a surprise sir, I wasn't expecting you to be here."

"I can see that Lieutenant. Thank you for going to such extremes to ensure the safety of this meeting."

"Yes sir." Sanders knew this was the beginning of a long day.

"You've all come a long way and I'm sure you're hungry. My wife has prepared something for you to eat and some coffee. Would you like it now, before you begin your meeting?" Gabe asked.

"Yes, that would be nice, thank you for thinking of us," General Grant said gratefully.

"Please be seated then, rest assured you'll be safe for as long as you are here. The food will arrive shortly.

"We would like for you to attend this meeting Mr. Lyon. We want you to know what's going on in case we need your help. Will you do that?" General Grant asked.

"Yes. Excuse me. I'll be right back."

Gabe could only imagine the ribbing Sanders would be taking from the other soldiers because of his skin tone. He only hoped it wouldn't be too bad for him. Entering the kitchen, Gabe informed Josie and Liza the men were ready to eat.

After eating a meal of hot biscuits, ham and coffee, the men were more ready to sleep than to have this meeting. Gabe listen while the men around the table talked of their strategies, and how they would be needing a place to stop over. Most needed was a place to store weapons and soldiers.

While the soldiers made their plans, Gabe glanced toward the window, bored. To his surprise, Gabe could see a glowing near the window. Not outside of it, but inside next to it. Smiling to himself, he watched as Michael appeared and put a finger to his lips signaling for him to be quiet. Michael walked slowly over to Gabe, causing a slight stirring breeze as he did. Gabe was fascinated by the flickering of the candles and lamps in the room as Michael moved to his side.

"They can't see me. Only you can," Michael informed him.

Gabe gave a slight nod and smiled.

"Interesting meeting, you humans need to understand warfare better." Michael said causing Gabe to look up at him.

"Tell them you have the perfect place for them to store the guns and keep the soldiers. Tell them you're buying the Broussard Plantation and it will be available for their use."

"I'm buying the Broussard Plantation?" Gabe asked in a whisper trying not to move his lips.

"Yes, you are. You only have to think your questions and I'll understand. Otherwise these people are going to think you're losing your mind," Michael said laughing loudly.

"Just where am I going to get the money?" Gabe thought.

"God will provide! Go ahead, tell them," Michael commanded.

Clearing his throat, Gabe said, "Excuse me gentlemen. I believe I have the answer to your problem."

CHAPTER 9

JOSIE SAT ON THE FRONT porch in a rocking chair looking out over the front lawn of New Canaan. How she wished her father were here. The closer it came time to have this baby, the more she missed him. The fan in her hand required more energy to use than the relief it gave. What she wouldn't give for a nice cool breeze for just a few minutes. Just as she had given up on ever feeling cool again, a sweet light breeze began to blow. Josie closed her eyes and thanked the Lord for such a wonderful gift.

With her eyes closed, Josie heard a voice say, *"Send for your father."* She opened her eyes slightly to see who had been talking, but saw no one. Closing her eyes again, she sighed and heard the voice repeat. *"Send for your father."* Keeping her eyes closed, Josie smiled and thought to herself, Yes, I'll send for Father. Then she slipped into a comfortable well needed sleep.

Josie opened her eyes. She was home, yet she wasn't, though she still sat in her chair on her front porch. The sun shone brightly, but amazingly it wasn't hot. Standing to her feet, Josie walked down the steps of the porch that led to the yard. The cool breeze blowing was sweet and felt wonderful! The grass was a bright green and the sky was a pure blue. Flowers were everywhere she looked, in glorious colors that glisten in the sun as if they were made of crystal. Walking over to a red rose, she gently touched it. The flower was so perfect and the color was so brilliantly, clearly she felt she could see through it.

As Josie looked around, she saw a little boy of three sitting under the trees playing by himself. Josie started toward him, and then as if he sensed her presence, the little boy looked up, smiled and waved. Josie wondered who he was. As she stood watching the child, she felt a hand on her shoulder. Turning to see who had touched her, Josie was surprised to see Michael standing beside her. "That's your son."

"My son?"

"Yes. His name will be William Ezra Lyon," Michael told her.

"He looks like his father."

"He will be a mighty man of God!"

"You do know, I knew you were an Angel don't you?' Josie asked smiling, as she watched the little boy play.

"Yes, I knew." Michael couldn't help but laugh.

"You also know, I knew this baby was a boy."

"Yes, that's true," Michael replied.

"Why have you brought me here?"

"I didn't bring you here Josie, the Father did. He wanted you to see your son. You'll be going through a lot in the next few months and God wanted to give you this to help you through those times."

"Thank you, Father!" Josie said as tears of happiness slid down her cheek.

"Missus! Missus, wake up! You shouldn't be out in this heat," Hannah said as she shook Josie awake.

Gabe knew he had to buy the Broussard's plantation, and knowing Broussard, it wasn't going to be easy to negotiate the price. Gabe was grateful he'd be dealing with Richard Begnaud, the banker, instead of Broussard directly. Taking a deep breath and saying a quick prayer for favor, he walked into the bank for his appointment.

"Mr. Lyon!" Mr. Begnaud said as he greeted Gabe with a handshake.

"Mr. Begnaud, thank you for meeting with me on such short notice. I hope I haven't taken you away from anything important."

"Not a problem! Please, do come in and let's talk." Mr. Begnaud led the way into his office. Taking a seat across from the large desk, Gabe said, "I guess you're wondering why I've asked to talk with you."

"As a matter of fact, I am."

"I've come to ask about the Broussard plantation. I understand you're handling all inquiries."

"Yes, I am. Are you interested?"

"I've been thinking about it. I was wondering how many acres are in the plantation and the asking price."

"There's one thousand acres of land and of course the house. The barns no longer stand, but you know of the tornado damage." While he talked, Mr. Begnaud pulled out a map of the estate. "It looks like it joins your land!

This could be quite the asset for you if you bought it!"

"I'm just looking at my options right now," Gabe told him. "Do you know the asking price?"

"Let me see, if I remember correctly, Mr. Broussard just wanted to get rid of it. He didn't leave an exact price. Though in all fairness, I will be acting on Mr. Broussard's behalf. I couldn't let it go for an unfair price."

"Again, Mr. Begnaud, how much is the selling price?"

"Well now, let me see…How much are you willing to give for it?"

Tired of playing this cat and mouse game with the man, Gabe stood suddenly. "Mr. Begnaud, I'm very much aware no one around here wants to buy that land. Unfortunately, with the war that's going on, no one wants to part with their money. I'm willing to offer ten thousand dollars in gold for the whole thing. You think about it and give me an answer in the next couple of days." Gabe then turned to leave the office.

When he had reached the door, Mr. Begnaud stopped him. "Wait!" I can give you your answer now. Please come and sit down Mr. Lyon and we can seal this deal."

"Then you agree to the price?" Gabe remained standing and didn't move.

"Yes, it's more than fair. It's more than Mr. Broussard thought he'd get for it. If you don't mind waiting, I'll have my man draw up the bill of sale and deed for you."

"That will be fine, thank you," Gabe said as he sat down again.

Josie could think of nothing but her dream. Dream is what she decided to call it, but she knew it was a vision provided by the Lord. She was glad Michael was there. She just had to let him know she knew about him. The thought made her smile. The blessing was seeing her son's smile. How it filled her heart and mind. The moment of him smiling at her had been itched into her very being and could be recalled in an instant. She liked it very much.

"Whatcha be a thinkin Miz Josie?" Liza asked as she watched her closely.

"Oh, about the baby."

"Ya be thinkin bout a name?"

"I know his name."

"What be it?"

"William Ezra Lyon."

"We's be callin him Will?"

"Yes Liza, that's what we'll be calling him. I like the nickname Will."

"What ifin it be a girl?"

"Its not, it's a boy. I know it."

"How ya be knowin that Miz Josie?"

"The Lord told me. I guess you think I'm being silly, don't you?"

"No, I's don't. The Lord tells us what he be wantin us ta knowd. Ya been blessed Miz Josie, jus keep dat in ya heart. Havin a babe aint easy, but it be worth it."

"You know Liza, my mother passed away sometime ago. Since I've been here, you've filled the emptiness it left me. You've accepted me and guided me as if I were your own daughter. Not many would've done that. I want you to know I love you. I know why Gabe has loved you all his life, and that his fondest memories are of you."

"Oh Josie girl," Liza cried, as she wrapped her arms around her. "I's love ya too!"

Gabe went looking for Josie. He wanted to talk to her about buying Broussard's plantation. Since he'd already done it, he thought he should go ahead and confess it was a done deal. He found her in her sitting room writing a letter.

"What are you doing?" Gabe asked her.

"I'm writing a letter to my father. I want him to come here. It's alright with you, isn't it?"

"Of course it is. I was wondering if he shouldn't come down when the baby is born. Is that what you're asking him to do?"

"Yes, I miss him. It seems the closer the time comes for the baby, the more I want to see him. Silly, isn't it?"

"Not at all. I think he'd love to come. I know he misses you. After all, I just whisked you away. It's had to be hard on him to adjust to living alone."

"I didn't think you would mind," She told him as she continued to write.

"When you get through with your letter, I need to talk to you."

"I'm finished now. What do you need to talk about?"

"I want to tell you what I've done today. I'm asking you to hear me out before you say anything."

Smiling she shook her head slightly. "What have you been up to that you're apologizing before hand?"

"I bought Mr. Broussard's old plantation today," he confessed.

"Whatever for?"

"It's what the Lord wanted me to do. It's going to be a help to us in the long run. Just how, I haven't been told yet. When General Grant was here, he and his men where talking about needing a place to hide soldiers and arms, and it's big enough for that purpose. It'll be a good place for them to have their meetings and it won't be in our house."

"What are we going to do with it in the mean time, Gabe? People will be expecting us to farm it, and maybe even buy slaves. How can we?"

"Just pray God tells one of us what to do!"

Professor Hall walked the floor in his study, thinking. Turning to Charles he said, "I'm going to Baton Rouge. My grandchild is going to born in the next few months and I want to be there. I miss Josie and I'm going to her!"

"Are you sure? After all there is a war on now," Charles told him.

"I know, but for some reason I feel the need to go. I've been praying and I know I should."

"If your mind is made up, I'm going with you. No sense in you going by yourself."

"I don't believe the deep South is where you should be, Charles. You should pray before volunteering. I'd enjoy your company, but I don't want you to place yourself in a dangerous situation."

"I don't want you to go by yourself either. I'll pray about it. Just wait a couple of days before you do anything. Would you do that?"

"Yes, I will but only two days. Maybe I'll get a letter from Josie by then."

Lieutenant Sanders was happy to see the little church in the woods, as he got closer to Lyon's home. He'd wait here until night fall then, proceed to the house unless he ran into one of the workers. Sanders was amazed at how they operated the plantation. Never had he seen anyone doing the will of God like Gabriel Lyon. The loyalty these people had for one another, and God, made him want to join them. Not many people knew he was a Christian, but he was, and had been since he was a boy. Even in time of war he continued to pray and read his Bible. It didn't matter where he was; he knew God did not leave him nor forsake him. God had proven it over and over many times. Hiding in a thicket for the shade and protection from being seen, Sanders closed his eyes to sleep until night fall.

Sanders woke with a start, it was already dark. He hadn't meant to sleep so soundly. Making his way from the woods and across the fields, he had the feeling of being watched. A high pitch whistle went through the night air, which he answered back.

"Ya be rite noisy Jacob!" Jonah said, stepping out into the moon light.

"I knew you'd be watching, I just wanted to make sure you knew it was me." Sanders laughed as the men shook hands.

"Ya be needin ta see Mr. Gabe?"

"Yeah, I've got a message for him."

"Come wid me afor ya getcha self inta trouble," Jonah said as he took the lead to the house.

Entering through the back door, Jonah stopped and knocked on his parent's door.

"Pa, be Mr. Gabe in de study?"

Ben opened the door, and wasn't surprised to see Lieutenant Sanders with Jonah. "Yez, he be there. We's goin ta have more company?"

"No sir, just me," Lieutenant Sanders told him.

"Go ahead on then."

Jonah knocked on the study door before entering. "Mr. Gabe, it be Jonah, and de Lieutenant."

"Come on in," Gabe said.

"Mr. Lyon, it's a pleasure to see you again," Lieutenant Sanders said as he shook Gabe's hand.

"Good to see you Sanders, have a seat. I don't believe you've met my wife, Josie, this is Lieutenant Sanders."

"It's nice to meet you Lieutenant, I've seen you before and my husband has told me all about you."

"Yes, ma'am, it's an honor to met you personally." Sanders said politely.

"Thank you. Now if you gentlemen will excuse me, I think I'll retire for the evening." Josie quickly kissed Gabe on the cheek and left the room.

"I didn't mean to interrupt your evening sir, but I have an urgent message for you from General Grant," Sanders said as he took a seat.

"Needing another meeting?"

"Yes sir. But this time we need to leave a few men behind to blend into the town."

"How are you planning on doing that? Most men are signing up for the Confederate army. I don't know how I'm going to be able to hide them."

"We's can get de walnut stain," Jonah offered.

"Yes, we can do that, but I don't think its going to be necessary right now."

Sanders said laughing, "Do you know how long that stuff lasts?"

"Yes, I do," Gabe said laughing with the two men.

"We also have some wounded men who aren't seriously wounded, but they're holding us back."

Just then the study doors opened and Josie walked in. "Excuse me gentlemen, but I left my Bible. I'll just be getting it and leave."

"No, please stay and maybe you can help us with this little problem," Gabe said.

"What problem would that be?" She asked.

"General Grant wants another meeting, and he has some wounded men he'd like to leave with us, along with some men he wants to blend into town to gather information. I don't see how we can manage with the wounded or helping the other men blend into town. Any ideas?" Gabe asked.

Thinking as she went to pick up her Bible she turned and smiled. "Yes, I know exactly how to help."

"How?" Lieutenant Sanders asked.

"Gabe just bought the neighboring plantation. It needs work. The wounded could stay there, and the others could be used to help make its repairs. That way they would be going into town making the necessary purchase for materials and no one would be the wiser."

"That's a great idea!" Gabe said.

"No sir, its not. For one thing, the men just can't show up. People are going to wonder how they got here. Other than that, it would've been a good idea," Sanders said.

"That problem is easily solved," Josie said seriously.

"How's that?" The men asked in unison.

"Simple. Lieutenant Sanders, just where are the men now and how many?"

"Scattered ma'am. Some are in Texas, and some are in Mississippi, and some in the northern part of Louisiana. The wounded traveled with me as far as I could bring them. They're hiding out in your woods now. We've done all our traveling at night, hiding in places you don't want to know about. I've got five wounded with me, and we want to bring in about ten more soldiers to infiltrate different areas where we need information. For the meeting with General Grant, it will be the same as before, fifteen."

"Then this is what you do, Lieutenant. Have the men you want to come and stay with us get on a train with papers saying their destination is here to work for Gabe. Of course they wouldn't be in uniform. No one need know about the wounded. Liza and I can care for them. This way only the first to arrive will have to come by train. You can trade them out as often as you want after that. No one will know any difference, as long as we keep the same number of men. They can go into town with the workers from here, so people will get used to seeing them. If that doesn't make you feel any better Lieutenant, we can always stain their skin." Josie smiled sweetly and said good night.

Professor Hall got his letter from Josie asking him to come to New Canaan.

He was delighted he was going. All he needed to do was tell Charles, who would be arriving any minute. Quickly Professor Hall wrote a response to Josie telling her he would be coming soon. He would probably be there a day after she received his letter. He couldn't wait. He was leaving the day after tomorrow.

Charles felt he should accompany Professor Hall. He'd prayed for the past few days. He knew what he would tell the professor tonight at dinner. Whether the professor liked it or not, he'd be going with him. With his mind made up, Charles grabbed his hat and set off for Professor Hall's house.

Liza and Josie looked at each other as the wounded men filed into the house. Not only were they tired and hurt, they looked like they hadn't eaten in a long time.

"I think we should keep the wounded men here in our house, don't you?" Josie asked Liza.

"Be lots easier fo us ifin we did fo shoor," Liza replied, watching each one carefully.

"Lieutenant Sanders, let's take the men to the east wing. There are plenty of empty rooms on that side, and if they need to make a hasty exit, they can use the back stairs that lead down to the kitchen."

"Here ma'am? I thought you wanted them to stay at the other house."

"I've changed my mind. As you can see, I'm not able to ride a horse or walk long distances like I use to without it causing great discomfort. Liza and I can care for them better here."

"Yes ma'am, I understand," Sanders said with a blush showing on his face.

"Let's get them settled in up stairs, so Liza and I can get you and your men something to eat. Please follow me."

Josie took the men and Lieutenant Sanders up the back stairs to the east wing. As they came to the top of the stairs, Sanders said, "It's a dead end Mrs. Lyon. The stairs end in a wall."

With a smile, Josie pushed a panel that opened the wall allowing them to enter into the hall of the east wing.

"That's great!" Sanders exclaimed as the wall closed behind the last one. "How do you open it from this side?"

"It's the same panel on this side." Josie showed him how to work the hidden door.

"You see, Lieutenant, apparently the designer didn't want the servant's entrance to be noticeable so he hid it. I haven't been to the other house, so I don't know its secrets. But I do know this one's. If I were you, I would go over to the other house with Gabe, and check it out for this type of thing. It may prove to be helpful in the future."

"Yes ma'am, I certainly will!"

Sanders and Josie helped the men settle into the five rooms nearest the hidden door. It made them all feel better knowing it was so close. Liza and Hannah brought up clean clothes and water for the men to wash in. Liza took this time to look at wounds so she would know what medicine she needed. Josie went back to the kitchen to check on the food that had been started. These poor men didn't know what to do first. Sleep or eat. She'd make the decision for them. They'd eat first. They needed food to heal and keep their energy.

Professor Hall and Charles boarded the train heading for Baton Rouge, Louisiana. They were like two little boys let out from school. They were ready for this adventure.

The next three days kept both Josie and Liza busy with the extra mouths to feed, and taking care of wounds. Liza had Hannah cleaning wounds and applying poultices while she mixed the herbs. Though no one said they knew the wounded soldiers were there, Josie knew everyone on the plantation knew it, because she didn't have to ask for help. Delia and the other women just came and helped with whatever needed to be done. It was such a blessing.

Gabe couldn't believe the furniture that had been left behind in the new house. Broussard had truly been in a hurry to leave. Most of the bedrooms still had beds which he was grateful to see. Now the soldiers would have a choice of staying the night after their meeting. Sanders went through each room like a boy at Christmas knocking on walls, looking for hidden panels, and secret stairways. Soon Gabe was joining him in the fun. They didn't find hidden doorways, but they did find a trap door in the main dining room under the rug that the table stood on. They explored it and found a tunnel leading outside into a flower garden. It was enough to make Sanders happy.

"We're here Charles!" Professor Hall exclaimed as the train pulled into Baton Rouge.

"I'm so glad. I don't believe I could last another day on this train," Charles told him as he helped the professor gather his things.

"I'm sure we'll be able to get directions to New Canaan from the ticket master inside the station, and then I will see about getting us a buggy to drive to the house."

"I was hoping they knew we were coming and would be meeting us here." Charles said.

"Not to worry my man, it can't be too hard to find."

Professor Hall handed Charles his case and walked to the ticket counter.

"Excuse me sir, I'm wondering if you could give me some directions."

"How can I help you?" Mr. Fontenot asked.

"I'm here to visit with my daughter and son-in-law. Perhaps you know them? They're Gabriel and Josephine Lyon?"

"Yes sir, I sure do! So you're Mrs. Lyon's father. Welcome to Baton Rouge! I'm Steven Fontenot, ticket agent and post master. You're about seven miles from their plantation. Across the street is Allen's livery stable. You'll be able to hire a buggy there."

"Thank you so much, and it has been a pleasure to meet you, Mr. Fontenot."

"Pleasure has been mine." Then lowering his voice and looking quickly at Charles, Mr. Fontenot asked, "Why do you dress your slave so well? He'll give the others the wrong idea!"

Professor Hall froze. How dare this man think Charles was a slave! Quickly thinking he replied, "Mr. Fontenot, I don't think I know you well enough to tell you this, but I am. My Father is the richest man you'll ever know if you ever met him. He owns more gold and cattle than you can imagine. I can dress anyone anyway I choose!" With that, he turned and left Mr. Fontenot looking shocked.

"What did that man say to you?" asked Charles as they crossed the street.

"He wanted to know why I dressed my slave so well."

Charles stopped in mid stride. "What?"

"You're in the deep south now Charles, we have to be careful until we get to Gabriel and Josephine. I told you, you might not want to come here, but don't get offended yet. Just take a look around you! You're seeing slavery for the first time in its truest form. We've got seven miles to go until we can be in a safe place."

"I'm going to keep my mouth shut. I can promise you that!" Charles assured him as they entered Allen's Livery Stable.

Mr. Allen looked from Charles back to Professor Hall. " Can I help you?"

"I need a buggy to drive to my daughter's home. Mr. Fontenot told me you rented buggies."

"Yes I do. Who's your daughter?" Mr. Allen asked.

"Josephine Lyon. My son-in- law is Gabriel Lyon, do you know them?"

"Yes sir, I do. They own the New Canaan Plantation just seven miles down the road. Rumor has it your son-in-law just bought the adjoining plantation. Is that true?"

"I wouldn't know, sir. He doesn't tell me everything, and with me traveling for the past few days, he had no way of letting me know."

"I was just wondering. I don't know what he would be doing with the extra land. After all, he doesn't have enough slaves to tend to it."

"I'm sure you're right, now about that buggy?"

The arrangements were quickly made for the buggy. Charles and Professor Hall were very glad to be on their way.

"It should be just around this bend." The professor knew he'd followed the directions carefully.

"I've never seen a plantation before. I wonder what it'll be like," Charles said, more to himself.

"I have no idea, lots of land and a big house from what Josie's told me." The professor slowed the buggy down and turned off the main road. Charles and Professor Hall said at the same time. "It's beautiful!"

"Just look at these trees! Look at that house! I didn't know Gabe was this wealthy. Did you?" Charles could see the question threw the Professor.

"I didn't think, I mean, no. I knew he sent us the money up front for all the books and sewing machine and such. But I didn't really know!" Professor Hall continued to follow the drive to the back of the house and stopped. Running toward them, was the biggest black man he had ever seen.

"Ya be here ta see'd Mr. Gabe?" Big John asked as he held the horses while the men stepped down from the buggy.

"Yes, I'm Professor Hall, Mrs. Lyon's father and this is Charles Wood, my friend."

"I's be proud ta meetcha! I's be Big John. Mr. Gabe be in da study. Ya'll jus goes thru dat door and Miz Liza be showing ya de way."

"Thank you John, It's been a pleasure to meet you," Professor Hall said.

"Yo be Mr. Gabe's best friend?" Big John asked Charles.

"Yes, we are. I'm pleased to meet you." Charles shook Johns hand before following Professor Hall to the door.

Liza wiped her hands on her apron as she went to answer the knock. Opening it, she was surprised to see two men standing there. What a sight it was. Both were dressed elegantly, but one was a white older man and the other was the most handsome black man she had ever seen, besides her Ben. She thought her eyes were playing a trick on her.

"Hello, Miss Liza?" Professor Hall asked.

"Dat be me," she answered trying to clear her eyes.

"I'm Professor William Hall, Josephine's father. Is she or Gabriel here?"

"Oh yez sah, dey both be here! Come on in. I's showed ya the way. Who be this wid ya, sah?"

"This is my and Gabriel's friend, Charles Wood."

"Yo be my Gabe's best friend?"

"Yes ma'am and you are Gabe's Liza. I've heard many stories about you."

"Dat be me! I's hope ya got good stories bout me cause dat boy been hard ta raise."

"Yes ma'am, they were," Charles told her laughing.

"Ya'll comes wid me now, dey be in the study." Liza led them through the house to the study doors. Knocking wasn't necessary because the doors were open and both Josie and Gabe sat on the sofa talking.

"Lookie here what I's brung ya, Miz Josie!" Liza announced with excitement.

"Father!" Josie shouted as she jumped up and ran to him throwing her arms around him for a hug.

"Charles! Professor Hall! When did you get here?" Gabe asked as he went to them.

"Just now. I bet you didn't receive my letter telling you we were coming," Professor Hall said as the men shook hands.

"No sir, we didn't. Please come and sit down. I see you've met our Liza."

"Yes, we have!" Charles said. "Later I'm going to see if she'd tell some tales on you!"

"I's be morin glad to," Liza said as she left the room.

"I can't believe you're here!" Josie told her father. "I have missed you. Have you been taking care of yourself? Who's been cooking for you?"

"My dear girl. You needn't worry about me. I've been doing just fine. Ask Charles, he'll tell you. We have dinner most evenings together."

"It's true Josie. Your Father has finally learned to take care of himself. His cooking is terrible but he can do it. We bachelors have been doing very well since you left.

"You don't appear to have lost any weight, neither one of you!" Josie exclaimed.

"Let's not talk about weight. You seem to be carrying a little extra," her father told her teasingly.

"Father! How can you say such a thing? This extra weight is William Ezra Lyon, your grandson!" She pretended to be offended.

"I love the name. Are you telling me you know this baby is going to be a boy?" The professor was pleased his grandson would be named after him.

"You've already picked out a name?" Gabe asked.

"Yes to both your questions. This baby is a boy and William Ezra will be his name!

"I like it," Gabe said. "He'll be named after both his grandfathers."

"Me too, but couldn't you put a Charles in there somewhere?" Charles asked laughing.

"Not this time Charles. Maybe next time," She answered him.

"But what if the next one is a girl? You can't name a girl Charles."

"Let's get this little one here before we start talking about the next one." Josie told him, as she gave them all a big smile.

"Just how do you know this baby is a boy?" Her father asked.

"I know because the Lord told me. He also gave me his name."

"You didn't tell me about this," Gabe said to her softly.

"I had a dream. In this dream I saw a little boy playing under the trees on the front lawn. An angel came to me and told me the little boy was my son and his name would be William Ezra Lyon."

"Josie, why didn't you tell me?" Gabe asked.

"It isn't that I intended to keep it from you my love, but it was my special present from the Lord. I've been holding it in my heart. Besides, when have we had the time? We've both been busy lately," she reminded him gently.

"I'm sorry. You're right. We haven't had much time to talk have we?"

"No and I don't feel neglected either. I think we'd better fill Charles and Father in on what's going on. They're bound to find out soon enough."

"Yes, you're right," Gabe said as he turned his attention to Professor Hall and Charles.

"You wouldn't believe what's been going on with us. I think we just need to show them Josie, how about that?"

"Show us what?" Professor Hall asked.

"Let's start by going upstairs. Besides, we need to get you settled in your rooms before dinner." Gabe stood and the others followed him.

"I've got a lot of questions for you Gabe," Charles said as they went up the stairs.

"I've got the answers for you my friend. Just be patient. This won't take long."

After showing Charles and Professor Hall their rooms on the west wing, Gabe took them toward the east wing. There he told them about the men staying in the rooms. As they walked down the hall, Hannah came out of the last room and stopped. "Hannah, this is my father and our friend Charles from Maine. Father, Charles, this is Hannah." Josie was happy to make the introductions. "Hannah is Liza and Ben's daughter and is helping take care of these wounded men. She's a healer just like her mother. She knows all about herbs, sickness and wounds. I don't know what we would do without her."

"It's nice to meet you," Professor Hall said.

Charles could hardly say a word. This was the most beautiful woman he'd ever seen. All he could do was smile at her and nod a greeting.

Hannah smiled back. "I be down in de kitchen ifin anybodies need me." She turned toward the wall and touched the hidden panel, causing the wall to open, and disappeared inside, leaving both Professor Hall and Charles astonished.

"Gabe, this house is great!" Charles exclaimed, causing them all to laugh.

After checking with Liza and learning they had plenty of time to go for a walk before dinner, the three men ventured outside while Josie lay down for a quick nap. As they walked, Gabe talked. "There isn't one slave on this plantation, Charles. All these people have their freedom papers but they chose to stay and work for me. They are paid wages for their work."

"Everyone?" Professor Hall asked.

"Everyone! Wait until you meet them. These are the greatest people you'll ever know."

"How did you do it?" Professor Hall asked.

"That's a long story. I'll tell you about it later. I've got a lot to show you," Gabe said as he led them to the workers quarters.

"These homes are just like cottages," Charles pointed out as they passed by.

"They all have their own flower and vegetable gardens. Does Hannah live down here?"

"No, she lives in the house with her parents in the household quarters. I can't wait for you to meet the rest of her family. As a matter of fact, here come her brothers." Gabe made the introductions to Caleb and Jonah. "Caleb takes care of the horses and Jonah takes care of security," Gabe's grin brought laughter from Jonah and Caleb.

"If you aren't busy why don't you join us?" Professor Hall asked.

"Thank ya sir, we's be done fo de day," Jonah said as he smiled at his brother. "Caleb here be goin ta see'd his girl."

"It'll wait," Caleb told them blushing.

So the group walked on together toward the church in the woods. Gabe explained to them about the Church and school as they went. He filled them in on what had been accomplished and how proud he was of everyone involved. Professor Hall and Charles were excited for them and said so. When the tour ended the group headed back toward the house. Caleb invited Charles to come and see the horses the next day, which he accepted immediately.

When they had reached the house, dinner was ready and Josie joined them. After eating, Ben, Liza, and Hannah joined the group at the table where they all talked and laughed until late in the evening.

CHAPTER 10

"I'm so glad you and Charles are here," Gabe confided in Professor Hall as they sat talking in the study.

"I'm glad we're here too. You know Gabe, what you've done here is nothing short of a miracle. I don't know how you've done it."

"It wasn't me. God did everything, and now I'm involved in a war," Gabe stood and walked to stand by the window.

"I know, God has a reason for everything he does. No telling what your real mission is in all of this," Professor Hall said.

"Sometimes I feel overwhelmed. It's good to have you to talk to. Josie's been a rock through all this. She's just followed my lead and never asked why." Gabe turned from the window and paced the floor.

"She knows what's from God and what's not. Have you been confiding in her about everything?" Professor Hall inquired.

"Yes, but now it's different. I don't want to worry her, now that it's getting closer to having the baby."

" You're right, but now that I'm here, I'd like to help anyway I can. I know Charles will want to as well."

"I'm glad to hear it. I've got to get things ready for the next meeting with General Grant over at the other house. I haven't gotten word yet when the soldiers will be here. I've been hoping Sanders would show up soon."

"What's your concern about having the soldiers over at the other house?" the professor asked.

"I don't have a good reason why I bought the house and extra land; much less have a reason to fix it up. I've got to have an explanation should anyone ask. Right now, I've got nothing." Gabe stopped his pacing and stood before the professor. "You being here will divert questions for a while, but after you leave people will start getting nosey."

"Then I won't leave!" the professor exclaimed.

"What do you mean?"

"As you said, you need a reason for buying the other land. So, I can be your reason. Charles and I will move over there and stay."

"You mean you're willing to move here... and stay?" Gabe asked in disbelief.

"I don't want my grandson to grow up without knowing me! All I have in Maine is an empty house."

"What about your position at the College, your friends, and your home?"

"What about them? Nothing is more important than family, you know that!"

"It'd certainly solve the problem, and be a great cover for sure. What about Charles? He'd be leaving a good position, he wouldn't be able to have the same rights in the south, and we don't know how this war is going to end. Things will be uncertain for him." Gabe voiced his concern.

"You just need to talk to him. If he doesn't want to stay, he'll tell you. Even if he doesn't, that doesn't take away our cover story," the professor explained.

"You're right, I don't know,... maybe we should just pray about it and see what God wants us to do." Gabe offered.

"I've been praying about this for months. Why do you think I'm here? Charles hasn't any family but us, so I know he'll stay. It's right Gabe, let's just do it."

"Let's talk to Charles before we decide his life for him, Gabe said laughing, but we'll go ahead with you staying."

"Good! I'll send a letter to the college letting them know I've resigned, and that I'm staying here. You go find Charles and talk to him. I'll find Josie and fill her in with what I've decided to do. By the way Gabe, the College is very proud of you and what you've done here."

"They're proud of me? It's God, not me!"

"That's true, but you did what He's asked you to do. The Lord loves obedience and I've let the College know it."

"That means a lot to me, thank you," Gabe said gratefully.

"You're welcome! Now, you go find Charles and talk to him. I'm going to go see Josie and tell her my good news!"

Gabe found Charles in his favorite place, the barn, with Caleb. He stood watching the two men, and realized these two men came from very different worlds. Caleb had been a slave most of his life, while Charles had been fortunate to be a student and then a teacher. Now Charles was a student again and Caleb was the teacher. They both shared a love of animals, especially horses.

"Excuse me gentlemen, but I need to have a word with Charles," Gabe told them as he strolled into the barn.

"Shur, Mr. Gabe, we's jus be talkin bout horses," Caleb said.

"You get any closer to that end of the horse Charles, and she'll kick you," Gabe warned.

"No she won't. She's gentle as can be, Caleb said so," Charles informed him.

"Alright, if Caleb says so then it is. I've got a question to ask you Charles."

"Ya be needin me ta leave?" asked Caleb

"No, its okay, you can stay, Gabe assured him.

"What's your question Gabe?" Charles asked.

"Professor Hall and I have been talking, he wants to stay here for good, and move into the other house. He thinks you might want to do the same thing, and Josie and I would love it if you did. You don't have to answer now, but would you pray about it? See if it's what God wants you to do."

Charles didn't know what to say. He hadn't told anyone he had resigned as headmaster from Silver Springs Academy, because he felt God was leading him in a different direction. He'd only been filling in until the new headmaster arrived when Professor Hall told him he was coming to see Josie. This would be a great place to wait upon the Lord.

"I can give you my answer now, Gabe. I would love to stay! I don't want to be a burden to you and Josie though. I'd like to move in with the professor."

"Are you sure Charles? I mean, you haven't prayed about this. It's a big decision to make so quickly."

"You've no idea what a blessing you've given me! I've been feeling, for sometime now, that God has been pulling me in a different direction in my life. I'd already resigned from my position at the academy before I found out Professor Hall was coming here. It just all fell together, so I came with him. As for praying, Gabe, I've been praying for months!"

"Don'tcha loves it when de plans cum together?" Caleb asked grinning.

"Indeed I do!" Gabe exclaimed happily.

"Let's go tell Josie and the professor it's a done deal!" Charles said excitedly.

Gabe and Charles found Professor Hall and Josie happily talking in the sewing room. Gabe could tell how happy she was at knowing her father would be staying from the way she glowed. When Charles informed them he would be staying too, Gabe thought Josie was going to cry. She stood and threw her arms around Charles in a big hug. "Now my family is all together. We're one big team for God!"

Professor Hall and Charles moved into the house with only those things they brought with them. Though they'd sent for their other things, it would be a couple of months if not longer, before they arrived. Hannah offered to be their housekeeper much to Charles' delight. Ben asked Jonah and May to move with them because it wasn't proper for Hannah to be alone with the men. Jonah would be needed when the soldiers arrived, and May would help with the cooking and cleaning. Gabe agreed with him. Josie and Liza went through the kitchen gathering things Hannah needed until they could go to town to buy her new ones.

"Hannah, ifin there be trouble, ya getcha self here fast!" Liza told her.

"Yez, ma'am, I's be lookin out fer it," Hannah promised.

"If this is too much for you, let us know. We can get you some help," Josie offered as she helped pack extra dishes.

"I's be tellin ya ifin it's so," Hannah promised again.

"I's be ridin over wid ya ta see what's be needin fo the rest of the house. Might be we's can move sum of de hurt men over soon. Dey be getting restless," Liza said.

"That's a good idea. The ones that can be moved should be. That way they'll be able to join the other soldiers, and move out when Sanders comes."

"Miz Josie, I's be thinkin dat three of'em can move, but dey aint healed enough ta go warin," Liza said showing concern.

"We can let Lieutenant Sanders know, and he can decide what to do," Josie suggested. The women agreed.

Gabe and Ben were walking toward the house for their lunch, when they saw Little John running towards them. "Dey's be a rider comin, Mr. Gabe. It be Mr. Allen!" Gabe could tell by the expression on Little Johns face he was scared.

"It's okay Little John, you go on home; I'll see what Mr. Allen wants."

"Eli ran ta de house ta tell the Missus," Little John explained.

"I'll send Eli home as soon as I get to the house. You go on now and don't worry."

"Yez sah!" Little John said as he turned and ran towards home.

"This is all I need. What could that man possibly want now?" Gabe said sighing.

"He jus bein nosey, dat's all," Ben told him grinning.

"Mr. Allen! What brings you here?" Gabe asked trying hard to be polite.

"I just thought I'd ride over and see how you were doing. I haven't seen you in town in a long time."

"We've been busy here and just haven't had the time. But, it's nice of you to come by. Why don't you come in and have some lemonade?" Gabe asked hoping the man would decline, but knew he wouldn't.

"Well, that's mighty fine of you! I sure would love something to drink." He dismounted his horse quickly.

"I's go an tell Liza," Ben said, trying not to show his amusement, then left quickly.

"Your place sure is nice! You've done a lot of work on it since I was here last. Your crops look good in the fields too," Mr. Allen stated as they walked to the house.

"We've been working hard."

"I heard you bought Broussard's old place" Mr. Allen said bluntly, as they entered Gabe's study.

"Yes, I did."

"You don't have many slaves on this plantation, how you going to tend to the other?"

"Well my father-in-law is here as you know, and he's living there now."

"Oh, so you bought it for your father in law? How nice of you! He sure has a fancy slave. Fontenot told me your father-in-law comes from a rich family," Mr. Allen said as he took his drink from the tray Liza offered.

Taking a minute to let that sink in, Gabe looked at Liza and asked, "Is Eli in the kitchen?"

"Yez sah," Liza answered, making a face that almost made Gabe laugh out loud.

"Would you send him to Big John for me?" Gabe asked, trying to look in control.

"Yez sah," Liza said as she turned and left the room.

"How's Judah working out for you?" Gabe asked changing the subject.

"He's a stubborn horse, you know! I haven't ridden him in a long time. Why? Would you want to buy him back?" Allen asked too quickly.

"I could be interested in buying him back. How much would you want for him?" Gabe felt he'd had this conversation before with this man.

"We could swap back what was traded initially. I'll take Little John for him."

Hearing a soft cry from the doorway, both men turned to see Josie standing with her hand over her mouth. She looked as if she was going to cry.

"Gabe, don't you dare trade Little John! He's been with me since the day I arrived here! He helps me so much and… I won't be without… him!"

"There, there Mrs. Lyon, I wouldn't think of taking Little John away from you. I'm sorry to have even brought it up." Mr. Allen stood quickly.

Gabe was amazed at how Josie just turned this difficult situation around. Josie was putting on a show for Mr. Allen!

"I need to be going now," Mr. Allen headed for the door and Gabe walked with him outside.

"I'm sorry I upset your wife. I forgot, you're expecting your first child. I remember how my wife was when she had our children. I sure feel sorry for you. How about we talk about the horse later, when you come into town?"

"That's a good idea. Thank you, Mr. Allen."

"If you need anything, just send one of your slaves and let me know."

"Oh, wait just a minute. I'm wondering if you can do me a favor," Gabe asked.

"Sure, if I can," Mr. Allen said with a nervous smile.

"My father-in-law hired some men to do repairs, remodel his house and to build some barns. If they come into town, the first place people come to is your place for directions. Would you send them out this way? Of course, if they need a ride out here, we'd be more than happy to pay for it."

"Why sure, be glad to do it. Why isn't he buying any slaves for that?" Mr. Allen asked.

"He doesn't have any place to put slaves right now. He wants to get everything in order before buying any. He has a certain way he does things, and that's how it has to be."

"He does things all fancy like, doesn't he, of course, I'm just judging by the way he dresses his slave. It must be nice to have that much family money. You were wise marrying Mrs. Lyon. One day all his money will be yours!"

"Thank you Mr. Allen, we'll talk about Judah soon!"

Mr. Allen nodded, turned his horse, and headed down the drive.

Lieutenant Sanders showed up at New Canaan just before dusk. What a busy day! Gabe thought as he led him into the study.

"How've you been Lieutenant?"

"I'm fine, just tired. It seems this traveling will never end."

"I sure don't envy you; I know it must be hard," replied Gabe.

"It is. Anyway, what I've come for is to let you know the first soldiers will be arriving in three days time, all by different trains."

"Are you going to be here when they do?" Gabe asked.

"Yes, I have to be here for the last meeting with General Grant. I'll be getting new orders."

"When's the meeting?" Gabe inquired.

"Tomorrow night, General Grant should be arriving then. I've told them we would be meeting at the other house. Jonah and I've already talked, and it seems he has everything under control there."

"Good, I'm glad you've got everything organized." Gabe was relived.

"I'm going to tell you something, it's only my thoughts, not a fact. I believe the war is going to be on your front doorstep soon, but that's just from the information I've gotten from our sources. I thought you should know."

"We'll just have to pray, Lieutenant. It's about all we can do now."

"I know. I just want you to be prepared. You might want to have your wife moved to a safer place."

"She wouldn't leave even if the President asked her. My wife is stubborn, Lieutenant, and I wouldn't have her any other way," Gabe said chuckling.

"One day, I hope to meet someone just like her. She isn't afraid of anything! I see how she always stands by you in whatever decisions you make."

"The secret of our marriage is, we put God first," Gabe informed him.

"That's how I want it to be with me, too."

"You're a Christian?" Gabe asked.

"Yes sir, since I was a boy. How else do you think I've survived crossing enemy territory like I have? I've been hidden in Christ!"

"You mean, you go to other places besides here?"

"Yes sir, I gotta tell you, you've been an answer to my prayers! You don't understand how nice it was the first night I slept here. It was wonderful to sleep in safety! I know now I have a place to go should I need it at anytime."

"I'm glad God has allowed us to be here for you, Lieutenant Sanders. It makes this whole messy business worthwhile."

Charles was like a love sick puppy! All he could do was follow Hannah through the house, asking if he could help her. Hannah liked the handsome young man very much, but he was getting in her way. She didn't know if she should talk with the Missus or her mother. Something had to be done!

There was just too much to do right now. It's not that she didn't like the attention, she did, but too many things relied on what she had to do today.

Seeing Professor Hall in the parlor, Hannah decided she would talk to him.

"Excuse me sah, I's be needin to talk wid ya a minute. Does ya have de time?"

"Most Certainly, Hannah, come and have a seat." Professor Hall motioned to a nearby chair.

"Thank ya sah, I's won't be long, but dar be a problem, I be thinkin ya can help me wid."

"What would that be?"

"It be bout Mr. Charles, sah. I think he be right nice and helpful, but today he be gettin under foot. Could ya jus see'd ifin ya can give him somethin ta do fer a while? Jus till I's get my work done?"

Her request brought a rumble of laughter from Professor Hall. Looking at her he said, "I think he's smitten with you Miss Hannah. He doesn't mean to get in the way."

"Wid me?" She asked in surprise.

"Yes, with you! I'll give him some task to do to keep him out of your way for awhile. I really shouldn't have laughed, but I've been wondering if you noticed how much he likes you."

"I's knowd that he be mighty helpful, but I's surely not guess he be smitten!" She said blushing.

"Well, now you know. Don't you dare tell him I've told you! He wants to tell you himself."

"I not say a word sah, jus don't ya tell him I's asked ya ta keep him from underfoot!"

"Not to worry, it'll be our secret," Professor Hall assured her laughing.

"This was going to be fun to watch develop," the professor thought as Hannah left the room. He could see she was as taken with Charles as Charles was with her. Today Hannah needed his help in keeping Charles out of the way for the big meeting tonight, but tomorrow was different!

Jonah and Lieutenant Sanders were in their hiding places as the sun went down over the bayou. It was a beautiful sight to watch as the sky filled with yellows and reds, as the sun set then darkened with the night. The full moon and the glistening stars filled the sky, as the bayou night air rang with the music only nature makes. It would have been a perfect night just to sit, and enjoy what God had made; if it hadn't been for the fact they were there to meet General Grant and his men. Both men kept a watchful eye on the water, waiting for the first sounds or sights of the boats coming in. This was a new meeting point for the Union Army, and Lieutenant Sanders was nervous. Though it had been easier for them to come this way, it hadn't been tested in advance, and left him uneasy. Too much was at stake.

The boats came in through the night by the light of a full moon. When they had reached the shore, Lieutenant Sanders stepped from his hiding place, and without a word, gave the signal for the men to follow him. Jonah remained hidden until after the last man fell in behind Lieutenant Sanders. Then, he slipped out to make sure they hadn't been followed.

Josie laughed at Gabe as he tried to tie the tiny bootie she'd just finished.

"My hands are too big!" Gabe complained.

"You'll get use to it by the time the baby outgrows them," she informed him.

"I don't know. If the size of this bootie has anything to do with the size of the baby, I might have to wait until he's grown some before I hold him!"

"He'll be little, but his feet are tiny. You'll do just fine. Are you going to the meeting tonight?"

"Yes, I should be leaving now. I think this will be the last meeting for awhile. Will you be okay while I'm gone?"

"Of course, I have Liza here, and you're only a mile or so away should I need anything. I've been thinking, we should come up with a name for the other house. What do you think?" She asked.

"Sounds like a good idea to me. I'll have to ask your father and Charles if they have any ideas."

"We can do that tomorrow. You be careful tonight and don't stay too long."

"Why? Are you feeling bad?"

"No silly, I'm just tired and I don't like sleeping by myself!"

"I'll be back as soon as I can," he told her, "I'll probably be back before you're asleep."

The ride to the other house was quick and easy, more time went into saddling up the horse than the trip there. "Next time I'll walk," Gabe thought to himself as he went up to the door. Not bothering to knock, he let himself in knowing his arrival had already been noticed. He found Professor Hall and General Grant talking in the library.

"Gabe, I'm glad you're here. We've been waiting on you," Professor Hall said.

"Hello Professor. Nice to see you again, General," Gabe shook Grants hand. "I think we should join the others, and get this meeting started."

"I'm staying out here with Professor Hall, Mr. Lyon. I already know what this meeting is all about, and they don't need me. They already have their orders. But, go ahead and join them. They want some input from you," General Grant informed him.

"Very well, I'll join you afterward." Gabe left the library and made his way to the meeting room.

"Would you care to have a seat?" Professor Hall asked the General.

"Thank you. That would be nice," he said as he sat down. "You're a lucky man professor!"

"Whys that?"

"You're here with your family. I miss mine very much."

"I'm sure you do. You're away a lot, aren't you?"

"Yes I am, too much so I'm afraid. I hate it! I miss my wife, Julia, very much. I know being a General you wouldn't think I would, or at the very least, I'd be used to it. But I'm not; she's the love of my life."

"I know what you mean. When my wife passed away, I thought I'd never get over it. If it hadn't been for Josie, I don't know what I would've done. It's hard, because it leaves such a void in your life."

"That's what I feel, a big void. I don't believe I'll ever get use to it," replied Grant.

"I hope you don't, sir. Not many people find the love of their life, but I believe you and I did," Professor Hall said mostly to himself.

The men continued talking while the meeting upstairs carried on.

Gabe couldn't understand why he'd been needed at the meeting tonight. Other than informing them he wanted Lieutenant Sanders at New Canaan to organize the movement of the soldiers, he couldn't think of any reason. He'd even paid special attention to where the Confederate army was located, noting they weren't close enough to New Canaan to worry just yet. The soldiers hadn't shard much information with him, and that bothered him.

He was tired, yet restless, as he climb into bed next to his sleeping Josie. Quietly saying his prayers, he closed his eyes and was asleep within minutes.

The last two days had been hard on everyone. You could cut the tension in the air as they waited for the first soldiers to arrive from the train station. They began to come in at noon. First it had been two, and then three came, and so on, until all ten were at New Canaan. Lieutenant Sanders waited till nightfall to move the new soldiers over to the other house, along with the few wounded who were well enough to join their troop. It was a busy place, but so far no one from town had asked any questions, or paid any visits.

"We need to come up with a name for this place," Gabe said as he and Professor Hall walked to the back of the house. Gabe wanted to see how Lieutenant Sanders was organizing the men.

"It would be nice to have something to call it other than, "the other house." Have you any ideas?" Professor Hall asked.

"No, how about you?"

"I've been thinking about it, and I think Mount Haven would be a great name, after all it is a refuge. What do you think?"

"I think it's great! From now on that's what we'll call it. I can't wait to tell Josie!"

Charles went looking for Hannah. He hadn't seen her all day, and he was worried she was working too hard. He hoped today he would be able to tell her how he felt about her. He had tried a couple of times before, but her beauty had taken his breath away. The way she smiled at him made his stomach flip, and he couldn't say a word except for some nonsense. "She must think I'm crazy!" he thought as he found himself in the kitchen. But she wasn't there. Continuing his search through the house, he found her changing bandages. He watched her as she worked on a young soldier who wanted to join the rest of his troop. She was giving him words of encouragement, telling him that soon he would be able to be alongside the others. Charles wished he could talk with Hannah as easily as the young soldiers did. "Can I help in anyway?" Charles asked.

Turning toward him, Hannah smiled. "No, we's be done here." Then she turned back to the young soldier and said, "Jus another day or so an yo be just fine." Then she stood to her feet, and gathered her things and walked toward Charles.

"Don't ya be tellin me ya be hungry again!" She said smiling,

"No, I'm not hungry, but I would like to talk to you, if you have the time. I don't want to take you away from anything important."

"Walk wid me whilst I put thangs up, an we's can talk."

As they walked down the hall, away from the young soldier's room, Charles could feel his heart beating in his chest. It was now or never! So, taking a deep breath he began, "Hannah, I've been waiting to talk to you for some time now, and never seemed to find the right time or place to do it."

Hannah smiled to herself, maybe now he would let her know how he felt about her. "Whatcha been wantin to say?" She asked.

"Well, Hannah, I don't know any other way to say this but out right. I really like you, and I want to know if you're seeing anyone right now." Then he winced as he realized he had said he really liked her, when in fact he wanted to tell her he loved her.

"No, Mr. Charles, I's aint seein no one. I's really like ya too. Are ya asking we's be friends? She smiled sweetly at him, loving the way he was squirming.

"No... Yes... I want us to be friends, but I'd like for us to be more than friends, Hannah. But if you just want to be friends, it would be okay with me," Charles said with defeat in his voice.

Hannah came to a quick stop and turned to face Charles. "Now ifin ya be askin me ifin ya can court me, my answer be yes. But ya need ta be askin my paw," she said, then turned leaving a happy Charles standing by himself.

"Oh no! I've got to talk with her father. I've never done that before!" Charles said out loud. Hearing a chuckle, Charles turned toward the sound to find the young soldier laughing at him. Apparently the young man had witnessed the whole conversation.

"It's really easy," the young soldier said, "All you have to do is ask her father if you can court her. He will give you a hard time about it if he likes you, and then say yes. If he doesn't like you, he'll say no right off."

"Sounds like you've done this before," Charles said embarrassed. Smiling, the young man shook his head yes, and went back to his room, leaving Charles alone to think about what he had to do.

Charles wasn't one to let things wait. As evening approached, he knew Hannah's father, Ben, would be at the house at New Canaan. He decided that walking over would give him time to prepare what he wanted to say to Ben. He played the conversation over and over in his mind as he went. He hoped by the time he arrived at New Canaan, he'd know what he was going to say. But it didn't work. The closer he got, the worse he sounded to himself. How in the world did Gabe do this with Professor Hall? He should've asked Gabe before he left. But then again, he hadn't wanted anyone to know before asking Ben.

Going to the kitchen door, he knocked. Liza greeted him when she opened it. "Mr. Charles, why ya be a knockin? Come on in here. Mr. Gabe be at your place."

"I know Miss Liza. I've come to talk with you and Ben if you have the time now."

"Anythang wrong?"

"No ma'am."

Liza stood back and looked closely at Charles. He appeared as nervous as a long tailed cat in a room full of rocking chairs. Walking over to the door, she called Ben. "Have a seat Mr. Charles. Ben be here in jus a minute."

Taking his seat Charles said, "Please call me Charles. We're all friends here."

"I's be morin glad ta." Liza smiled, still not sure why Charles wanted to talk with her and Ben.

"Mr. Charles, you be needin something?" Ben asked as Charles stood and shook his hand.

"Yes sir. I need to speak with you about something that's important to me."

"What can I be helpin ya with?"

"Well sir, I've come to ask you if...... well, would it be alright with you....

Well could I..." Charles started.

"Jus say it boy! What be wrong wid ya?" Ben asked.

"Nothings wrong sir, I just wanted to ask you if I could court Hannah?!" There, he'd said it. Actually, he just blurted it out! Things weren't going as he"d planned.

Ben just sat there with a surprised look on his face. He hadn't seen this one coming, but he reckoned not many fathers did. Charles watched the expressions on Ben's face change from surprise to seriousness in a matter of seconds. Quickly Charles looked over at Liza about the same time Ben did. He couldn't read what Liza was thinking. She didn't show any signs of being happy or unhappy. Quickly Charles looked back at Ben who was still looking at Liza. Then Ben looked back at Charles and said, "Ya be wantin ta court my Hannah?"

"Yes sir."

"What be ya intentions?"

"Why, I want us to get to know each other. I'm hoping she'll come to love me as I love her."

"Ya love my Hannah?"

"Yes sir, from the time I first saw her."

"She knowd ya love her?"

"I haven't told her yet, but I did ask her if I could court her, and she said yes, but I'd have to get permission first."

"She be a good girl, an fears the Lord! Does you?"

"Yes sir, I love the Lord, and I'm a Christian. I would make her a good husband."

"Ya be takin her up north anytime?" Ben interrogated him.

"I don't believe so. I feel God wants me here. He just hasn't told me why yet. But I do know that one reason was so I could meet Hannah."

"Ifin ya court her, it be done proper. Jus cause ya be over at the other house wid her don't mean ya haves liberties. Understand?"

"Yes sir. It'll be done proper, I promise you. So may I court her?"

Ben waited a few minutes as if he were thinking before he answered. "Yez, ya can, but proper like, an we's see'd ifin she learn ta love yo as ya say ya love her."

"Thank you!" Charles stood to his feet, grabbing Ben's hand shaking it. Then he turned to a smiling Liza and kissed her on the cheek, saying his good byes to hurry and tell Hannah. After he left, Liza and Ben hugged each other laughing at how excited Charles was when he was given permission. "De Lord always provides!" Liza told Ben, who could only nod while he laughed.

Josie thought Mount Haven was a good name for the new plantation. She liked it very much. Only time would tell if it would live up to it's name.

Liza and Ben agreed with her and prayed for Gods blessing. Josie and Liza thought they should have a party and dedication for Mount Haven. Gabe and Professor Hall agreed. As soon as the renovations were complete, they would do just that.

The days passed quickly with all the work that was being done to Mount Haven. The tents in the back became a permanent sight to anyone who passed bye, or got close enough to see them. All the while, Union soldiers moved back and forth in secrecy. Strategies for battles were made, and messages sent back and forth to the leaders of the army. All this was done while barns were being built, according to plan.

Soon all the renovations would be complete, but that didn't bother Lieutenant Sanders or Gabe. Slave quarters needed to be built to fool the public and buy them more time. When they were completed, God would show them something else to do. After all, he'd seen them through a lot already. Gabe and Lieutenant Sanders knew God wouldn't let them down.

The day the last barn was completed the soldiers moved inside the barn nearest to the bayou. It was a day of celebration. Liza and Josie had decided they would have a big dinner and everyone was invited.

"Does ya think maybe ya shud lie down fer a spell, Josie girl?" Liza asked as she and Josie worked in the kitchen.

"I feel just fine. As a matter of fact, I haven't had this much energy in months!"

Liza just smiled at her. "That's why ya need ta be restin some."

"Oh Liza, I need to help you. After all, tomorrow will be our dedication for Mount Haven."

"I's done asked Delia and de others ta help. Dey be cookin too. We's got us a powerful lot to cook for by tomorrow. Ya go ahead on, and lays down fo a spell. I's call ya ifin ya be needed."

"I don't want to sleep long Liza. Would you wake me in an hour?"

"I's be goin ta see'd ifin Hannah be needin help settin thangs up at de new place. When I's get back, I's will."

"Let me know how things are progressing with Charles and Hannah when you do. I've never seen Charles so much in love!"

"I's tell, ya dey both be love sick puppies! Liza said laughingly. Josie laughed with her as she left to go to her room.

Professor Hall was so excited about the dedication of Mount Haven. He had a surprise himself! No one knew about it but him, and he was going to keep it that way. Even if he told Charles, he doubted if he would even remember. Charles was so much in love with Hannah, he couldn't do anything but talk about her." Professor Hall shuffled his papers, placed them back into the desk, and locked it. Grinning to himself, he went to see what he could do to help with tomorrow's party.

Josie was lying on her bed trying to go to sleep, but was unable to do so. She found when she lied down her mind went into a whirlwind of activity.

She began to think of things that had been done, and things that needed to be done, for the school. Right now all was well, but soon the summer break would be over, and another school year would begin in a month. Emlee had been a blessing. Josie believed she'd always think of Emlee and blessing as being the same word. That was how much Emlee had helped. Why, even this summer Emlee had arranged to have classes, and the children loved it. Each area of the plantation had been taught to the children, from taking care of the animals, carpentry, sewing and cooking. The adults loved it as much as the children did. Even Big John showed the boys how to build bird houses. The older boys, after chores, were being supervised by him in building a cabin. So far it was going well. "Thank you Lord," Josie said as she closed her eyes.

The morning dawned with lots of activity between the two plantations. Tables were set up while the hired hands and soldiers worked side by side. Everyone was excited and it showed. Gabe walked with Ben, trying to decide where they should start building houses for the imaginary slaves. It made both Ben and Gabe laugh when they talked about it. If they had to, they could always rely on Liza's stain, and paint every white soldier that came through there.

"I's be thinkin dat we's build em over by de edge of de woods, Mr. Gabe. Dat ways dey be easy ta come, and easy ta go ifin dey had ta."

"You know what? You're right Ben. It's just a little further from the house than where the old one's stood. It would be protection just outside their door if they needed it."

"Does ya think de war be comin our way?" Ben asked seriously.

"We've been blessed so far Ben, with it being all around us. But yes, I think we'll be seeing it soon. Lieutenant Sanders left me a map where all the battles are being fought. It looks like it could be a matter of weeks before it'll be here."

"Erya scared?" Ben asked.

"No, not scared so much, I'm just worried with the baby coming next month. I know we've done all we can do to be ready, and I believe we are. How about you? Are you scared?" Gabe asked.

"Naw sir, not me. De Lord be with us. I's grateful when He took ya paw dat He gave us you and Miz Josie. I's knowd ya be listenin to Him, and ya prays afore we's does sumthin. Sumtimes I's see'd ya walkin and talkin ta de Lord. We's all have, and we's knowd dat ya be a listenin ta Him fo de answer. Yez Mr. Gabe, I's be proud of ya so would ya pa ifin he could see'd whatcha be a doin here."

"Why thank you, Ben. You've no idea how I needed to hear that!"

"We's be prayin fo ya, Mr. Gabe. Ya gots lots ta think on," Ben assured him.

"Do you really think my father would be proud of me?" Gabe asked uncertainly. " After all he was a slave owner."

"De massa not knowd any different. He jus done what his pa done. Tis all he knowd. I's believe de Lord let my Liza raise ya so ya could see'd peoples are jus peoples. Makes no difference what color de skin be! Ya loved my Liza jus like ya love a Ma, didn't ya?"

"Yes sir, I sure did, and still do. I can only imagine what kind of person I would've been if it hadn't been for her. Then you, why I believe if you hadn't taken me out behind that old woodshed and given me a good talking to as many times as you did, I'd been some kind of a brat!" Gabe told him laughing.

"Ya never told a body about it, and dat showed me ya knowd I's done it fo ya own good!"

"I've learned a lot from you and Liza. I just thank you for being there to raise me the right way."

"Ifin ya tellin me I's did good, no need. I's see'd de man ya are, and dats morin enough fo me!"

Gabe was surprised! It meant a lot to him for this man to say he was proud of him. It was something he'd treasure until his dying day.

The morning passed quickly, and the time had come to bring everyone to the tables for the dedication. It was a perfect afternoon. The wind was blowing and the heat didn't seem so bad. It sure was a good idea to place the tables under the big shade trees, Gabe thought, as he looked upon all the smiling faces that helped make this a special day. Gabe stood and looked out over his family. There were so many God had placed in his trust. Soon they would all spread their wings as children do, and go off on their own. He truly believed that day would be as hard on him as any father whose children grow up and leave.

"Today we dedicate this plantation to God," Gabe began. "Please bow your heads for prayer. Lord, we ask that you bless everyone here today. Keep them safe and sound as they work or fight battles. We ask that you bless Mount Haven as you have New Canaan with many friends and new family members. We dedicate Mount Haven to You, for Your work to be done in any way You see fit. Lead us and guide us as we go about Your business. We all know that no job is too big or small. Both are equally important to You, and we can rely on You to help us. I ask You to bless this food we are about to receive in the Name of Jesus, amen."

Gabe then raised his glass and said, "To Mount Haven!" Everyone did the same and shouts went up from the crowd. After everyone settled down, Professor Hall stood saying, "I have something I want to say. I want to thank you all for allowing me and Charles to become a member of this big family. We both love being here. Well... Charles really loves being here!" This caused a roar of laughter to go through the crowd. It seemed everyone knew about Charles and Hannah.

"Gabe, Amherst has asked me to present you with your diploma of Theology. They feel what you have accomplished here has more than made up for the days you missed at the time of your fathers illness. Congratulations! This may be a dedication, but it's also your graduation."

Gabe's heart was full as he accepted the diploma from Professor Hall. There in bold letters was his name. Until this very moment he hadn't realized how much it meant to him. Taking a moment to regain his composure, he said, "Thank you Professor Hall, I don't know what to say." Then looking out over the crowd added. "You don't need a diploma to do what God calls you to do. There is something about a diploma that makes you want to work harder. I'm so glad I've been able to share this moment with all of you."

Before he could say anymore, Josie stood and went to her husband's side, giving him a kiss she whispered in Gabe's ear, "Where's Liza?"

"She's sitting beside Ben over there. Why?"

"I have to go home, now! You're about to become a father."

Gabe jumped into action, taking Josie by the arm and looking at Professor Hall saying, "Get Liza and come to the house quickly. Josie's having the baby!"

Gabe stood outside the door of his bedroom pacing and praying. Josie had been in labor for hours. The baby wasn't due for another month, and that had him worried. All he could hear from behind the closed doors was Liza's voice giving orders to Hannah, and an occasional cry from Josie.

He just wished Liza would come out and tell him how things were going. He needed to know something! As soon as the thought went through his head, the door opened. Hannah hurried out, trying not to look at Gabe.

Gabe stopped her and said, "What's going on? Is everything all right?

"Maw be out ta talk wid ya," Hannah answered and hurried down the stairs.

Gabe was beside himself with worry. He knew for Hannah to say her mother would be out to talk with him, meant something was wrong! Professor Hall and Charles had left hours ago to go pray. He didn't know what he would do if Josie were to die. She was the love of his life. How does one live without the one they love? His father had done it, but he had become a lonely old man in the process. Professor Hall had done it, but he had Josie to fill his void. All he knew to do was pray, and so he continued his prayers until the door opened and Liza stepped out. Gabe could tell by her countenance she was concerned. Hurrying toward her, he asked, "Liza, please tell me what's happening. I need to know the truth! He could still hear Josie's soft crying behind the door.

"It be a hard birth, I won't lie ta ya Mr. Gabe. I's be doin all I's can now. De baby aint turned right and he be early. We need de help of de Lord. Pray Mr. Gabe, just pray!" Liza then turned and went back into the room.

Gabe fell to his knees and bowed his head and prayed, "Lord, please don't leave me now. I ask you to bring both my wife and child through this trial. It is so important to me this baby know his mother and for Josie to know her child. Please Lord, please be with Josie and baby William. Bring them through this safe and sound." Once again, he began to pray silently to himself, remaining on his knees. He didn't know how long he had been praying, when he felt a touch on his shoulder. Lifting his head, he saw Michael, the angel, standing in front of him. Quickly rising to his feet, Gabe said, "Michael, you're not here to take Josie are you? Please ask God not to take my Josie or my baby." The emotions he held back for so long ripped thru him as he poured out his petition for his wife and child's life.

"Fear not Gabriel Lyon, for the Lord has heard your cry! *I say to you, that if two of you agree on earth about anything that they may ask, it shall be done for them by My Father who is in heaven.* The Lord says to you Gabriel, *"For where two or three have gathered together in My name, I am there in their midst."* Fear not! Your family prays for your wife and child as I speak. The church in the wood is filled with the prayers of the Saints. The encampment of the soldiers sing God's praises. Your home is on Holy ground Gabriel Lyon, remove your shoes!"

Gabe quickly removed his shoes. As he stood again, the room glowed with the brilliance of the presence of angels. One by one they slipped through the closed door, to be with Josie in her room. Gabe fell on his knees again, and began to thank the Lord for saving his wife and child. Tears flowed along with his praises. Michael never left Gabe's side as the Lord God Almighty's presence filled the house. Even Michael bowed to his knee. Gabe felt it as surely as he felt Michael at his side. Gabe had no idea how long they had remained on their knees, but he knew when he heard the baby cry. Quickly jumping to his feet, he ran to the door and opened it. There stood Liza, holding the smallest baby he had ever seen.

"It be a miracle from the Lord, Mr. Gabe! Dis babe turned and be born lickity split! He be jus fine and so be my Josie girl!"

Gabe ran to Josie's bed side, and took her in his arms, kissing her and thanking God for their miracle. Gabe never noticed when Michael or the other Angels left, all he could do was thank God and hold tightly to Josie and his son.

CHAPTER 11

LIZA LEFT JOSIE AND GABE alone with the baby while she went to find Ben. She ran as fast as she could for a woman of fifty something, across the back lawn, then the cotton field toward the church in the woods. She knew they would all still be there waiting to hear about the baby. Reaching the church, she stopped to regain her breath, then went inside. All eyes were upon her when she entered. "De babe be a boy!" She announced to everyone. "An he be jus fine!" People jumped out of their seats and began shouting, thank you Lord and clapping their hands.

"Big John, I be needin ta talk wid ya fer a minute," Liza said after she found him in the crowd.

"Yez ma'am?" Big John asked, as he made his way toward her.

"I's be needin ya ta help. De babe be small and afore his time. I's need ya ta make him a special bed." Taking a piece of chalk from one of the nearby seats and a slate, she drew Big John a picture of what she needed, while explaining at the same time. "It be needin ta be small wid de sides whole. De bottom needs ta be big enough ta place a warm brick inside ta keep de babe warm, but somethin ta cover de brick so's de babe don't get burnt."

Big John studied the drawing while listening. "I's can do it! When ya be a needin it?"

"The babe be needin it now! How long ya think it be afore ya have it?" She asked.

"I's be getting rite to it!" He said, as he turned and hurried on his way.

Liza then turned to Ben and said, "I's done fergot ta tell de Professor de babe be born! I's best be gettin back. Ya comin wid me?"

175

"I's be right along, ya jus gos. I be wantin ta see ifin Big John be needin help first." Ben told her.

Liza walked back to the house quickly, stopping briefly to ask Caleb to go to Mount Haven to let them know the baby had been born.

Professor Hall and Charles had already reached New Canaan. They heard the baby cries and ran upstairs to Josie's room. Knocking on the door they let themselves in.

"Here's your grandson father," Josie said as she held the baby out for him to see.

Taking him gently into his arms, Professor Hall began to bless his grandson.

"The Lord will always be with you. He will always have His hand upon your life. You will be a mighty man for Him and will find favor in His sight as He will find favor in your sight." Then he kissed his grandson on his head and passed him to Charles. At first Charles didn't know what to do with him. He just stood there holding him awkwardly, but smiling.

"You better get use to it Charles!" Gabe told him. "Soon you'll be having your own family."

"If Hannah will agree to marry me, I hope so," Charles said as he quickly handed the baby back to Josie. "I'm thankful all went well," Charles said to Josie. "I think I'll go now. I just had to see you were all right."

"Thank you Charles, for all your prayers," Josie told him smiling.

"Anytime, just remember to return the favor," he said smiling as he backed his way out of the room to leave.

The next thing that happened was Liza, like a mother hen protecting her chicks, she shooed everyone, including Gabe, out of the room.

"Liza, Will won't nurse!" Josie exclaimed with worry in her voice. "What are we going to do?"

"There be ways, now, don't be worrin jus yet. He be born early an he's needin ta learn. Ifin he don't, I's send Mr. Gabe ta get a babe bottle from de general store. We's be needin ta gives him time."

"He has to eat something. I can't stand the thought if he's hungry!" Josie was almost in tears.

"I be sending Mr. Gabe ta get de bottle now, but we's not use it lessin we be needin ta. Okay?"

"Okay, that'll make me feel better. Would you go ask Gabe to get it now?"

"Yez ma'am, then I's be back."

Liza found Gabe and Jonah talking in the study. Jonah, like his father, had morning meetings with Gabe to bring him up to date on the activities that were going on at Mount Haven.

Liza stood at the open door and said, "excuse me Mr. Gabe, but I be needin ya to go ta Hebert's General Store ta get the babe a bottle. He be havin trouble with nursing and the bottle will give Miz Josie peace of mind. Does ya think ya could go soon?"

"Of course Liza, I'll go now!"

"Wouldcha care fer company Mr. Gabe?" Jonah asked.

"That would be great; we can finish our meeting on the road. Let's walk to the barn and see if Caleb can saddle us a couple of horses."

As Gabe and Jonah rode toward town, they talked about their concerns for the safety of New Canaan as the battles were coming closer to home.

"I's been watching and listening ta de soldiers Mr. Gabe, and I's be fearin we aint gona be ready for the fightin dat be comin our way!" Jonah had worry in his voice.

"How does one get ready to be surrounded by war and death Jonah? All we can do is pray and ask God for His protection. It's our faith that'll see us through. I believe we're here to help, as servants of God, He will be with us. If it's coming, it will come. All we can do, as I said before, is pray," Gabe said with more faith than he felt. As far as Gabe was concerned, he was calling things that be not, as though they were. It was one of the Bibles verse's he stood on. If the men of the Bible could do it, so could he!

"I's be prayin fo shur, but I's be watchin too!" Jonah said.

When Gabe and Jonah reached Hebert's General Store, Gabe went inside, but Jonah remained outside stating he had some errands to do. Agreeing to meet at the store, Jonah made his way toward the livery stable. He had noticed for sometime now, when he had come to town, that Mr. Allen always had company. Not that it was a bad thing, except these people weren't from around here. They always seemed to try to hide their faces from anyone who entered the livery stable. Jonah knew this from the many times he had to come to the livery for the plantations, and from the looks of things, Mr. Allen had more company today!

Quietly Jonah made his way behind the livery and through the back corral. He was grateful the horses were in their stables. Looking around for entry into the livery, Jonah saw the back door was opened, just enough for him to slip through. That was all he needed! Quickly Jonah looked around to see if anyone was watching, and then he raced toward the opened door. Once inside, he had to give his eyes time to adjust to the dim lighting of the livery. Quickly he ducked behind some bales of hay which just happened to be at the door. "If dat not be de Lord, I's don't know what is!" Jonah thought to himself. There he remained until his eyes adjusted.

Slowly he got up on his hands and knees lifting his head over the bales to see if anyone was there. Seeing no one there, he made his way quietly down the livery hall, staying close to the wall. Hearing voices coming from Mr. Allen's tact room, he stopped and listened. Jonah didn't recognize the person talking.

"We're going to be needing more horses soon Mr. Allen. How many can we get from you?" asked the unknown voice.

"Just depends on how many you need and when you need them. You've taken all I had except for the three I need. It's not easy to find good horses on such short notice. How much are you willing to pay for them?" Mr. Allen asked eagerly.

"You should be willing to give them to the Confederate Army. After all, we are fighting for your way of life as well as our own. If you can't supply us with them, do you know of anyone who could?" asked the unknown voice.

"We've got plenty of people around here that raise horses, but none finer than Gabe Lyon over at New Canaan Plantation. He's got some good horse flesh. I don't know if he would be willing to part with any of it. You see, he inherited the plantation from his father. His father was known for his horses.

"Do you think he would be willing to donate any to the cause?" He asked.

"I don't really know. You could go over there and ask if you want. I'm sure he'll talk with you. You should know, before his father died, he was away at school to become a preacher. He isn't one to take sides with war."

"You know I can't go and talk with the man myself! That's what I pay you for! After all, we can't trust anyone right now. You know me and my troops are here in secret. Everything we've done up to now depends on keeping it that way. All I need is for the Union to find out we have a camp on the back of your land! We'd never catch the Union soldiers passing through this way and you know it!"

"Now General, don't get upset. I'll go over there tomorrow and talk to him myself. You'd better get that telegram off if you're going to, and get back to my place before I have anymore customers come in. I don't think anyone believes we're cousins! You sure get nervous if anyone is around. It's bad for business. If we need to talk, come up to the house after I get home." Mr. Allen told him.

"I have to come to town sometimes, and you know it! I can't always wait for you to get home when something important comes up. You just talk with this Lyon fellow, and get back with me as soon as possible tomorrow. Don't come here to the livery. Come straight to the camp after you do! Is that understood, Mr. Allen?"

"Yes general, you've made it quite clear. I'll see Lyon in the morning."

Jonah couldn't believe what he'd just heard. He needed to get out of there as quickly as possible. Jonah made his way toward the back door praying the whole way, as he tried to be quiet, and hurry all at the same time. He could hear Mr. Allen and the general moving around and talking, but he was too far away to hear what they were saying. Just a few more steps and he would be at the door. Just as he neared the bale of hay at the doorway, the livery cat jumped out and ran in front him, causing Jonah to trip and fall. To him, it seemed as if he fell in slow motion, as he grabbed at anything to keep from falling. On his way down, he knocked over the shovel and a bucket hanging on the wall at the side of the door. The loud commotion caused Mr. Allen and the General to come running from the tact room, just in time to see Jonah stand to his feet. "Oh Lord, please help me," Jonah prayed quickly. As Mr. Allen approached Jonah, he yelled, "What are you doing here?"

"I's be Jonah sah, frum New Canaan. I's come ta bring de news dat de Massa's babe be born last night. Ya Missus be wantin to knowd." Jonah couldn't believe what had just come out of his mouth, though it did seem to put Mr. Allen and the General at ease.

"This is one of Gabe Lyon's slaves," Mr. Allen informed the man standing next to him with a wave of his hand.

Jonah knew this man was the General he had overheard talking to Mr. Allen. He was glad he had a face to go with the voice now. "Sah, I's also be comin bout de harness de Massa ordered. Be it ready?" Jonah asked innocently.

"Not for another week. I had to special order the leather. Tell your Master that it won't be much longer than that," Mr. Allen informed.

'Yez sah, I's tell him," Jonah said as he turned to leave, feeling his heart beating as if he'd run a mile.

"Wait a minute!" Mr. Allen said stopping Jonah.

"Yez sah?" He asked turning slightly to face him.

"Tell your Master I'll be paying him a visit tomorrow morning," Mr. Allen said sternly.

"Yez sah, be that all?"

"Yes, you go on now. Don't forget to deliver my message!"

Jonah didn't bother answering. He just hurried on his way to meet Gabe at Hebert's Store. He knew he was late already, and he would have to tell Gabe everything that had just happened.

Mr. Allen and the General were having their own conversation after Jonah left. "I can't believe how well Lyon dresses his slaves. Why he even had good shoes on! Do all Lyon's slaves dress this way?" The General asked.

"I don't know, never paid much attention to it. I was just over at his place a month or so ago. Just in the house. I haven't been out on the grounds in sometime. But what does it matter anyway? The man's father-in- law has got money! If you think that was well dressed for a slave, you should see the Professor's slave. He wears a suit! Don't say anything to Professor Hall about it though, he'll just tell you he has the money to do what he wants, and its nobodies business. Besides, what do you care? It's Lyon's horses you want."

"I guess I've never seen anything like it before. I know Adams does well by his slaves, but I figured he was the only one. Like you said, my only concern is the horses. Do you think the slave heard anything we were talking about?"

"You saw him; he just came thru the door! He couldn't have heard anything, besides, we were already finished. You know, if anyone gives you away, it's going to be you. You're too skittish!" Mr. Allen said as he turned to go to his office.

Gabe had spent too much time in the store. Mr. Hebert was full of questions and was way too slow at finding the baby bottle for him! If only the man would lose a few pounds, he might be able to move faster! Gabe thought as he listened to the endless dribble that poured out of Mr. Hebert's mouth. Gabe didn't even have to answer him. It wasn't as if Mr. Hebert was giving him time to anyway. After taking all the nonsense he could, Gabe said, "Mr. Hebert, if you don't have a baby bottle here, I'll just go find it somewhere else. I need that bottle now, not later."

"Here it is, here it is, Mr. Hebert said, still moving slowly. "Sorry it took so long to find. We just don't get many orders for baby bottles. Let me see now, the last time I had an order for a baby bottle was in….." Mr. Hebert started but was interrupted by Gabe. "I have to be going, just tell me how much I owe you for the bottle."

Mr. Hebert quoted the price and Gabe paid it. "I really have to be going now. My wife will be worried. Thank you for finding it for me," Gabe said as he hurried out the door.

Once outside Gabe looked for Jonah. " Where has he gotten off to?" Gabe thought as he looked up and down the street for him. Seeing Jonah coming across the street, Gabe mounted his horse and shouted to Jonah, "Let's go. We need to be getting back before Josie gets worried." Jonah ran the rest of the way to his horse and mounted. "Where have you been?" Gabe asked.

"I's be tellin ya soon as we's get down de road cuz, I's got some good news, and I's got bad news," Jonah told him as they rode out of town.

Gabe listened while Jonah told him about what happened during his visit to Mr. Allen's livery stable. Gabe couldn't believe the Confederate Army had a camp so close! If this was the good news he could only imagine the bad news. Waiting until Jonah had finished, Gabe asked, "So what's the bad news?

"Yo be having company come tomorrow mornin," Jonah told him grinning.

"Company? Who?" Gabe asked with concern showing on his face.

"Mr. Allen!" Jonah informed him. He wants your horses for the Confederate army. Then with a wave of his hand Jonah headed for Mount Haven while a confused Gabe turned into New Canaan.

Liza was tickled with the bed Big John had made for the baby. It was perfect. Little Will had been asleep now for three hours. He was nestled warmly among the soft blankets and the warming brick was in the false bottom of the bed. "So far so good," Liza thought, as she slipped out of the room leaving Josie and her baby sleeping soundly.

Gabe met Liza on the stairs. Seeing the smile on her face brought relief to his worried mind. "Don't ya go waken dem two up now! Let'em sleep tills they wake," Liza whispered to Gabe.

"I've brought the bottle. Do you think he'll have to use it?" Gabe asked with concern in his voice.

"Only ifin he don't learn ta suckle, then we be usin it. We's don't want him ta loose weight bein as he's be so small now. I's been prayin bout it and so you should be too," Liza took the bottle from Gabe. Looking it over closely she said, "Aint never thought we be needin one of these thangs."

"What are we going to put in the bottle if we need to use it?" Gabe inquired.

"I's done showd Miz Josie what ta do ifin we's gotta. Now don't be a worrin so. Ya be sleepin in de study tonight.

"Is that where you want me to sleep tonight?" Gabe asked.

"Yez, I's be stayin with Miz Josie and de babe. You be needin ta rest from de looks of thangs. Don't ya be fussin wid me, jus do it! Liza pointed a finger at him.

"Yes ma'am. You'll know where to find me if you need me," Gabe told her, then gave her a quick kiss on her cheek. He then turned and went down the stairs toward his study. He needed to do some praying.

Hannah and Charles sat in the kitchen of Mount Haven talking about the new addition to the family. "Little Will has a lot of people who love him," Charles said to Hannah.

"Yez and he don't even knowd it."

"Can you imagine? He's got aunts and uncles in all different ages, size and colors!" Charles said laughing as he sat down at the kitchen table.

"He be loved powerfully," Hannah said as she poured Charles and herself some lemonade.

"Have you ever thought about having a family?" Charles asked shyly.

"Yez, why?" Hannah asked.

"I've thought about it too. I'd like to have a big family. Would you like a big family? You know, lots of children?"

"Charles, why all dis talk of chil'lin?"

"I don't know. I guess seeing Gabe and Josie with Will. Did you know I got to hold him? Not waiting for an answer, Charles continued. "It's not just seeing them together; it's also being in love with you. Hannah, will you marry me?" Charles reached over and took her hand.

"Oh my yez, I love ya Charles."

Still holding her hand, Charles stood to his feet, pulling Hannah up from her chair to him. Taking her into his arms he kissed her softly, and then whispered how much he loved her.

Jonah had to wait until Jacob, Lieutenant Sanders, was alone to tell him what he learned. He wasn't sure what it meant to have the Confederates so close. One thing for sure, it meant change was coming. He knew it as sure as he knew his own name.

When Lieutenant Sanders was finally alone, Jonah approached him, "Jacob, I's gotcha some news ya be needin ta knowd."

"Hello Jonah. I'm sorry, I didn't hear you come up," Lieutenant Sanders said as he ran his hand over his face worriedly. "What have you got for me?"

"Last few times I's been ta town, I's see'd dat Mr. Allen be havin lots of company. Dey aint from around these parts, so's dis mornin when I's rode ta town wid Mr. Gabe, I's slipped on over ta de livery ta see what be goin on. Sur enough, Mr. Allen be havin company! I's heard him an a fella he be callin, general, talkin. Seems dis general and his men be staying on at Mr. Allen's place. Deys knowd datcha men be slipping back and forth, but des don't knowd when, where or how dey be doin it." Jonah informed him.

This information had Lieutenant Sander's attention. How could this have happened right under his nose without him knowing? He had let his guard down and he'd gotten too comfortable. "Do you know how long they've been there?"

"Naw and dey didn't say, but dat aint all. Mr. Allen be comin ta see Mr. Gabe tomorrow mornin bout horses. Deys be needin horses, and Mr. Allen gona ask Mr. Gabe ta help de cause by givin' em sum."

"I'll need to talk with Mr. Lyon then. Did this man have a uniform on?"

"Naw, he be dressed regular, nothin fancy like."

"You're sure they were Confederates?"

"Yez, I's sure Jacob. De man said that he not be wantin de Union ta finds out where dey be! He be payin Mr. Allen ta stay at his place, and ta get horses fer' em."

"Thank you Jonah! This is really important information. It tells me we need to get out and find these men."

"Whatcha gona be doing when ya fine's em?"

"Nothing right now, I just want to know where they are. I'd love to find out how long they've been over at Allen's place. You wouldn't know the layout of Mr. Allen's land, would you?" Lieutenant Sanders asked.

"Jus ya gives me a couple days and I's has it fer ya. Den I's take ya over and shows it ta ya."

"Good, that's a great idea. Just don't go and get yourself caught, Jonah."

"I's be quite as a mouse but smart as a fox. I's be leavin tonight."

"I'll be praying for you. You just be careful." Lieutenant Sanders said.

"I's be fine. Ya need ta see'd Mr. Gabe and tells him what I's be doin."

"I will, you best get some rest before you leave tonight. I'll see you when you get back."

Jonah nodded in agreement, and smiled as he waved his good bye, and made his way toward the house.

Charles and Hannah couldn't wait to tell Professor Hall the good news. He had just returned from seeing Josie and the baby and was sitting in his study relaxing.

"Professor Hall!" Charles said, as he and Hannah entered the study, "Are you busy?"

"No, not at all. Come in and have a seat." He motioned to the sofa.

"We've got some good news for you, and we wanted you to be the first to know," Charles told him grinning from ear to ear.

Professor Hall looked from Charles to Hannah. Charles was grinning and Hannah was smiling shyly, and blushing. From the way things looked, he knew what they were going to tell him.

"What's your good news?" Professor asked, after the two had taken a seat.

"We're getting married!" Charles said in a rush.

"Congratulations to you both!" Professor Hall stood and shook Charles's hand. "Have you asked Ben and Liza for permission to marry their daughter?"

The smile left Charles's face and went to a look of concern. "No, not yet. I'll speak with him tonight." With that decision made, the smile returned to Charles's face.

"Have you two set a date yet?" Professor Hall asked.

"No, we haven't." Charles turned toward Hannah and asked, "When would you like to get married?"

"I be wantin Miz Josie ta come. I's need her help in makin de plans. After ya talk with my mama and pa, I's be knowin more. Can it wait?"

"Of course. We need to talk with your mother and father first anyway, then we can make plans," Charles told her softly, causing her to blush.

The couple sat with Professor Hall and talked about their hopes for their future. Professor Hall listened, enjoying being part of their lives.

Lieutenant Sanders and Gabe talked for a long time about the information given to them by Jonah. Gabe was in agreement with Lieutenant Sanders. Jonah was the only one who could find out where the Confederate's were hiding, and the layout of Mr. Allen's land without getting caught. As for the visit from Mr. Allen tomorrow, Gabe was honest with Lieutenant Sanders by telling him he had no idea what he was going to say. He knew he wouldn't be supplying the Confederates with horses, but how he was going to get that across to Mr. Allen without giving himself away, he didn't know. That was another thing he needed to pray about, If only he could just get by himself!

As Gabe and Lieutenant Sanders left the study, they heard excited voices coming from the kitchen area. Going to investigate, the two men found Charles, Hannah, Liza and Ben in the dining room. Everyone was smiling, and Liza and Hannah had tears in their eyes. Surprised to see everyone, Gabe asked, "What's going on here? I see smiles and tears. Just what does this mean?"

"We's be gona have a weddin, Mr. Gabe! My Hannah be marryin Charles!" Ben told him with pride in his voice.

"Congratulations, Charles! It's about time you married this young lady. When's the big day?"

"We're going to wait until Josie and the baby are better. Hannah wants Josie to help her with the wedding plans, and Liza wants to make the dress. We're thinking in about two months," Charles told him.

Gabe looked over at Liza questionably. Liza understood his questioning look and shook her head yes, Josie and the baby would be fine by then.

Hannah slipped away from the group to talk to Josie. She was so excited! She wanted to share it with her now. Knocking softly at Josie's bedroom door and hearing Josie's "come in," Hannah entered the room.

"Hannah, how nice to see you, I've missed you," Josie told her. "Come sit beside me and let's talk."

"I's come wid some news fer ya. Charles done asked me ta marry up wid him!" Hannah told her excitedly.

"He did?! When? Tell me all about it!"

So Hannah told her all about Charles' proposal, even the kiss that took her by surprise. They wouldn't be married until Josie could attend.

"Oh Hannah, I'm so happy for you, congratulations! Thank you for wanting me at your wedding. We'll have a big wedding for you. We'll invite everyone. Your wedding will be the first in the new church! I can see it all decorated with flowers and bows."

"That's what I's be wantin ta talk wid ya about. I's be hopin dat ya could help my mama wid my dress. I's like it ta be fancy an all, and de way ya fixed de flowers fer de women at de big weddin, when ya first come here is how I be wantin my flowers ta be, as purdy as dat."

"Oh they will be, only better. We'll have such fun planning this wedding Hannah!"

"Now I's be askin another favor, Miz Josie. Charles be a learnt man, and talks rite nice, and dresses fancy. I's don't knowd how ta does them thangs. Does ya think dat ya could help me wid talkin and dressin proper? I's be wantin ta said my weddin promises proper befo de Lord and Charles," Hannah said with hope filled eyes.

"Yes, I believe I can help you with both request. First of all, we'll make you some new dresses, and while we sew we can work on your speech, if it's truly what you want."

"Yez ma'am, dat's what I's desire!" Hannah told her with excitement ringing from her voice.

"Then that's what we'll do," Josie assured her.

Baby Will chose that time to start fussing and crying. Reaching over to take him, Hannah placed him gently into his mother's arms and said, "Me and Charles be talkin how lucky dis babe be. He got's more lovin bout him than he be knowin."

"Pray he learns to nurse soon, Hannah, I don't want him to use that old bottle," Josie said in a soft tone as she nuzzled her baby.

"Jus ya be calm. He be knowin when ya be in a twitter. He knowd what ta do," Hannah assured her.

The two women talked softly of wedding plans and flowers, as Josie tried to relax and get Will to nurse.

Jonah waited until nightfall to begin his surveillance. He was excited that Lieutenant Sanders had faith in him to seek out the enemy, and bring back important information. Jonah walked with ease across New Canaan fields, enjoying the cooler night breeze. Then he paused, and looked up into the starry night sky. How bright the stars looked as they twinkled, making Jonah realize what a mighty God he served. It never ceased to amaze him how God wonderfully decorated something as big as the sky. The day sky held the bright sun with its white floating clouds. The night sky brought the moon and all its twinkling stars, each one having its own job to do. "Jus like me," Jonah thought as he started walking again toward the woods, praying for the guidance and protection he would need to complete the task before him.

Josie could hear baby Will moving restlessly in his bed. She knew soon he would be awake, crying to be fed. "Please Lord, let him nurse, just let him nurse and help me to be calm," she prayed as she watch her son moving in his small bed. Liza heard him too. She was quick to be by the baby's bedside to make sure all was well.

"He be wantin ta be fed soon," Liza whispered, to Josie knowing she too was awake.

"I know. I've been praying he'll be nursing tonight," Josie whispered back.

"Now Josie girl, he be needin ta learn, and dat's what he's gona do tonight. Even ifin we's gotta give him de bottle," Liza said softly as William began to cry.

Liza picked the baby up and handed him to his mother. She hurried to get another warming brick for the bed. Josie looked at her son and said,

"William, I'm your mother, and we need to have a talk. I know learning to nurse is new to you, but it's new to me too. We have to work together on this, and with the Lord's help, we can do it. Are you ready to try my little one?" Almost as if to answer, he yawned and wrinkled his little nose to cry. This time Josie was determined, she would do what it took to get her baby to nurse. Talking to him softly, she began telling him of all the people that loved him especially, God, all the while urging him to nurse.

Liza returned to warm his bed with the warming brick, and listened to Josie softly talking to her son. Suddenly, Liza had an idea. Pulling a chair close to Josie's bedside, she sat down and started talking softly to her. "Hannah tol me dat ya be helpin her wid de weddin. I's thank ya muchly fer it."

"I hope it's alright with you. She wants me to help her make some dresses too." Josie said softly.

"I's be wantin ya ta help wid the weddin plannin. Ya knowd, I's aint never did nothing like this afore. We's gona be needin ya help greatly."

"I can't wait to get started. It's going to be so much fun to do. I've been thinking about it since she told me. We need to see what kind of cloth we have, and what we need to buy as soon as possible. Have you thought about her wedding dress?"

"Yez, I's have. I's be wantin ta ask ya ifin ya had yo weddin dress wid ya. I's aint see'd one afore so's I's be in a quandary bout it."

"Yes, I'd forgotten about it. It's in my trunk. Hannah can use it! Oh Liza it would be just perfect for her! You'll have to take it in some, because Hannah is smaller than I am, but if she wanted to, she could use it! Josie said excitedly.

"Dat be takin a load off 'in my mind ifin she would. I's be askin her in de morin, but I's knowd she be proud ta wear it. Thank ya fer de offer," Liza said in a whisper.

The two women continued making plans for the wedding. Talking softly, they shared ideas to make Hannah's wedding the most perfect ever. Neither noticed just when baby Will finally started nursing, but Liza knew when she saw the sudden surprise in Josie's eyes. "Hallelujah and praise the Lord!" Liza said softly. All Josie could do was nod her head as tears rolled down her cheeks.

"You knew what you were doing all along didn't you, Liza?" Josie said softly.

"Jus makin ya be restful by talkin to ya is all. I's tol ya he knowd what ta do," Liza said smiling at both of them. "I's gots more questions fer ya so's lets us go on wid de plannin. Liza and Josie talked while baby Will continued to nurse, until all questions had been answered. Placing the baby back in his crib, Liza covered him with his blanket while offering up her thanks to God along with Josie's.

Gabe was delighted with the news Will was nursing. The only thing that ruined this perfect morning was knowing Mr. Allen would be arriving at any time. Hurrying to the stables, Gabe asked Caleb to move most of the horses over to Mount Haven. Saddling his own horse, Gabe rode on ahead to talk with Professor Hall. Finding him eating breakfast, Gabe sat down to have a cup of coffee with him. "Mr. Allen will be coming to New Canaan soon, so I need to fill you in on what's going on. By chance do you have a dollar on you?"

"A dollar? Yes, I have a dollar, why?" Professor Hall asked confused.

"Would you just give me the dollar, please?"

Reaching into his pocket, Professor Hall pulled out a dollar bill and handed it to Gabe.

"You are now the proud owner of fifteen of the finest horses in this parish!" Gabe proclaimed.

"Have you lost your mind? What are you talking about?" Professor Hall asked. He was really concerned about Gabe now.

"You've just bought most of my horses. The ones left are the ones I need to run the plantation." Then he went on to tell the professor how Mr. Allen was coming by to ask him to sell or give horses to the Confederate army. Professor Hall was shocked. Then he started laughing. He started laughing so hard that he in turn caused Gabe to start laughing, until they both were holding their aching sides. When they were able to regain their composure, Gabe continued with further explanation of the conversation overheard by Jonah in the livery stable.

"How did you ever come up with the idea to sell me the horses?"

"It's nothing but the good Lord, professor. I could never come up with something this simple and easy. I just prayed about it. To tell you the truth, I've prayed about it a lot. Then it just came to me. I honestly believe my guardian angel is working overtime! God has just got to give my angel a promotion after this!" Gabe exclaimed, causing both men to start laughing once again. Finally, Gabe excused himself and rode back to New Canaan.

Caleb and Big John passed Gabe as they moved the horses toward Mount Haven. Gabe stopped them long enough to ask Caleb if he would mind moving to Mount Haven to care for the horses. "Just think about it. Have a look around, and see if you think you would want to make the move." Gabe told him. "It'll be fine if you don't. I thought I would make the offer to you first. Just let me know what you decide."

"Yez sah, I's letcha be knowin," Caleb assured, him then rode off to join Big John.

Gabe was glad Mr. Allen's morning visit actually came in the early afternoon. Gabe watched for him from his window in the study. Today Gabe was ready for anything that Mr. Allen could throw at him. Seeing

Mr. Allen ride up to the front of the house, Gabe asked Ben to go outside and meet him.

"Afternoon Mista Allen," Ben said as Mr. Allen dismounted.

"Afternoon, is Mr. Lyon about?" Mr. Allen inquired.

"Yez sah, he be in de study. Miz Liza be takin ya to him," Ben took the horses reins.

Standing at the door was Liza, waiting for Mr. Allen to enter. Taking him to the study, she announced his arrival, then left the room closing the doors behind her.

"Gabriel! How are you?" Mr. Allen asked with exuberance.

"I'm fine and how are you?" Gabe asked calmly.

"Fine, just fine. How's the new baby? Mr. Allen inquired wondering if he was going to be asked to sit down.

"He's doing just fine and so is my wife. Thank you for asking. Tell me Mr. Allen, what brings you to New Canaan?" Gabe asked, motioning for Mr. Allen to sit down.

Taking a seat in a nearby chair, Mr. Allen answered, "You always know how to get straight to the point. I like that in a man. I've come to talk business with you."

"What kind of business?" Gabe leaned against his desk.

"Well, it has to do with buying horses," Mr. Allen said somewhat nervously.

"Mr. Allen, I'm not selling my horses," he told him looking him directly in the eyes.

"Actually, they're not for me," Mr. Allen said hesitantly. "They're for a friend of mine. Well, that's not really true."

"Just what is the truth, Mr. Allen?"

"The truth is, the Confederate army has asked me to ask you if you'd be willing to donate horses to the cause. If you're not willing to donate them, they might be talked into buying them."

"Let me see if I got this straight. You've come to ask me to give my horses to the Confederate Army, and they don't really want to pay for them? Is that right?" Gabe asked with firmness.

"Yes, that's it," Mr. Allen told him.

"Mr. Allen, first of all I want to show you something, and then I'm going to tell you something you already know. Come with me."

Mr. Allen stood up and followed Gabe out of the study and out of the house. Gabe took him toward the stables, without saying a word, noticing Mr. Allen was paying close attention to everything around them as they went. Finally, breaking the silence, Mr. Allen said, "You've made a lot of changes around here since the last time I was here!"

Gabe stopped quickly, and turned toward him. "Mr. Allen, I don't believe the improvements I've made here are any of your concern. To put any further concerns you may have to rest, I will tell you this. I don't believe in wasting money. If you have an investment in slaves, then you should treat them just as you would any investment. You see that they are properly attired and have plenty to eat. You give them a sound place to live where they are happy and can stay healthy, which will increase their ability to work better. If the improvements I've made here are offensive to you, then you don't have to come here. Now that your curiosity has been satisfied, we'll continue to the stables. With that he turned, leaving Mr. Allen standing by himself, trying to figure out what had just hit him.

When Mr. Allen finally entered the stable, he found Gabe waiting for him.

"As you can see, Mr. Allen, I've sold all my horses. The only one's I have left are the ones I truly need to run my plantation, as for selling or giving any of these away, the answer is no. You can return and tell your friend what I've said. I run my plantation as God would have me to do. It's that plain and simple. You already know this, so my question is, why would you come all the way out here to hear this again? I also know, you know, my wife gave birth just a few days ago. This meeting with you about business is not only rude, but improper. So why are you really here?"

Mr. Allen's face had gone from a pallor white to an embarrassed red.

"I…ah…I'm sorry Gabriel, I just didn't think. You must be under a lot of stress. Please forgive me. I'll give your answer to my friend as soon as possible. It is the only reason I'm truly here," he explained.

"Thank you, Mr. Allen and I accept your apology. Please tell your wife that Mrs. Lyon would love for her to come by in a few days." Gabe had forgiveness in his voice.

"I'll tell her. Maybe she can give your wife some helpful advice. Again, I'm sorry to have bothered you in this stressful time," Mr. Allen told him.

The two men walked back to the house with Mr. Allen saying good bye in the yard. Before he left, Mr. Allen mounted his horse and asked one more question. "Who did you sell your horses to?"

"I sold them to my father- in- law. It won't do you any good to ask him about the same business offer, but you can try." With that, Gabe turned on his heels and headed into the house.

Jonah was pleased with the progress he was making. In the last few hours he had crossed over New Canaan's boundaries, and onto Mr. Allen's land, without being detected. He even found the perfect hiding place in a thicket, which had all the appearance of a deer's resting place. He made himself a bed and lay down. The way the branches of the bushes came together, forming a perfect dome, was more than he expected to find. From here, he could sleep during the day, with the shade to protect him from the hot sun, and it would be the perfect place to come back to after he had been spying during the night. God had provided once again. Jonah fell asleep quickly knowing, that this was truly a place of protection.

Lieutenant Sanders was becoming worried because he hadn't heard from Jonah, but it had only been one day. Sometimes he forgot how big New Canaan was, and how long it would take for someone to walk across to the adjoining land. If Jonah didn't return by the end of the week, he would go looking for him. He felt responsible for sending his good friend out on this assignment alone. He knew Jonah would be able to make this journey quicker by himself. Lieutenant Sanders prayed for his friend, knowing God knew better than he how to protect Jonah.

"Come on Liza. Just let me sit in a chair for a while. This bed is hurting my back. When will I be able to sleep with my husband again? He's been on the couch in his study since Will was born!" Josie was starting to be a little whiney.

Laughing Liza told her, "I's be lettin ya sit in de chair fer a few minutes whilst I's change ya bed. Gabe be doin jus fine in de study, ifin he be wantin a bed, dere be beds galore in this house. He be havin his pick, but not in yours until de time be up. Ya knowd dat, Josie!"

"I'm sorry about being so fussy Liza. It's that I miss him. I know he's busy, but I'm use to seeing him more than a couple of times a day. Will you ask him to come see me more often? I'm feeling so much better."

"I's knowd dat ya be and I's told him. Did ya knowd dat he stands by de door and peeks in on ya?"

"Does he really?"

"Yez em. Bein as he be a new father, it be all he can does ta stay away like he be doin. It be hard on him too," Liza assured her. "Now yo come on, and lets me help ya ta de chair. Ya might be light in de head when ya's stands, so's hang on ta me."

Josie loved sitting in the chair. So much so, that she begged Liza for a few more minutes, which she gave her. When Josie returned to her nice clean bed, she fed Will. With his little stomach full, he fell asleep quickly, but so did his mother. Putting Will into his bed, Liza knew that she loved these two as if they were her own. It never ceased to amaze her how much a mother's heart could love.

Caleb and Emlee walked hand in hand toward the school. Soon Emlee would be teaching again, and Caleb would be moving to Mount Haven. Emlee was saddened she wouldn't be seeing Caleb as much as in the past. This was a good move. Caleb had already picked out a new cabin that would soon become their home after they married. The good part was Caleb would be training Eli and Little John on how to take care of the horses left at New Canaan. The two boys were excited about it and Ben had agreed they could do it as long as they came for help when they needed it. Caleb would check in on them regularly. Charles was excited Caleb was coming to Mount Haven, because he knew Caleb would teach him all about horses. Charles wanted to learn all he could, because someday he knew he would own his own place.

Just before nightfall, Jonah woke up to the sounds of foot steps. From his location he was able to see four Confederate soldiers walking past his hiding place. They were an arms length away from him, and they didn't even know it. To Jonah's surprise, the men stopped at a fallen tree and sat down while one soldier lit a pipe.

"How much longer are we gona be here?" complained a young soldier.

"We'll be here for as long as it takes!" said the soldier with the pipe gruffly.

"We've done been here three weeks, and it seems like it's been three months. When are we going to see some action?" asked the young soldier.

"You'll see enough killing before long, and then you'll be complaining about that!" Said the tallest of them.

"Yeah, you'll be wantin your mama by then!" Laughed the pipe smoking soldier.

They all laughed except for the youngest one who said, "We've been through these woods and down to the river for the past few weeks and we aint found no signs of them Yankees anywhere! I think the general is barking up the wrong tree. I don't believe there's anyone coming through here."

"We'll keep doing it until the general tells us to stop. It's getting dark so we better get back to camp. I wonder what we're eating for supper tonight," the pipe smoker said as they all stood and headed toward camp.

Jonah waited in his hiding place until their voices faded. Quickly he came out to follow them. It was so easy. It was if they had become so used to their surroundings, they didn't even know someone might be watching.

When Jonah reached the camp, he remained in the woods. He counted a hundred tents. That could mean there was between a hundred to two hundred men at least, figuring two men to a tent. Noticing a barn in the distance he prayed it didn't house any more men. Making his way a little closer, he saw the General from Mr. Allen's Livery stable and he looked upset. Mr. Allen was with him and the two men were talking. Jonah wanted to hear what they were saying, so he moved closer, staying in the shadows, keeping away from any campfire light. He was able to skirt the outside of the camp to where Mr. Allen and the General were standing. Quietly he got closer. All he had to do was reach out and he could tap the General on the shoulder, but he resisted the urge. It made him smile to think how startled the General would be at discovering how close someone could get to him without his knowing. Remembering why he was there, he listened closely to what they were saying.

"I told you he wouldn't want any part of this, but I asked him anyway. He's sold all his horse, all the good ones that is. He only has work horses left." Mr. Allen explained to the general.

"Who did he sell them to? Or did you even ask?" The General demanded.

"I asked him! He sold them to his father in- law. Lyon's told me he knew his father in- law wouldn't sell them, but we could ask anyway."

"No, that won't be necessary. If we need the horses badly, enough we'll just take them. I don't need their consent if the army says we need them. How are you doing with some of the other owners?"

"I told you, we can get about twenty right now, and that'll do just fine. You don't need to steal from anyone. Lyon's horses were the best, and you don't need the best for war."

"Look, I've got to get men to Leesburg, Virginia before October, and disperse men to Fort Jackson and New Orleans before the beginning of the year. Not to mention the fact I've got to keep men here in Baton Rouge. So don't tell me what I need or don't need. You just get me those horses and get them soon! I've wasted too much time with this!" barked the general.

This was more than Jonah bargained for. He had all the information Lieutenant Sanders was going to need for the next few months.

"I'll do what I can. That's all I can do, unless you're going to embarrass the Confederate States with thievery. That's something I hope you don't do General! It would cause you more trouble than you could handle if you did," Mr. Allen informed him. "Are you going to make my land your camp much longer?"

"I am! This is where we're going to disperse our men from now until the end of the war, so get used to it!"

With nothing else to say, Mr. Allen turned and made his way out of the camp. Jonah, pleased with all his new information, quietly made his way back into the woods toward his own hiding place. He quickly gathered his things and headed toward home.

CHAPTER 12

IT HAD BEEN THREE MONTHS since finding out about the Confederate Camp on Mr. Allen's land. Lieutenant Sanders and Jonah had visited it twice. He waited patiently for most of the troops to be moved out, according to what Jonah had learned. From what he could tell of his last visit, all was going according to plan. Soon he'd be able to move his soldiers in, and take over the camp. Waiting was hard to do. Lieutenant Sanders hated waiting on anything, but today he would enjoy the wedding festivities of Charles and Hannah's marriage. One day, he too, would like to be married. Hopefully, when this war was over, he would be able to find someone. Right now, he needed to leave or he'd be late.

The church was decorated beautifully. The benches were replaced with pews made by Big John, especially for the occasion. They were decorated with white satin bows at each end. Down the middle aisle was a white runner that ran from the door to the front of the church where it met with a canopy of ribbons, white mums, white roses and white Periwinkles. The whole church was lit with white candles, which cast a soft glow over the room. Everything was ready.

Charles was nervous! He rattled on and on about nothing in particular, which caused Professor Hall and Gabe to question his sanity. "I remember you making fun of me when I got married!" Gabe teased Charles.

"I remember it too! I just never dreamed you'd get the chance to do it to me!"

"It's something all men do, we either pace or talk non stop. I've known a few that's done both!" Professor Hall informed them laughing.

"I wonder if Hannah is nervous," Charles asked.

"I'm sure she is," Gabe told him grinning.

195

Hannah was nervous. She couldn't believe today was her wedding day. Liza and Josie were helping her with her hair.

"Where's Will?" Hannah asked.

"He's with Delia right now. I'll get him after the wedding." Josie told her.

Then she asked, "Are you ready for your dress?"

Smiling at both her mother and Josie, she softly answered, "yes."

Josie was proud of Hannah's speech. Lord knows, she practiced so much she nearly drove everyone crazy! Occasionally, she would slip back to her old ways, but that wasn't a worry for today.

Josie and Liza helped Hannah step into her wedding dress. It was beautiful! You couldn't tell it had at one time been Josie's. Not only had Liza altered it to fit Hannah's slimmer figure, but she'd also added lace to the bodice. A white satin bow was added at the end of the pearl buttons which ran down the back of the dress. Liza made Hannah's veil to not cover her face and it was held in place by a comb Liza's father had made for her mother.

Josie and Liza stood back and admired Hannah, who was looking at herself in the full length mirror in Josie's room.

"Ya be prudy as can be," Liza told Hannah softly.

"You're beautiful!" Josie added as she backed out of the room to give mother and daughter time to be alone.

The Church was full. Everyone was dressed for the occasion. Josie even noticed many of the women had new dresses to wear. The children were excited, but well behaved. Josie looked over to where her husband and Charles stood as she walked down the aisle. Charles was standing tall and proud. Gabe was deep in thought as he remembered the day he and Josie were married. When Josie took her place in front of the church, everyone turned to see the beautiful bride walking down the aisle as Emlee began to sing. Soft awes were heard from the guest as Hannah walked to Charles. Taking her hand, they faced the pulpit. Gabe left his place at Charles side and stepped in front of the couple. Asking everyone to bow their heads, Gabe prayed for God to bless the happy couple. Then, taking his Bible, he read the vows with the couple promising to love and cherish each other for a lifetime. Josie could see Hannah glowing as she repeated her vows in perfect English. No one missed the surprised from Charles as she did so. When they'd sealed their vows with a kiss, Gabe announced, "I now present to you Mr. and Mrs. Charles Wood!"

The reception was held in the ballroom at New Canaan. Even the soldiers from Mount Haven came to wish the couple well, and to enjoy the food.

Charles and Hannah took jokes in stride as they mingled with the guest. It was well into the night before the party broke up. Charles and Hannah went back to Mount Haven and Professor Hall stayed at New Canaan to give the newlyweds some privacy.

"We'll clean this up tomorrow," Josie told Liza, as they walked toward the kitchen with left over food. "We've got enough food to feed the soldiers for a week! Wouldn't they just love that?"

"I's shur deys be happy jus ta eat regular like."

"It was a beautiful wedding wasn't it?"

"Yez, it be morin I'd knowd ta say," Liza said softly. "I's be proud ta have Charles in de family."

"I know he's proud to be in your family. It's all he could talk about. I know he misses his mother and father. He wanted them to be here and meet Hannah. Maybe after this war is over they'll be able to do that."

"Could be, I's jus not be a wantin dem ta up an move. I's wana see'd my granchillin growd up."

"I don't think you have anything to worry about, Liza. Those two will stay here long after the war. They may make a visit or two up north, but I have a feeling Charles doesn't want to be anywhere but here," Josie assured her.

The women began putting away the food, while talking about what the future might bring. They laughed at the thought of how Charles would handle becoming a father.

Lieutenant Sanders left the party early. He had a lot on his mind. It was hard to decide what should be done about the Rebel camp. Lieutenant Sanders walked to the church and entered. Falling on his knees, he prayed and sought God's guidance in the matter. He prayed with all his might! After an hour or so he decided he would wait upon the Lord for an answer. He didn't move. Waiting was waiting no matter where you did it as far as the Lieutenant was concerned. There was something about this church that gave him comfort, and waiting here was right.

Gabe had the feeling something was about to happen. He felt it in the depths of his soul. Slipping away quietly from his loved ones, he made his way to his study to pray. Feeling he needed to go somewhere more private, so he wouldn't be interrupted, he made his way to church. As he, walked he prayed silently, asking God to show him or tell him what he needed to know. The closer he got to church, the heavier his burden seemed. He knew this prayer time was of the utmost importance.

Entering the church, Gabe saw Lieutenant Sanders on his knees, praying. Being as quiet as he could, he joined him. No word was exchanged between them. Gabe didn't know what problems the Lieutenant was praying about, but he did know God wanted him to be there.

Lieutenant Sanders believed he had his answer from God. Now would be the time to attack the rebel camp on Allen's farm. It all made sense to him now. It would be easier, and there would be less bloodshed, since all but fifty men had moved out. After praying, and talking over his decision with Gabe, he knew there was no time like the present. So he hurried to gather his troops for their pre dawn attack. Sanders was thankful he'd sent for additional soldiers. In doing so, he had more boats for transportation sitting in the bayou. He'd also sent a message to a nearby Union regiment; captured soldiers would be needing transport to a prison camp soon. Everything was set.

The hours slipped away, as the night did, with the dawning of the new day. To Gabe, the early morning was the most exciting. It represented the wondrous handy work of the Lord. The sky was painted with the purest of colors. The air was filled with the sounds of woodland creatures, big and small, as they sang out their praises to the Lord. It truly was the perfect time to talk to God. It was at this time God began talking to Gabe, deep within his soul. What bubbled up from there was comforting, as Psalm ninety one washed over him with the promise of God's protection. *The security of the one who trusts in the Lord* was whispered into his heat. Gabe no longer worried about the war. He knew the Lord was with him.

Lieutenant Sanders and his troop surrounded the Confederate camp while the soldiers slept. "They've gotten too comfortable," Sanders thought, as he watched their sentry guard sleeping with his back against a tree, and his gun barely in his hand. Motioning for his men to move in, he stepped into the edge of the camp. First the sentry guard was abruptly awakened with a firm hand placed over his mouth, while his gun was removed from his fingers. The startled soldier was then tied securely to his sleeping tree and left.

"How could they have gotten so lazy as to have only one sentry?" Sanders wondered. He moved forward quietly, making his way deeper into the camp. Only an odd man here and there needed to be restrained, as they slept near an extinguished camp fire. Both surprise and fear registered in their eyes, as they were quickly tied and gagged without a sound being made. By the time it was done, each Confederate tent was covered by Union soldiers, who waited for their signal. When the Lieutenant saw all his men were in place, he slowly raised his hand. Then, with a prayer flowing from his lips, he lowered his hand swiftly. Suddenly, confusion rang out in the early morning air as the startled cries of the Confederate soldiers, and the commands of the Union soldiers, filled the sleepy camp. Sanders and his men took control without one shot being fired!

Lieutenant Sanders marched his prisoners toward the river. "I would love to see the look on Mr. Allen's face when he visits the camp and finds no one's there," he thought. He led their descent down the embankment to the waiting boats. At first, Lieutenant Sanders had been concerned Mr. Allen and his family might hear the commotion. It had been done so quickly, and the house was far enough away, their attack went unnoticed. As the last man was loaded into the boats, Sanders gave a sigh of relief. It was almost over. The prisoners would be moved up the Mississippi to a waiting Union Army regiment, who would take them on to a prison camp. His part was done.

A week later, Mr. Allen ventured down to the Confederate camp to collect what was owed him for their stay. He was amazed to find no one there. Thinking perhaps they were on some sort of mission, and would return soon, he left promising himself, to come back for what was due him.

The sugar cane and cotton had been harvested, and new crops were planted for the next year. It took nearly everyone to accomplish this. The hired hands were eager to have it done to enjoy some downtime. In just a few days, it would be Thanksgiving. Even though it wasn't a decreed holiday, it was one New Canaan celebrated, for they were thankful for many things. It was a time of fellowship and praise. This year's would be especially joyful, because it was Will's first.

Will looked more and more like his father each day. Josie had made her mark upon him too, for he had the bluest eyes that twinkled with joy. It didn't matter who he was with, he was content. To him, everyone was family. "That's just how I feel," Josie thought as she watched Will playing on his blanket with the other babies. She and Liza and Delia were busy preparing food for their Thanksgiving feast.

"I've never seen so many healthy babies at one time," remarked Josie as she worked.

"We's shur got us sum! I's aint see'd a sickly chil in a long time. De good Lord be wid us fo shur," Liza agreed.

"En dere be mor acomin," Delia added.

"Yez, it be seemin so," Liza replied.

"Miz Josie, I's be wantin ta ask ya fer sum time now ifin ya be thinkin dat war be comin des way? My John be watchful, an he be sayin he see'd de signs of it comin near. Whatcha knowd dat ya can share?" Delia asked.

"I see the signs just like Big John, Delia, but I don't know anything for sure. Gabe hasn't mentioned anything about it in a long time. I'll ask the first chance I get, and let you know what he says. I pray a lot and ask God to keep it away from here. I know it's all around us in the west and some parts of the east, but I really don't know anything else."

"Jus wanta be ready is all. I's thank ya fer askin Mr. Gabe bout it. Jus told him we's be needin ta knowd sumthin." Josie could tell Delia was worried.

The women continued their work and no one brought up the subject of war again. Warm laughter filled the house, as the women cooked and watched the babies play.

Gabe loved to hear laughter in his house. It filled his heart with such joy. He understood the meaning of laughter doeth good like a medicine. He knew first handed, it lightened burdens, healed a broken heart, and mended a broken spirit. Gabe followed the happy sound to find his son trying his best to roll over on his stomach, while lying on a blanket. Strong determination could be seen on Will's little face. When he finally succeeded ,after many attempts, the women all clapped and gave out praises for a job well done.

Looking up, Josie saw her husband standing in the doorway smiling at the accomplishment of their son. She was grateful Gabe had been able to see it. Sometimes, she didn't know if her heart could hold all the love she had for her husband and son, as it grew daily. Sensing her watching him, Gabe turned, Josie could see the love shining in his eyes. He was truly the best gift, along with her son, God had given her. Standing to her feet, she walked over to greet her husband.

"How about you and I have a little talk?" ask Josie.

"Of course. Come with me for a walk?" replied Gabe.

"Liza, would you mind watching Will for me?" Josie asked.

"Ya knows dat I's be jus happy ta!" Liza smiled. "Ya jus go ahead on en takes ya time."

Walking arm in arm, Josie and Gabe strolled through the flower garden, enjoying each others company until they reached the garden bench. Josie sat down. "Big John and Delia are worried about the war getting closer. She asked me today if I knew what was going on. I told her I would ask you."

"Things are changing my love. It could be here at any time. No one knows for sure. All we can do is pray and be prepared. I think Lieutenant Sanders' capture of the Confederate camp at Allen's farm will put off the war for a while; at least until the General returns to see no one's there."

"How long do you think it'll be until someone notices?" Josie asked.

"I really don't know. I guess I need to bring everyone up to date on what's all happening. I'll talk with Ben about it in the morning. Then we'll decide what to do. You're not worried are you?"

"No, I'm really not. Don't look so surprised! I know God's in control. He's the only one who can do anything about this war. He's watching out for us Gabe."

"I know, I just keep forgetting how strong you are. You amaze me sometimes." He kissed her softly, and then changed the subject to Thanksgiving. "Have you and Liza planned a big celebration?" Gabe inquired.

"Yes, we have. It's going to be wonderful. Lots of food and lots of family! I've even been thinking about Christmas. How about you?" Josie asked.

"You're just like a small child when it comes to Christmas. I've already made some plans!"

"What kind of plans?" She asked excitedly.

Laughing, he put his arms around her. "You'll just have to wait and see Josie Lyon!"

It was Thanksgiving Day! Excitement filled the air. The soldiers from Mount Haven were the most excited about the celebration. They were many miles from home and this was an answer to their prayers. It wasn't being at home, but it was with friends.

Lieutenant Sanders' men supplied the turkeys for the day's festivities. Hannah was shocked but very pleased with the gift. The soldiers had even cleaned them for her. They were so appreciative of being invited to the family affair; they wanted to do anything they could. The soldiers wanted to help so much so, they were almost underfoot. Hannah didn't have the heart to shoo them out of her kitchen. When everything was ready to go to New Canaan, Hannah asked the men to help load the food. She felt like she was the mother of these twenty young men who teased her, and each other. Occasionally she would fuss at them to keep their hands off the food, which only caused them to aggravate her more.

When they arrived at New Canaan, the men were busy setting up tables and chairs in the ballroom. There was so much food they needed three long tables for all of it. The children ran about playing, and the men gathered in groups talking of everything but the war. The women went about making sure all was ready. while they talked of children, husbands and the things women share with each other in general.

Finally came the time to eat. Gabe walked to the head of the table and called for everyone's attention. "Let's bow our heads, give thanks and ask God to bless our food." The room became silent as everyone bowed their heads.

"Father, today we are especially thankful for the blessings you've bestowed upon us. We thank you for all of the new additions to our family, and our health. We thank you for our bountiful harvest and prosperity. Most of all, Lord, we thank you for keeping us out of harms way of the war. We ask that your mighty hand be with those who are fighting, and we pray this conflict comes to an end soon. We also ask you to be with the soldier's families, and give them peace and comfort. We ask your blessing upon this food we are about to receive. We ask you to bless it to the nourishment of our bodies, and our bodies to your service. In Jesus name, amen."

A resounding amen was heard through the room, as all that were gathered gave their voice in agreement. Soon the room was alive with the activity of celebration. Stories shared, and laughter rang throughout. It indeed was a joyful time of fellowship and thanksgiving. To end the celebration, was the dedication service to the Lord of all the babies born that year. It truly had been a blessed year.

It seemed the end of the year was coming fast. The cooler weather of December felt wonderful. The children were impatiently counting the days to Christmas. They were definitely up to something! Gabe and Josie, with little Will in her arms, stood on the porch as the children of New Canaan seemed to be having a meeting of their own under the trees.

Deep in conversation, the children had not seen Gabe and Josie watching them until little Sarah looked up. The group stood to their feet, laughing and waving, as ran back to their homes with secret smiles on their faces.

"I'm wondering what they're up to now?" Josie asked with a chuckle.

"I'm sure it has to do with Christmas," Gabe said grinning. "It seems no matter where I go, the children are whispering about Christmas and gathering in small groups. Why, I've even found them pretending to help Little John and Eli with chores in the barn. They're definitely up to something!"

"I think it's funny. They haven't a clue we know they're planning something," Josie said as she, and Gabe turned to go back into the house.

Gabe and Ben walked together as they did every morning over the land and discussed the projects needing to be done.

"Ben, I'm thinking we need to start some planting over at Mount Haven. It's time to let our neighbors see some crops growing."

"It be a fine idea, Mr. Gabe. We's gona havta git sum able bodied men over dar ta work it."

"I know. I thought I'd give everyone the chance to choose where they wanted to live and work. I've wanted to talk to you about it. We'd be cutting our work force in half and finding more workers will be hard."

"Ya means hard ta buy em cause it be agin ya?" Ben asked.

"I don't want to buy anyone! I don't know what to do just yet."

"Mr. Gabe, ifin ya does buy'd somebodies, ya be buyin dem freedom. Ya be a Godly man. Ya be givin a body a chance. Ya needin ta prays on it" Old Ben advised. Shaking his head in agreement, the two continued their walk.

The children of New Canaan met in the barn for their Christmas meeting.

Emlee had been invited because she was the best planner of all and could keep a secret.

"We's be a wantin ta surprise Mr. Gabe and Missus fo Christmas, an we's be needin ya help Emlee," Little John said in a low voice.

"Whatcha be wantin ta do?" Emlee asked trying hard not to laugh.

"Dat's what we's be needin ya fo. We's gots sum ide's ifin we's all can agree. We's wanta does the bestest. So here dey is." Little John handed her the slate with the list. "Ya need ta read em and ponders on it. We's all met back here when ya makes ya mind up."

"I's see'd ya gots sum goodly thangs rite here. I's jus gots sum questions," Emlee informed the group. She motioned for the children to gather around her as best as they could to hear her questions. There the plans for the Christmas surprise began to unfold. They didn't have long to prepare, so they needed to start right away.

Josie was making her own Christmas surprise. She made her list quickly. Soon she would go to town so she could get started. This year was a challenge. A present for the baby was easy, but for the rest, she had her work cut out for her. Talking to Gabe would get things started.

It was their first Christmas together, and Hannah was excited. She knew Charles would be missing the snow that was normal this time of the year in Maine. He hadn't said anything to her, but she'd over heard him and the professor talking about it last night. She was determined to make it a special Christmas for both of them. Mount Haven would have their own Christmas tree. It was just last year when she had her first tree, and she'd made herself a promise that no matter what, she'd have one every year.

Emlee had Caleb rolling in laughter, as she told him about the children's ideas of having a Christmas surprise. She'd sworn him to secrecy on the children's behalf, because she needed his help. Emlee had gotten the Christmas surprise list down to two for the children to choose from. She seemed to know down in her heart the one they'd pick. So Caleb's help was very important.

Lieutenant Sanders and Jonah were busy with Christmas plans as well. All but ten soldiers had been moved to other locations, and something needed to be done for those that had been left behind.

"Mr. Gabe and the Missus be havin Christmas celebration, an I's knowd they be askin ya'll ta come," Jonah told Sanders.

"The Lyon's have always been good to my men, but I feel I should do something for them too. I just haven't decided what yet."

"Dey's be plenty fo everybody, jus as was Thanksgiving. Dey be missin family but nothin ta do fer dat," Jonah said.

"I know, but something will come to mind for me to do," Lieutenant Sanders said with confidence.

Jonah shook his head in agreement. Just at that time, a knock sounded at the door. Jonah opened the door to find Gabe and Ben standing there.

"Cum on in, Mr. Gabe and pa," Jonah stepped back, allowing the men to enter. Lieutenant Sanders rose from his chair, and greeted them with a hardy handshake.

"Are you busy? We could come back later," Gabe asked as he took a seat.

"Actually, we've been talking about Christmas," Lieutenant Sanders said

"Seems as if everyone is," Gabe said with a laugh.

"What can I do for you, Mr. Lyon?" Lieutenant Sanders asked.

"If you don't mind, I'd like to wait for Professor Hall and Charles before I tell you. I've asked Hannah to have them meet us here. It shouldn't be too long."

"Must be serious," Sanders said.

"It is, and it involves all of us. So the decision has to be made with everyone in agreement," Gabe said.

The men talked about small matters as they waited. Before long, another knock sounded, informing the group of the arrival of Professor Hall and Charles. After everyone was seated Gabe began, "As you know, the repairs to Mount Haven have been completed. The good people of

Baton Rouge will soon be asking questions as to why we haven't started growing crops. That's the reason for this meeting. In order to grow crops at Mount Haven, we'll need more help. I'm not expecting the military to help with this. In order to get the extra help, I'll be needing to buy slaves." Gabe paused at this and waited for his last statement to sink in. If he had to go by the expressions on the groups faces, with the exception of Ben, he knew they were having a hard time dealing with it.

Finally Ben spoke up and said, "I's knowd whatcha be a thinkin. Ya'll be needin ta knowd dat I's told Mr. Gabe he ougta do it. Cause he be buyin dem slaves a chance fer freedom. Dey aint gotta chance ifin he don't!"

"But paw, it aint rite!" Jonah exclaimed.

"Aint rite ta let dem others be lost! Ifin buyin em be de onliest way, I's say do it!" Ben said directing his answer to his son.

"They'll have the same opportunities as everyone else. It's not like they'll be slaves as slaves are on other plantations," Gabe added.

"I understand what you're trying to do here, Gabe. I know you need these people to keep my cover in place. You do understand I'll need to keep men here anyway," Lieutenant Sanders stated.

"I understand, Lieutenant. You do know the men remaining here will either need to stay out of sight or….. Gabe started, but was interrupted by Jonah, who with a laugh said, "Or go see'd my ma!"

This caused the group to laugh, except for Professor Hall and Charles, who had no idea what they were talking about. Lieutenant Sanders turned toward Professor Hall and said, "When I first came here, Miss Liza stained my skin with a walnut stain so I would blend in."

Charles was first to get the idea and began to laugh. Then Professor Hall caught on quickly, and laughed so hard tears ran down his face. Shaking his head when he finally could speak, he said, "Now I've heard it all! I bet it took a long time to wear off!

"Yes sir, it surely did. The worst part was the way I was treated by white folks. I truly learned what it was like to be a black man. It made my reasons for fighting this war more important," Lieutenant Sanders told him thoughtfully. "It's something one truly can't experience as a white man; I knew the stain would wear off and I would be white again."

"It's different in the northern states. You're given the chance of education for both black and white. Depending on what state you're in, your job opportunities are greater. It comes down to this, in the north you're not a slave, and you can't be bought or sold because of the color of your skin!" Charles stated firmly.

For a few minutes the men were quiet. Then Gabe spoke, "Is there to be a discussion about us buying workers for our plantation?"

"I agree with Ben," Charles said.

"Me too," Professor Hall added.

"Alright then, I have to attend a Plantation Owners meeting on Friday. I'll put the word out that I need some workers," Gabe stated.

"Have you talked with Josie about this yet?" Professor Hall asked seriously.

"No I haven't but I will tonight. I may need your help. As a matter of fact, I might need all your help!" Gabe said grinning.

This statement brought laughter from the group of men. They all knew Josie was dead set against slavery. They all offered up encouragement to Gabe but none offered to be with him when he told her.

Gabe went in search of Josie. He knew he had better go ahead and tell her. Especially since someone might let it slip before he could tell her himself.

He found her in the nursery with Will in her arms. She was getting the little fellow to sleep by rocking him and singing softly. She looked up and smiled at Gabe but didn't stop her song or rocking. Gabe silently mouthed the word "study" to her and Josie nodded her head as she continued with her job at hand.

It was sometime later when Josie descended the stairs to the study to see Gabe. Seeing her in the doorway, Gabe rose. "I never tire of seeing you with Will in your arms. It overwhelms my heart," He told her, still holding her close.

"I feel the same way just holding him. God has blessed us so much Gabe. He has given us a wonderful family. A wonderfully large family," she added softly laughing.

Slightly pulling away from her, Gabe said, "Our family is about to get bigger."

"What do you mean?" She asked confused.

"I have to talk to you about something I need to do," he said, then went into the explanation about buying more workers. Josie listened quietly and didn't say a word. Gabe couldn't tell what she was thinking from her expression, which was unusual. He knew she didn't like it, but he would wait for her to say so.

"So there you have it, I want to know what you think," he said.

"Are you sure there's no other way?" Josie asked as she walked over to her chair and sat down.

"No my love, there's no other way. We need to start farming the other land, and it will be too much work for Ben and the hands to farm both."

"I hate the thought of buying humans! But then again, it will remove slaves from the other plantations and give them freedom. Have you talked with Ben about this?" She questioned.

"Yes, I have. As a matter of fact it, was Ben's idea! He said it would be saving at least some from slavery, and here they would have a chance."

"He's right you know," Josie said deep in thought. "Have you decided how many you will need?"

"Yes, I'm thinking we'll start out with five families."

"I'm glad you're getting families so they'll be staying together. What about those that aren't wanted? You know, like little Eli was. Will you be looking closely for that too?"

"Yes, I promise I will. So don't worry," Gabe assured her.

"I don't like it, but if it will give the slaves their freedom and help the war by keeping Lieutenant Sanders cover then…. go ahead and do it. Oh Gabe, I wish slavery didn't exist," she cried.

"I wish it too my love, but it does and there's no other way."

"When will you do this?" She asked.

"I'm going to the Plantation Owners Association meeting tomorrow night and put out inquires then."

"Well… be sure to pray for God to give you direction and I'll do the same."

"Why don't we pray right here together?" He asked.

"Yes, we need to do that," Josie said, as she bowed her head, and Gabe began to pray.

The news of new workers being bought, swept through New Canaan's like a wild fire. Everyone had questions. Big John went to both Gabe and Ben to ask for a meeting, to explain the situation before rumors got out of hand. All the men and their families were waiting at the church. It took both Ben and Gabe to assure them that adding slaves was not the goal. They only needed more help, and the new arrivals would have the same advantages as they did. Gabe asked everyone to help with the adjustment these new people would be facing, and make them feel welcome. He assured the group absolutely nothing would be changing, except the family was growing. Gabe asked everyone to pray for him as he sat out for this adventure. As the meeting ended, Big John and Delia stood together saying, "Des people's be needin help knowing how we's does thangs here, what's dey cans say and what dey cants. I's say we's divvy up, en help em."

Gabe stood and watched as the former slaves divided into groups, each being responsible to teach something to the new arrivals. It never ceased to amaze him how much his family had learned.

"The Baton Rouge Plantation Owners Association meeting will now come to order," The new president of the association, Mr. Simoneaux announced.

"Are there any announcements before we begin?"

Gabe stood and said, "Yes sir, I have an announcement to make."

"Come on up Mr. Lyon. You have the floor," Mr. Simoneaux said wavering his hand.

Gabe took his place behind the podium and said, "As you know my father- in- law has Mr. Broussard's plantation. He's finished with all the repair work, and is looking to buy slaves. If anyone has any for sale, please see me after the meeting. Thank you."

"We'd all like to meet your father - in- law Mr. Lyon. It would be nice of him to start attending our meetings," Mr. Simoneaux informed him.

"He's asked me to handle the majority of things for now because he's so busy. I'll tell him and get him to attend the next meeting," Gabe promised as he left the podium and returned to his seat.

For the next hour and half, Gabe listened in amazement, as he found out the majority of the plantations in the area were in trouble. Crops had failed, and sickness had taken live stock. Crop yields were down and no one knew why. Gabe knew it was by the grace of God his own plantation had flourished.

After the meeting, two men approached Gabe with news they were selling slaves. Gabe agreed to come to each plantation and made appointment times. He couldn't believe how fast things were moving. He really didn't believe anyone would seek him out so soon, but then he hadn't realized what a hard time the others were having.

On Saturday morning, Gabe set out on horse back with Ben following behind in the big wagon. As they approached Mr. LeBlanc's plantation, Gabe stopped and said to Ben, "Are you ready to do this?"

Ben smiled and said, "Yez sah Massa, I's ready!" This statement brought a surprised look from Gabe, and then both men broke out laughing.

"I don't believe your heart was in that!" Gabe said to Ben chuckling.

"No sah, my heart aint got nothin ta do wid it," Ben replied which caused both men to laugh harder. After a few minutes, they were able to regain their composure to continue on.

Gabe thought Mr. LeBlanc's plantation was beautiful. He loved the way the trees formed a canopy over the driveway. Water fountains were placed strategically throughout the landscape of the front lawn, with flower beds lining the front of the large house.

Mr. LeBlanc was waiting for him as he arrived. Gabe was greeted warmly by the man and was introduced to Mrs. LeBlanc. She was a charming woman who was very much with child. So it came as a surprise to Gabe when Mr. LeBlanc led him to the slave quarters. The conditions there were sad, but not as bad as he thought he would find them. In the middle of the quarters, several men, women and children were waiting, clinging to each other with fear in their eyes.

"These are the ones I wish to sell," Mr. LeBlanc informed Gabe.

"Are they families?" Gabe asked.

"Some are, but not all of them," Mr. LeBlanc said.

Gabe walked over to the first man who appeared to be in his early thirties. He smiled then asked, "What's your name?"

The man looked at Mr. LeBlanc for permission to speak, which Mr. LeBlanc gave with a nod of his head.

"My name be Peter. sah," he replied with a lowered head.

"Is this your family, Peter?" Gabe asked.

"Yez sah," Peter replied.

"Is it all of your family?"

"Yez, sah. Dis be my woman Rose, en dis be my boys Matthew and Tom. Dis here be my girl Rosie. Gabe looked to where Peter pointed. Matthew looked to be about fifteen. Tom appeared to be twelve and little Rosie was about five years old. Nodding, Gabe went down to the next man. This man was almost as big as Big John, and about the same age. "What's your name?"

"I's be Zach, sah," he answered.

"Is this your family?"

"Yez, sah. Dis be my woman Ginny. Aint got no chilin sah," Zach said not looking at Gabe.

Gabe nodded and moved to the last group, approaching a short slim man of about thirty something, and asked, "What's your name?"

"I's be called Dancy, sah," the man replied.

"Is this your family?" Gabe asked.

"Yez sah, des be my woman Hildie. De little'ins be Ludie, Jasper, Bar and Clem, sah. Dey aint blood sah, the chilin's ma en paw died en we's be wantin ta stays together.

"Dancy!" Mr. LeBlanc shouted. "That's enough!"

Quickly Dancy lowered his head, and didn't say another word. Gabe walked back to Mr. LeBlanc and stood quietly. Gabe was sure Mr. LeBlanc thought he was thinking about who to buy, but in fact he was praying to control his anger due to the way Mr. LeBlanc had talked to Dancy.

When Gabe's anger subsided he turned to Mr. LeBlanc and said, "I'll take them all. You and I should go and finish our business together, while they gather their things. Ben will help them and show them to the wagon. With that, Gabe and Mr. Leblanc left to finish their business.

Ben walked over to the group that huddled together before him, and said, "It be a blessin ta ya dat Massa Gabe bought ya. Don't ya be a fearin." The group had only confusion and fear in their eyes. Ben offered encouragement to them as he led them to the wagon.

Gabe was sick at his stomach. He didn't know if he was going to be able to get through the purchase. All he could do was pray. Every time he looked at those frightened people in the wagon, he felt the guilt of his forefather's sins.

He prayed and asked forgiveness for them, and himself as they headed for Mr. Chaumont's plantation.

Gabe didn't even notice Mr. Chaumont's plantation. He was too busy praying and asking God for His help. As they approached the front of the house, Gabe noticed Mr. Chaumont was waiting. Standing beside him, was a big heavy set sweaty man with a whip in his hand. "Oh no Lord, please, help me through this," Gabe prayed silently. When they came to a stop, Gabe turned to Ben. "Wait here please. No need for you to come around until I call for you."

Ben nodded and said, "Yes sah."

Gabe dismounted from his horse, and was immediately greeted by Mr. Chaumont firm hand shake. "Mr. Lyon, welcome to Chaumont Plantation!"

"Thank you, who's this gentleman with you?" Gabe asked.

"This is my overseer, Townson," Mr. Chaumont said with pride. "Would you like to come in for some refreshment?"

"No, thank you sir, I need to be heading home soon. I'd like to see what you have for me," Gabe said quickly.

Gabe wasn't prepared for what he saw. It was a horrible injustice. Mr. Chaumont's animals had a better place to live than his slaves. The clothes these people had on were nothing but rags held together with a hope and a prayer. Their cabins looked more like rickety old shacks. He could almost see right through them. Gabe felt the nausea rise in his stomach. He was so glad he had Ben and the others wait in the side drive. In the middle of the slave quarters, a large group of men, women and some children stood waiting. As Gabe and Mr. Chaumont came toward them, Townson went over to the group, and grabbed the first man by his arm, and practically threw him on the ground at Gabe's feet. The slim man stood to his feet slowly with his eyes on the ground. Gabe looked at Townson and said, "I can handle this myself, thank you. I'll call you if I need you." Townson looked confused, and looked over at Mr. Chaumont, who motioned for him to come to his side.

Gabe walked over to the slim man, and asked, "What's your name?"

"I be Ephrom ,sah," the man said with his eyes on the ground.

"Ephrom do you have family?"

"No sah," he said.

"Would you go with me and introduce me to the others?"

"Yez sah," he said and walked with Gabe to the group.

There Gabe met Leola, a young girl of about eighteen and Woodley, a thin man of about twenty five, and his young wife, Joy, who was with child. Then Polk and Myra, husband and wife of about nineteen, with one small child of two, named Ella. Next were three brothers, Venell was about fifteen, Hess was about seventeen, and Roy, who was the oldest, at eighteen years of age. Gabe asked each one if they were leaving behind any family, and all answered no. Satisfied with his answers, Gabe turned and joined Mr. Chaumont. "I'll take all of them. You and I will go finish our business while they gather their things. I'll have Ben take the wagon down to help."

"No need. They don't have anything but what's on their backs. They can walk to the wagon," Mr. Chaumont told him.

Gabe and Mr. Chaumont walked to the house, and as they came within hearing range of Ben and the wagon, Gabe said, "Ben, would you go gather everyone and get them in the wagon? We'll be leaving here as soon as we're finished."

"Yez sah," Ben replied taking the reins of the horses, and moving toward the back.

Josie, Hannah and Liza, along with the rest of the women of New Canaan, were busy as they prepared for the new arrivals. An inventory of extra clothes and shoes had been made, and brought to the church. Every family had donated something that might be needed by the people arriving shortly. A large meal had been prepared for everyone, and would be eaten outside as a welcoming gesture. Not sure how many people Gabe would be bringing back, the women had gone out of their way to make sure their feast had lots of extras.

Gabe needed to talk with Ben as soon as they were a safe distance from the Chaumont plantation. He hadn't planned on buying so many slaves today, but he couldn't leave them in the sad situations he found them. For once, he felt better about buying slaves, only because he knew they wouldn't be slaves long. Their lives were about to improve one hundred percent. Judging from the sad expressions, and fearful eyes of these people, they didn't know the good, and probably expected only the worse.

Slowing his horse, Gabe waited for Ben to catch up to him and stopped. Dismounting from his horse, he went to Ben and said, "I think we're a safe distance away from Chaumont's, and I don't expect we'll pass anyone on this road. That wagon looks like it's about to bust with all those people. I think I'll put some of the children on my horse, and if you would, please move Woodley and his wife up here with you. Joy has to be uncomfortable riding back there, being with child. If you don't mind, how about walking with me for a while so we can talk?"

"Yez Mr. Gabe, I be believin we's needin ta sort sum thangs out," Ben answered.

Gabe nodded, and Ben began to make the changes in the wagon, while Gabe walked to the back and asked Dancy, "How about Bar, Jasper and Ludie riding my horse for a while? Will that be okay with you?"

Dancy looked confused. He looked from Gabe to the horse, then back at Gabe and said, "Yez sah Massa, but what is you riding?"

Smiling, Gabe said, "I'm going to walk the rest of the way. This wagon is too crowded, and we need to make it more comfortable."

Still confused, Dancy nodded at the children, who had heard everything, and helped them out of the wagon. Gabe lifted them one by one onto his horse. He couldn't get over how little the children weighed, and how boney they felt through their clothes.

Ben had moved Woodley and Joy to the bench of the wagon, and asked Myra to sit with them with her baby daughter Ella. "Would ya be a mindin, Woodley, ta de take rein? I's be needin ta speak wid Mr. Gabe."

Woodley nodded in agreement, and took the reins. "Jus be keepin on dis here road. I's tell ya ifin we's need ta change."

Ben walked over to Gabe while he led his horse with the children.

"I didn't know I was going to be bringing twenty four people home with us today," Gabe said looking to Ben for some sort of comfort.

"Ya did goodly, Mr. Gabe. Our'in family be having thangs ready when we's git home. My Liza an your Josie be good women, and dey gots thangs in hand," Ben assured him.

"I know. I sure hope you're right about them having things in hand! Mine and your idea of having things in hand is different than Josie's and Liza's," Gabe laughed.

Woodley watched as Gabe and Ben walked together. He had never seen a slave and his master walk and talk together, much less laugh as if they were friends. Joy leaned over and whispered, "Aint never see'd any thang like dat afore. Dey's be laughin like friends, an de Massa wantin me an Myra en de chil ta be sittin easy like! Aint never see'd it afore," she repeated with a slight smile.

Gabe and Ben had finished their conversation, and were walking in a comfortable silence the way old friends do, each lost in their own thoughts.

They weren't aware of the eyes that watched them closely. A slight hope had been planted in their hearts that this Master would be good to them. The slaves talked softly among themselves about Gabe, how he spoke kindly to them, and wanted to make them comfortable in their wagon ride.

Gabe was happy to see New Canaan in the distance. This long weary day would soon be over. He truly hoped the slaves would be happy here and at Mount Haven. He would tell them later where they would be living. Right now he knew he was thirsty, and if he was, everyone else was too.

As they made their way down the drive of New Canaan and to the back, they were met with a big surprise. For there waiting for them, was all the people of New Canaan, and enough food for an army. Everyone was smiling and waving as the wagon was brought to a stop.

Delia and Big John came to the wagon and introduced themselves immediately to the new comers. Caleb took the reins of the horses, while Jonah helped everyone out of the wagon. Liza and Josie made over the babies, while Little John and Eli encouraged the boys to join them under a shade tree. Emlee offered drinks of lemonade, as they were surrounded with well- wishers.

"I think it's time to eat," Josie said to Gabe. "How about you make the announcement?"

"I think I will," Gabe said, dropping a kiss on her forehead, then walked to the steps of the porch. Picking up little Will Gabe said, "If everyone is ready, let's ask God's blessing upon our food."

Immediately the group became quite and Gabe prayed, "Father, we thank you for this day. We thank you for the new members of our family, and ask that you remove their fear, and give them peace. We thank you for this food, and ask your blessing upon it. In Jesus name, amen."

"When we're finished eating, we'll be going to the church where I'll introduce everyone to you, but for now enjoy your meal."

The slaves were shy and overwhelmed at first, but as the meal progressed, they seemed to relax and enjoy themselves. Gabe's heart strings had several tugs, as he watched the ones that had been so mistreated, eat their fill for the first time in a long while. He noticed the children were making attempts to hide bread for later, in the rags that were supposed to be clothes. He couldn't wait until they got new ones. With that thought he leaned over to Josie and asked, "Do we have some clothes for these people?"

"Of course, Gabe! Liza, Hannah and I have taken care of everything," she said with a smile that reached her eyes.

"Ben said you ladies would have everything under control," he said smiling back.

"Ben is wise and I thought you would be too, oh ye of little faith!" She answered laughing.

"There's twenty four of them. I just couldn't leave them in the conditions I found them. Mr. Chaumount has an overseer that carries a whip. I can only imagine what some of them have been through."

"That's in the past now. They're here with us, and they won't be slaves any longer," she said looking at him with love in her eyes. The fact was she had been praying that Gabe would leave no one behind. She prayed God would have present only those He wanted Gabe to take. God answered her prayers.

Gabe stood at his window and thought back over the past few weeks. So much had happened. He would never forget the surprise in the new slave's eyes as they received new clothes and shoes for the first time. He didn't know which hit him harder, the look on their faces when they received their new clothes, or when they walked into their new homes. It pulled at his heart remembering the way the women and children touched everything.

At first they were apprehensive upon learning they would be going to Mount Haven, and not staying at New Canaan. Then they met Professor Hall, and it seemed they had an instant bonding with the white haired man, and all was well. Gabe thanked the Lord for this. The three brothers, Venell, Hess and Roy where living with the young bachelor, Ephrom, at Ephrom's request. Apparently they had been friends when they lived at Chaumont's plantation.

Then Ben, Big John, and Henry took over. They explained to them the way things were at New Canaan and Mount Haven and why. It seems, according to Ben, they were more than willing to keep the secrets, and took the mark without hesitation. Liza and Hannah helped the new women with sewing, and Emlee started right away with getting the children settled in school. Since the family had grown, Charles volunteered to teach the adults. This made Emlee responsible only for the children, twelve years of age and younger. It seemed as if everyone was helping, and everything was working out well.

"Are you busy?" Josie asked from the doorway of the study.

"No, just thinking. Come on in," Gabe said, as he turned from the window to greet his wife.

"Are you worried?" She asked as she put her arms around him.

"No, I'm not. I was just thinking how well everything is going."

"Our God, is good isn't he?"

"Yes, He is. I don't know what I'd do without Him."

"Me either. I know it hasn't been easy on you lately. Everyone's trying to lighten your load."

"I'm aware of that, and very thankful. What is it that you want dear wife?"

"I wanted to tell you what Hannah told me earlier today.'

"What was that?" He asked holding her closely.

"She wanted us to know how the new hired hands were so thankful for being here. They want you to know they'll work hard for you, and for themselves, to pay you back for their freedom."

"Josie, they don't have to pay me for anything. I'm going to give them their freedom papers as a Christmas present. I don't want to ever buy another human being! I don't think I can do it again. It was the hardest thing I've ever done," he confided in her.

"You won't have to. I think everyone will be staying. I don't believe I've seen so many smiles in all my life. I've gotten so many flowers from the little ones, I could replant the flower beds," she said laughing.

"That's probably where they came from," Gabe said grinning as they sat down on the sofa.

"It doesn't matter if they did. I like getting flowers."

"The new shoes for Christmas have come in. Caleb picked them up for me yesterday. I think he's hidden them in the barn at Mount Haven," Gabe informed her.

"Yes he told me. Caleb also said the books and slates came in today. I'm glad because Emlee and Charles will be needing them."

"Christmas will be here soon! Have you been good?" Gabe asked her.

"Yes I have, just ask my husband!" she answered playfully.

"Is everything ready for Christmas Eve?"

"Yes it is. What a great Christmas this will be too!" she informed him.

"Yes it will be. Knowing you, and the ladies, it will be a big one!" Gabe teased.

"You're right! This Christmas will be a testimony to all of our blessings!"

"You and Will are the greatest blessings of all. I could never thank God enough for you two." Gabe told her softly.

It was Christmas Eve, and excitement filled the air along with the aroma of good food at both New Canaan and Mount Haven. Jonah had taken the children of Mount Haven to cut a tree, while Caleb had taken the children of New Canaan to do the same. Caleb had moved back to his old home now that the new workers had come, and Ephrom had taken over the barns.

Emlee was extremely happy about this, and so was Gabe. Gabe felt better having Caleb supervising Eli and Little John in the barns though; they proved to be excellent workers.

Gabe could hear laughter coming from the great ballroom. He knew Caleb and the children had brought in the tree. Making his way there, he stood and watched unnoticed as Josie handed each child a decoration to hang, which was different from last year. Little Will was on Josie's hip, laughing as the decorations went on the tree. Henry and Big John were busy setting up the tables, while James and Jerome, with the help of Dave and Dan, brought in the chairs. Susie and Nolee were busy decorating the room with candles and flowers. Tamis and Laney were busy putting tablecloths on the tables as fast as they were being set up. Everyone was singing, laughing and talking. It appeared that getting ready for Christmas was just as much fun as Christmas itself. For the first time in a long time Gabe felt at peace.

Professor Hall was laughing more than he had laughed in a long time. Just watching Charles and Hannah did his soul good. Jonah and the children had brought in the Christmas tree, and along with it, the excitement only a child knows at Christmas. Charles and Hannah included the children in decorating the tree. Professor Hall couldn't tell who the children were from who were the adults, for both were excited. Charles was doing his best to sing Christmas Carols, but his best was pretty bad. The man never could sing and it caused the children to laugh out loud at him. It didn't seem to bother him, as he continued making his joyful noise unto the Lord.

Hannah teased him making him and the children laugh. It was a wonderful sight and Professor Hall knew Charles and Hannah would make good parents.

Everyone from the two plantations had gathered in the great ballroom of New Canaan. Even Lieutenant Sanders and his soldiers were there. Laughter rang out through the room as everyone enjoyed the fellowship.

Finally, Gabe stood next to the tree that was laden with presents, and said, "Lets ask God's blessing upon our food." When every head was bowed, he prayed, "Thank you, Father, for what we are about to receive. We thank you for our families health, and prosperity, and all the blessings you have given us. I thank you Lord, for each and every person here and ask you to continue to be with us and keep us safe. In Jesus name, amen." At that, a group amen rang through the room.

Dinner was wonderful and truly enjoyed by all. The children ate quickly and gathered together at the back of the room. Clearly they were up to something.

At Josie's urging, Gabe stood and went to the tree again and said, "This year was our best year ever, even with buying Mount Haven and making all the repairs. To show our appreciation, Josie and I would like to give each family their own cow and chickens. If you will see Caleb, he'll go with you, so you can pick them out. If you would like sheep instead chickens, you can do so. Josie and I want to thank you for a wonderful year. For our family at Mount Haven, we also want to give you five acres of land, along with your cow and chickens. Would Peter, Rose, Zach, Ginny, Dancy, Hildie, Ephrom, Leola, Woodley, Joy, Polk, Myra, Venell, Hess and Roy please come up here?"

The group came up shyly with questioning looks upon their faces.

"Peter and Rose, these are your freedom papers, not only for you, but your children as well. Thank you for your hard work." Gabe then went down the line and gave everyone their freedom papers, and their children. When he reached the three brothers they were crying. Gabe spoke softly to them as he handed them their papers. As Gabe gave Roy his, all three brothers wrapped their arms around him, and pledged their loyalty to him and Professor Hall. It was all Gabe could do not to cry. He looked over at Josie for help, but saw she too was in tears. He stood there in the middle of these three brothers, telling them that God loved them so much that He picked them to be part of His family, and of the Lyon family. After a while, the boys regained their composure and let Gabe go.

As Gabe walked to the tree, Peter stopped him and said, "Massa, we's not worked as long as de others fo our'n freedom." Gabe placed his hand on Peters shoulder, and turned to face the room and said, "In the Bible, Jesus tells a parable of a man who needed workers for his vineyard. So, he goes out in the morning to hire the laborers. He agreed with them that for their labor, he would pay them a denarius, which is a day's wage. Then he went out about noontime, and saw others just standing in the market place, so he told them, you go also into my vineyard and whatever is right I will give and so they went. Then in the evening, he found others just standing around, and he said to them, why have you been standing here all day long? They answered him by saying, because no one hired us. So, he told them to go to his vineyard too. Well, when late evening came, he called his overseer to him and asked him to gather all the workers, and pay them their wages, beginning with the last group to the first. The last group each received a denarius. When the first group came, they thought they would receive more, but each received the same pay as the last. This made them angry and the landowner heard them saying, the others didn't work as much as they did, but he paid them the same. The landowner said to them, I did you no wrong. Did you not agree to work for a denarius? Take what is yours, and go, but I wish to give to the last the same as you. Is it not lawful for me to do what I wish with what is mine? The last shall be first, and the first shall be last. There is no difference."

"I's thank ya Massa, fo usin all," Peter told him with tears in his eyes.

"You're welcome, Peter. All of you are welcome. I'm not your Master, only God is your Master, and He's mine. Please call me Mr. Gabe."

"Yez sah, Mr. Gabe, what does we'ins calls him?" Peter asked pointing to Professor Hall.

Professor Hall stood, "You call me Mr. Hall or Professor Hall. It doesn't matter which." Smiling Peter nodded his head then led the group back to the tables.

"Let's give out the presents!" Gabe said cheerfully as he and Ben began to read out the names. After a long while everyone finally had their presents. Everyone received a book, fitting for their age, along with new shoes. The women received bolts of cloth, along with a sewing basket, laden with needles and threads. The men received tools of all kinds, such as a shovel, saw, hammer and nails. The smaller children received wooden toys, a bag of candy and new clothes. While the older girls and boys received the same as the adults along with new clothes.

After a while, Gabe reached behind the Christmas tree and brought out a bag. The head of each family received their portion of the profits from the crops. The new hired hands were amazed at holding money for the first time in their lives. The three brothers' portion was divided into thirds, as they had no head of their family.

Gabe gave Josie a golden pendant, and Josie gave Gabe a leather journal. Little Will got a rattle made from ivory and wooden blocks. Ben and Liza would be joining Hannah and Charles for their present exchange at Mount Haven along with the rest of their family. Professor Hall was delighted at receiving the latest best seller, and a pen set from Gabe and Josie.

They all stood side by side smiling at the blessings God had given them. The children came forward in a single file, singing Christmas Carols at the top of their voices. They'd been practicing for weeks. Only their sweet voices filled the room, for everyone else had become quiet to listen to the words of their song. As Gabe look around the room he saw a glow from the corner of his eye. As he turned to look closer, there appeared before him, Michael, in his brilliant white. He smiled and then with a nod of his head, he was gone. When the children had finished their Christmas surprise, Gabe read them the Christmas story from the Bible. Not even the smallest child made a sound as they listened about Jesus Christ's birth, for which this day is celebrated.

CHAPTER 13

THE SEA OF BLACKNESS ENVELOPED Gabe as if he'd been plunged into death itself. He couldn't see where he was, or where he was going. He only knew he was running as if his life depended on it. The darkness was so thick, he could feel it brush against his skin as he passed through it. Something strong was driving him forward, and he could feel the weight of it on his back.

Shouts of men, along with gun fire, filled his ears. The noise was so loud it hurt, but he couldn't lift his hands to protect himself. "Why am I here?" he cried out to the nothingness. Only the sounds of confusion answered him. It worsened as the shouts of unseen men turned to terrible cries of agony and pain.

The darkness thickened and he ran faster. His heart was beating so hard, he felt it would burst in his chest. Suddenly, a loud explosion rocked him! Gabe was jerked up in bed as if something or someone had yanked him to an upright position. He was breathless and fought to breathe while blinking his eyes rapidly to adjust to the darkness of his room. "A dream, I was having a dream!" he thought, as a flash of lightening lit the room, then plunged him into darkness as a mighty roll of thunder shook the night air.

Jumping from his bed, he quickly lit a lamp. First, he checked on Josie, who lay sleeping in their bed undisturbed by the noise of the storm. Then he looked over to little Will's bed. He watched the even rise and fall of Will's chest as he slept soundly. Gabe sighed in relief. His family was safe. Dressing in a shirt and trousers, Gabe picked up the lamp and made his way downstairs.

Gabe sat in his study as the storm raged outside. With his head in his hands, Gabe tried to figure out his dream. Was God trying to warn him about something, or was it just the storm that made him dream crazy dreams?

As he sat deep in thought, the Grandfather clock in the next room chimed the four o'clock hour.

Gabe told no one about his dream. He knew if God was trying to tell him something, He would keep on until he got it. The storm turned into a gentle rain, as morning dawned. "There wouldn't be much farming done today unless the rain stopped soon," he thought, as he made his way outside.

Ben met Gabe as he rounded the back of the house, "Mornin, Mr. Gabe, de storm wake ya?"

"I heard it well enough! Josie and Will slept right through it. Beats all I've ever seen."

"Dey's dat rest in de Lord ain't got nothin ta fear," Ben assured him.

"Truer words were never spoken. So tell me, what are we going to do today?"

"We's be needin ta ready de ground fer fall plantin. Not much ta do's less' in de rain stops. Woodley en Pete be askin ifin dey could have a wurd wid ya."

"Sure, I'm going over there later this morning, you want to go?"

"Naw sah, I's be needed here. Woodley en Pete be good workers, en de knows what dey be's a doin."

Together the men finished their morning ritual of checking the barns, talking with the workers, and getting the daily reports. The sugar cane had weathered the storm quite well, but the ground was too wet to work.

It continued to rain as Gabe rode over to Mount Haven to talk to Woodley and Pete. He was sure the two men were going to need some extra help. The improvements that met his eyes as he rode down the drive, were wonderful. He could tell the men put a lot of work into the yard and house. It made him smile. Professor Hall would soon be taking over most of the management of the plantation. Then, hopefully, he would be able to take over completely, and run it by himself. That was the day Gabe longed for. When that happened, he could get back to concentrating on God.

Gabe rode around to the back of the house and headed his horse towards the barns. Thinking he would stop by and say hello to Lieutenant Sanders first, he passed the small barn. Then he headed toward the wooded area where the largest barn stood just at its edge. It was the perfect disguise for the Union Army headquarters. As he drew near, Gabe noticed there was more activity than usual. As he looked closer, he noticed more soldiers and horses, which made him nervous. Dismounting from his horse, he quickly made his way inside the barn. The barn, which up until this time held only a few soldiers, seemed to be bulging at the seams with new faces dressed in blue. All eyes were upon Gabe as he walked swiftly to Lieutenant Sander's office.

Not bothering to knock, Gabe opened the office door and entered. As his gaze traveled the room, he found Lieutenant Sanders and several high ranking officers bent over a map, deep in conversation. Other soldiers moved about the room in a hushed quiet as they went about doing what appeared to be official business.

Gabe cleared his throat. "Lieutenant Sanders, is there something you need to be telling me?"

Startled, the group of men around the map looked up at Gabe. The expressions on their faces were both surprise and aggravation at the intrusion upon their meeting.

"Mr. Lyon, you can see we have some business to deal with right now. As soon as I'm finished here, I'll talk with you," Sanders said in his military voice.

"Who is this man, and why is he here?" A captain demanded impatiently.

"Sir, this is Gabriel Lyon, who has been so gracious to help us by allowing us to use his land," Lieutenant Sanders explained.

"Correction, Sanders!" Gabe said using his voice of authority. "When I met with President Lincoln at the White House, he asked me to help and that's why you're here!"

This unknown fact brought an immediate change of attitude from the officers, and they began introducing themselves. Gabe was polite, but he wanted answers, and he would not wait!

When introductions had finished, Gabe continued. "Gentlemen, let me be clear. I answer to no one except God and President Lincoln! Is that understood? While you're on my land, I'm to be informed of everything that's going on here. Don't let me be surprised again! Lieutenant Sanders, you and I will indeed be talking today!" Gabe turned and walked out of the room leaving the officers in a daze.

Gabe entered the barn and found Woodley and Pete working along side of Ephrom. The three men paused and looked up as Gabe entered. They could tell from the look on Gabe's face he wasn't happy.

"Howdy, Mr. Gabe," Pete said with caution.

"Hello Pete. Ben told me you and Woodley needed to talk to me."

"Yez sah, we's be fearin dat ya not knowd bout dem soldiers a comin," Woodley explained.

"You're right, I didn't."

"We's not rightly knowd what ta do Mr. Gabe. Dis here ain't never cum up afore," Ephrom told him. "But we knowd ya needed ta be tol!"

"If you ever at anytime, from here on out, think I need to know something, you get on a horse, take a wagon, or run to where I am and tell me. You have full access to everything on this plantation to use as you need. You don't have to ask for permission for one thing. This is your home! Understand?"

"Yez sah," the three answered in unison.

"Do you have any idea where Jonah is?"

"He up and left afore them boys in blue showd up. Dat Lieutenant sends him on sum kinda errand," Pete informed him.

"Does Professor Hall know about these soldiers being here?"

"Naw sah, we ain't tol nary a soul. Ephrom here be goin ta de house ifin ya hadn't showd," Woodley said.

"How long have they been here?"

"Cum sum time afore day light. De storm musta slow'd em sum, I's reckon." Pete said.

"Keep an eye on them while they're here. Let me know if anything changes. Professor Hall needs to know too. When Jonah gets back have him come see me. By the way, the plantation really looks good. Would you pass that on to everyone?"

"Yez sah, we's surely will," Ephrom said with a proud grin.

"I'm going to see Professor Hall, and then back to New Canaan. Oh, do you think we should take the fence down between New Canaan and Mount Haven? Think about it and get back to me. I don't know if it's a good idea or not, and I need advice." Gabe waved good bye and headed to the house.

Professor Hall was beside himself! How could he not know about the soldier's presence? The professor decided he needed a more active part in the activities at Mount Haven. From now on, he and Pete would walk the grounds as Gabe and Ben did. That way he'd know the workings of the plantation, and get to know the hired hands. After all, he considered himself to be a smart man, and he knew he could run this plantation. Yes, it was time to start earning his room and board!

The rain began to fall more heavily during the evening. Not much had been accomplished, and Lieutenant Sanders had yet to talk to Gabe.

So Gabe decided to spend the rest of the day with his wife and son. Seeking them out, he found both in the kitchen with Liza. The women were enjoying a cup of tea while watching a very active eleven month old showing off his new skill of walking. When Gabe entered the room, Will's little eyes lit up with joy at seeing his father. His son quickly forgot about walking and crawled as fast as his little hands and knees would carry him saying, "dada dada!" Picking him up, Gabe made an announcement. "Liza, take the rest of the day off! My wife and I are going to spend some time with our son."

"Now ya might be agivin me de rest of de day off, but I's knowd cum time ta eat ya be a hollerin loud," Liza's laugh filled the room.

"Not this time!" Gabe in a loud whisper added. "That's why I have a wife!"

Liza laughed and Josie rolled her eyes saying, "Men!"

Little Will thought it was funny too, and clapped his little hands and giggled as if he sided with his father, which caused the grownups to laugh.

Little Will fell asleep in his father's arms, because he was all played out. Gabe really enjoyed the time with his family. He promised Josie that as soon as her father learned the plantation business, they would do it more often.

Josie and Gabe were heading up the stairs to bed when they heard a knock at the door. Gabe kissed his wife, "I'll be up soon, you go on to bed."

"Don't be too long. It's been a long day and you're tired too," she reminded him. Smiling in agreement, he turned to go and answer the door.

Gabe greeted Lieutenant Sanders and showed him into his study. He was tired and didn't feel this conversation was going to go anywhere, and it hadn't even begun.

"I've come to apologize to you, Gabe," Lieutenant Sanders began. "I should've let you know they were coming."

"Yes, you should have, but that's the past now. Tell me what's going on?"

"It seems the general returned to Allen's farm, and found all his men gone. He couldn't tell if they'd been captured, or just up and left. Anyway, he's calling in troops."

"So what's that got to do with all the blue at Mount Haven?"

"We're getting ready for battle," Lieutenant Sanders said, looking Gabe directly in the eyes.

"Then you best get some rest, it might be the last for a while."

"Yes sir. I'll leave you now," Lieutenant Sanders turned to leave the room.

"Jacob?" Gabe said, using the Lieutenants first name.

"Yes Sir?"

"We'll be praying for you."

"Thank you, Gabe, I'll need it."

As soon as Sanders was gone, Gabe jumped into action. Going to Ben's door, he ask Ben to join him in the study. Then he was out the back door to stop the first person he saw. Seeing Little John, he called to him, "Little John?"

"Yez sah, Mr. Gabe!"

"Would you go get your father, and Caleb, and have them come to the house? Tell them I'll be in the study waiting for them."

"Yez sah!" Little John assured him, and ran to do as he was asked.

Gabe returned to his study to wait. Falling on his knees, he asked God to give him guidance and direction. He asked God to protect his family and keep them safe. He asked for the right words to use so he wouldn't cause panic.

Within a short time all were gathered in Gabe's study. Explaining the situation quickly, he asked for suggestions. It seemed everyone had one. The best came from Ben who said, they should go to Mount Haven and have the meeting there. Then Gabe wouldn't have to repeat himself. "Best ta be a plannin wid de others," he stated, and Gabe agreed.

"I'm going to tell Josie where we'll be, and why. I suggest you tell your wives too. We'll meet out front in fifteen minutes. I know it's late, and we have a lot to do. I just want to take this time to tell you how much I appreciate each of you, and to thank you for all your help."

"We's be fambly, en dat's what fambly do's," Caleb told him, then asked,

"We's be a needin de wagon or horses?"

"The wagon please, that way we can talk on the way. Quickly they went their separate ways, knowing they only had fifteen minutes before meeting at the front of the house.

Josie was on her knees praying before she heard the door close, as Gabe left.

She placed her petition before God with confidence. He would not only hear, but answer her. Then with the peace only God can give, she climbed into bed and went to sleep.

Professor Hall answered the door in his night robe. He didn't understand why the men were on his porch.

"We need to talk," Gabe said immediately. "We need Charles, Pete, Woodley, Ephrom and Jonah here before we start."

"Okay, but Jonah isn't back yet," Professor Hall informed him.

"I's get Pete and de others. I's be quick bout it!" Caleb said, and left the room in a hurry.

Gabe explained the situation at hand to the men. No one seemed surprised to hear a battle was coming. Together they made plans. The women and children would all be moved to New Canaan at daylight. The men would stay and move the cattle to a safe pasture to the back of the plantation. Caleb and Ephrom would move the horses back to New Canaan's barns, then bring extra food from the storehouses to the kitchen.

"Mr. Gabe, I's been thinkin bout de fence we's talk bout. Ifin we's take a portion down in de woods dat joins de two lands, we's be makin a short cut from here ta New Canaan. Dis ways we's not be needin ta take de road," Woodley informed him.

"Then let's do it. If you'll show me and Professor Hall, we will get started on it. If anyone comes up with anymore suggestions, please share them. I guess we'd better get busy men. We've got a lot to do before we sleep."

By late afternoon the two plantations merged into one. Liza and Hannah made a late lunch for the hard working men. Emlee kept the children out of the way by playing with them at the church. The women from Mount Haven moved their belongings in with the assigned families at New Canaan. They were ready.

Josie kept busy making bandages at Liza's request. She cut so much cloth that her hands were getting sore, but she continued on. Her thoughts were on how to keep the children and women safe during the battle when it came. The only answer she could come up with was to move them into the house. If anything were to happen to one of them, she would never forgive herself. She stopped long enough from her task to find Liza and tell her about the plan. Liza was in agreement, and the word was passed when the time came everyone was to come to the house, bringing only what they needed.

By the next day, everything was in place. Everyone knew what they're assignment was. Life settled into an easy pace with the women and children at New Canaan, and the men working both plantations as a team. Professor Hall loved being in the same house with his grandson, and Liza loved having Hannah and Charles at her side.

Jonah rode as hard as he could toward Mount Haven. He knew if he was seen, he'd never get the information to Lieutenant Sanders. He thanked God for the darkness of the night, and the light of the moon. "Lord, I's be askin ya ta git's me home alivin!" he prayed as he pushed his horse faster toward home.

Riding into Mount Haven, Jonah didn't notice all the changes. His mind was occupied with important information for Lieutenant Sanders. Bringing his horse to an abrupt stop, and whispering his thanks to the Lord, he dismounted and ran toward Lieutenant Sander's office. It wasn't long before his information was delivered and the troops were called to arms. The soldiers sprang into action when they learned Confederate troops were just outside of Baton Rouge.

It began in the early morning hours. Gun fire and cannon explosions could be heard all around them. Gabe jumped to his feet and dressed while Josie threw on a robe and got little Will from his bed. When they arrived down stairs, Ben hurried to him. "It be a startin, we's best be get de women and chilin in de house! Charles and Hannah, already dressed, went to see if they could help move things along faster. Soon Gabe's family was in the safety of the house.

The women seemed calm as they took over. They comforted the frightened, and brought in the things needed for the night. Emlee gathered the children together and kept them occupied so they wouldn't be scared. Liza started making biscuits, and Josie sliced the large ham Caleb brought by the kitchen. Hannah had Will, and gathered the women with babies to her side speaking words of comfort. The men ran back and forth doing only the necessary chores, and then returned to the house.

Smoke could be seen rising over the tops of the trees coming from the town. Cries and shouts could be heard as the battle gained force. Rapid shelling sounded from the direction of the river, letting the men know this was not only a battle on land, but on water too. Gabe and Ben looked at each other with concern. Soon the noise from the battle got closer as the Union and Confederate armies moved across the surrounding countryside.

Gabe stood outside on the porch, and gathered the men together. Taking his Bible, he turned to Psalms ninety one and began to read out loud God's promise of protection. After the reading, he prayed and asked God to do as his word promised. When he finished, he said, "Let's take our places. As we do, be careful and stay safe. We'll meet back here in two hours." Nodding in agreement the men turned and stepped into the yard to leave, but stopped suddenly in their tracks. No one said a word as they stared in amazement at the sight. Angelic beings surrounding the grounds as a wall of protection, stood shoulder to shoulder. Professor Hall was the first to find his voice saying, "Look! They're surrounding the house from all sides!" Then falling on his knees, he prayed out loud his thanks to the Lord. The others quickly followed his example.

Gabe looked up and saw Michael coming toward him in a brilliant light. Gabe jumped to his feet and ran to met him. Professor Hall and the other's watched with excitement as the two greeted each other with an embrace. Pulling away slightly, Michael proclaimed loudly, "Fear not, for the Lord has heard your prayers. Know this! Though you can not see us, we shall always be protecting you from harm. There are more of us, than of them. Then bowing, the angelic beings faded away, leaving each man knowing that God was in control and his angels were protecting them.

Fear was no longer present at New Canaan as the men quickly scattered to their assigned places. Each man left with the knowledge that no harm would come to their families. They were excited knowing they had truly experienced a miracle from God. A truer knowledge of God was etched into the hearts of every person who witnessed the sight. They knew they would never be the same.

The battle raged on as night fell. Soon, reports came of wounded men lying on battle grounds that had been left behind, as the battle moved forward.

"De's be men a cryin in pain, Mr. Gabe, whatcha be think we's ta do?" Woodley asked.

"They've just been left to die?" Gabe ask in disbelief.

"It be lookin like it."

Calling Josie and Liza to the kitchen, Gabe informed them about what happened. "We need to do something Gabe; we can't just leave them to die!" Josie exclaimed.

Liza was thoughtful as she listened, then said, "I's knowd we's need ta help dem soldiers. Des what I's be thinkin. We's can get em an take em to de other house. Me an Hannah can see'd to em there."

"Bring them to Mount Haven? Do you think that's wise?" Gabe asked with concern.

"It's all we can do! We just can't leave them! With Liza, Hannah and myself working together, we can do this," Josie said with determination.

"What about Will? He needs you," Gabe reminded her gently.

"Will is going to be fine. I'll ask Delia to watch him while I'm gone."

"You don't know how long that will be once you get started, my love," Gabe said softly.

"I's send her home as soon as I's can. Den maybe Ginny can cum an help," Liza told him.

"I'll go with them," Professor Hall said. "That way the ladies won't be by themselves. If you can spare another man or two to go along with us, it would help."

"I see you're determined to do this, and I know in my heart its right. Okay, go. Take Dancy, Zach and Big John with you. We'll give you time to get there before we start bringing the wounded to you. Josie, are sure you want to leave Will tonight?" Gabe asked one more time.

"He's asleep right now. He's so used to Delia he won't miss me. I promise to be back before long."

"Alright then, gather what you need. I'll get Caleb, Woodley and the others together, and let them know what we're doing. Maybe we're here for such a time as this."

Nodding, Josie kissed her husband and hurried to find Delia. Liza went to retrieve her trunk of herbs and bandages, and to get Hannah. Professor Hall went to find Big John, Dancy and Zach. Soon the group was moving through the night toward Mount Haven, determined to accomplish God's will.

Gabe and Woodley stood at the edge of battle field that now lay silent, except for the occasional cries of the wounded, and the distant sound of gunfire. The battle had moved forward toward the river. Never had Gabe seen such bloodshed in all his life. He didn't know where to begin. Quietly, he and Woodley made their way through the field, checking for life among the bodies that lay scattered in all directions.

Woodley approached Gabe and whispered, "I's be gathering dem dat be cryin out, first. Ifin ya want ya can be checkin dem dat be layin near em."

Taking their lanterns, they began to search. The stench of blood filled their nostrils as they moved bodies, searching for life. Gabe paused and looked about. He listened for any noise that would let him know someone was still alive. As he lifted his foot, something grabbed him by the cuff of his trousers. Looking down, Gabe came face to face with a young soldier covered in blood, whose leg was badly mangled. The young man cried weakly to Gabe saying, "Please...please help me." Quickly Gabe called Woodley to him. Together they picked the young man up and carried him to Caleb and the waiting wagon.

"He's bleeding badly. I don't think he'll be able to wait. Take him up to the house, but hurry back Caleb! Bring back some bandages and water. I have a feeling we'll need them."

As Caleb left, Gabe and Woodley moved over the field. There was more dead than alive. After a while, they began to find soldiers that were breathing. The one that bothered Gabe most was a soldier that couldn't have been more than fifteen years old. The child was scared and crying like a baby.

"What's your name, son?" Gabe asked as he checked the boy's wounds.

"Tim... my name...is Tim. Are... you an... angel?" he asked between sobs.

"No Tim, I'm just a man," Gabe assured him.

"I've been praying... someone would... find me," he said weakly. "I thought I was.... dying and God sent an angel ...to come get me."

"God answered your prayers, he sent me. My name is Gabe, and I'm taking you to my house to get you some help."

"Thank you," the boy whispered just before he lost consciousness.

As Gabe carried the boy he became aware of the sticky ground.

"Where's this mud coming from? It hasn't been raining, Gabe asked, directing his question to Woodley.

"It ain't mud cause frum water, Mr. Gabe. It be frum de blood," Woodley said sadly.

Gabe couldn't say a word. He was sick. He could only imagine how much blood had been spilled to cause the ground to be so wet. He lay the boy down where Caleb could find him, and went back to searching.

Gabe and Woodley continued. Gabe had noticed Woodley would occasionally stop and throw up. The badly mangled bodies of the dead often lay over those who were alive. It was this that caused their stomachs to be rebellious. For some reason, they couldn't find anyone who could walk or that was lightly wounded. Gabe reasoned those soldiers were helped by their friends, while those that were badly wounded were just left behind to die.

Josie, Liza and Hannah readied the rooms for the arrival of the wounded, as Professor Hall and Big John kept watch outside. Zach went between the two groups, helping where he was needed. Soon Caleb arrived with the wounded soldier. Zach and Big John helped carry the young man to a room, while Professor Hall went for the bandages Caleb requested.

"Ya be needin more bed's maw. Deys be lots ta cum," Caleb informed his mother.

"Ya jus be's careful en bring em in," Liza whispered.

"Yez em, I's be back soon."

The young man was in terrible pain and rightly so. Working quickly the women removed the filthy uniform covering his leg. Liza and Josie began to wash his wounds, while Hannah retrieved the herbs that would stop the pain and fight infection. This was only the beginning of a long night that would test the strength of the women who worked hard at saving lives.

Caleb arrived at the battle field to find men lying at its edge. With the help of Gabe and Woodley, he loaded the wagon and began his trip back, promising to bring Zach when he returned to made things go faster.

That's how the night proceeded. Gabe and Woodley looking for wounded, while Caleb took them to the house. The women worked feverishly tending to wounds. They offered comfort, words of encouragement, prayers and led souls to salvation. The beds in the house quickly filled. Soon palettes were placed on the floor of the ballroom, as more soldiers arrived. Professor Hall was sent to New Canaan to get more help, as the number of wounded became more than the three women could handle.

As the sun rose in the morning sky, the sounds of battle began to diminish. Gabe and Woodley were exhausted, but they weren't alone. Everyone involved was tired. Gabe walked toward Woodley who sat on the ground.

"I guess we can make one more pass to see if we've missed anyone."

"Mr. Gabe, we's ain't missed nary a soul. It be the Lord dat took us ta dem we's got. De rest be dead sorry ta say."

"You're right."

"I's be a pondering, Mr. Gabe. Does ya think dat sumbodies be comin ta look fer em?"

"I don't know Woodley, maybe…hopefully someone will."

"Den we's got trouble," Woodley informed him.

"What do you mean?"

"Me an yo pay no never mind ta de color dem boy's be wearin, but I's be thinkin, dem boy's or de body cumin lookin fer em will!"

Gabe groan out loud, and sat with a thud beside Woodley. "I didn't think!" he exclaimed.

"De Lord knowd ya wouldn't. Dats why we's be here. Ya surd beat all Mr. Gabe. Ya don't see'd color of skin, and ya don't see'd de color of war. Ya jus does what's be a needin. Ya Missus be de same."

"There's a lot of folks out there Woodley, that feel the same way. One day this war is going to be over and you'll see."

"When des war be over, I ain't gona go no place. I's be stayin here. Des be my home!"

Gabe stood to his feet and held his hand out to help Woodley up. "I guess we'd better be going to the house and getting rid of some uniforms. Whatcha think?"

"I's feel a chill in de air. I's be thinkin dat a fire would be right handy bout now," Woodley said with mocked seriousness.

Smiling with understanding, Gabe said, "You know Woodley, I think you're right. I feel a chill in the air too!"

With that, Gabe and Woodley exhausted, started toward Mount Haven. They had one more thing to do before they could rest.

Liza sent Josie home to get some sleep as promised. She herself was exhausted and wanted only to lie down for a few minutes. Hannah, seeing her mother struggle, went to her side and said, "Ma, go and rest for a while in my room. You look so tired."

"I's gotta see'd ta ya paw afore I's be gettin sleep."

"Ma, you know pa and Charles are handling things at New Canaan, and if they need anything they'll send for us. Now go sleep for a while, and when you wake up, I'll take a turn. Then we'll send the others one at a time until everyone is rested enough to keep working. We've a long day ahead of us."

"I's knowd ya be rite. Jus don't seem rite dat my girl be tellin me what ta do," Liza said laughing.

"I'm fully grown now and a married women. I'm doing what you would do," Hannah said teasingly, then added, "Now go before you fall over!"

Without further fuss, Liz did as she was told.

Ben couldn't believe he had fallen asleep sometime during the early morning hours. He was relieved to see Charles coming toward him.

"The women are hard at work in the kitchen fixing breakfast," Charles said. It was a good idea to put the children in the beds upstairs last night. Emlee said they fell asleep without any trouble," Charles continued. "Delia opened the nursery and put all the babies there, so they wouldn't be awakened by our talking. Pete took charge of the boys and went with them to tend to the animals this morning. Henry and his group came by and said the gun fire has died down. Even Josie came home. She said Mount Haven was running over with wounded soldiers, but everything was under control. The only one missing, is Jonah. No one's heard from him," Charles stated.

"De Lord be bringin Jonah home, I be knowin it! Ya did good Charles. Thank ya fer lettin me rest," said Ben.

"All I did was what you said needed to be done. It was nothing Ben, and you needed some sleep. I know you're exhausted. I also know you feel responsible for everyone even, Gabe. I just want you to know I'm here to help you." The call to breakfast stopped any further conversation, as both men went in search for a cup of coffee.

Gabe was glad Josie had gone home, and Liza was taking a nap. He and Woodley went through the house gathering up all the uniforms they could find. These poor men would be needing other clothes to wear, but for right now, a fire should to be started. Clothes would be a worry for another day.

Hannah went from one bed to another, giving sips of water and herbs for pain and infection. The faces lying before her broke her heart. War never did anything but help death do its job. These men were sons, husbands, and brothers to someone somewhere. One day hopefully, they would return home to them. Helping them get there was her job.

Hannah went upstairs to the room of the young soldier who was the first to arrive. It was time to check his wounds. Entering the room she found him awake. "How are you feeling?" She asked.

"Do you believe in angels?" he asked.

"Yes I do, why?"

"I think I saw one last night. I'm not sure."

"Why don't you tell me about it?"

"I remember being out on that field hurting like…well in a lot of pain. I was praying to God, begging him for help, when this light came over me. It was a bright light that shown all around. This angel told me not to worry, and help was on the way. I didn't know what to say. All I could do was look into his eyes. The longer I looked into his eyes, the better I felt. I don't know why… I just did. Then this man came. I know he was a real man because he carried a lantern. I reached out, and grabbed his leg and ask him to help me and he did. The next thing I knew, I was here."

"I believe you really did see an angel. What's your name?" She asked.

"My name is Anthony St. John."

"Well, Anthony St. John, I'm Hannah Wood. The man who brought you here is Gabe Lyon. He's a wonderful man of God that seeks the Lord for direction. The angel knew this. That's how God answered your prayers. If God sent his angel to you, then your life was saved for a reason. You might want to think about that."

"Yes ma'am, that's what I've been doing, until I go to sleep," he answered.

"Right now Mr. St. John, I need to check your wound and change your bandage. I'm not going to lie to you, it's going to hurt. Just bear with me, and when I'm finished, I'll give you something for the pain and to keep the infection away. Do you think you could do that?"

"Yes ma'am, I think I can," he answered weakly.

Hannah worked quickly at removing the bandage. The bleeding had stopped, but the leg still looked bad. Saying a silent prayer for healing, she applied a salve along with a clean bandage. Seeing the pain in his eyes, she quickly gave him the herbal tea to drink. She sat with him and waited for him to fall asleep. When he had, she left him and went to the next room.

Gabe woke Josie with a kiss. She smiled and slowly opened her eyes.

"Time to wake up, sleepy head, or you won't be able to sleep tonight, unless you're going back this evening to help Liza."

"No, I'm needed here tonight, but in the morning, I will."

"Good because I've missed you. Your son's missed you too, he keeps calling for you."

This tugged at her heart strings. "Liza and Hannah will need lots of help. Gabe there's about forty men over there," she informed him.

"I know, I gathered them, remember?"

"I remember. How could I forget? Gabe, how have you been handling all of the blood and pain?" she asked.

"I've been praying...a lot! We do have one small problem though."

"What's that?" she asked as she sat up in bed.

"We've got to get those men out of their uniforms as soon as we can."

"Why?" She asked not understanding.

"Because, we've got both gray, and blue over there!"

"Oh my, I didn't realize. I sure don't want them fighting between themselves as they get better," she said with understanding.

"It's more than that! Someone's going to come looking for them sooner or later. Right now the battle is what's keeping them away. It doesn't matter who wins this battle or this war, we could be in big trouble and so could the men who are not on the winning side."

"What are we going to do?"

"We're going to get rid of all those uniforms. Woodley and I gathered the ones we could this morning and burned them. We just need to keep them boys from finding out who is confederate and whose union."

"You know what? I'm not going to worry about it! God has brought us through so much, and I know He'll keep on doing it. Now, I'm going to go find my son. I've missed him. Kissing her husband, quickly she headed for the stairs.

Jonah only knew he had to get home, because there he could find help for his friend. Jacob Sanders was hurt and needed attention. His maw would be able to help. Jonah prayed as he carried his friend across the field. Thinking his mother would be at New Canaan, he made his way in that direction. Tears of joy came to his eyes as he saw the house standing in the distance.

"Jacob, can ya heard me?"

"Yes," he answered weakly.

"Home be in sight. I's gona laid ya under des here tree en goes fo help. I's promise ya I's be right back." All Lieutenant Sanders could do was nod his head then closed his eyes.

After making Jacob as comfortable as possible, Jonah took off running toward the house. When he finally reached the back door, he leaped to the porch without touching a step. Throwing the door open, he shouted into the kitchen, "Maw! Paw! I's be needin help!"

People came running from all direction at his cry, with Ben leading the way. Seeing his father, Jonah continued, "Paw it be Jacob cum quick like, an bring maw. He be hurt somethin awful!"

"Charles, we's be needin a wagon! Little John, go wid Charles.

Where be de Lieutenant, son?" Ben asked quickly. All Jonah could do was point in the direction of where he'd left him.

Big John carried Lieutenant Sanders into Gabe's old room and laid him down gently. Gabe and Jonah followed behind them. Liza shooed everyone from the room, except Big John, who has done more than she could have ever expected. He'd proven to be her favorite helper. She was glad the others were busy, and it would only be the two of them. Big John was the calm in the midst of the storm. Quickly removing Lieutenant Sander's shirt, she began to examine his wounds.

Charles, Gabe and Jonah waited in the hall. As they sat with their backs against the wall, Jonah began to tell them what happened. "Dem Confederates was gona surprise usin but we's found em out. Deys be

wantin ta fight anyway. Cum daylight, we's be in de middle of de town. Dem Confederates be group in two parts north of us' in. It be a mighty fierce battle. Dat General Williams got killed right off. Sum Colonel took over and sent Jacob wid de men out dis way. We's ta keep dem Confederates frum cumin. We's battled wid em till evenin time. We's won too! Then Jacob gets offin his horse ta see'd ifin he could help dem dat be hurt. He be at dis confederate soldiers side tryin ta help em. Anyways, dis boy be havin a gun en Jacob not knowd it. Dis boy shot him whilst he be tryin ta help. I's not knowd why. He jus did. Then I's jus gots Jacob here fast."

"You've done all you could possibly do Jonah. Jacob knows that too," Gabe said gently.

The door opened, and Liza stepped out. Gabe could tell by the look on her face that it wasn't good news. "Ya best be a sayin ya good byes. He be wantin ta talk wid ya's. Best come on whilst dey's be time."

Gabe stood on one side of the bed, and Jonah on the other. They could tell Jacob didn't have long for this world. Jacob opened his eyes and looked at Gabe and gave a slight smile. "I want to thank you…for making me…a part of your family. You gave me…shelter and rest. You…helped me see God… clearer than I ever have."

"You'll always be a part of this family. You're our hero! My son will know his Uncle Jacob and what he did for this family," Gabe said softly.

Then Jacob turned his head toward Jonah and said, "We're the… best of friends. I… never had many… friends so I… thank you for…the honor. You always… make me laugh, I'll …be waiting for you… so don't mess up!" He said with a weak laugh.

"I's be de one doin de thankin. I ain't has a friend like ya afore. Yo en me be bothers. I's promise ya, I's be seein ya soon an friends be keepin promises," Jonah said with a broken voice.

Everyone but Jonah left the room to give the friends time to talk while they could. It wasn't long before the door opened, and Jonah told them his friend had gone home to see Jesus.

The Union Army regained control of Baton Rouge in two days time. The battle claimed more lives than Gabe could count. He'd lost a good friend and a dear brother in Christ. Lieutenant Jacob Sanders would never be forgotten.

CHAPTER 14

THE UNION FORCES NOW OCCUPIED Baton Rouge. The town was severely damaged, but saved from the destruction many other cities faced at this time. It seemed despite an economic downturn, New Canaan flourished. Since the battle, Gabe had combined the two plantations into one. Mount Haven became Haven House of New Canaan. The land was farmed as one, with the workers teaming together. The idea, which had been sent by God, seemed to please everyone. Now, New Canaan was truly one big family.

Professor Hall and Gabe sat in the professor's study talking when angry shouts and yelling interrupted their conversation. Leaping to their feet, they ran toward the loud commotion. Upon entering the grand ballroom where the wounded were staying, they were met with the sight of two angry soldiers in verbal combat. Others joined in from their sick beds.

Hannah and Josie, wide eyed with fear, tried to calm the situation, but to no avail. Anger washed over Gabe at the sight. He and Professor Hall rushed toward the angry soldiers. Professor Hall whisked Josie and Hannah out of harms way. Gabe quickly stepped between the two men. With all his might he pushed one, then the other down to the floor.

Gabe's anger gave voice as he said, "This is God's house! How dare you violate it in this way! Is this your way of saying thanks!?"

"He's a no good rebel! How can you have him here?" the soldier asked bitterly.

"In this house there's no blue and no gray! All God's people are the same. Color of skin and color of uniform isn't seen here. Look around you! Who is taking care of you? Who has fed you? Who has comforted you?

239

I'll tell you who, both black and white! Color doesn't matter. Don't you understand?" Gabe shouted.

The room became as quiet as a church, as Gabe continued, "Tell me, did your fellow soldiers come to your aid when you were wounded? NO! They didn't! They just left you to die on that bloody field and they wore the same color as you. Answer this, who's given you a second chance at life?"

"You have," said a nearby soldier.

"No! Not me. God has, and you better be thinking on that! For some reason God's chosen each and every one of you to live! He wouldn't have allowed us to find you if He hadn't. Now, you've got a choice to make! What are going to do with your second chance? Are you going to do something with your life that will make God proud of you? Or are you going to waste it on color differences? If you choose the latter and this bickering, you'll leave here now! If you feel good enough to fight, then you feel good enough to leave! Is that understood?"

An echo of "Yes sir," came from the group.

"One more thing Gentlemen, when you leave here each man is on his own! You can rejoin your unit, or go home. It doesn't matter to me, but know this, if you rejoin your troops and tell them what we've done here by helping you, God will deal with you! I for one wouldn't want to be in your shoes. So gentlemen, don't temp God!"

Walking to his wife, Gabe took her by the hand, and led her from the room as Professor Hall and Hannah followed.

Josie and Hannah were visibly shaken. Leading them to the study, the professor stopped long enough to ask someone to fetch Charles. Once the women were comfortable, Gabe went to fix them some tea. He felt spent. Never had he experienced anger like he did today. He knew he should start sending the soldiers back to "where ever" soon. Picking up the tea tray, he returned to the study.

Charles was comforting Hannah, and Professor Hall was holding his daughter's hand when he entered the room. "We've got to start sending the soldiers out soon, Gabe," Professor Hall informed him.

"I know, I've been thinking about it too. Hannah, are there any ready to go?"

"Of course the two who were fighting! Their wounds are healed enough. There're others too. I've just been waiting because I knew they wouldn't be eating as well if they left."

"Then it's time. I'm sorry about today, ladies. I knew something like this might happen, but I'd hoped it wouldn't, however I was wrong." Sadness engulfed Gabe.

"It's not your fault, Gabe. We all feel the same way! You've apologized for nothing," Charles informed him.

"Its okay, husband, we're strong women!" Josie informed him confidently.

"You didn't look so strong when we first saw you!" Professor Hall said in amusement.

"You should have seen your face Josie! Never have I seen someone's expression go from surprise, to fear, then to anger so quickly. It's a good thing your husband showed up, or those soldiers would be the worst for it!" Hannah exclaimed.

Caleb and Emlee sat quietly in the flower garden enjoying a little time to themselves. This was something rare for Emlee. The children seemed to think of her as their own, and were always with her. She really didn't mind, especially when Caleb was busy with work.

"I's be wantin ta ask ya sumthin," Caleb said breaking the silence.

"Umhum?" Emlee replied dreamily.

"I's be thinkin me and yo be knowing each other sum time now…en I's love ya…en it be bout time me and ya up an married. Ifin ya be incline ta."

Emlee smiled, "Dat ain't no question!"

"Awh Emlee, ya's makin dis here hard on me! Whatcha say?"

"Still, ya ain't ask a question," she giggled.

"Emlee, will's ya marry's up wid me?"

Throwing her arms around him she exclaimed, "Yez Caleb, I's will!"

Taking her in his arms, he kissed her. "Ya ain't got no pa ta be askin, so's I reckon we's jus up and does it!"

"Ya be askin somebodies fer permission, ya be askin Mr. Gabe an missus Josie! De's be my family, an I's ain't doin it till ya does," she told him firmly. Seeing how determined she was, he agreed. They would go talk to them this very evening.

With Charles by her side, Hannah went from one soldier to another. She pointed out to him the ones ready to leave and those that had to stay. The soldiers they told this didn't want to go. They knew what would be facing them on the outside. One soldier expressed his concerns to Charles.

"You're families will be thinking you're dead. You need to let them know you're not. The army isn't going to want you back because of your injuries, but your family will! I suggest you go back home."

"I don't know how I'll get there! I don't have a horse much less clothes to wear out of here," the soldier informed him.

"We'll see to the clothes and God will provide the way. You'll just have to have faith," Charles assured him.

The other soldiers listened as Charles answered questions and offered answers with words of encouragement. They really knew, deep in their hearts, it was their own fault they had to leave. It was something they'd just have to accept.

Josie and the women of New Canaan banded together. They started making new shirts and trousers for the leaving soldiers. "Thank God Gabe and Woodley hadn't thrown away their shoes," Josie thought as she sewed. Out of the forty, fifteen would be leaving as soon as the clothes were ready. Josie prayed asking God to supply the soldiers with transportation home.

Gabe and Ben rode into town. The destruction they saw made them more thankful they'd been spared. Stopping at the train station to see if any mail had arrived, they were greeted by Union soldiers. Making his way inside, Gabe looked for Mr. Fontenot. Not seeing him, he asked the young woman behind the counter if Mr. Fontenot was about. The young woman began to cry and shook her head no.

"My father died. He joined up with the Confederate's a few months back and was killed in the battle of New Orleans."

"I'm so sorry Miss Fontenot, tell your mother Gabe Lyon talked with you today. If there's anything I can do, just let me know."

"Thank you Mr. Lyon, I will. Forgive me for crying, I just can't get used to father being gone. I'm sorry, you're here about your mail," she said sniffling.

"Yes ma'am, but I'm not expecting anything."

"You do have a letter," she said handing it to him.

"Thank you and again, don't forget to tell your mother what I said."

"I won't," she promised. Assured she would, Gabe went back outside to join Ben.

"We's be goin ta de livery stable?" Ben asked.

"Not this trip. Let's go to Hebert's store, and see how things fared there. It looks like Mr. Allen's place did fine."

As they rode to Mr. Hebert's, they could see where the battle had taken place. Scorched ground was the only thing remaining where buildings once stood. Large holes in remaining structures were patched with new lumber, to block out the weather. Gabe knew it would be some time before the town would be back on its feet.

Gabe was surprised to find Hebert's store in better condition than most. When he entered, he was shocked to see the empty shelves. Mr. Hebert looked as if he'd aged ten years since he'd seen him last.

"Hello Gabe," Mr. Hebert said without his usual cheerfulness.

"Mr. Hebert, how are you?"

"Doing fair," he replied.

"I'm here to get a few things, and to see if you know of any news of the war. I just heard about Mr. Fontenot."

"It's a shame, just a shame! With you not being in town much, you didn't know. Hebert began to tell Gabe of the downfall of the economy, people missing, and plantations that had gone under. Mr. Hebert also told him about people leaving the area, moving either to the north or to the east. Everyone seemed to be seeking safety somewhere else. When he'd finish, Gabe just shook his head.

"I'm so sorry to hear it." Again Gabe noticed the empty shelves. Changing the subject quickly, he asked, "Do you have any flour? My wife wanted me to ask. Our son will be having his first birthday soon and she wants to make a cake." Gabe silently asked God to forgive him for this untruth.

"No flour right now, I'm expecting some soon. Just depends if the train doesn't get confiscated, or blown up on its way here. Can't tell these days what's going to happen."

"How's your business doing?"

"Not too well. I don't have much to sell as you can see. Even if I did, no one's got the money to buy."

Looking around, Gabe sought out anything he might buy to help the man. Seeing bolts of cloth, Gabe went and gathered two. Seeing a few other things he could use back at the house, he quickly retrieved them.

Ben, who had been quiet up to now, picked up on what Gabe was doing.

"We's be needin some nails and such. We's be getting mighty low."

"Let's get them while we're here Ben, no sense in having to come back in a few days. Do you see anything else we need?"

Their purchases made Mr. Hebert excited, especially when Gabe paid him in gold. Following them to door as they left, Mr. Hebert chatted happily and standing outside he shouted, "Ya'll come back soon!"

They were almost home when Gabe said, "I didn't realize things had gotten so bad."

"Yez sah, it be pretty bad. De good Lord be takin rite good care of usin. We's be protected like ifin deys be a wall round us. Just like de good book says," Ben answered.

Gabe knew what Ben was talking about. Not only was he talking of God's promise from the Bible, but he was reminding Gabe of the miracle God sent with the angels. They continued home counting their blessings.

Hannah wanted to talk to her mother. It was just like her to be out when she needed her, but she knew it wasn't planned, it just happened. This of all days, Hannah really needed her mother. Fixing herself a cup of tea, she sat at the table to wait. No matter how long it took, she wasn't going to move till her mother came back.

Caleb was in a hurry to get his work done. He had to slow himself down several times to make sure he did it properly. Now, of all times, he didn't want to do anything wrong. He wanted to have a feeling of accomplishment when he went to see Mr. Gabe.

There weren't many times Liza could enjoy a walk by herself. There weren't many times she just went for a walk. Today though, she needed to talk with the Lord. To her, there was no place like the outdoors to do it. As she walked, she talked out loud as if the Lord Himself walked right beside her. It didn't matter to Liza if anyone saw her talking to herself, or if they might think her crazy. The Lord knew the truth, and that was all that mattered.

"Lord, ya be givin us a good day, en I's thank ya fo it," she said. "I's comin ta ya wid a heart full of love an gladness. Thank ya fer bring de family through de battle. Ya takes a good man home ta ya, when ya took Lieutenant Sanders. I's thank ya fer bringin him ta de us' in, an ta Jonah. Jonah be needin a good friend, an I's reckon Lieutenant Sanders did too. Ya knowd what we's be a needin afore we's does. Dat be fo sure! I's love ya, and I's thank ya fo ever thang." She continued her walk singing praises to the One she knew she would be seeing in person one day.

Josie and little Will were outside when Gabe and Ben arrived back at New Canaan. It seemed, to Gabe, Will grew more with each day. Now that he had Professor Hall's help, he was able to spend more time with his son. Stopping where Josie and Will stood, Gabe reached down and took Will from Josie. Giving Josie a smile, he sat Will in the saddle with him, and rode toward the barn. Will was excited to be riding with his father.

It did Gabe good to see his son this happy. When they'd reached the barn, Gabe handed Will to Caleb before dismounting. When he had done so and taken Will back, Caleb asked Gabe for a minute of his time.

"What can I do for you, Caleb?"

"I's be a wonderin ifin me an Emlee could cum talk ta ya and de Missus?

"Sure, when do you want to do this?"

"I's like ta does it soon, ifin it be's okay wid ya."

"You come anytime Caleb. We haven't talked in a long time, and I'll be at the house the rest of the day."

"Thank ya sah, we's be dere soon as de works done," he promised.

"Then I'll see you and Emlee after while," with Will in his arms, he left the barn.

Gabe and Will made frequent stops on their way to the house. Gabe allowed Will to walk as much as his little legs would let him. This meant stopping to closely examine a rock, a blade of grass, or a pretty wildflower. When Will decided to taste a bug, Gabe picked him up and said, "Your mother will not approve of you eating those!" Swinging Will high in the air, he carried him the rest of the way to the house.

Liza returned to find Hannah waiting on her, which was a surprise for Liza. Looking closely at her daughter, Liza tried to guess what had brought Hannah to her kitchen.

"Dis be nice ta find's ya a sittin at my table!" Liza said gleefully.

Laughing Hannah said, "Maw, I need to talk to you. Have a seat and please answer some questions for me."

"Last time somebodies be needin answers ta questions des be havin a babe. Dat be'd Miss Josie askin de questions," she said smiling at the memory.

"Well Maw, it's me now!"

At this news, Liza shouted and jumped to her feet. She threw her arms around her daughter, and showered her with kisses and tears. After a while, Liza settled down, and Hannah was able to ask her questions. She was able to confirm for Hannah, she was indeed having a baby. Now all she had to do was tell Charles.

Caleb went to get Emlee. They both dressed in their finest for their meeting with Gabe and Josie. Caleb was getting nervous as they neared the house, though Emlee didn't seem to notice. As they entered the kitchen together, they were surprised to see Hannah. Jumping to her feet, Hannah quickly hugged her mother and told her she would be back soon. Then she grabbed her bother, Caleb, and gave him a big hug before going out the door.

"My, ya be lookin mighty purdy Emlee. Ya be lookin rite handsome too son," Liza informed them.

"We's getin married, Miss Liza!" Emlee half whispered to her.

Quickly she looked at Caleb. When he nodded in agreement, Liza laughed and said, "Lordy this be a day of surprises!"

"We's be here ta speak ta Mr. Gabe and Missus Josie," Caleb said. "Maw bring pa en cum wid us."

"Ya'll go ahead on, an I's get ya pa," Liza promised. "Dey's be in de study."

Caleb knocked on the study door even though it was already opened.

Seeing them standing in the doorway, Gabe rose from his chair to greet them. When the greetings were done and they were all seated, Gabe asked,

"How are you two doing?"

"We's be fine sah. Ifin ya don't mind, I's like ta wait fo my maw and paw afore we's tell ya why we be here," Caleb requested.

"That's just fine with us," Josie said cheerfully. "Emlee, you're doing so well with the school! I don't believe I've ever thanked you for all you've done. Those children truly love you."

"Thank ya Miss Josie, I love doin de teachin."

"Now Caleb, what is it you and Emlee need to talk to us about?" Gabe asked when Ben and Liza came into the room.

"Well sah, I's be a comin ta ask fo Emlee's hand in marriage!" Caleb squeaked out.

"Why are you asking me? Have you asked Emlee?" Gabe questioned him.

"Yez sah, I's did, but she say I's be needin ta ask ya'll fo de permission," Caleb told him.

"Why?" asked Gabe.

"Cause ya be the only family I's got," Emlee said softly.

"Do you want to marry Caleb?" Gabe asked.

"Yez sah, I's does."

"Josie, do you agree with this marriage?" Gabe asked.

"Yes, I do! They've loved each other a long time, and have waited patiently."

"Then you have my permission. When do you want to get married?" Gabe asked.

Emlee and Caleb looked at each other smiling as they held each others hand. "I's don't rightly knowd. We's ain't got that far!" Caleb said. The whole room broke out in laughter.

Liza jumped up and pulled Emlee to her feet and wrapped her in a big hug. "I's be so happy fo ya! Ya be a fine wife fo my Caleb!" Everyone offered their congratulations as they circled the happy couple.

Professor Hall hurried toward the sitting room. He could hear loud shouts coming from that direction and it sounded like Charles! As he entered the room, he knew they were from Charles! He was laughing, as he whirled poor Hannah around and around in the air.

"Charles, you've scared me out of ten years growth with all that yelling. Put that poor girl down before she gets dizzy!"

"I'm the one that's dizzy!" he said as he sat Hannah on her feet. "We're going to have a baby professor! Hannah just told me, I'm going to be a father!"

"Congratulations, Charles! Hannah, I'm so happy for both of you," Professor Hall said with delight.

"I can't believe it, Professor. Isn't this wonderful?" Charles said.

"Yes it is, but Charles, you can't go around swinging that dear lady around like this, or your baby will grow up walking in circles!" The professor informed him laughing.

"Thank you, Professor! I have a feeling I'm going to need another level head around to help keep this man in line," Hannah laughed.

"We need to get you some help, there's too much for you to do here," Charles said seriously.

"Charles, we've lots of help here already, what more do you want? I promise I'll take it easy."

"You know," Professor Hall said thoughtfully, "Pete and Rose could move into the staff quarters here, like Ben and Liza at New Canaan. After all, Pete and I work together like Ben and Gabe do. What do you think?"

"Ask them if it's something they would like to do!" Charles exclaimed.

"I will, as soon as I think you're calm enough to be left alone with your wife!" said the professor.

Nothing could have made Ben any happier than knowing he was going to be a grandfather! It did his heart good to know his grandchild would be the first in the family to be born free. This child would never know the fear of being sold away from its family, or to feel the sting of a whip. Not that he would here, but it was just the thought knowing it would never happen.

Then, there was knowing Caleb and Emlee's children would be born the same way. He was proud of Caleb for picking a wonderful girl for his partner in life. All of his children made him proud; he only wished Jonah could find the same happiness as Caleb and Hannah.

Caleb and Emlee had a beautiful fall wedding. They didn't want anything fussy at first. They just wanted to be married. Josie explained to

Emlee her wedding day would be the one memory that would bring them through the hard times in the future. The love they felt for each other, and the way they looked on that day, would be forever etched in their minds.

After the wedding, Caleb and Emlee moved into the house that was closest to the school. Some day, they would build a home on the additional acres Caleb purchased from Gabe, and raise a family.

Ben and Gabe walked the fields checking the crops as they always did. Soon the sugar cane would be harvested and they could rest a while. Repairs would begin after the harvest to homes, barns and tools. Horses needed to be trained, and cattle needed to be brought to closer pastures. Ben and Gabe always saw to these things themselves, and worked along side the other hired hands. Neither Gabe nor Ben ever told their wives how much they enjoyed doing it. As they walked, they began making plans for the down time, as they referred to it. They laughed at how the women always fussed over them when they came back from working so hard.

"It be a fine sugar crop des year, Mr. Gabe!"

"It sure is! I wonder if we'll be able to get a good price for it with this war going on."

"We's get what de Lord be wantin us ta have. God be in control, or does I have ta remind ya?"

"No sir, I remember and I have faith we'll sell it for top dollar."

"Don't go an be greedy, Mr. Gabe. We's all knowd dat times be hard an dem wounded soldiers added more mouths ta be fed. Ain't no worry amongst de hired hands."

"I tell you Ben, I was glad to see the last of the soldiers leave. God never ceases to amaze me, not only did they all leave with places to go, but they left with a way to get there."

"Why's does what God do's fo ya surprise ya so, Mr. Gabe? Seems ta me dat a man of God be expectin dem thangs."

"I think because I let the worries of this world get to me. I need someone like you to keep me in line. You always put me back on track. I thank you for that."

"Den I's knowd whys I be here!" Ben exclaimed laughing.

As they continued to walk, Gabe began to notice a change in Ben. His breathing became shorter and his pace slowed. Gabe made an effort to stop frequently, which allowed the man to catch his breath and rest. Gabe began to worry when it didn't help. Finally, he asked, "Ben, are you feeling okay?"

"I's be fine. I's be feelin poorly today fo sum reason. Woke up dat way. It jus be ole age, I reckon."

"Let's start back. We can finish this another day, when you're feeling better," Gabe assured him.

"Dat be fine by me," he said without a fuss.

Turning back, Gabe's worry increased as Ben's breathing became worse. He even thought about leaving him, and going to get a wagon, and said so.

Ben wouldn't allow it.

"Are you hurting anywhere?"

"I's got a feelin in my chest, but it aint too bad."

"Lets sit awhile. You need to rest," Gabe looked around to see if anyone was near enough to call. He was really worried now.

"I's jus need ta rest. Dontcha be fussin so," Ben said as he sat down on the ground.

Seeing Big John and Eli coming from the back pasture, Gabe stood and shouted for them. Big John could tell by Gabe's voice that something was wrong and took off running toward them.

"We need a wagon. Ben isn't feeling well!" Gabe told Big John when they had reached them.

"Eli. goes fetch Caleb an de wagon. Run fast as ya can boy. Go now!" Big John said urgently.

By now. Ben was sweating, pale and needed to lie down. Gabe and Big John tried to make him comfortable, each praying fervently!

"You hang on now, help will be here soon," Gabe assured him.

"Ain't.. gona.. make it boy… I's see'd.. de angel. He be cumin fo me… So's listen ta me. Ya be de best thang …ta happen ta me. I's love ya as.. Ifin ya was my blood. I'd knowd God be usin ya… when ya be a chil. Jus member what.. I's told ya this day. God be in control."

"Don't talk. Save your breath," Gabe told him as tears slid down his face.

"Ya need.. ta listen Gabe. Ya keep on.. wid de Lords work an ..ya takes care of de family...ya heard me?"

"Yes sir," Gabe was sobbing, now unable to argue with the man.

"Ya tell.. My.. Liza ..I's love her.. an I's be seeing ..her sum day." He was so weak all Gabe could hear was words in a whisper.

"Yes sir, I will." Trying to control his sobs, he continued. "You've been just like a father to me. I love you and thank you for always being there for me. You stood with me through thick and thin." Grief over took Gabe and he could no longer speak.

"It be.. easy.. ta do. Tell's… my Hannah's babe…bout… me."

249

"Yes sir, I promise," Gabe said between sobs, now holding Ben in his arms.

"It be… alrite… It.. be alrite…. "Ben whispered, then closed his eyes as his last breath left him.

Gabe was inconsolable as he sat there on the ground holding his dear friend. He cried harder than he had at his own father's death. Big John sobbed along with Gabe, as he bent and picked up Ben's lifeless body, and carried him toward the house. The wagon was too late.

The funeral for Ben was the hardest thing Gabe had ever done. He did not know why this fine man had to die. Josie and Emlee had become pillars of strength during this time. She and Emlee just took over, making sure everything ran smoothly. Gabe and Jonah talked long into the night after the funeral. Gabe asked Jonah to take his father place with him, running the plantation, and he agreed.

Later Caleb confided in Gabe he wanted to become a preacher. Gabe was surprised at Caleb's knowledge of the Bible. He asked Professor Hall to take Caleb under his wing and teach Caleb as he had taught him. The professor was please to have the opportunity. Charles stayed close to Hannah and Liza's side, offering words of comfort and seeing to their every need.

Liza was a strong woman in the Lord. She knew she'd be seeing her Ben again one day soon. This knowledge allowed her to shake her sadness and put it to a better use. At first, she began saying the promises of the Lord about seeing our love ones in heaven. Then as the days passed, she began to thank God for her blessings. After a while, she could be heard singing praises to God. As she got better, so did the rest of the family. They missed their Ben, but life goes on. They knew Ben would have wanted it that way.

Gabe and Jonah walked the fields of New Canaan, just as Gabe did with Ben. They talked of many things, but mostly about Thanksgiving. The holiday was upon them. It would be their first Thanksgiving without Ben. They both were wondering how Liza would handle it.

"I's be thinkin Maw do jus fine, Mr. Gabe," Jonah said.

"I think she will too. She and Josie are already planning meals."

"Yez sah, she be jus fine. Ya knowd, Mr. Gabe, I's been ta town a few times en dere be sum changes."

"What kind of changes, Jonah?"

"De soldiers be buildin sum de places back. Ain't see'd many folk bout ceptin sum hungry lookin black folk."

"Things must be bad for the others, then. I've been wondering how other plantations have been doing. I was hoping their sugar cane and cotton sold as well as ours."

"Fum what I's be hearin, dey ain't many fairin."

"I'm sorry to hear it; we need to pray for them. We need to ask God to answer their prayers, and see to their needs."

"Dat's what I's be a praying fo. I reckon de Lord be answerin prayers in His way, in His own time."

"He does that, Jonah. It may not be in the way we want, but He does answer them. He's never late, and He's always on time."

"Yes sah, I's be knowin dat since ya be here," he said smiling.

"I miss your father," Gabe said as if they had been talking about him.

"Yez, I knowd ya does. I's does too." As they continued their walk, the conversation turned to farming and the plans for the next year.

Professor Hall and Pete finished walking the fields surrounding Haven House. They were excited about next year's crops. The sugar cane had been planted, and the fields readied for the spring planting. November was a good month to rest, and spend time with the family. The two men took the short cut through the woods to meet with Gabe and Jonah. The four of them had a lot of farming to talk about.

Liza and Josie began checking the storehouses of New Canaan, while Hannah and Rose checked the ones at Haven House. They needed to make sure they had enough food to last them until the gardens could add to their supplies. The women were pleasantly surprised to see the storehouses were not only full, but packed tightly.

"Liza, look at this! I don't think we've ever had this much food before. There's no space opened to put anything else in here," Josie exclaimed excitedly.

"Hannah say's it be de same at Haven House."

"What? Even after feeding those soldiers for so long?"

"Yez, dat's what she say. Why dat be a surprise ta ya? Jus ya think on how de Lord fed de folk wid jus two little fish an five loaves of bread. Member de widow wid her boy? She be makin dere last meal wid de last of de flour. She even say's, I's reckon we's be dyin cum tomorrow. Den de prophet showd an say's ta her, cook dat fer me. She tol him, dis here be de last of it then me an my boy be dyin. Then de prophet says, ya cook dat fer me first, an then cooks fo yo an ya boy. Ifin ya does de, Lord be makin shur ya be havin plenty ta eat. De widow did like she be told, an den she has plenty frum then on. I's knowd ya knowd de story, Josie Girl! We's be jus like dat widow. We's fed many a folk so's de Lord be blessin ya. Ain't no surprise ta me," she said as she turned to go back to the house.

Josie looked upward and said, "Thank you Lord for the food and Liza."

Afterward, Josie, Liza, Hannah and Rose had their own meeting. It had nothing to do with farming; it had everything to do with eating. The women were excited about Thanksgiving.

"This is going to be our first Thanksgiving in a long time with just our big family. I want to make it special!" Josie said excitedly.

"I's love ta smell de cookin at Thanksgiving. I's specially likes de eatin," Rose said giggling.

"Me too!" Hannah chimed in.

"We's be needin ta plan sumthin special. Ya makes the best cinnamon apples Rose. How's bout ya doin dat?" Liza asked.

"Yez ma'am, I's be proud ta. What's ya specialty Missus Josie?"

This question brought a round of laughter from the women sitting at the table.

"I'm sorry, Rose. You have no idea how hard it's been for me to learn to cook the basic Louisianan dishes! My specialty is bread. I can cook the best bread ever!" Josie said laughing.

"Can't sayd ya ain't one ta try, Josie Girl. Ya's be willing, but ya jus ain't took hold yet. How's bout yo, Hannah? Whatcha be bring ta de table?" Liza asked.

"I think I'll make pies this year. I know cakes feed more, but I sure would like a pumpkin pie," she told them.

"Dat be de babe a talkin! I's thank de pies be a good change," Liza said.

"I can bake a cake. How about I be in charge of the bread and the cakes?" Josie asked grinning.

"We's need ta get all de women together and plans de meal. Everybody be helpin des year. Whatcha say?" Liza asked. The ladies all agreed, then got down to the business of planning a menu.

Thanksgiving Day arrived with the excitement of being together as one big family. This year the grand ballroom was decorated with pumpkins, hay stacks and flowers. A scarecrow stood in the corner beside a haystack, dressed with wild flowers. Extra tables had to be set up to hold all the new dishes they made this year. Even in the back yard, a large kettle of crawfish sat boiling. The women were extremely proud of what they had accomplished. Everyone had something they were thankful for this year. One was they had this large family to share their blessings with.

Gabe and Josie, with little Will in her arms, mingled with the group. Joy coming from the house, could be heard outside by anyone who passed by. Professor Hall was thankful he knew each person by name. He shook their hand, and thanked them for all their hard work. He even remembered the jobs they did. You could see the pride shining from their faces, as Professor Hall acknowledged their accomplishments.

Just as they were beginning to gather at the tables to give thanks, Little John came running into the room and called out, "Mr. Gabe, ya best cum quick. Ya gotta see'd out front!"

Leaving his place at the table, with Will still in his arms, he and Josie followed Little John to the front lawn. What met him there left him speechless. His yard was filled with former slaves, men, women and children of all ages. Making his way to the front steps as Josie followed, he saw the family gathering at the side of the house to watch. Standing on the steps so he could see everyone, Gabe said, "Good afternoon." When no one responded he asked, "Can I help you?"

A tall elderly gentleman, of about sixty, walked through the crowd to the bottom of the steps, and said, "My name be Moses, sah. I's be speakin fo de folk here. Gabe stepped down and held out his hand, "It's nice to meet you Moses, I'm Gabe Lyon, and this is my family."

The elderly man took Gabe's hand, then said, "We's knowd ya be a good man. We's been watchin ya when ya cums ta town wid ya slaves. We's knowd dey's be happy here, an see'd dat ya hold em dear ta ya. We's cum ta ask ya ifin ya be needin help."

Moses stepped back and looked down at the ground. Josie's heart was about to break! They looked hungry, and Lords knows they needed clothes instead of the rags they were wearing. Gabe didn't know what to do. He was at a loss for words because this was a pitiful group. He looked out over the sea of desperate faces. All he could see was fear, hopelessness and despair in their eyes. These forgotten people stood before him, asking him for comfort.

Looking at Josie, he knew what she wanted to do. Then he made eye contact with Jonah and saw him smiling. Jonah nodded, and made his way through the crowd to Gabe's side. Leaning toward Gabe, he whispered, "These be de folks we's be a prayin fo. Member God answers prayers. Sumtimes not de way we's want, but He always does in He's time." He had quoted Gabe word for word.

Smiling Gabe looked over at Josie and said, "Well my love, it would appear our family is growing." Turning to the crowd of about sixty to seventy five people he said, "Here you are not slaves, you are family. Here you'll be working for wages, not a master. Here you will have your own home as long as you choose to work here. Some of you will be living here at New Canaan; others will live at Haven House. No families will be split up. You will go to school, and be taught to read and write. We do things here according to God's word, with everyone going to church on Sunday. Is this agreeable, Moses?"

Gabe could see hope spring into the eyes of those standing before him. Moses turned to the crowd, "God be answerin our prayers." Then turning to Gabe, he nodded, "Yez sah, we's be blessed ta be joinin ya."

"Then welcome to New Canaan! Come; join your family for Thanksgiving dinner."

At those words, the members of New Canaan ventured out into the crowd of newcomers. They went about introducing themselves, and offering words of encouragement as they led their new family to dinner. Peace seemed to cover them as they went. Gabe and Josie looked at each other realizing this very day a new ministry began; a ministry of restoration.

Before joining the others, Gabe gathered Josie, Professor Hall, Charles and Hannah, Liza, Jonah, Big John and Delia, Pete and Rose, Caleb and Emlee into a circle on the lawn. Holding hands, they bowed their heads as Gabe prayed. "Lord, we thank you for this day. We ask your blessing upon each person here. We thank you for our new family members. We ask that you grant them the desires of their hearts, and heal their hurts. Lord, I ask you to bless those in this circle. I ask you to lead us and guide us in this new adventure you've set before us. We thank you for this opportunity as we grow in the knowledge of you. We do all things to your glory, in the name of Jesus," and all Gods people said, "Amen"

To be continued.........

NEW CANAAN LEGACY
The Journey continues

BY
GLENDA ALLEN REID AND LUANN ALLEN PAYNE

CHAPTER 1

MOSES

JOSEPHINE LYON LOOKED AROUND THE room at her very large family. Smiling, she remembered the first day she came to New Canaan. Never in her wildest dreams did she ever think God would give her and Gabe such abundant blessings. Here, twenty five years later, she sat gazing over the living miracle before her. The dark skin and the light skin relatives all laughing and talking, just enjoying each other's company as they had over the many years.

As she looked about, her gaze fell upon Moses. How the children loved him! They gathered around him every chance they got to listen to his stories, and today was no different.

The children, setting before him, reminded Josie of the keys on a piano. This thought made her laugh. Just then, Moses looked up and caught her gaze and smiled. He knew what she was thinking because he was thinking the same.

Hearing his named being called brought Moses back to those who sat before him. "Moses, would you tell us a story?" Joshua asked with pleading eyes.

"Yes please! Tell us a story Moses! Please?" The children all chimed in with excitement.

"Would ya be a wantin a tale, or would ya be wantin a honest ta goodness true one?"

"A true one!" The children shouted in agreement.

"Well now, let me see'd." His eyes, aged with the wisdom of his years, twinkled as he began. "It be twenty five yeers past taday when it happened.

It be such a day as dis here!" Josie moved closer to listen. She knew the story he was going to tell.

As Moses began his story, the memories flooded his mind taking him back. He felt as if he, with just a thought, had stepped back twenty five years into that very day.

Moses walked wearily toward the town of Baton Rouge. In all his sixty odd years he had never seen such misery, but that's what war leaves behind, pure misery. The Civil War brought nothing but this and hunger. Hundreds of souls were left without work, food or a home. Work…the thought of work brought mixed feelings to him. His master had been cruel to all his slaves.

The Civil War not only brought devastation to his master's plantation, but it also took the lives of his two sons. The plantation had been brunt to the ground. Then with the Emancipation Proclamation issued, hundreds of freed slaves were left on their own. They had no work, no food and no prospects of getting either. Living off the land instantly became a reality for them all.

Lifting a prayer to the Lord, Moses left the main road and walked toward the river to rest. The woods on the edge of the river provided some relief to his eyes. The beauty of Gods handiwork enclosed about him as if the Lord Himself had wrapped his arms around him. It was that comforting peace only a father gives to his child. Moses stopped were he was and closed his eyes as he enjoyed the embrace from his Father. "Thank ya Lord," Moses whispered softly, then continued on his way to the river.

As he walked out of the woods to the clearing, Moses was surprised to see a group of former slaves camping next to the river. As he came nearer, he recognized many faces from the plantation where he had lived, and slaves from neighboring plantations he'd seen in town. As he approached the group, a young man rose and called to him. "Moses! Cum an rest yor bones! I's be mighty proud ta see'd ya be alivin!"

"Samuel! I's be morin proud ta see'd ya too, I's thank ya!" Moses said as he sat on the ground beside Samuel.

"Dis here be a pitiful sight. Whatcha be doing wid all des peoples here?" Moses asked.

"Aint got no place else ta go Moses. Least wise here we's got water an can hunt fer food," Samuel answered.

"Be poor huntin fer shoor en dem woods! Why dey aint much ceptin maybe's a rabbit or a squirrel or two."

"We's got fishin at hand Moses!" Samuel assured him. "What's we ta do? We's got mouths ta feed."

"I's be believin de Lord be havin better fer usin. Dem woods ain't gona feed dis many folks fer long."

"Whatcha thinkin de Lord be wantin usin ta do? I's surely be a prayin He be sendin a sign or sumptin. Dey's more than jus dese here. I's never see'd de likes of it. More hungry lost souls than I cares ta see'd. My Maddie here be a worrin bout de chil'lin." Samuel glanced at the children playing near by, then looked back at Moses.

"I's tol ya, we's need ta pray," Moses said. "We needs ta get every able bodie man en woman tagether atter the chil'lin be a sleepin, an prays bout it together. Den we's need ta talk. I's jus knowd en my knower dat de answer be rite under our'n noses!"

"I's be passin de word along. Ya be de Godliest man I's knowd, Moses. Ifin ya says ta pray, den we's be a doin it! Ya jus rest. I's be back shortly."

Moses lay back on the ground and closed his eyes. Samuel went about the group spreading the word about the meeting after the children were asleep. But Moses only appeared to be resting. In fact, he was praying with all his heart for God to guide him and give him wisdom.

Night fell on the small encampment by the river, and as the children slept, the grown ups made their way toward the light of Samuel's campfire. A seed of hope had been planted in their hearts. Moses was known for being wise, and walking with the Lord. Hopefully, he would be able to help with their present dilemma.

When everyone had gathered in a circle around the fire, Moses began. "I's see'd we's be needin ta ask de Lord fer de path ta follo. Everbodies be agreein we's need help?" Moses asked, then waited for an answer. The groups reply came quickly with a resounding "Yez".

"Den everbodies take aholt de one aside ya's hand, whilst we pray." Taking a deep breath, he began to pray. "Lord, we's be a needin ya help bout now. We's be askin ya ta showd usin what we's needin ta be a do' in. Ya knows we ain't got no place ta lay our'n head, no regular food, and no work ta does ta get it. We's be askin ya ta showd us de path ya be a wantin usin ta take. We's thank ya fer de answer afor hand cause we's knowd ya be a answerin. I's thank ya again fer dis here day, en fer dis warm night, en all ya has givin us, amen."

"Moses, what we be a needin is work. Ain't no work ta be had in dese parts," Samuel said as soon as the amen faded into the air.

"Don'tcha be a talkin like dat! We's jus ask de Lord fer help en ya goes an confesses wid ya mouth, he ain't. Whats de matter wid ya? Ya ain't got a knowin fer what de Lord be workin fer usin rite at dis here minuet! Ifin ya can't be a sayin sumptin goodly, keeps ya mouth closed!" Samuel was taken aback, but knew Moses was right.

"Now as I's see'd it folks, we be a missin sumptin here. Dey's gotta be sumbodies round here be needin our'n help en we jus not knowd it," Moses informed them. "Who be doing goodly wid farming here? We's all knowd how ta farm an such." Moses searched the faces before him as if the answer could be found there.

Samuels's wife stood and faced Moses shyly. "I's knowd who I's like ta work fer," Maddie said softly. "I's like ta work fer de Massa ob New Canaan.

"Why?" Moses asked.

"Cause I's see'd his slaves in town. Did ya knowd all his slaves gots shoes?"

"How ya knowd dis here?"

"I's be a waitin fer de Missus one day, en I see'd de Missus frum New Canaan cum inta de store with her slave. De slave be carryin a babe wid her. I's think it be de Missus babe, but no, it be de slave girl's babe! De babe be swaddled in a prudy blanket, jus like new! I's ask ta see'd de babe, and de girl showd me. It be her babe, an it be wearin booties on its feets! I's looked rite quick at de girl's feets, en she be a wearin shoes too! I's mean shoes dat be a fittin, not sum hand me down. Den I's sees' her dress! She be a wearin a clean whole dress, not nary a tear in it, en it be a fittin too! Den, her Missus comed out, en she smiled at me afore she ask de girl ifin she'd be a wantin ta cum inside ta pick out her cloth. I's tell ya dat girl peered happy ta me!" With that, Maddie sat back down.

"Anybodies knowd anythang else bout des family?" Moses asked curiously.

"I's knowd sumptin," said a young man.

"What be ya name?"

"I's be Luchas, sah. I's knowd de peoples ya be talkin bout. I's see'd de quarest thang oncet wid dat Ole Ben frum New Canaan en his Massa. I's be in da woods a huntin one day an I's see'd Ole Ben an his massa stopped in de road. Dey's had em a wagon load of slaves I's never see'd afor. Anyways, de Massa got off his horse an started putting de little uns on his horse ta ride whilst he walked! Den, he en Ole Ben started walkin side by side a talkin and a laughin. It be a sight! Here dis Massa be leadin his horse whilst three chil'lin be ridin all de while laughin en talkin ta Ole Ben."

260

"Ya see'd anythang else?" Moses asked.

"Yez, sah. I's follow em fer a while, and dey prut much walked all de way home. De wagon Ole Ben was a ridin in be drivin by one ob de new slaves. Ole Ben walk rite along side wid his Massa. It be a sight, I's tell ya! I's see'd dem slaves in town sumtime later en Miss Maddie be rite. Dem folks be dressed in new clothes, and dey had shoes dat be a fittin."

It seemed all the slaves gathered there had a story to tell about the Master of New Canaan. "I's heard de Massa traded a horse for a slave boy so's he could be back wid his family," someone said. "I's heard he be a preacher but his pa died en he took over," another said.

"I's tell ya what I's knowd," said a young woman.

"What be ya name?" asked Moses.

"I's be Bella sah, en my ma been de housekeeper fer de Broussard's. I's knowd dat de Massa ob New Canaan give de slave, Jonah, freedom papers long afor de war cum bout. I's knowd too dat dem at New Canaan got a special mark. Not one like dis here burn." Bella lifted the sleeve of her blouse to show a cruel burn scar of a B on her shoulder. "Dey's got this tiny cross tattoo on de right hand, bout here," she pointed to the top of her wrist.

"Hows ya be knowin dis?" Moses asked.

"Cause my ma heard Massa Broussard a talkin bout it ta de Missus. Said sumptin like dat be de only way he got dat boy back cause ob dat tattoo. I's knowd Broussard done sumthin bad ta de boy. Ma said he be beat. Den rite atter de big twister dem people came ta help clean up. De Massa of New Canaan worked rite along side, and Massa Broussard give him de boy Eli. We's all see'd de Massa frum New Canaan take de boy aside an feed him! I knowd rite den de man be a good man! Ole Massa Broussard say we ain't ta fed de boy, cause he be too small ta earn his keep an not fit ta feed.

Moses sat quietly for a few minuets. The others gathered around didn't know if he was ever going to speak again because he had gotten so quiet. Then after awhile, he said, "Anybodies got anythang else ta tell bout dis man?"

"I's does sah, I's be called Clem. Afor de war I be a huntin in de woods over near dis mans plantation, and I's heard singin. I's got rite curious bout it, so I's just follo de singing. Dere in de wood be a church, en it be full! I's sit myself down on the ground outside a opened window en jus listenin ta de singin. Den, I heard de preachin so I's listen fer a spell. Den I's thought I's best be movin on, but I's gots ta thinkin, I's go see'd de rest of dis here place. What I's see'd be de prudiest cabins an I's knowd dey be fer de slaves. Why dey be two times bigger dan any I see'd afor and tightly made. Why I betcha nary a raindrop gets through dem cabins. Dey even gots glass in de windows! Dey weren't a slave around ta catch me either. Dey all be in church."

"Clem, ya be tellin de honest truth?" Moses asked.

"Yez sah! I's see'd it wid my own two eyes!"

"Moses, I be Abby. Every slave dat see'd de man and his slaves knowd dat he hold em dear ta his heart. Why, he smiles at em, and touches em like dey be friends an such, more like dey's be family. I's been de slave ta Massa Fontenot, an I's see'd de man plenty. De man name be Gabriel Lyon. My Massa told his missus dat Lyon bought de Broussard ole place afor de war."

"Ya be shoor on dat?" Moses asked.

"Yez sah!" she assured him.

"Den we's got's sum prayin ta do. We be gathering again tamorrow night, same time. Dis here jus might be our answer."

The meeting broke up with the promise from each person to pray about what they had talked about. As far as Moses was concern, all he needed was a sign from God to tell him this was the way to go. New Canaan, the promise land was just what they needed.

The morning dawned with hope for the first time in years for Moses. He walked slowly along the river banks praying and asking for a sign that going to New Canaan was what God wanted them to do. It was all left up to Moses. These people would follow him anywhere. But the anywhere needed to be where God wanted them. As he stood there praying at the water's edge, with his eyes closed tightly, a breeze blew gently across his face, and with it came *"go to New Canaan."* Quickly Moses opened his eyes and looked around. He was truly alone. "Lord, ifin it be ya a sayin go to New Canaan, den when I's close my eyes ya be sayin it again, okay?" Closing his eyes he waited for a reply. After what felt like a life time, but was only a matter of minuets, Moses felt the gentle breeze returned once again. It blew across his face and then he heard, *"I Am Who I Am! Go to New Canaan!"*

Moses didn't need any further encouragement. He quickly turned and ran back to the campsite. It was later said, from those who witnessed Moses running, that he ran like a sixteen year old, not a sixty year old man. Quickly he called everyone to gather near him. "We's be goin ta New Canaan! Everyman come wid me. We be going ta town ta gather de lost ones ta cum wid us ifin dey be so inclined. We's need ta be getting de word out. Ifin dey's be wantin ta cum, deys need ta be here in de morin, or met us on de road on de way." Soon Moses, Samuel and five other men were on their way to spread the word!

Moses stopped everyone he saw, and invited them to join him and the others. He was surprised at how many thought he had lost his mind, or just out right said no. But it didn't stop him. He knew this was from God ,and he was going to do his best to get those he could. He just knew in his knower this was what God wanted them to do! Some came back with them, and others said they would met them on the way. He didn't take time to count the number of people who agreed to go with them. He only knew they'd said yes to coming. His heart was full of joy and gladness, as he and Samuel and the folks made their way back to the river.

That night, Moses told his story of how God talked to him, not once, but twice. He told them how important it was to always pray and ask God for direction in everything they do. Moses could see hope in the eyes before him. This would be a sleepless night for him, for his soul was full of thanksgiving.

The next morning, Moses and his group started out toward New Canaan. As far as he could tell, he had thirty people in all with him. How glad he was he had learned to count. His first master's son had taught him, as if it were some kind of game. But it hadn't been a game to him!

As they walked, people began to join them here and there along the way. The closer he got to New Canaan, the more the group grew. He felt panic rise within him. Then he'd feel the words *Fear Not* more than hear them, and the panic would leave. But now, as he stood at the drive of New Canaan, he wasn't too sure about anything. All he knew was God wanted him here. Most of his doubt laid in the fact he hadn't expected this many people to join them. He hadn't counted them in the last seven miles or so but the group was large. At least seventy five in all. With prayers flowing from his heart, he led the people down the drive to the front lawn of New Canaan.

Moses could tell the plantation was having a celebration of some kind. He could hear the laughing and talking from where he stood. Most of all, he could smell the food! He thought he'd been hungry before, but now his stomach ached and grumbled from the lack of it. He also knew if his stomach was doing this, so were the many others and his heart hurt for the children with them.

Moses didn't know what to do next. He didn't know if he should go around back or just knock on the door. He was trying to make a decision when the Lord took it out of his hands. A little boy came running around the side of the house and stopped still. His mouth dropped opened and his eyes widen, then he turned quickly and ran back the way he came. Moses wasn't given the chance to say anything. His heart fell. What was he going to do with all these people should this man not accept them? *"Fear Not"* came in a quiet whisper to him and left him with peace within his soul. So Moses and his group just stood there. No one said a word. They just waited.

Moses saw the man come from the back of the house. He carried a small boy in his arms. This must be him, Moses thought. The man stood before the large crowd and said, "Good afternoon." No one answered, not even Moses.

"Can I help you?" The man asked again smiling.

Moses stepped forward. "My name be Moses sah and I's be speakin fer de folks here."

The man stepped toward him and said, "Its nice to meet you Moses. I'm Gabe Lyon and this is my family. Then the man did something Moses never experienced before. He held out his hand to him. It was the first time Moses ever shook a white mans hand. Moses then said, "We's knowd ya be a good man. We's been watchin ya when ya cum ta town wid ya slaves. We's knowd dey be happy here, and see'd ya hold em dear ta ya. We's cum ta ask ya ifin ya be needin help."

Moses then stepped back and bowed his head saying a quick prayer quietly to himself, then raised his head. Out of the corner of his eye he saw a large group of people standing at the side of the porch, listening and watching. He returned his gaze to Gabe Lyon. Moses saw the man look at his wife, then quickly to the crowd at the side of the porch. A young negro man, of about twenty five, smiled at Gabe as he made his way to him through the crowd of people. This young man stood beside Gabe Lyon and whispered in his ear. The man smiled and turned to his wife. Whispering a quick word, he then turned and faced Moses.

"Here you are not slaves, you are family. Here you'll be working for wages, not a master. Here you will have your own home as long as you choose to work here. Some of you will be living here at New Canaan, others at Haven House of New Canaan. No families will be split up. You will go to school and be taught to read and write. We do things here according to God's word with everyone going to church on Sunday. Is this agreeable, Moses?" Gabe asked.

"God be answerin our prayers. Yez sah we's be blessed ta join ya!"

"Then welcome to New Canaan. Come! Join your family for Thanksgiving dinner."

To Moses' amazement the people listening and watching came out into their group. They introduced themselves and lead them to the Thanksgiving feast. There was more food than any of them had ever seen before at one time. Moses quickly turned back to thank Gabe Lyon for accepting them. As he came to the side of the house, he stopped. In front of him was Gabe Lyon and members of his family, both black and white, gathered in a circle holding hands praying. Moses couldn't believe his ears when he heard Gabe Lyon thank God for bring him and his group to join his family. It took a lot to make Moses cry, but this made him weep like a small child. He would thank Gabe Lyon later. Now wasn't the time. He quietly returned to join the rest of the family, giving thanks to the Lord for this Godly man.

Josie and Gabe joined the others last for dinner. First they went about introducing themselves to the new members, making sure everyone had gotten enough to eat, and to let them know this was now their home. Moses was amazed, but so were the people in the group he'd brought. He hoped they would understand what a wonderful thing God had done for them. Maybe with Mr. Gabe's, help they would finally understand the love God had for each of them.

"Moses! Moses! What happened then?" Joshua asked.

The call of his name brought him back to the present time and the children before him.

"What?" He asked.

"What happened after that? How does the story end?"

"Jus ya be lookin bout des here room. Dat be what happened! De story don't end. It be going on wid each en every soul dat be here. Member de story en pass it on. Dat way it be livin fer ever."

"Tell us another one, please?" The children asked.

"Mayhap another time, be off wid ya now," Moses laughed as he shooed the children out to play.

Jose walked over and sat beside Moses. "Those children love your stories. When you tell them, I can see it all over again as plain as the day it happened," Josie said with a smile.

"Twas de happiest day ob my life! I's never told ya, but I's be mighty thankful ta be here. De Lord did good when He put ya in my path. I's shoor enjoy a livin my ole age here, surrounded by so many love ones. Did I's ever tell ya bout de first night I's be heer?"

"No sir, I don't recall that story," Josie said.

"Ya don't member cause I's never tol a soul. But I's be thinkin I's can be trustin ya wid it."

"Thank you! What happened?" Josie was excited to hear his story.

"Mr. Gabe as I calls him back then, took me ta de nicest home I's ever had," he began, and in his mind he flashed back to that night.

Moses walked beside Gabe as they left the last of the new members in their new homes. It had been a long day and night for the both of them. Gabe could tell Moses was tired because he'd become quiet, but Gabe needed to talk. "I hope everyone will be happy here."

Moses looked up quickly at Gabe and smiled. It pleased him for Gabe to talk directly to him and tell him of his hope. "Dey's be powerful happy at whatcha does fer em Mas…" Gabe interrupted him by stopping quickly and placing his hand on his shoulder.

"Please Moses, call me Gabe. If you have to, you can call me Mr. Gabe, but I'd be honored if you'd just call me Gabe."

Moses was thoughtful for a moment. "I's try ta sah, but I's don't knowd ifin I can. Ya gotta knowd it be hard ta be a slave one day and den de next, cause sum man I's don't knowd says I's freed, dat I's really be free. Does ya see'd what I's be sayin?"

"I'm trying to understand what you're saying and what you're feeling, but to know how you feel? To really know? I don't. I've never been a slave."

"It be de mind, sah. De mind says yo be a slave, but ya knowd ya ain't no mo. But it be feelin de same. I's no different dan afor. Think on it. Member when ya married up wid ya Missus?" Moses asked. Gabe nodded. "Well sah, ya just be happier ta be wid her, but ya still be de same mind ya was! Be takin a spell afor ya be thinkin married. It be de same wid freedom."

"It kind of grows within you. I think I understand," Gabe said softly.

"Jus ya takes what we's be a doin dis very minuet. I's ain't never in my sixty sum yeers walked en talk wid a man like ya afor. Why, we's be a talkin like we be pa an son. No Massa ever allows it. Never got de chance ta does it wid my boy. Dis here be new, an it be rite nice, ifin ya be askin me."

"Yes sir, I think its right nice myself," Gabe said and both men laughed.

The two men talked as they walked toward a small cottage nearest the main house. Gabe stopped in front of it, and said, "this is your home Moses, for as long as you want it. Lets go in and I'll show you around."

Gabe opened the door, and quickly lit the lamp. He could tell by the look on Moses' face that he had become overwhelmed.

"This is your sitting room here, and a little kitchen is just to the right there. That door leads to your bedroom. I see you're tired, so I'll leave you to get some rest. I'll see you in the morning. Good night Moses."

All Moses could do was nod his head. Gabe left him standing in the middle of the sitting room, and quietly closed the door behind him.

As soon as the door closed, Moses fell to his knees and sobbed. He thanked the Lord for all He'd done for him. Then he started talking out loud.

"Lord, I's never had such a place. Why Lord, I's never had my own sittin chair afor. I's thank ya fer dis here home wid a wooden floor. I's thank ya fer de sittin chair." Moses ran his hand over the rug beneath him. "Dis be a rite prudy rug too Lord, en it be warm as can be!" Moses got to his feet and walked through his home. He touched everything he came to, and thanked the Lord for it. When he opened the door to his bedroom, he couldn't believe his eyes. Never in his wildest dreams had he ever imagine he'd have his own above the ground bed, with a mattress and quilt. His heart was full. So much had happened to him in the last few days. So many changes, that night was the best night of all. It was the first time in his life he'd ever been by himself. It was the first time he'd looked a white man directly in the eye. It was the first time he walked beside a white man and talked like friends. It was the first time he'd ever felt like family, and it was the first time he felt he was home."

Josie's sobbing brought Moses back to the present. "I's not mean ta make ya cry, Josie girl! I's jus wantcha ta knowd what it meant ta me is all."

Josie couldn't stop the tears. She threw her arms around him and said, "I love you Moses Lyon, more than you'll ever know!"

"I's love ya too girl. Now stop dem tears else I's never tell ya a story agin!"

Gabe looked across the group of smiling faces and found his wife. He could see she was crying with her head on Moses' shoulder. He walked toward them smiling. Josie loved Moses' stories, and they always made her cry. When he came to them, Gabe said, "Now Josie are those tears I see?"

"Yes they are, and don't you dare say a word Gabriel Lyon!"

"Are you telling stories again, Moses?" Gabe asked.

"I's always got a story! Now don't ya mind her none, she be alrite." Moses assured him.

The two men laughed at her as she dried her tears. "I'm just going to leave now that I've made you two laugh, and see what the children are up to. See if you men can stay out of trouble!" Josie turned and walked away with her head held high as Moses and Gabe continued to laugh. They both knew Josie loved to tease and be teased.

"She be a mighty fine woman, Gabe. She loves ya truly! Ya be a blessed man," Moses told him.

"Yes sir! Of that I am sure. What story did you tell her to make her cry so?" Gabe asked .

"Jus told bout you an me dat first nite I's cum here."

"That sure was some day, wasn't it?" Gabe asked.

"It surely was. It be de nite ya saves a wondering people," Moses told him seriously.

"I disagree with you. It was the night you saved us all! Why if you hadn't been here, we'd lost the crops that year. You're the one who knew what to do to save the corn. If memory servers me right, you're the one who knew how to save the orchards from that late cold snap. Why we would've lost it all if it hadn't been for you!" I could go on and on. One thing about it, no one knows farming like you. Then, when Professor Hall made his trip to Georgia, you just took over and ran Haven House so smoothly. I never worried about it. I tell you this, just between you and me, I was glad Professor Hall decided to let you take his place in running things. You doing it gave me peace of mind. If we had a problem, you had the answer. Plus, you allowed me to spend more time with my son and wife. Why, you gave Professor Hall the chance to start teaching again. I knew he missed it, but I didn't know how much until he came back from Georgia. I tell you Moses, he sure was glad you were willing to stay on."

"Farming be easy ta me, an a blessin. De Lord truly be de Massa of it," Moses said.

"Why didn't you want to move over to Haven House?" Gabe asked.

"Cause it not be my home. My home be de one I's got dat first night," Moses assured him.

"There's nothing like knowing you're home," Gabe said laughing.

"Yez sah, en I's done mor wonderin den I's care ta member afor I's got ta my promise land. Ain't de Lord good? I's got me a home, en a last name all in one journey. Jus like de good book says, delite yoself in de Lord an he be givin ya de desires ob ya heart!"

Gabe smiled and said, "All I can say to that Moses is….. Amen!"

CPSIA information can be obtained at www.ICGtesting.com
Printed in the USA
LVOW060831010612

284144LV00002B/3/P